SECRETOCRACY

Secretocracy

A novel
by

TOM GLENN

BOOKS

Adelaide Books
New York / Lisbon
2020

SECRETOCRACY
A novel
By Tom Glenn

Copyright © by Tom Glenn
Cover design © 2020 Adelaide Books

Published by Adelaide Books, New York / Lisbon
adelaidebooks.org

Editor-in-Chief
Stevan V. Nikolic

For any information, please address Adelaide Books
at info@adelaidebooks.org

or write to:

Adelaide Books
244 Fifth Ave. Suite D27
New York, NY, 10001

ISBN: 978-1-951896-96-6

Printed in the United States of America

Contents

Foreword **11**

PART ONE
Damage Control **13**

The Tank **15**

Chapter 1
The Grand Inquisitor **19**

Chapter 2
A Riddle Wrapped in a Mystery **43**

Chapter 3
The Eichmann Defense **70**

Chapter 4
We're Gentlemen Here **96**

Chapter 5
Obstruction **120**

PART TWO
Triangulation **141**

Chapter 6
Manifest Destiny **143**

Chapter 7
The Coon Fairy **162**

Chapter 8
Playing the OSCI Card **183**

Chapter 9
Manifest Obstructionism **203**

Chapter 10
Secretology **227**

Chapter 11
Manifest Insubordination **254**

PART THREE
Isolation **275**

Chapter 12
Shame **277**

Chapter 13
Manifest Debauchery **296**

PART FOUR
Redux **321**

Chapter 14
Unraveling Reinterpretation **323**

Chapter 15
Faithful Toadies and Good Worms **353**

Lexicon of Government Organizations **367**

About the Author **371**

The liberties of a people never were, nor ever will be, secure when the transactions of their rulers may be concealed from them.

—Patrick Henry

Foreword

Secretocracy is fiction. None of the characters in the story is based on a real person, and the principal organizations are imaginary. The Federal Intelligence Budget Office (FIBO), the National Preparedness Office (NPO), the Senate Preparedness Subcommittee, and the Bryson Building do not exist and never have. The budgeting process described is drawn from real procedures but has been greatly simplified and compressed.

PART ONE

Damage Control

The Tank

So it had come to this. August 2018. Trump in the White House, and Gene Westmoreland out on his ass.

Gene kicked his way through fast-food wrappers and single-shot vodka bottles. No sidewalks. Only clogged gulleys. He slung his suit coat over his shoulder. Sweat from the heat blurred his vision. He passed a burned-out building, houses with boarded windows, abandoned warehouses. No one on the pot-holed streets. Too hot. No sound except the occasional siren of an unseen police car. The stink from the polluted Anacostia River rolled over him in waves.

He turned down a nameless street and squinted at the D.C. map Harry had given him. The Bryson Federal Building was one of the few World War II temporary structures still standing. It was literally on the other side of the tracks, in Anacostia south of the freeway. He searched both sides of the street for the entrance, all the while enjoying the gray air of a Washington summer. The only opening he found was a shack extending from a graffiti-covered wall. Its door was glass with tape running from corner to corner and crossing in the middle. After several attempts, he forced it open and entered a windowless room. A fluorescent lamp flickered above a security guard who looked up from his magazine.

"Is this the Bryson Building?" Gene asked.

The guard picked up his phone and punched numbers. "Guy here for the tank." He went back to his reading.

Gene folded the map and put it into his briefcase. He had to work on his flagging spirits. *When you make mistakes, you learn.* One of his foster parents had told him that. What had he learned? Nothing. Sexual orgies, Harry had said. Who had made the accusation? What was the evidence?

A middle-aged woman in a business suit came through another taped glass door. "Doctor Westmoreland? Come with me."

Gene followed her into a cinder block hall and down a flight of steps lit by bulbs in cages to another hall darker than the first. As they passed a plate glass window, she selected a key from a hoop in her jacket pocket and opened a door. "Hasn't been used in a couple of months, but the cleaning crew is scheduled to do the basement first week in September."

The room was narrow, three walls of gray plaster, the fourth taken up with the window looking out to the hall. A desk and chair with a telephone sat at one end. The air was musty, as if no one had opened the door for months. She flipped a switch in a metal box. Fluorescent tubes plinked to life and filled the room with shadowless light.

"What's the window for?" Gene asked.

"I've only been here eight months."

He pulled out the chair. Standard old-fashioned federal desk of enameled gray metal, the top a cork-like composite material. He opened the drawers. Fragments of paper, scattered paper clips, and rubber bands.

"Fill out these forms," she said, "and leave them with the guard on your way out. We recommend that you not park on the street. I had a wheel taken off my Nissan in broad daylight. The Anacostia Metro station is a few blocks up. I wouldn't walk there in the dark. You might want to leave the building with the group."

"Can I get paper and pencils? How about a computer?"

"Supply is on the main floor, up the same stairwell we came down."

"What else is in this building?"

"Mostly old files waiting to be destroyed."

Gene ran his hand over the gritty desktop. "Who had this . . . office before me?"

"A gentleman from the Pentagon. He's since left the federal service. During my tenure, there were three others."

"Who'll keep my time card?" Gene said.

"Your home office."

"Can I come and go any time?"

"The guard's on duty twenty-four hours a day, but he keeps the door barred except during daylight. I recommend you not work nights or weekends. Your time is your own. Your home office wouldn't have assigned you this space if they needed to keep tabs on you."

Gene frowned at the window. "Is there a way to block the view?"

"You can close the curtain on the outside."

"Is there a key for the door?"

"We don't lock it when the space is in use. If you need anything, I'm on the main floor up the hall from Supply."

When the woman left, Gene dusted the furniture with his handkerchief and eased into the chair. Enforced idleness until they got around to firing him. The ideal punishment for a workaholic. After almost twenty-five years . . . He'd done this to himself. *Pride goeth before destruction, and an haughty spirit before a fall.* He should have sat down and shut up and done what he was told.

Tom Glenn

Two workmen in overalls and a woman in slacks watched him through the display window. They talked and laughed, then moved on. Gene went to the hall, searched among the folds of synthetic canvas for the pull cord, and tried to draw the curtain. It stuck, leaving a foot-wide gap. He carried the chair into the hall, stood on it, and tried to repair the mechanism. The curtain was stretched taut on both sides of the opening. That was as closed as it got. *My breach of privacy.*

Back inside, he dropped into the chair, raising a cloud of dust, and chuckled. This morning he'd had an office, all polished wood and computers, on the seventh floor of the New Executive Office Building, around the corner from the White House. He'd been respected, even feared. Dust settled on his shoes.

But he wouldn't crumble, no matter what. Okay, maybe he *was* too proud to knuckle under. Never mind that now. Where would he start to rehabilitate himself, restore his reputation, clear his name? He had to review every incident, every moment. Had the president's yes-men really expected him to grovel? They accused Gene of vainglory, but what kind of monumental arrogance was it for *them* to assume that they knew what was best for the country in violation of the constitution? He couldn't reveal what he knew—they'd prosecute him for divulging classified information. How could he fight the whole administration?

Go back over it. When was his first inkling he was in trouble? The day last March when he was named Senior Budget Reviewer for Nuclear Defense Intelligence. Everything began that day, starting with lunch out with his boss.

Chapter 1

The Grand Inquisitor

Gene had been at his U-shaped desk since seven that March morning in what he had laughingly called his "office" for the past eleven years—a twenty-by-twenty sound-proofed cubicle with elevated teak cabinets, a combination safe, three computers, and a large window that would have provided a fine view of Seventeenth Street Northwest were it not painted black. Michael's high school graduation picture, goofy grin and all, sat next to the keyboard, and the scant bare walls between the cabinets were covered with Gene's awards. He went over the figures in National Security Agency's proposed budget supplementary for the third time. Why did data mining require another forty million for remote computers to be used in the PRISM program? The NSA documentation didn't specify where they'd be located, but Gene suspected they'd be clandestinely stashed in commercial telephone hub installations on both coasts to speed up the scanning of intercepted calls.

The secure intercom buzzed.

"Hey, professor." Clem's voice. "What's on your calendar for the rest of the day?"

"Meeting with the fiduciary guys from NSA at three—"

"Cancel it. I'm taking you to lunch."

"Clem, they're driving in from Fort Meade."

"I'll be by your cubicle in ten minutes. Nettie'll have a cab meet us downstairs."

"Can't we walk?"

Clem laughed. "To Georgetown? I've got reservations at the Chez Maigret."

"Wow. That's a little beyond my penury level."

"I said I was taking you."

The weather was muggy, the sky a gray glare, so they headed past the wrought iron sidewalk tables and pink awning and asked to eat inside. The hostess seated them in a booth surrounded by dark polished wood and cut glass. When Gene ordered his perennial pinot noir, Clem suggested he have a gimlet instead. "I know you like them very dry."

"I have to work this afternoon, remember?"

Clem's smile was almost giddy. "Today, we're going to celebrate." He turned to the waiter. "We'll both have gimlets, short on the lime juice. And the crab-and-artichoke dip."

Gene folded his arms. "Okay, chief, what's going on?"

"I have the honor," Clem said, "to address myself to the Federal Intelligence Budget Office's new Senior Budget Reviewer for Nuclear Defense Intelligence effective March 2018."

Gene's heart pumped. "Me?"

"As of this morning."

Gene caught his breath. "I thought I didn't have a chance."

"It was nip and tuck, actually more nipping than tucking. The National Security Council guys and Office of Management and Budget had pretty much settled on General Hacker's nominee, despite my objections. Senator Prowley was pushing hard to get him named. Then yesterday Hacker's guy withdrew. Word on the street is that he ran into some security problem or other. You were second on the list."

Gene breathed deeply. "Thank you."

Clem waved off the gratitude. "I got what I wanted. For once. In this man's government, the agency head doesn't have the deciding vote in who his direct subordinates will be. You have to scheme and twitch and wriggle. I've gotten good at it."

"What happened to Hacker's man?"

"I hear he lost his clearances. Hacker had sent him on a trip to Riyadh. Something happened while he was there. The minute I got the word, I started calling the movers and shakers at NSC and OMB. Said I had to have someone in the job immediately, now that previous reviewer has already left. It worked."

Their drinks arrived.

"Who'll be taking my old job?" Gene asked.

"Mark Forrester. He'll need mother-henning to learn his way around the Signals Intelligence budgeting world."

"So Mark will make it into the Senior Executive Service," Gene said. "I can't wait to congratulate him on his SES5—"

Clem swiveled toward the fireplace. "Not instantaneously. He'll have to earn his spurs."

"I thought it was automatic. To put us on a par with our counterparts at the agencies and in Congress."

"The administration is rethinking that policy," Clem said.

"But, Clem, not promoting him would smell fishy. You know, equal opportunity for those of color. His credentials are as good as mine—Ph.D. from Cornell, years of experience here, awards for excellence. And he'll be starting off on an uneven playing field. The current administration isn't known for its progressive views. The White House regularly refers to African Americans as unqualified or dumb or low IQ."

"You've got balls of brass. Not afraid to speak up. But down pedal the mouthing off. You'll need all the humility you can muster. The person you have to worry about first in the executive branch is Lieutenant General Pete Hacker, the director—he calls himself the commander—of the National Preparedness Office. He's the president's handpicked lackey."

Clem toyed with his gimlet. "On the legislative side, the congressional people come in all stripes, but they're used to getting what they want. Watch out for Senator Herman Prowley. He has the determination and political skill of Lyndon Johnson minus the ethics. He's been chairman of the Senate Preparedness Subcommittee for six years. That's his specialty, and he doesn't take kindly to peons mucking in his bailiwick. And just because you're an SES3, only two steps short of the top rank, doesn't mean you're not a peon."

"Any specific issues ongoing?" Gene asked.

"Can't get into anything classified here. For now I want to lay out some principles for you. First, hold National Preparedness Office to its charter. Hacker's trying to push the envelope. Second, don't let NPO or the Preparedness Subcommittee allocate funds for anything that violates the law or conflicts with treaty obligations. Finally, remember that the Federal Intelligence Budget Office is an independent agency. We don't work for Prowley, and we're not in Hacker's chain-of-command."

"Where have I heard that before?"

"And, Gene," Clem said, "think in context. This is 2018. We're in the second year of the administration. The press maintains that the president has told more than four thousand lies. And he's attacking the press, calling it 'the enemy of the people.'

North Korea's rattling its sabers. Our international relations are in tatters. The Republicans deliberately refused to consider Obama's nominee for the Supreme Court and then confirmed an arch-conservative, weighting the court to the conservative side. A special prosecutor is wrapping up his investigation into Russian interference in the 2016 election—and there's at least an inference that the president's campaign worked with the Russians. The president has accused without evidence his predecessor of wiretapping him during the campaign. He's encouraging the use of torture as an interrogation technique, attacking the civil rights of immigrants, and excoriating the FBI and the Justice Department. His attacks on us, the intelligence community, get fiercer every day.

"Should I go on?"

"Your point being?"

Clem grimaced. "When the going gets rough, the powerful get desperate. The damage will be lethal. We have an old saying: 'When the rhinos are making love, stand clear.'"

"You said you need all the help you can get. Does that have to do with the rhinos?"

"Maybe." Clem leaned back and sighed. "I can retire in another year and a half at max benefits. I don't want anything to overturn my applecart. Julia . . ." He paused long enough to wipe the moisture from his eyes. "Julia's had to put up with years of doing without me because I was working ten-hour days and weekends. She's always yearned to see the Parthenon. Finally, she'll have a chance." He ran an index finger under his nose. "And when I go, you'll be the obvious choice to replace me—if you keep your nose clean. Questions?"

"When do I start?" Gene said.

"This afternoon. Mark's ready to take over your old office, and your new digs are next door. Hacker will arrange for an orientation for you on National Preparedness Office—he always calls it NPO— operations. If he drags his feet, push him. Anything else?"

"Just one thing. Any chance of a promotion to SES2? Hugh got his when he moved to the NPO Chief of Staff slot."

"Don't be so anxious," Clem said. "You're already of equal rank with Hacker."

"I'd like to outrank him."

"Gene, in the view of the military, civilian rank doesn't exist. I'm an SES1. That means I outrank a lieutenant general, but Hacker still talks down to me. Let people pull rank all they want. Treat them reverentially—for example always use 'sir' with Hacker. All that matters is that we can veto their programs with impunity. I'm hungry. Let's order."

Clem insisted on the pan-seared salmon with Hollandaise. "Celebrate while you can. It's going to get rough."

Close to two, they arrived by cab back at the New Executive Office Building. In the elevator, Clem told Gene to come by the front office to get cipher lock and safe combinations. As they came through the double doors to the director's office, Nettie looked up from her computer. Her face bloomed. "Man of the hour." She swept from behind her desk and threw her arms around Gene. "I'm so happy for you."

Flustered, Gene returned her hug and stepped back.

"Doctor Yancy," she said to Clem, "General Hacker wants you to call him right away."

Clem made for the door to the inner office. "Gene, wait until I get Hacker off my back, then come on in." He went in and closed the door.

"When did you find out?" Nettie said, all smiles.

"At lunch," Gene said.

"The office is ready for you. Hugh cleaned out his stuff last week. You going to move in today?"

"Hadn't thought about it. Didn't think I had a chance. Figured Hacker's man would get it."

Nettie appraised the ceiling. "Probably shouldn't tell you this, but after Hacker's nominee withdrew, a certain member of the Senate Preparedness Subcommittee who shall remain nameless intervened—"

"Not Prowley?"

Nettie laughed. "Heavens, no." She leaned close to his ear and whispered. "Senator Danley."

"I'll be damned. I've only met him half a dozen times—while I worked with his staff during that fracas about using classification to hide illegal operations."

Nettie faked a shudder. "The agency heads are still pissed."

"I figured my involvement gave me a permanent black eye. Rumor had it I was on Prowley's to-be-fired list. Clem never pushed to get the administration to act on the findings. My guess is that the president told him to sit down and shut up."

Nettie's phone rang. She rolled her eyes. "March madness, and I don't mean basketball." She picked up the receiver. "Doctor Yancy's Office. No, sir, he's on the other line. Of course, sir. One moment." She pushed the hold button and the intercom. "Sorry to interrupt, Doctor Yancy, but Senator Prowley's on the outside line." She pushed buttons and hung up. "Now Hacker will be mad at me, but senators have precedence over generals."

Gene lifted the desk portrait of two teenage girls. "How are they?"

"What can I say?" She shook her head. "Ever since their father left, my bedroom has become the family hangout. Can't keep them out of *my* clothes, but I wouldn't be caught dead in the outfits *they* buy."

The intercom buzzed. Nettie picked up the phone. "Yes, sir, General Hacker's still waiting. Line one secure." She listened, nodded, hung up. "Hacker's steamed about something. Prowley, too."

"Steer clear. A wise man once told me to stay out of the way when the rhinos are making love. That was less than two hours ago, or I wouldn't have remembered it."

The intercom sounded. Nettie picked up. "Yes, sir." She scurried to open the door for Gene. "You're on."

Clem sat frowning at his desk.

"You don't seem happy," Gene said.

"Sorry. Got a senator and a general taking umbrage."

"What's happening? They're the primary players in my new portfolio."

"Later." Clem's frown deepened. "Your new job will take guts, but I know you—you're made of pith and vinegar."

"Thanks for the vote of confidence."

"Harry will read you on for the nuclear defense compartments when we're through here. They all have their own codewords and require individual clearances. You'll keep some of your signals intelligence clearances."

"Okay. Which snakes will bite me first?"

"That will be obvious as soon as you start reviewing the correspondence. Here's the cipher lock and safe combinations. Harry reset them both. I'll be out of town from 23 to 30 March, so you'll have a couple of weeks to bounce things off me before you have to fly solo."

"Thanks again for the boost, boss. Great lunch. I owe you."

Clem raised a hand, palm outward. "Final bit of guidance, Gene. Beware Hacker. Never give him anything he can use against you."

From Clem's office, Gene headed downstairs to security. Harry read him on for the new clearances, witnessed his signature to documents swearing never to reveal his knowledge of the compartments, and gave him the combination to open the key cabinet in his new office and the passwords he'd need to access the compartmented computer files. Gene climbed the stairs to the seventh floor. At the entrance to the secured spaces of the Federal Intelligence Budget Office, he slid his badge into the reader. The barrier arm lifted. He clipped the badge to his lapel, nodded at the guard, and headed through the dark-paneled hall until he came to the door marked "Nuclear Defense Intelligence." He found the cipher lock and punched in the six-digit code Clem had given him. The system answered with a reassuring two-tone welcome. He leaned his shoulder against the door and swung it open.

His new office was a twin to his old one, next door. He tried the keys Harry had entrusted to him— "Remember, Gene, no copies"—one for each cabinet, then hung them in the key box on the wall, locked it, and reopened it with the combination. He booted the computers and tried the new passwords, as Harry had instructed, and opened the safe. Time to study.

First came the Charter of the National Preparedness Office (NPO), classified Top Secret under the codeword Magenta. NPO's job was two-fold: to monitor nuclear threats to the United States; and to analyze U.S. preparedness to cope with a nuclear attack. The president chose its director from a list of candidates drawn up by The National Security Council after the Office of Management and Budget had approved the list and had received the advice and counsel of the Senate Preparedness Subcommittee. Gene shook his head. *Pro forma* gobbledegook. What it meant, when the niceties were stripped away, was that the president names the NPO chief. So Hacker was definitely the president's man. Gene checked the charter's date. Revised in January 2017, right after the current administration took power. Queasiness seeped through his bowels. His instincts were warning him of—what?

He searched the safe in vain for anything describing the thirteen compartments Harry had cleared him for. Commanding his stomach to cease its rumbling, he dug into the correspondence which filled the bottom drawer of the safe and pieced together a fuzzy image of NPO and its structure.

Finally, using the password for each compartment, he read the computer files Hugh Shafter had left behind and found vague descriptions of the operations. Concentrating on the budget proposals, add-ons, supplements, and corrections, he discovered that the NPO headquarters was in the Pentagon, with various offices scattered around the Washington area, many in covert locations. Its staff was around twelve hundred in three main divisions—operations, research, and planning—with other functions carried out by headquarters staff. Congress funded it at just over six billion for 2018, and the 2019 budget came in at just under seven billion.

Gene puzzled over the numbers. Why were they so large? He went through the NPO programs one by one and found nothing to explain the extravagant funding.

Past five. After memorizing the cipher lock code, the passwords, and the safe and key box combinations, he sanitized—switched off the computers, assured that all classified information was under lock and key, and shredded classified waste. He emptied the shredder into a burnbag and sealed it. On his way out, he dropped the bag into the classified trash chute and took the stairs rather than the elevator, part of his fitness regimen.

He loosened his collar as he passed Farragut Square, even though it was unseasonably cool. On the Metro, he took off his suit jacket. The tie came off during the ten-block walk along Sixteenth Street from the Silver Spring station back to Shepherd Park in the northernmost part of D.C. By the time he turned down the hill on Jessamine Street, he was moist. Disgusting. He sweated more than any man he knew. At the circular driveway, he dropped his briefcase and mopped his forehead. The daffodils were bright and cool.

The grounds of the old mansion, surrounded on three sides by Rock Creek Park, cried out for maintenance. The forest was encroaching; the Hinoki cypresses, arborvitae, and yews along the foundation looked like they hadn't been pruned in years; and what once must have been a beautiful lawn was ragged with chickweed—crabgrass and dandelions wouldn't be far behind. Maybe this year Gene would ask his landlord, George, to let him work in the yard, because George was probably too old for that kind of work. The thing Gene missed most from his days in Takoma Park was working the land with Michael, nurturing growing things, bringing new life from the earth. The father and son, working together, had achieved their masterpiece: the new lawn they'd planted four years before all around the Victorian three-decker.

As Gene let himself into the coolness of the entrance hall and slammed the door behind him, Scarpia barked from somewhere. Three steps up, George was vacuuming the foyer with long swaths, starting at the arch leading to the living room, past the double doors to the dining room and both sets of stairs, and finally to the den entrance. Humming to himself, George went on working, simultaneously wiping sweat from his short-cropped white kinks and chocolate skin. When Gene walked up the steps, George looked up, startled, and switched off the vacuum.

"I didn't hear you. Priss called on the house phone. Twice."

"Sorry, George. I'll call her."

"Want to join me for a salade Niçoise and a touch of Pouilly Fuissé?"

"Thanks, but I can't eat before I work out."

Gene climbed the spiral stairs to the second floor, where his three housemates had bedrooms, then headed up the narrow curling staircase to his room in the attic. Tossing damp dress shirt and underwear into the bathroom, he carried his suit and shoes into the bedroom. When he had opened windows on three sides of the room and flipped on the pedestal fan, he retrieved his cell phone from his jeans. One message.

"Hi, handsome." Priss' smoky voice. "Elizabeth's at her father's to celebrate her thirteenth birthday, so you could stay the night and go straight to work from here. Give me a buzz."

His gypsy temptress. She'd told him the truth when they met: she was too smart to be prissy. Incisive and sometimes acid, she was well-read and knew theater, music, and painting—she worked for the National Endowment for the Arts—and like Gene and Michael, she delighted in picaresque phrasing but was better at it than either of them. When she was good, she explained to Gene, quoting Mae West, she was very, very good, but when she was bad, she was . . . wonderful.

She wore her black hair loose so that it blew in the wind. Her olive skin and high cheek bones betrayed her American Indian ancestry. He thought he'd seduced her after the New Years' Eve bash where Carl had introduced them between piano sets. Now he suspected he'd been the seducé.

He could be with her tonight. No, he had to be rested before his second day on the new job, and no night spent with Priss was a good night's sleep. He dialed her number.

"Can't do it tonight, Priss. Just started a new job."

"Elizabeth will at her father's Friday night through Sunday."

"Your place or mine? You've never stayed overnight here."

"Might upset the guy who owns the house," she said.

"George?"

"That's him. I can never remember the names of people who don't like me."

"He's never met you," Gene said.

"He was pretty uppity on the phone. Actually, I did meet him once. Carl introduced us."

Gene laughed. "George takes some getting used to. He's deaf. Has a lot of trouble with the telephone. He's got the house phone rigged up to an old school bell, the kind that sounds in the hall to tell you it's time to go to class. And the doorbell is Big Ben with the volume nob set to eleven."

A pause, then she cleared her throat. "Gene are you, you know, seeing anyone else?"

He tried to keep the irritation out of his voice. "The answer is still no. As I said, that doesn't mean I'm ready for an exclusive relationship. Let's go on as we are, enjoy each other and let it go at that."

"That's what I want, too," she said. "Okay. We'll get together Friday night. I'll call you later in the week—"

"Not on the house phone, okay? It annoys George."

"You never answer your cell."

"I can't take it into the office," he said. "No cell phones allowed in classified areas. You know that."

"See you Friday."

He put down the cell and picked up his workout shorts and tank top. He wished he understood these games better. When he met her, he hadn't dated in twenty years, but he'd read the signals right—she was attracted to him and available. He should have paid closer attention to Carl's warning. "She hangs on with talons that would give an eagle pause." Rumor had it, Carl had told him before their second date, that she'd gone after the guy she rented a room to, and he barely got away with his balls.

A casual relationship, no commitment. That's what she said she wanted. It had been his first sex since leaving the marriage. Priss had been a revelation. Nothing like Donna, with her notes next to the bathroom sink on Saturday mornings: "Wake me early." For one of their rapid, efficient encounters with a condom because she was afraid of the Pill. She'd have done her duty. He'd have no grounds for complaint. Down time, she'd called it. That had infuriated him. "Say 'lovemaking.' Or copulating or even screwing. How about 'fucking'?"

He could hear her voice. "You make me sick."

Remembering saddened him. He put on the workout clothes and descended to the cavernous living room on the main floor, furnished with Carl's Steinway grand, a workout bike, benches and dumbbells, and Hank's dismantled motorcycle laid out on a tarp. One of these days, George would tell Hank to get the damned thing out of there. The scent of motor oil mixed with smell of his own sweat. Bizarre, but nothing compared to the rest of his life. He spread a mat in front of the dead fireplace and went through the stretching regimen.

He was on his last set of curls when Hank Shelby bounded down the stairs into the foyer. His pale red hair was still wet from combing, his frame lankier than ever in dress shirt with bow tie and black trousers.

"Going to work?" Gene called.

Hank hurried down the steps to the front entrance and out of the house, slamming the door behind him.

Gene put the barbells down with a thud. *The guy's a prick, all right? Get over it.* He finished his routine and stretched. He was toweling off when the front door opened and Carl Swenson, in his army major's uniform, materialized in the foyer. Framed by the arched doorway, broad enough for a four-man color guard, he looked more diminutive than usual.

He gave Gene a brilliant smile, all teeth. "Doing the macho thing again?"

"You ought to see about bulking up," Gene said. "Might improve your love life."

"If my love life gets any better, it'll kill me. Besides, I don't have time. After I change, battlefield martinis will be served on the veranda. Can't be long, though. Got a gig tonight."

Gene dried his hair. "Going to be here for dinner? I'm cooking."

"In that case, no. Actually, I'm supposed to play at the piano bar for the after-dinner crowd. The restaurant gives me dinner."

Showered and in post-workout scrubs, Gene skipped down the servants' stairs in the rear of the house to the kitchen and made his way through the French doors from the dining room to the ancient stone veranda. He settled in a plastic chair and scanned the maples and birches in Rock Creek Park below him. Carl appeared with a tray. Blond and blue-eyed, in a white evening jacket and red bow tie, he was like a live-action figure of a Barbie's Ken, minus the sun tan.

"I've been meaning to ask," Carl said. "What's with the scrubs? You moonlighting at Washington General?"

"I go on sweating for a long time after I finish lifting," Gene said, "and sweat clothes are too warm."

In the twilight, a blur of black appeared on the grass just inside the property line, tore around the stone barbecue, then bounded up the stairs to the terrace, circled, and dashed up the steps to the veranda.

Carl extended his hand, palm out. "Scarpia, stop."

The German Shepherd slid to a rest against Carl's legs.

"How'd you do that?" Gene asked.

"George taught me how to give the 'stop' and 'back' commands." Carl pushed Scarpia away. "Don't get my jacket dirty." He scowled at Gene. "When that dog's on his hind legs, he's taller than I am."

Gene gave Scarpia a wave. "Come over here, boy." Scarpia wagged his way to Gene who scrunched under the chin and evoked a grateful growl. "Scarpia and me, we're buddies. When he stands upright, he and I see eye-to-eye. Same with Michael."

"Gigantism runs in your family, right? That's okay. Don't apologize."

"Spoken like a true boy-toy," Gene laughed.

"Hey, be nice."

"Why start now?"

Scarpia placed his head on Gene's knees. Gene scratched behind both ears. Scarpia rumbled somewhere between a growl and a purr.

"You're his favorite," Carl said. "Except for George, of course."

"Scarpia loves everybody."

"Not Hank." Carl dumped gin over the ice in the cocktail shaker and added three drops of red wine. "The only time I ever saw Hank happy was when he was tormenting Scarpia."

"George let him do that?"

Carl dropped an olive in each stemmed glass. "George had to restrain Scarpia. He was going to eat Hank alive."

"So it's unanimous: nobody likes Hank. Wish he'd finish fixing the motorcycle and get it out of the living room."

"Nothing like playing at the Steinway while Hank cusses and tinkers with the bike and swills beer." Carl shook the martinis and poured. "The more he drinks, the madder he gets. Last week he threw down his wrench and screw driver and staggered out. I cleaned up the empty bottles."

Gene lifted his martini to Carl. "Sounds like some people at the Pentagon."

"Nobody I know. Hey, compared to the budgeting business, work in Defense is nothing but sparkle and excitement. How's life in the gray world?"

Gene brightened. "Started a new job today. My client is a classified organization headed by Lieutenant General Peter Hacker. Ever run into him in J4?"

"Never met him, but I monitor acquisition and provisioning for his compartmented accounts, the ones I'm cleared for. J4 is the gossip mill of the military, so I know about Hacker. The Air Force logistics guys refer to him as the Grand Inquisitor—call him GI for short—and have an office pool on who he'll send to the stake next. He takes no prisoners."

Gene shrugged. "He can't touch me."

One corner of Carl's mouth turned up. "Won't need to. He never does his own dirty work."

"Enough about Hacker." Gene sipped. "I'm off duty. You gettin' any these days?"

"As we say in the Army, I don't let my heartache get in the way of my hardon. Sharon will be here for the weekend. If I can't get what I want, I take what I can get."

"Guess we all do," Gene said.

"Uh-huh, and how *is* Priss?"

"She'll probably be here this weekend, too."

Carl gave his head a fast shake. "Priss is high-maintenance, low-confidence, with an industrial-strength ego and serious castration tendencies. Other than that, she's a sweet kid."

"With a contralto voice that melts rocks."

"She melted my rocks once. Still have claw marks on my back."

"I can handle it. How're your boys?"

Carl's incandescent smile returned. "They're driving my ex's live-in boyfriend crazy. Can't wait for their weekends with Dad. I let them go native. How's Michael?"

"Cramming for mid-terms and working part-time for Troiano Construction. They'll need him full-time for the summer. Donna didn't want him to work—says a young man of his breeding should enjoy his leisure. The last thing I'd want is to delay his senior year for lack of money. Now if I can just get him to save up and not spend everything on his love interest of the moment—"

"So there *is* a skirt-chaser in the Westmoreland family," Carl said. "I'd begun to suspect that gigantism squelches the libido. Took you two years to break out of celibacy."

"Michael doesn't have a bad marriage behind him to slow him down." Gene chuckled. "I don't think he ever saw a skirt he didn't like. He's got hormones by the quart in every vein."

"Never mind. George would enjoy having him here. He likes my boys." Carl consulted his watch and gathered the glasses and cocktail shaker. "The glamorous life awaits me. Keep the Grand Inquisitor on your radar, Gene. He has thumb screws and knows how to use them."

Gene maintained his usual schedule for the rest of week, arriving at FIBO by seven and leaving after five. He buried himself in the National Preparedness Office files, memorized pertinent data, and did a classified search on Hacker and Prowley. Hacker was the president's protégé all right. But unlike the president, he'd been in government for more than thirty years and had ensconced loyal supporters throughout the bureaucracy to assure his programs sailed through without snags. Hugh Shafter,

Gene's predecessor as Senior Budget Reviewer for Nuclear Defense Intelligence, had originally come from NPO. Now he'd been reassigned back to NPO as Hacker's chief of staff. The man Hacker had supported to replace Hugh at FIBO was also from NPO. Vince Dellaspada, chief of staff for the Senate Preparedness Subcommittee, was a retired Air Force Officer. He'd been Hacker's chief of staff at NPO before he was hired by Prowley. Gene shook his head in admiration. The president and his hand-picked men sure knew how to work the system.

The classified bio of Hacker told him little, but a Google search unearthed an HGTV "Dream Home" video on the Hacker residence in Georgetown and three news articles, from the *Washington Post,* the *New York Times,* and the *Los Angeles Times,* dated February 2011. They reported allegations that Brigadier General Peter Hacker, then at the National Reconnaissance Office, had lied to the Senate Select Intelligence Committee. His major defender, according to the articles, was Senator Herman Prowley, then the ranking Republican on the committee.

Further hunting produced texts of speeches Prowley had made. All stressed the need for vigilance against the enemies of the United States and the importance of enhancing nuclear deterrence. Prowley had sponsored three different bills, all defeated in committee, to expand and modernize U.S. nuclear armaments, arguing that "repair and maintenance of old warheads is expensive, dangerous, and counter-productive." His name appeared in four articles about the hiring and firing of Paul Manafort as the president's campaign manager.

Late Friday, Gene dialed Hugh Shafter at NPO on the secure line.

"This is Colonel Pierce," said a voice with the inflection of a classical music radio host. "Mr. Shafter will be right with you. Your name please?"

"Gene Westmoreland."

"Sorry, sir. I need your full payroll name for our records."

"Eugene Burrell Westmoreland."

"Excuse me, sir. Noise on the line. Could you repeat that slowly?"

"Eugene. Burrell. Westmoreland."

"Thank you, sir. One moment."

Shafter said Gene wasn't cleared for the documentation in NPO's budget justification, transmitted separately to Clem. Gene asked what clearances he needed. Shafter would have to get back to him on that.

The Senate Preparedness Subcommittee scheduled the first hearing on the 2020 budget for the second Tuesday in March. "Just a *pro forma* session," Clem explained. "They'll make broad policy pronouncements with lots of 'good-of-country' and 'in these grave times' phraseology. We'll do the same."

On the appointed day, Clem, with fact book and the 2020 budget in his locked briefcase and Gene in tow, got to the Russell Building at eight thirty-five. Clem showed his security pass, and the guards let him through but thoroughly ransacked Gene's briefcase. At the dark wooden door to the classified hearing room, Gene rang the bell beneath the cipher lock. The door opened. Inside, the guards at a long counter examined IDs, photographed Gene and Clem, went through Gene's briefcase again, and asked them to wait. Hugh Shafter nodded to them from another bench. Beside him sat a balding Air Force colonel and a baby-faced man with buzz-cut blond hair and an olive-drab suit.

Gene tilted his head toward the blond. "Who's the kid?"

"Lieutenant Cutter. Hacker's gopher. He's the general's favorite."

"And the lugubrious Colonel?"

"That's Pierce," Clem said in an undertone. "Always strikes me as a refugee from a funeral home."

Four of the seven senators on the subcommittee, each with a coterie of staff, passed through a door labeled SUB-COMMITTEE AND STAFF ONLY at the end of the room. Senator Prowley bustled in, sporting the famous bristling white hair, wild eyebrows, and a belly that strained his dress shirt under an open suit coat. He was accompanied by Vince Dellaspada, black hair graying at the temples, and a self-confident young man in a pale blue summer suit. The swag of dark hair over his forehead reminded Gene of Gainsborough's *The Blue Boy*. The three had just gone through the subcommittee-only door when Senator Willis Danley, ruddy and plump, ambled in with a woman in a business suit. He spoke briefly to Hugh, then turned to Clem and Gene. They stood.

"Doctor Yancy, good to see you again. Doctor Westmoreland?" Danley grasped Gene's hand. "What a pleasure. So you're now part of the preparedness community?"

"Barely, Senator. New to the job. So much to learn."

"Indeed," Danley said. "And so many clearances." His joviality wavered. "Has NPO cleared you for everything?"

"He'll soon have them all," Clem said before Gene could answer. "Red tape, bureaucracy, you know—"

"After two weeks? Horse feathers." Danley scowled. "Mavis, telephone Hacker before the session begins. Tell him I expect Westmoreland to be cleared before close of business." He swung to Gene. "Call me in the morning and let me know if the clearances have come through." He started away, then stopped. "Westmoreland, keep me in the loop. I want weekly updates. Mavis?"

She nodded. "I'll make a note of it, Senator."

They headed for the door.

At nine-fifteen, the Blue Boy appeared and greeted all the players except Gene. Clem introduced him to Gene as Dennis Hodgings, staff assistant. He shook Gene's hand in passing.

Dennis led them through the unmarked door into a windowless chamber reminiscent of a small courtroom. Facing them on a platform was a long desk of shining wood—the aroma of wood polish clung discreetly to the filtered air. Seven microphones stood by seven brass nameplates. "Senator Prowley" was dead center. A dark floor-to-ceiling curtain covered the wall behind the desk. Clem and Hugh sat side by side at a mahogany table with five heavy chairs, five microphones, five water glasses, and a frosty carafe. Gene took a chair to Clem's right, and Colonel Pierce placed himself to Hugh's left. The blond kid sat in the back row of the darkened gallery.

"What's Danley's problem about your clearances?" Clem whispered.

"During the classification hearings last year," Gene said in an undertone, "several agencies, NPO among them, stonewalled granting clearances to the investigative staff. They were hoping to hobble the study or get Danley to call it off. It finally took a face-to-face showdown between Danley and the agency directors. He doesn't take kindly to resistance."

Gene opened the combination lock on Clem's briefcase and handed him the fact book and the 2020 budget. As he did, the red jewel light on the microphone in front of him lit. A door closed. The Blue Boy and Vince Dellaspada came through the curtain, then faced each other and parted the curtain for the entrance of Prowley. Danley and four other senators, each with staff people, followed and took seats behind their nameplates.

Prowley opened the meeting declaring that the nuclear threat to the United States and its allies had, if anything, increased because of North Korea's intransigence. The funding of the National Preparedness Office was more urgent than ever, he said, and he encouraged Hugh Shafter to feel free to bring forward proposals. Danley spoke next, agreeing with Prowley but stressing the need for justification. "We are here to watch over the interests of the taxpayers."

At the invitation of Prowley, Clem outlined the Nuclear Defense Intelligence budget proposal, gave the figures, and declared that FIBO had scrubbed NPO's programs to assure that each was justified and economically sound. He was ready to work with the subcommittee staff as needed. Hugh added that NPO was prepared to assist.

Danley asked why it was necessary to add three new compartments, each with its own codeword, to the litany NPO already was using.

"Because of the extreme sensitivity of each of these operations," Hugh said.

"Perhaps," Danley said, "but with so many compartments and codewords and separate clearances and discrete budget items for each, keeping track of NPO is becoming well-nigh impossible. I'm going to recommend folding these operations into a single archive under one rubric. How many different clearances does NPO control?"

"I'll have to get back to you on that, Senator," Hugh said.

Danley's frown deepened. "Are we talking dozens or hundreds?"

"Senator, I'll convey that information to the subcommittee's chief of staff."

"By the end of the week, please. Vince, see me Friday and confirm that you've received the list. I'll want to spend time on it next week. Mavis—"

"Noted, Senator," Mavis said.

"Willis," Prowley said to Danley, "I'd rather have the staff handle minutiae off line."

"Allow me my idiosyncrasies, Herman," Danley said.

Prowley frowned into his notes. "Anything else? We're already overtime . . ."

"I have nothing else for the moment," Danley said.

Prowley stood. "Thank you, gentlemen." Vince and the Blue Boy parted the curtain, and Prowley passed through the opening.

Chapter 2

A Riddle Wrapped in a Mystery

As Gene stepped into his cubicle after the hearing, his secure line rang.

"Harry Breighton, Gene."

"My faithful security officer. What's up?"

"One of Hacker's people will be over to give you the security clearances for new National Preparedness Office compartments. He kindly agreed to stop by here afterwards to let me know what the hell's going on. How about checking with me to be sure he gives me a complete list?"

"How come you're not reading me on?"

"NPO insists on doing their own for these compartments. 'Too sensitive for non-NPO personnel to administer,' they said. Call me after he signs you up."

The doorbell chimed at one o'clock precisely. Through the peephole, Gene recognized the blond kid who'd been at the Prowley hearing. Gene secured all classified material and admitted him.

"Lieutenant Cutter, NPO, sir," the boy said with a wooden smile. He laid his photo ID on Gene's desk. The picture showed the same lineless face. "Would the gentleman be kind enough to show credentials?"

Gene pointed to the picture badge attached to his collar.

"If the gentleman wouldn't object," Cutter said, with a mechanical prosody that sounded like a voice-activated phone tree, "I need an additional ID. Regulations."

Gene pulled his Federal Intelligence Budget Office identification card from his wallet.

"Thank you, sir." Cutter unlocked his briefcase. "If the gentleman would be kind enough to read the following material, then sign on the last page. I'll sign as witness."

Gene read the indoctrination page for a compartment called CLANGDON. It told him little beyond the fact that the compartment dealt with "special techniques" for obtaining atmospheric footprints of radioactive activity. He signed the last page, and Cutter countersigned, taking pains to avoid smearing the ink. Next Cutter presented him with six more packets like the first, each with a different code name. Gene read each of them and signed.

The last was FIREFANG. Its accompanying text was only two paragraphs. The first emphasized the importance of the United States' preparedness for a first-strike nuclear capability. The second was a single sentence: "Initiation and scope of actions covered by this compartment remain the purview of the national command authority and may be communicated verbally."

Gene frowned. "What does this mean?"

Cutter's face stayed blank. "The gentleman will have to take up inquiries with Mr. Shafter and General Hacker."

After signing the document, Gene started to write the compartment names on scratch paper.

Cutter confiscated the list. "My apologies, sir. That's against regulations."

"The FIBO security chief, Mr. Breighton, asked for a list of the clearances."

"I remind the gentleman that the codewords themselves are compartmented. The only other cleared personnel within this organization is Doctor Yancy. I will speak to Mr. Breighton on my way out and supply him with the requisite data. The National Preparedness Office will provide the gentleman with an approved safe to store the material from these compartments. The files are not to be interfaced with other materials. The safe is scheduled for delivery tomorrow. An NPO representative will change the combinations weekly. With the safe will come a list of passwords to allow the gentlemen access to the compartments in the FIBO computer system."

With that, Cutter slid the papers into his briefcase which he secured with a cipher lock and left.

Gene dialed Clem.

"Hacker's security man just read me on for seven new clearances, Clem. Guess Danley knows how to make things happen."

"Word of advice, Gene. Don't cozy up to Danley. He's in bad odor with the president. He's on the administration's hush-hush list of senators to be defeated in November."

"How do you know? You're not part of the conservative old boys' network."

Clem huffed. "Went to a mandatory PowerPoint presentation last week in Commerce."

"Doesn't the Hatch Act forbid that kind of thing?"

"Not my business. I'm a bean counter. Anyway, steer clear of Danley. And, Gene—" He paused. "An old rule of thumb in dealing with Congress: Never answer a question that hasn't been asked, and never volunteer information. Don't forget. You work for the executive branch."

That evening, the house was empty. Carl was probably playing at the Côte d'Azur, and Hank was tending bar at the Dandelion. No sign of George. Gene changed into his workout clothes, grabbed a towel, and started down the staircase. A clang and a curse echoed through the casement window. "*Merde*," a voice said. "*Il s'en faut de beaucoup.*" Three stories below, George, shovel in hand, stood staring at the flat strip of land to the rear of the garage. Gene called to him but realized George couldn't hear him.

Gene hurried to the yard. "What are you up to?"

George shone with sweat in the twilight. "I'm too old, Gene. The ground is too hard."

"For what?"

"To plant climbing roses along the garage wall."

"I could help." Gene glanced at the sky. "A little late in the day, though. How about if I tackle it over the weekend?"

George gave him a sour smile. "And deprive you of time with Priss?"

"She's taking her daughter to Williamsburg."

"I'm going to wash up," George said. "Montrachet in the wine chest. Glasses in the credenza. Meet you on the veranda in twenty minutes."

Gene tossed the towel into the living room. He wouldn't be able to work out after wine, and George obviously needed to talk. By the time George came out to the veranda, Gene had the wine opened, glasses ready, and popcorn popped. Scarpia was lying obediently next to George's chair.

"Popcorn?" George scowled. "With Montrachet?"

"All I had. Sorry."

"God. Impecunious divorcés."

"I'm not divorced yet," Gene said. "Besides, I'm a man, not a divorcée."

"Divorcé. One e with an *accent aigu*. The feminine has a double e."

"*Touché.*"

George looked faintly sick. "For an educated man, you lack both passable French and palate finesse. On the other hand, I have no foie gras or oysters. Priced beyond my reach."

"And Montrachet isn't?"

"One makes one's choices and lives with the consequences. Including popcorn." George poured the wine. "Life without Montrachet is a life wasted."

Gene chuckled. "I have trouble taking you seriously."

"That makes two of us."

"About the roses. Michael's supposed to be over this weekend. He could help me prepare the bed. Maybe you could give us dinner. Got to warn you, though. Michael's more into sodas and hot dogs than wine and hors d'oeuvres."

"One must make allowances," George said. "Seriously, I'd be grateful to you both. I promised Alex I'd plant roses—"

"A former tenant?"

"The owner before me. He always wanted to keep the place up, especially the garden. I haven't been able . . ."

"Sounds like there's stuff besides roses you'd like done," Gene said.

George opened his arms. "Where to begin? Pruning, landscaping the semi-circle inside the driveway, replacing the dead shrubs. You know what I'd love to do? Put in a real lawn from the terrace steps to the property line. When Alex owned the house, it was genuine grass. Now it's nothing but—" George's nostrils flared. "—a meadow."

"If you want to do it, the earlier in the spring you get it in—"

George stopped him with a wave of his hand. "You have any notion of what it would cost to hire workers to dig up that tract?"

"Maybe Michael and I could take it on."

"If you could—"

"I have a favor to ask in return," Gene said.

"For a lawn gardener, anything."

"Carl tells me you taught him commands for Scarpia." Scarpia raised his head and wagged expectantly. "I'd like to learn how to control him."

George squinted into the darkness. "You're a mind reader. He's getting—" He took a deep breath. "Scarpia's a pup at heart. I got him just before you moved in because I needed a guard dog. Built him a doggie door from the party room and taught him to stay on the property with an electronic collar. Training is a life-long pursuit with a dog. He's getting sloppy because, between my arthritis and emphysema, I can't keep up the constant review." He hesitated. "I'll be eighty-two this year, Gene."

"What do you need me to do?" Gene said.

"Assume mastership over him. Take over the regular training sessions."

"I'd enjoy that. Meanwhile, you're supposed to be cooking tonight. What's the menu?"

"Hot dogs and sour kraut," George mumbled.

Gene laughed. "A meal with genuine palate finesse."

"Sorry. It was on sale."

The first day of spring. As Gene ate eggs and toast on the veranda the next morning, he glanced at the *Washington Post* front page. House Republicans reported that their investigation showed no collusion between the president and Russia. Stormy Daniels offered to repay the $130,000 given to her a hush money for covering up her affair with the president. A string of firings and resignations at the president's behest. Gene sighed. It got worse every day. At least there was nothing new about the president's attacks on the intelligence community.

The new sun touched the trees on the hill beyond Rock Creek. The first warmth of the day brushed across his skin. His sap, like that of the trees, was rising.

With the vigor of newness came melancholy. Why didn't hormones adjust to the realities of life? More to the point, why couldn't he be like Carl and compartmentalize his sex drive from his life needs? Why didn't the human heart accept the slings and arrows of outrageous fortune and move on?

His life with Donna had been finished for years, long before the separation. He'd been over their history endlessly, trying to find an answer. Why now, on a spring morning with fresh life intoxicating him, did he have to relive it yet again? Why, having learned as a foster child not to depend on anyone, had he depended on Donna?

As he'd climbed the executive ranks, she'd become the proud executrix. She quit her job at NSA, took up tennis and cocktail parties, signed on as a docent at the Pfeiffer Galleries, and finally volunteered to counsel cadets at Saint Boniface Military Academy. A woman of arresting beauty, she fed on the adulation of her peers and the envy of the *hoi polloi*. In a moment of startling revelation, Gene heard her murmur, after she'd received an award at the Saint Boniface celebration banquet, "I wish my father were here."

Gene doubted her father would have been impressed. An investment banker in Philadelphia, Dexter Cantwell spent minimum time with his wife and children. Even during the years of Donna's wine and roses, he'd never visited. Gene had spent the worst Christmas in memory at Dexter's country place in Satterfield when Michael was an infant. Dexter treated them with rudeness masquerading as preoccupation with business. Gene had wanted to cut short the visit, but Donna insisted they stay. Gene had never gone there again—though Donna had taken Michael up to spend the vacations there half a dozen times—and Gene's relations with his father-in-law cooled.

Maybe Donna was emulating her father. As her social prominence grew, Gene and Michael became little more than a nuisance. The final episode had been Michael's mononucleosis his freshman year at George Washington. He'd passed out in class and was taken by ambulance to the emergency room. When the hospital telephoned, Gene ran there, only ten blocks from his office, immediately. Donna, loathe to miss the premier soirée of the season, postponed visiting him.

Gene understood now, as he had not then, that he'd been a substitute father, a man who gave Donna a sense of self-worth that her real father had withheld. As her social life brought her the respect of the high and mighty, she'd lost interest in Gene. Left more and more to his own devices, he engrossed himself in work. The twelve-hour days and weekends in the office led to promotions. The nice thing about intelligence budgeting was that the work was never done.

Michael had never counted with Donna, even in the early years. As Donna's career in the haut monde gathered momentum, she exploited him—showed him off at afternoon teas and lawn parties as her handsome, articulate little boy—but never had time to talk to his teachers, attend his track meets, or host birthday parties for him. Those tasks, along with getting him in bed at night, fixing his breakfast, getting him off to school, and, most important, baking him cookies at Christmas, fell to Gene. Father and son had grown close, consoling each other without ever saying so.

Gene finished his eggs. The traffic from Sixteenth Street was still dormant, and he could hear the babble of Rock Creek at the foot of the hill. He filled his lungs with the sweet smell of spring. Yeah, his fancy was turning. And making him face his vacuous existence. Work still protected him most of the time from moments of yearning when the emptiness of his life came out of hiding. Priss was no substitute for Donna. And, wisely, he'd never depended on her for anything but sex. Their affair was, for both of them, a temporary solution to a permanent problem.

He was seeing her less often, thanks to his workload and her daughter Elizabeth's presence every other weekend. Their love-making was still magic, but out of bed Priss was getting to be a royal pain. She'd taken to pouting over imagined slights—like Friday night when he didn't bring her flowers because he'd come straight from work. Carl had been gracious, but she was bratty. She treated George as if he needed a bath. And the questions about who Gene was seeing besides her buzzed around like ravenous mosquitoes. Her saving grace was greeting Scarpia like an old friend, sitting on the floor with him, and accepting his adoring kisses. Gene suspected it was an act to please him.

He put his plate in the dishwasher, packed his lunch, and left for the Metro.

Mid-morning Cutter arrived with two enlisted men carrying the promised safe. Gene made room for it by moving his coatrack and umbrella stand, which he never used anyway, into the hall. Cutter furnished him with the double passwords to open secure network files he was now cleared for and taught him to open and close the triple-combination safe. Finally,

Cutter burdened Gene with a sheaf of documents, which, Cutter made clear, must be kept in the new safe.

"I understand," Gene said, "that I am to receive an orientation."

"The gentleman will have to speak to Mr. Shafter about that."

Left alone, Gene stowed all classified material in the two safes and flipped off the computers, then went into the hall and verified that his door was locked behind him. At the cubicle next to his, labeled "Signals Intelligence," he rang the bell below the cipher lock. The peephole darkened, and the door opened three inches. Mark Forrester's luminous eyes—set in skin so black it was almost purple—peered at Gene.

"Hey, Professor," Mark said. "Let me sanitize."

The door closed with a metal click. The reverberation of a safe door slamming came through the wall. Mark swung the door wide, pushed it closed after Gene, and yanked it to be sure it was firmly engaged.

"Getting used to the catacombs?" Gene said.

"Claustrophobic, but anything for admission to the Senior Executive Service. Did they have to black out the windows?"

"The paint stops prying eyes. The window is double glass with copper screen between panes to prevent electronic emissions and sonic eavesdropping. You'll be handling some of the most sensitive information in the government, especially now with the administration pushing PRISM, what we used to call the Terrorist Surveillance Program, lovingly referred to as the TSP."

"There's more to the PRISM than wiretapping?"

"Much more. When your clearances come through, you'll see what a snake pit you're in. The president has expanded PRISM and uses it for monitoring of internal U.S. telephone calls and emails. Clem and I did the best we could to withhold funds on the grounds that it was illegal. The president gave

Clem a direct order to support the PRISM, even the parts we thought were illegal."

Mark quailed. "Mama in heaven pray for me. What have I gotten myself into now?"

"The NPO material is even more serpentine," Gene went on. "I have to maintain a special safe to store compartmented documents. Which brings me to why I'm here. Can you use the coatrack and umbrella stand in the hall? I don't have room for them."

"Perks provided to SESers? How soon will I be assigned a parking space?"

Gene hesitated. "You can use mine. I take the Metro. And—" Gene fumbled. "Acceptance into the executive service takes time."

"I thought it came with the job."

"Looked in the mirror lately, Spear Chucker?"

Mark's face hardened.

"This administration is the last bastion of 'family values,' Mark, especially since both houses of Congress and the White House are run by the president's insiders. How many blacks do you see in the executive ranks in the FIBO and NPO? For that matter, how many Latinos or Jews? Any leftists? Gays? Anybody in therapy? Any females?"

"If I believed . . . I'd go to the EEO Commission and—"

"You can't, Mark. We're an excepted service, remember? You make a stink and instead of being invited to join the Senior Executive Service, you'll find yourself cranking an adding machine in Commerce. If I knew when I first came here twenty years ago . . ." He took a breath and held it. "Beware security."

"Harry? He's a straight shooter—"

"Harry does what he's told. The president withdraws clearances to get rid of critics and resistors. And if you're fired for violating security, you lose everything, including your retirement."

Mark frowned. "Clem didn't tell me—"

"Clem's a superb administrator and so bright it's scary. I admire his decency. The old guy's gone out his way to guide our careers." *He coached me like the father I never had*, Gene wanted to say. "For all that, courage and confrontation aren't among his strong suits."

"The pious procrastinator. Sounds like he's earned his reputation. Shit."

Gene put his hand on Mark's shoulder. "Hey, respect him for what he is. Never mind. Be patient for a while. If the promotion doesn't come through, we'll fight this together. The rhinos may still be 'southern gentlemen,' but most of us calves are growing up. We'll make it happen."

Back in his cubicle, Gene worked his way through each of the new compartments, reading the material Cutter had brought him and the documents on the network. The first six compartments each dealt with finite aspects of nuclear warfare and seemed to have nothing to do with intelligence. Finally he came to FIREFANG. What emerged was an entire organization within an organization. An office named "First Strike Operations," managed from a covert "war center" in the Washington area, had six divisions—FS1 through FS6—responsible, respectively, for personnel, intelligence, operations, logistics, plans & policy, and communications. FS3, operations, was the largest. NPO was a shell over the real organization, referred to *in toto* as First Strike Operations or FSO. Even the personnel roster was a sham. The real jobs were quite different from the cover job titles.

Gene rolled his chair away from the desk and put his hands behind his head. *Wow.* The entity the public knew by the name of the National Preparedness Office was a clandestine outfit whose real name was First Strike Operations. *A riddle wrapped in a mystery inside an enigma . . .*

Nothing spelled out the mission of FSO. He snatched a blank paper from his drawer, picked up his pencil, and began the reconstruction of FSO's purpose through fragments and unexplained references scattered throughout the files and documents. For the first time in years, he was grateful for the training in cryptanalysis and code recovery NSA had given him when he had worked there as a mathematician.

The piecing together took him most of the day. The preoccupation with missiles was clear. Among the FS3 documents were reports on the reliability of silo concealment, cost-effectiveness studies of covert international transportation of ICBM components, operations analysis and statistical profiles of the destruction envelope of warheads in various climactic conditions and topography in Europe and Asia.

What this had to do with intelligence to help the United States prepare for nuclear attack was lost on Gene. Why did FSO need to worry about what sounded like the construction of missile sites? Gene scratched his head. FSO. First Strike Operations. Maybe he'd misled himself, assuming that FSO dealt with intelligence. Maybe it was what the name said it was, an apparatus to attack first with nuclear weapons. What if FSO wasn't an intelligence organization at all?

By Wednesday, Gene had identified missile sites in Montana, northern Maine, Turkey, and somewhere in Africa. He found that FSO had created a shadow budget. Money to finance the clandestine operation was identified in the shell budget—the one approved by Congress for entirely different purposes—and transferred to the real budget to buy missile components and ship them disguised as everything from electronic gear to battleship parts. The sites were camouflaged as electronic listening posts and radar facilities, ostensibly designed to protect the interests of the host governments who were kept in the dark about their real function.

Gene dialed Shafter's secure line.

"Hugh, I've been reading the material covered by the clearances I got Tuesday. Technical issue: I'm coming across stuff that seems to be beyond the formal charter of NPO. Is there any documentation—"

"There's a compartmented annex to the charter," Hugh said. "I'll see if the general will let you take a gander at it. We don't make copies."

"Maybe I can read it during my orientation. Is that scheduled yet?"

"Have to get back to you after I speak to the general."

Frustrated, Gene hung up.

The secure line rang. Nettie. "Hang on while I put him on."

Clem came on the line. "Need your help, Gene. What's on your calendar tomorrow?"

"Nothing."

"Come up and let's talk."

"Great. I want to go over what I'm finding out about NPO."

Gene sanitized and went up the corridor. Nettie waved him into Clem's office.

"Grab a seat." Clem sat on the edge of his desk. "Here's the deal. Hacker's arranged a business trip for me, and I need a ride to Dulles tomorrow for a 5:00 a.m. flight. Can you take me? And pick me up Sunday at ten in the evening?"

"Sure. Where are you going?"

"Shanghai by way of Los Angeles. I'll be participating in a conference protesting U.S. efforts to curb the spread of nuclear weapons."

Gene cocked his head. "Wait a minute. *In favor of* proliferation?"

"Most governments are boycotting it, but non-governmental entities will be there *en masse*. They proclaim that the United States is ignoring its commitment in the Non-Proliferation Treaty to reduce nuclear arms. The Chinese are sponsoring the conference. And here's the key point. Their top scientists are going to be doing presentations on the Chinese nuclear buildup."

"You'll stand out like a sheik at a Hasidic wedding."

"I'm going under cover. I'll be Keith Simon, Ph.D., political science professor at George Mason. CIA has created credentials that will show me as a rightist extremist. I have the passport, driver's license, phony drafts of articles supporting proliferation, even something called pocket litter—matches from a bar close to the university, a Safeway card, the works. They've even cribbed data into the ATS—"

"You lost me," Gene said.

"The Automated Targeting System, a secret program to track travelers without their knowledge. Every time you travel by air, the airline is required to send info on you to the Department of Homeland Security. Their data base even includes the personal items you carried, what books you took aboard, and your race. You're the only person outside of NPO and CIA who knows where I'm going or that I'll be under cover. Nettie won't be told. My wife's not to know."

"Why are you telling me?"

"CIA is providing a car," Clem said, "registered in the name of Keith Simon, for the trip to and from Dulles. They don't want it left at the airport while I'm gone—too easy for someone to snoop. You'll be my driver."

"Why not have an NPO guy take you?"

"Might be identified. Hacker wants to be sure that I get to the airport and back with someone unconnected to his operation. We budgeteers are famously gray, uninteresting people. Nobody will pay attention to us."

Gene shook his head. "Sounds creepy. You really want to do this?"

"Have you audited our TDY account lately? Not enough to cover a trip to Baltimore. Hacker's paying. Besides, I've always wanted to go to China. Never would be allowed to because of the info I've been privy to. I'd be a prime kidnap target. I told Hacker I'd go if he'd add in time for sightseeing."

"What's Hacker get out of this?" Gene said.

"Information. You can't shut scientists up. They love to talk about their work. Even in China. And guys from Pakistan, India, Israel, and Iran are going to be presenting. The conference sponsors will be selling tapes of their talks and copies of their visuals. It's an info gold mine."

"Clem, this whole thing doesn't pass the sniff test. Seems so odd they'd be sending you."

"You're not used to the operational side of intelligence. In the covert world, you always do what the enemy least expects."

"Okay, boss, it's your call. Can we talk about another subject? I've spent a good many hours figuring out what NPO is really about. I don't have the whole picture yet, but the construction and shipping of missiles is a big part of it. Covert sites are being built in Europe and Asia. FIREFANG—"

Clem started. "Hacker cleared you for Firefang?"

"What's wrong?"

Clem moved to the window. He surveyed the White House and the Eisenhower Executive Office Building. "FIRE-FANG has always been limited to me and Prowley. The only other people cleared for it are Dellaspada and, since he moved to NPO, Hugh Shafter. Hacker never intended to clear you. Who handled it?"

"Cutter."

"That numb nuts?" Clem sighed. "He screwed up, Gene. Jesus. How long have you been working on the FIREFANG material?"

"Full time since yesterday."

Clem winced. "All right. Let's think this through. Too late to withdraw the clearance." He came from behind the desk and sat in the chair facing Gene. "You got it right. FIREFANG is the codeword covering the first strike initiative. Reagan started it covertly. It all but disappeared when he left office. The president revived it as a means of giving the United States the option of attacking enemies and potential enemies—that means our allies—with nuclear weapons from places they don't know about—Turkey, Indonesia, Taiwan, India, among others. The host governments are not to be made aware of the construction of missile sites on their land. Elaborate cover schemes have been developed and so far have worked. The sites have yet to be equipped with nuclear warheads, the most sensitive step."

Clem stared at the wall behind Gene's head. In the silence, Gene could hear his own breathing.

"I was opposed to this plot from the beginning," Clem said. "It's clearly unlawful, but I haven't been able to bring in the legal team because the president refuses to allow them to be cleared. It's unquestionably in violation of treaties with the host countries. Had I known it was going on, I would have stopped the funding, but Hacker padded his budget until I began to notice. By the time he and Prowley let me in on what they were doing, much of it was completed. That was a year ago. Since then, I've done the best I could do limit Hacker's supposedly legitimate projects to bleed funds out of FIREFANG. I've been remarkably successful. Hacker's plan to circumvent me was to hire Hugh Shafter out of the job as my principal watchdog and make him his chief of staff. Hacker intended to put his man into your job. When his candidate withdrew, I moved quickly to get you in place."

"I thought Senator Danley—" Gene began.

"Danley had nothing to do with it. I knew you wouldn't cave under pressure. The day you were named to the position of Senior Budget Reviewer for Nuclear Defense Intelligence, Hacker and Prowley both called me." He laughed. "You were sitting in the outer office while I listened to them howl. Prowley kept insisting that the president wants 'good Americans' on the FIBO staff."

"Why didn't you go to the National Security Council or the Office of Management or Budget?"

"Gene, I have a year and a half before retirement. If I got into a pissing match with the president, I'd be out on my ass. Hacker has a long history with the president, who's trying to cripple the intelligence agencies. Hacker's fiercely loyal. Besides . . ."

Clem hesitated as if choosing his words carefully. "In this administration, the network of insiders is more powerful than the chain of command. Half the members of the National Security Council and the Office of Management and Budget were hand-picked by the president. Law enforcers in the Justice Department have resigned or been fired *en masse*. The attorney general, the president's man, just fired Andrew McCabe, the former deputy director of the FBI, 24 hours before he was due to retire at full benefits. All the president has to do is drop a word or two to his buddies in the NSC or OMB and I'll be managing paper clip accounting at Agriculture. Or worse . . ."

"The president's up to date on Firefang?"

"He revived Reagan's old program, and he's pushing it."

Gene took a deep breath. "Okay. Now what?"

"I pulled strings to get you into your job because I knew you'd spot the padding and blow the whistle without knowing there was a shell budget. Now that you've been cleared—" Clem leaned forward. "Now, it's going to be up to both of us. We can't fight FIREFANG directly, but money for it is hidden in other compartments of NPO's budget. You'll detect the overfunding, and you can identify it from the FIREFANG shadow budget. Scrub each of those bloated line items and insist on justification for every penny. Hacker doesn't have justification. So far that's slowed him, sometimes brought him to a stop. Best of all, he thinks I've been helping him avoid detection by the likes of Danley. Before all else, watch for the first hint that nuclear warheads are being fabricated for the covert sites."

"Hacker will put out a contract on both of us," Gene said.

"Not if we play our cards right. Flatter Hacker, keep him happy, but don't let him stampede you. Now you know the real reason I'm making this trip for him. He'll owe me one."

Gene came home to an empty house. Carl had a gig, Hank had the early shift at the Dandelion, and George was doing volunteer work at a clinic. It would be just Gene and Michael, who would be staying the rest of the week and the weekend. Gene seasoned the pork chops, washed the potatoes, and made the salad. More than an hour to kill until Donna dropped Michael at the house. Not enough time for a workout. Gene opened a soda and headed down the two flights of steps to the open ground—that George grudgingly called the meadow—that surrounded the stone barbecue. Scarpia, tail wagging so hard his hindquarters were doing the rhumba, met Gene at the path into Rock Creek Park. Together they wandered into late afternoon quiet among the trees.

FIREFANG still had Gene rattled. A missile site here and a missile site there and pretty soon you were talking real potential for nuclear war. But he was a technocrat, right? He wasn't supposed to make policy. But FIREFANG was flat-ass *wrong*. How could he prevent it from going any further? Clem was right—if he took on the administration overtly, he'd get squashed faster than he could say nuclear kill zone. If he blew the whistle to the press, he'd be prosecuted for violation of security. He'd have to play it carefully. Bide his time. Wait for an opening.

At the creek, Gene sat on his favorite knoll above the water and stroked Scarpia. If he'd been willing to kiss a few behinds, he'd be an SES1 by now, in a job like Clem's. Instead, he'd always had to be the smart-ass, pointing out the flaws, asking the awkward questions—as he'd done working with Danley's staff last year exposing the rhinos' shenanigans. Every promotion Clem put him in for had been granted begrudgingly. And here he was, caught in a trap that would have been a golden opportunity for the lickspittles—at least until the president decided they weren't licking enough spittle.

All his life, from the time he ran away from his first foster home, he'd asked himself why people settled for so little. He supposed that was what really went wrong with his marriage. Other guys swallowed their heartache and muddled on. He had to be the one who wouldn't put up with half a loaf. Now he'd condemned himself to aloneness. *Damn.* He'd let himself slip into fretting about solitude in a world of happy couples. Scarpia glanced up as Gene shook his head. Why did people settle for so little? Now he knew. It made life a whole lot easier.

He ruffled Scarpia's fur. "Let's head home, buddy."

They were at the French doors into the dining room when the house phone's school bell rang.

"Tried to call you on your cell but got your voice mail," Michael said. "Mom doesn't have time to bring me by and won't let me use the car or the SUV. Can you come pick me up?"

"Be there in twenty minutes."

Gene pulled the Mustang into the driveway at the side of the Victorian house. The beige paint he'd applied before he moved was holding up, but two spindles in the fence along the wrap-around porch were broken. The lawn he'd planted and nurtured was half weeds, and the landscaping he'd taken such pride in was overgrown. It hurt to see the land he'd worked with such love sinking into unkempt decay.

Michael trudged down the steps and across the lawn. "Hey." He grinned as he got in. "You're lookin' good considering your age and the shape you're in."

Gene gave him a light punch on the bicep. "Wish I could say the same for you."

Gene felt again the mix of pride and peace Michael's presence evoked. Despite the domestic strife, his son was at ease in the world. Lean and athletic, Michael moved with a runner's grace, and his intelligence showed as much in his wit as in his schoolwork. Most of all, he was well on his way to becoming a decent man—if he could just stop leching after every female who crossed his path.

Gene brushed Michael's chin with the back of his hand. "Have you given up shaving?"

"Shaving's severely last year. Women like a little beard." He handed Gene a fistful of papers. "Bills."

Gene flipped through them until he came to one for five-hundred-twenty-one dollars. "For shoes from Nordstrom's? Oh, come on—"

Michael held up his hands. "Don't go postal on me. I'm just the messenger."

Gene jumped from the car and started for the house.

"She won't talk to you," Michael called after him.

Gene rang the bell and waited. He rang again. After half a minute he leaned on the bell and pounded on the storm door.

The inside door opened. Donna stood inside the storm door in a full-length royal blue robe. She'd redone her hair. It was swept to the top of her head where it lay in soft curls. She wore dangling earrings and full makeup and stood very straight.

"Yes?"

He opened the storm door. "You're going to talk to me? You've gotten a make-over."

"Things haven't been easy."

"I'm sorry."

"You lie so well," she said with dignity.

"What's this bill from Nordstrom's?"

"Even though you've abandoned me, I still have to appear respectable. I can't go to the academy dressed like a bag-lady."

"Give up the volunteer work," he said. "Get a job."

"I suggest you vacate the premises."

"I could ask if Clem would hire you."

She stiffened. "And face all the people who knew us as a couple?"

"Donna, we're too poor to worry about loss of face."

"Our money troubles are none of my doing."

He folded his arms. "I'm not going to pay for the shoes."

"They're charged in your name."

"Return them."

"Will you go quietly, or shall I call the police?" Her face showed no emotion.

"I still own this house. Legally I'm still your husband."

"Not for long." She bit her lip.

"You're taking action?"

"I have nothing to say."

"A surprise attack?" Gene said.

She took a deep breath.

"Donna, we'd be wise to work together on a divorce, not go at each other in a cat fight."

She stood immobile.

"Since we're talking," he said, "I want to tell you that I'll be giving you fifty less each month. My rent's gone up."

"The record will show your reduction."

"Go back to work. Michael needs money for school next fall. We're broke."

"That's entirely the consequence of your decision to leave me."

He watched her.

"Is there anything else?" she said.

He shambled down the steps, across the lawn to the driveway, and got in the car. Michael said nothing.

By the time they finished cooking, it was dusk. They decided to eat on the veranda. Scarpia lay at their feet.

"I love this time of day." Gene rubbed the fur at the base of Scarpia's ears. "The sun's out of sight and everything glows. Ever notice how the trees turn their faces for one last glimpse of the sun?"

Michael grunted and cut his pork chop.

"Over the weekend," Gene said, "let's hike to the creek at sunset. We haven't done that yet this year."

Michael nodded.

"When you're this quiet," Gene said, "I know something's wrong."

"Mom's lying to Grandpa about you, pretending you're still living together."

"After two and a half years?"

Michael pushed out of his chair and frowned into the woods. "As soon as school's out and she's off the hook at Saint Boniface, she's going to Philadelphia to see him, says I have to go. She told him you were going to be out of the country on business. Tells me I have to lie about you."

"God."

"I'm not going. Haven't told her yet. She's still furious that I helped you move out. She brings it up, over and over."

Gene tasted his salad, watched the darkening sky. "Maybe you and I could go shopping. Warehouses over by Andrews Air Force Base sell used hotel furniture. See if you could find a bed. Maybe a desk. I've talked to George. You can share the attic rent-free."

Michael narrowed his eyes. "I could move while she's gone."

"We'd be batching it together. Kind of like permanently camping out—"

Michael stared into the trees and inhaled, as if savoring the fragrance of the honeysuckle. "I'll start packing now. We'll move my stuff little by little so she won't notice." He turned to Gene. "You know something? For an old fart, you're pretty cool."

At three in the morning on Thursday, Gene pulled into Clem's driveway in Chevy Chase. Clem, in jeans and a tweed sport coat, was standing beside a white Pontiac. "My suitcases are in the car. Let's go." He handed Gene the keys. "Once we're underway, I'm Keith and you're Stan. No mention of work or the office. Got it?"

They rode in silence until they were on the beltway heading south.

"You've got my flight number," Clem said, "and time of arrival Sunday, right, Stan?"

"Right, Keith."

Gene wanted to laugh at the silliness of the charade, but Clem wasn't smiling. At Dulles they parked, got Clem checked in, and said good-bye. Then Gene dropped the Pontiac at Clem's house and drove his Mustang home.

Saturday morning, Michael put away his sleeping bag, threw on a pair of Gene's scrubs, and went down the servants' stairs for coffee while Gene dressed. As Gene was tying his boots, Michael came in, cups in hand, flushed. "Who's the woman?"

"You're out of breath from climbing two flights of steps?" Gene asked.

"She was in the kitchen in a sheer peekaboo robe thingy."

"Must be Sharon. Didn't know she was here. Honey-colored hair, prominent nose, and jugs that would make a speeding bullet change course?"

Michael blinked. "I didn't notice the hair and nose."

"She's Carl's current squeeze, stays with him some weekends."

Michael whistled. "Do Hank and George entertain—what was that quaint term—squeezes?"

"Hank does. A waitress he's worked with somewhere. Not George, though."

"And Priss stays here sometimes?"

Gene hesitated. "Not very often."

"Wow." Michael emptied his lungs in a whoosh. "I'm moving into a regular den of ubiquity."

"Iniquity."

"Ubiquity. They fuck all over the house."

"Sorry," Gene said. "Guess I should have warned you."

"Once I'm living here—"

"Forget it. You can sleep alone until you have your own place."

"Uh-huh. And what are you going to do when I'm sharing your quarters?"

"Resume abstinence," Gene said. "Anyway, I have the feeling that by then Priss will be history."

"Hitting a few snags, are we?"

"Get dressed. We need to eat and get going."

Michael had arranged to borrow a pick-up truck from another construction worker in exchange for a case of Corona and a tank of gas. He and Gene drove around the beltway to a furniture warehouse and came home with a bed, desk, chair, and lamp, all costing Gene less than three hundred dollars. Together they hauled their bargains up the two flights of steps to the attic. They divided the room with Michael's furniture on one side and Gene's on the other. After chicken on the grill with Carl, George, Sharon, and Hank, Gene and Michael hiked the trails through Rock Creek Park and watched the sunset from a rocky rise. Michael slept in his new bed that night on sheets borrowed from George.

Over breakfast, Gene broached the subject of George's lawn. "The poor guy's too old for much hard physical work. You think we could handle it?"

"How about week after next? Got no classes that Monday."

Gene grinned. "I'll take a day or two of leave. Meanwhile, are you up to planting roses this afternoon?"

Sunday night, after Michael safely home with his mother, Gene stood beside George in the waning light next to the barbecue.

"Okay," George said. "Now use the hand signal."

Gene beckoned. Scarpia trotted to him. Gene held out his hand. Scarpia halted. Gene waved his hand once, palm down. Scarpia sat.

"You're a born trainer," George said. "Now praise him."

Gene dropped to his knees and rubbed the fur on Scarpia's neck. "Good dog."

"Now the treat," George said.

Gene offered a Liva Snap. Scarpia lapped it up with one swipe of his tongue, chewed twice, and gulped.

"That's enough for tonight," George said. "Let's review. What're the three rules?"

"Use his name when giving a command but never when saying 'no.' Give the command only once. Always praise and give treats."

"Pitch-perfect. Next time we'll do 'ready' and 'play dead.'"

George started for the stairs. Gene followed. Scarpia took up the rear. At the terrace level, the sound of Carl at the Steinway floated to them through the open French doors in the living room. Scarpia cantered past and started up the steps, paused, looked over his shoulder.

"Tell him to come back," George said. "I need to catch my breath."

Gene signaled. Scarpia ran to them.

"Praise him. Give him a treat. He needs to know you're in charge. Now that we've started, it's important to keep the training regular. Let's work every evening before dark except Thursday. I'll be at the clinic. After that, you'll need to train alone with him at least twice a week."

Gene knelt and scratched Scarpia's head. "Good boy." He smiled up at George. "This is going to be fun."

Chapter 3

The Eichmann Defense

When Gene let himself in Thursday night after work, Scarpia was bristling, in the dining room doorway. Heavy metal rock all but obliterated the sound of canned laughter on the television. Scarpia wagged his tail, bounced across the foyer, and rubbed his head against Gene's free hand. Gene dropped his briefcase and wooled Scarpia with both hands.

Hank, his eyes red-rimmed, cigarette hanging from his lower lip, shuffled into the dining room doorway. "Geez, we just let anybody in here." He giggled and executed a shaky pirouette. "I liberated a couple of cases of Corona last night from the Dandelion. Get out of them funeral duds and come on down to the terrace."

"You guys having a party?"

"Carl's got a gig, and George is off at the fucking clinic. A clinic, for Christ's sake. Pussy work, right? He probably puts on a white dress and one of them little nurse's caps." Without waiting for an answer, Hank headed off through the dining room.

In the attic, Gene opened the windows and switched on the fan. Another of the endless messages from Priss on his cell. Something about a singles cocktail party she wanted him to go to so she could show him off. This was getting old. Out of his suit and into jeans and a moribund tee-shirt, then down the servants' steps to the kitchen. He resisted the temptation to switch off the blaring television and boombox in the dining room and passed through the French doors to the veranda. Below him, Hank sat in the dying rays of the sun beside a galvanized tub of ice and beer. Half a dozen bottles were scattered around him. Scarpia lay at the other end of the terrace.

"Grab a brewski," Hank called. It was the first time Gene could remember ever seeing him smile. The furrow between Hank's brows remained.

Gene descended to the terrace, took a Corona, and pulled up a chair. Scarpia bounded to him, licked his hand.

"Carl's too vir-tu-ous to belt a few with buddies," Hank slurred.

"He's got a gig, remember?"

"He's Tinker Bell. A fuckin' pussy. Plays the fuckin' piano. That slut, Sharon, she'll take him for all he's worth." He took a drag on his cigarette. "Bantams'll give anything for a little twat." He spat. "Jesus. You and me are the only men in this outfit. At least you do that weight lifting thing."

You could use exercise, Gene wanted to say. Appraising Hank's sparse frame drooped over the plastic chair, he estimated that Hank was his height and half his weight.

"Had anything to eat?" Gene asked.

"You mean food, as in dinner? Not hungry."

"How come you're off tonight?"

Hank tossed an empty bottle over his shoulder and reached for another. "Got sacked."

"Ouch. Lots of bars in town. Maybe—"

"Third time I been fired. After the second time, couldn't find work. Declared bankruptcy. That's when my wife dumped me. Claimed she was a battered woman. Took my last penny. Then last Thanksgiving she swore out a restraining order against me. Hos'll do anything to get even with you."

Hank took a long slug, wiped his mouth with the back of his hand, and threw his cigarette away. "Anything to hurt a man," he said as if talking to himself. He stared into the shadows. "Can't visit my boy. He's named for me, but we always called him Hal. Last time I saw him, he was six. Red hair and freckles. Him and me used to have a great time. We used to—" His voice faded. He ran a finger under his nose.

"I didn't know you had a son," Gene said.

"All the perverts out there, too, and nobody to look out for him. Them queers went after me when I was a kid. You got to have someone to scare them off." Hank sat immobile, watching a scene in his head. "Shit." He lit another cigarette. "I'm going to kill that bitch. Slit her throat and watch her bleed to death."

Gene considered ways to get out of the conversation gracefully. "I'm getting hungry."

"That woman of yours, Priss? She gonna be here this weekend? I always have to jack off when she's around. She's giving you blue balls?"

"Naw," Gene said, "she's cool."

"All whores're cool."

"Watch your mouth, buddy."

"Who you think you're giving orders to, *Big* man. Your cock big enough to keep her in your bed?"

"Can it." Gene's fingers tightened on the chair's arms.

Hank laughed. "When that cunt wears you out, I'll take her on and teach her what real fucking is."

Gene flashed. "Shut up, asshole."

"You man enough to make me?"

Gene kept his voice at a low growl. "Matter of fact I am. Don't make me prove it."

Hank let his cigarette drop, grasped his bottle by the neck, and pushed out of his chair. "Show me, big man. If you got the balls."

In one motion, Gene vaulted from the chair and swung. Hank dodged and swiped close to Gene's face with the bottle. Scarpia roared and leapt. Hank tipped over like a bowling pin. The bottle flew past Gene's ear. Scarpia went for Hank's throat.

"*Scarpia! Stop!*"

One command from Gene was enough. Scarpia withdrew his head, bared fangs dripping, but held Hank on the pavement.

"Scarpia, back."

Reluctantly, Scarpia eased off Hank's chest, still snarling.

Hank, pale, rolled onto his side and sat up.

"Scarpia," Gene said. "Come."

The dog, fur standing on end, walked to Gene and lay on his stomach, without taking his eyes from Hank.

Hank stood. "Friggin' alpha male, right? Next time leave the fucking dog out of it, and we'll fight it out man to man." He stomped to the tub and took two beers. As he reached the door, he turned long enough to give Gene the finger.

Cold roiled through Gene's belly. Hank was fused, cocked, and ready to explode.

At the crack of dawn on Saturday, Gene dressed in old jeans and boots. Before the sun had cleared the horizon, he was at work on the meadow. He began with the hoe and wheelbarrow, taking out the worst of the weeds and any rock on the surface. Next he broke the ground with the pick and turned it over with the spade. At ten, he drove to Takoma Park for Michael. On the way home, they stopped at Harry's Rent-All and brought home a gasoline-powered tiller. By mid-afternoon, the meadow was spaded. After they'd cleaned up, Michael took Gene to Priss' place, promising to pick him up at eight in the morning, and went home to get spiffed up for a date.

Priss greeted Gene at the door with a kiss that promised passion.

"Got a mite more primping to do." She headed up the stairs. "Cava in the fridge."

As he listened to her footsteps on the stairs, he moseyed through the living room to the kitchen and opened the cava. Glass in hand, he lowered himself onto a stool at the counter in Priss' Mediterranean kitchen—imitation brick floor, sandstone walls, chocolate brown café curtains. The air was tinged with coffee, an undertone of Pine-Sol, a fading hint of dishwasher detergent. Behind it all, like an invisible mist, hung Priss' scent.

A door at the end of the room opened. Elizabeth came up the last two stairs from the basement. "Hi, Gene." She was barefoot, in an oversized tee-shirt and jeans. Her dark hair hung loose to her shoulders. She had her mother's features, but her eyes were blue.

"You moving in?" She tugged at a hank of hair.

"*No*," Gene said louder than he meant to. "Your mother and I are just friends."

"I *know* that. So was Jeff Rolandi. He used to live here. How many kids you have?"

"One. Michael, remember?"

She slid onto the stool next to his. "Actually, the house is plenty big enough. Jeff was going to bring his daughter, but he moved."

"Oh."

"My dad's really cool. Maybe you've heard of him. Patrick J. Simmons, the real estate developer. He lives in Potomac. He's going to pay for me to go to college. I have a two-year-old half-brother."

Priss came in from the dining room. She'd let her hair down and replaced her earrings with dangling gold crescents.

"Behold who's arisen from the lower depths," Priss said with a solicitous smile.

Elizabeth moaned.

Priss kissed her forehead. "Homework's waiting."

Elizabeth tramped toward the living room door.

"Say good night," Priss said.

"Night."

As Elizabeth clumped out, Priss stared after her. "I'm terrified of losing her."

"She seems healthy enough," Gene said.

"It's her father. He'd do anything to get her away from me. Told the court I was a bad influence on her. Claims I have a personality disorder. Says she has mental problems and I'm making them worse." She turned to Gene. "I dared him to prove it. Mustn't give him any ammunition." She moved closer. "Anyway, we're alone now." She melted into his arms. "Do we have to wait 'til we get home?"

"The National Gallery doesn't stay open late."

She headed for the front door. "Meanie."

They took the Metro to the National Gallery to see a traveling exhibit of Impressionist paintings, then went by Metro to the tidal basin and determined that the cherry blossoms had not yet opened. From there they took a cab to the Two Pheasants for dinner—her treat. Back at her place they fell into her four-poster for passionate lovemaking. Afterwards, she brought chilled cava to bed. They propped themselves against her headboard beneath the canopy and sipped.

"Don't forget the singles cocktail party tomorrow night," she said, "I'm going to put you on display. You don't have to do anything. Just hang around and be beautiful. Connie and Emily will be green."

"Can't do it, Priss."

"You can't renege on me now."

"I didn't realize the party was tomorrow. I have to pick up my boss at the airport."

"Send someone else."

He tasted the cava. "I can't. Has to be me."

"You bastard. I knew something was wrong. You have a date or what?"

"It's a work commitment I can't get out of."

She leaned against the headboard with a clunk. Wine slopped over her knees. "Christ," she said to the ceiling, "here he is in bed with the most desirable woman in Washington, and he's got the jitters about work. For God's sake, get over it."

"I'm trying."

"You certainly are trying."

While she launched into a tirade about men and their selfishness, he put down his glass, took hers, put it next to his, and wrapped her in his arms. "Hush." He pressed his lips against hers, opened her mouth, and slipped his tongue in. Her stifled mumble changed to a moan. They slid into the rumpled bed clothes.

Sunday, Gene and Michael borrowed the pickup from Michael's construction worker friend, carted a load of sphagnum moss and manure from a farm north of Olney, and worked it into the soil. Finally, as the sun moved behind the trees, they hunted for holes and filled them and leveled the plot by dragging a section of chain-link fence.

That evening, Gene waited in the massive terminal building at Dulles watching bedraggled passengers flood though the arrival gate until he caught sight of Clem in the crowd. "Keith. I'm over here."

Something was awry. As Clem approached, his ashen color and lined face alarmed Gene.

"My God. You all right?"

Clem glared at him through blood-shot eyes. "I'm fine. Let's get my bags."

He led Gene to the lower level where they waited by the carousel. When Clem rubbed his cheeks, his fingers fluttered. Was he hung over? Gene detected no alcohol smell.

The baggage arrived. Each took a suitcase and headed for the parking lot. Once on the road, Clem relaxed.

"How was the trip?" Gene said.

"Uneventful."

"Did you, um, come away with any useful information?"

"Mm-hmm."

"Were you able to do some touring?" Gene asked.

"I'm exhausted, Stan. Can we talk later?"

At the house, Clem took his bags and went in without a word.

The next day, the first day of Gene's leave, he and Michael drove to a farm co-operative in Anne Arundel County and bought Kentucky bluegrass and red fescue seed and straw. After lunch, they did a final leveling with a rake. The following morning they sowed the seed using a hand-held spreader Michael found among the tools in the garage. Before dinner, they scattered straw under a darkening sky. Gene soaked the seeded plot with a gentle sprinkle. The trick now was to keep the soil moist.

It had been bone-crunching drudgery, but it felt good. He loved working with Michael, and he loved the earth. No fulfillment surpassed standing at the edge of new lawn with his son, tools in hand, his body tired, his mind satisfied, knowing that soon the meadow would again be George's lawn.

The March 2018 Monthly Intelligence Budget Overview started promptly at ten Wednesday morning in the secure large conference room of the New Executive Office Building, two floors up from the FIBO offices. Gene sat next to Mark in the gallery, a raised row of seats at the side of the room. Clem, obviously ill, chaired the meeting from the head of the polished table with the intelligence agency directors along the sides. General Hacker sat, as though at attention, behind the brass plate etched with his name and position, his tightened fists resting on the table before him. The three stars on each shoulder echoed the silver of his hair, combed back on both sides of his bullet-shaped pate. His unblinking eyes caught the blue of his uniform. His scalp flushed when Clem expressed ignorance of National Preparedness Office's proposed budget add-on.

"I transmitted it to you several days ago," Hacker said.

"My apologies, General," Clem said. "I was on TDY last week." His glance darted to the gallery.

Gene cleared his throat before speaking. "General, I've also been on leave and haven't had time to study your proposal thoroughly, but I foresee problems. For starters, my understanding of the November National Intelligence Estimate is that Russia is now considered an ally and is not likely to launch an attack. Have I misread it, sir?"

"There are other hostile nations," Hacker said.

"Excuse me, General. I haven't seen those reports—"

"Compartmented information."

"May I be cleared for those compartments, General?"

Hacker tipped his head toward Hugh Shafter, in the gallery two seats from Gene. "See my chief of staff."

"Thank you, General," Gene said. "Meanwhile, I believe that the NIE of February estimated that China's long-range missiles could reach the continental United States but currently pose no threat. Is there other information—"

"That estimate fails to take into account the vulnerability of the Pacific islands."

"Pardon me, sir. I want to be clear. Do we need to be concerned that China would launch a nuclear attack on, say, Guam?"

Laughter around the table.

Hacker's fists clenched. "Doctor Yancy, I do *not* appreciate Doctor Westmoreland's patronizing attitude."

Clem coughed, fumbled with his tie.

"General Hacker," Gene said, now on his feet, "I apologize for any ostensible lack of respect. My question was not intended to be mischievous. I'm simply seeking evidence to support the National Preparedness Office's case. My questions pale compared to what NPO might face during a Congressional inquiry."

Hacker turned to Gene for the first time. "Doctor Westmoreland, I suggest you leave Congress to me."

"Of course, General," Gene said, "but, as you know, any one of us might be called to testify. Prudence dictates that the executive branch be aligned behind a single, supportable position in dealing with Congress."

"I can see," Clem said, "that we'll need considerably more discussion. Since we have a full agenda this morning, I suggest that we pursue these issues off-line. Gene, work with General Hacker's staff and set up whatever we need."

When the meeting ended, Hacker came around the table to Gene as the others gathered their papers. "You look positively puny." He stepped closer but kept his volume high, as if in a play. "Is the single life wearing you down?"

How the hell did he know about that? "Doing fine, thanks."

"If you decide on therapy, give me a call. Friend of mine. Very competent."

Conversation in the room stalled.

"Thank you, General. It's been more than two years. I don't foresee—"

Hacker rested his hand on Gene's shoulder. "Therapy's nothing to be ashamed of."

The son-of-a-bitch. Gene's adrenalin spiked. "You speak from experience, General?"

Hacker, his pseudo-sympathetic smile locked in place, removed his hand with calculated calm. He pivoted toward the exit and gestured at the papers on the table. Hugh Shafter swept the stack into a briefcase, locked it, and trotted after the general.

Unnerved, Gene took the stairs down two flights. At his external computer, now an outstation on the NPO network, he entered his FIREFANG password and clicked on the revised budget proposal of the National Preparedness Office, dated Monday, March 26, 2018, the day before yesterday, the first day of Gene's leave. If he hadn't come in for the monthly meeting, the budget transmission would have gone only to Clem. Gene had barely had time to skim through it before the meeting.

It cost him the better part of an hour to inch his way through the document. Hacker was asking for another six hundred million to upgrade clandestine missile sites in Sweden, with corresponding phony increases in the shell budget. That brought his total request to over seven billion. The line items were still small enough to conceal in the total NPO shell budget, which had been transmitted separately, and then be hidden in the unclassified defense appropriation.

Hacker had probably tipped off Senator Prowley. Hacker and Prowley both knew that neither of them could increase NPO's budget unless the proposed add-on appeared in the president's budget, sent to Congress with the approval of the intelligence budget staff. If Prowley tried to augment the funds without the president asking for it, he wouldn't be able to muster the votes to get it out of the subcommittee.

Gene dashed a quick note to Clem. "Read Hacker's latest. Recommend you procrastinate until I can work my way through it." He transmitted the message as PRIORITY PRECEDENCE so Clem would get it immediately.

Gene sanitized, stepped into the hall, and pushed the button at the cubicle next to his. Mark's eye appeared in the peephole. A safe door slammed, and Mark let him in.

"You saw it," Gene said. "You heard the whole thing."

"Watch out for Hacker, Gene." Mark swung into his chair. "He's on your case. At the SIGINT Review with the Director—"

"Which director?"

"Director of National Intelligence. The DNI. *The* Director. Hacker asks me if you've gotten yourself together. He makes a point of letting everyone, including the DNI, hear the question. When the session's over, he asks if you're at the office. Says he thought maybe the doctors weren't letting you work full-time."

"What's he talking about?"

"I said you were fine and asked what he meant. He just nodded. Now the DNI thinks something's wrong."

"Hacker can't touch me," Gene said. "He's a remnant of the Reagan First-Strike folly. A has-been."

"That's not how the DNI and the president see him. From above, he has all the vestiges of a statesman and elder. From the trenches, we can see up his kilt."

"And?"

"Okay," Mark said, "but don't leave home without your ball protector. Or—" He gave Gene an edgy smile. "You could quit fighting him."

"I can't discuss it, but what Hacker and Prowley are up to smells like a fish market on a late afternoon in August."

"Who anointed you the moral guardian of the world, Professor? Make a deal. Support some proposals if he'll take out a few line items."

"I should blow the whistle on Hacker and the whole National Preparedness Office. Two weeks ago, Shafter told me there was a compartmented appendix to the charter and he'd see if Hacker would let me read it. Never happened. One of these days buried in the NPO budget will be funding for—" He started to say "nuclear warheads" and stopped himself. "I've said more than I should have. Forget it."

"We don't make policy, Gene."

"That's the Eichmann defense—'just following orders.'"

"At least show flexibility. *Quid pro quo.*"

Gene laughed. "Like the woman propositioned for a thousand dollars. She says yes. The man offers her a hundred. 'You think I'm a whore?' she says. 'We've established that,' her man says. 'Now we're dickering about the price.'"

Gene had stopped bringing Priss to the house—she upset George, tossed veiled insults at Sharon, and annoyed Carl, and Gene didn't like the leers Hank gave her. Worse, she responded to them. He needed his weekends to spend time with Michael, train with Scarpia, and work on landscaping around the house. Or so he told her.

Thursday, the day after the Monthly Review, he had just hung up from his weekly call to Mavis in Senator Danley's office when his outside line rang.

"Westmoreland."

"Hey, hunky, what you doing tonight?" Priss, for Christ's sake.

"I asked you not to call me here," he said.

"I tried your cell. Got the 'leave-a-message' bullshit. I thought maybe you'd left town. The bed is mighty cold without you."

"I've been in over my head."

"Yeah," she said, "the son, the lawn, the dog. Where do I come in?"

"Priss, I can't talk here—"

"I'll let you off the hook if you'll go to lunch. I'll even agree to Dutch treat."

"Can't do it today." He ground his teeth. "How about to-morrow?"

"Done. We'll catch the cherry blossoms at their peak then go to the Old Ebbitt. I'll get a reservation for twelve-thirty. I'll pick you up in a cab at the Seventeenth Street entrance at eleven."

Gene hung up and read again the advance questions over the signature of Vince Dellaspada. The testimony before the Senate Preparedness Subcommittee, called by the chairman,

Senator Herman Prowley, was scheduled for nine-fifteen the first Wednesday in April. Vince referred to it as a "special hearing." Gene, as before, would act as the silence behind the throne—he'd coach Clem in detail and prepare a fact book for him. He'd sit with Clem at the witness table to prompt him, but only Clem would speak.

What was going on? Nowhere in the questions was there any mention of the clandestine missile sites. He shut the question file and dialed Nettie.

"I need five minutes with him," Gene said.

"He's not due back from Langley until eleven," she said. "After that the calendar's full, and he has four calls to return."

"Is one of them to Hacker?"

"You know I can't tell you that."

"What did Hacker want?"

"None of your friggin' business."

"NPO is my portfolio. Tell me, and I'll return Hacker's call."

"You do, and my keister's in a sling."

"Okay. Tell the man I need to see him. Pencil me in during a head break or something. I'm on my way to see Shafter at the Pentagon. Oh, another thing. You're a single mother. Can you recommend a good divorce lawyer?"

"I saw that one coming. Name's Barry Tilden. He's in WASP—Washington Area Single Parents—with me. Buy me a drink after work and I'll fill you in."

"I won't wrap up here until after seven," Gene said.

"I can wait."

"Can't do it, Nettie. I'm cooking tonight. Have to get home."

Nettie paused. "Okay. I'll email you the details."

After his unsuccessful session with Shafter, Gene went over the congressional question file one more time while he ate his bag lunch. The door chime rang. Through the peep-hole, he saw Clem frowning as if from indigestion. He'd lost weight.

Gene secured and let him in. "To what do I owe this unusual honor?"

"I like to stop in from time to time." He sat next to Gene's desk. "How are things going?"

"Lousy. Shafter's waffling. Keeps finding excuses not to let me see the fabled compartmented annex to NPO's charter. Our meeting this morning was interrupted by an unscheduled conference call with the Department of Energy, the National Nuclear Security Administration, and 'the nuclear guys in Omaha,' as his military aide put it. What nuclear guys in Omaha?"

Clem picked up the framed photo of Michael. "Nice kid. You still his sole support?"

"And we have serious debts." He waited until Clem replaced the picture. "Would you consider hiring Donna? She used to work at NSA, had clearances."

"I'll have personnel see what we can do."

"That's generous of you."

Clem smiled for the first time. "Anything for a member of the FIBO family. Meanwhile—" His face turned serious. "—how about giving up the role of the caped crusader? Don't act so shocked. I'm only suggesting that you mellow a little. Even Hacker's been concerned about you."

"Hacker's on my case."

"You could compromise a little."

"I don't get it," Gene said. "You tell me you want me to keep NPO in line, hold them to their charter, stop the padding. Now you want me to back off? I heard snatches of Shafter's phone conversation before I left his office. He thought I'd gone, saw me, covered the mouthpiece with has hand and said, 'Would you mind?' Why is NPO all of a sudden interested in nuclear warheads and their destruction envelope?"

"Why shouldn't NPO be interested in nuclear blast pro-files?" Clem played with his tie. "Their business is calculating the destructive effect of nuclear devices delivered against the continental United States and U.S. possessions."

"And why doesn't Prowley's advance question list even mention missile sites? Doesn't he know what Hacker's up to?"

"Of course he does," Clem said with a reassuring chuckle, "but he hasn't seen Hacker's add-on yet. That's 2020 budget. We're still massaging it here. Besides, that's in the FIREFANG budget, not the overt one. Maybe Prowley knows all he needs to about that. You've been over the questions more than I have, but my impression was that he was homing in on the projected cost figures."

Gene flipped open the file. "Right. He doesn't think NPO has asked for enough in previous budgets. 'Preparedness continues to be the gravest national concern,' he says."

"Gene, let me give you a little advice. Watch the cockiness. I admire that in you, but you're pissing Hacker off."

"That guy is manipulating the budget for purposes charitably described as questionable."

"Gene, leave the national decision making to people of a higher pay grade."

Gene put his palms on the desktop. "Is that an order?"

Clem laughed. "I don't bark commands to executives." He got to his feet. "Give my best to Donna when you see her." He let himself out.

Was this the Clem that admired Gene's pith and vinegar, the surrogate father who entrusted Gene with keeping NPO in check? Clem had undergone a tectonic change—his physical deterioration was more evident each day. Worse, he'd lost the will to fight. *China.* Something had happened.

Late in the day, Gene called up his email. Nettie, good as her word, had sent Barry Tilden's address—on I Street, Northwest, within walking distance—and phone number. Gene called and explained to Tilden's secretary that he'd need help soon, since his wife might be filing. She said Mr. Tilden had a cancellation Monday afternoon, April 2.

"I'll be there," Gene said.

Gene had barely settled at his desk with his coffee the following morning when Priss called again. "Elizabeth is throwing a tantrum. Something about never going to school again. This is going to take a while, Gene. I have to cancel lunch. Call you over the weekend."

Saved by the belle, even if only a thirteen-year-old one. Gene settled in to go over the answers to Dellaspada's questions. He wished he'd brought his lunch. Now he'd have to find a street vendor. He'd been looking forward to the Old Ebbitt. Hadn't been there since he took Michael to celebrate his high school graduation. A quick call confirmed that Priss hadn't cancelled the reservation. He dialed Mark on the intercom.

"Can't do it, Professor. I'll be at Fort Meade all day."

He called Nettie.

"No," she said, "Doctor Yancy is lunching with General Hacker in the Pentagon Executive Dining Room while I eat leftover tuna casserole at my desk."

Gene had walked right into that one. "Oh, well, um, maybe you could leave the noodles in the fridge and go to the Old Ebbitt with me."

"You buying?"

"Would you go halves with an indigent X2B?"

She laughed. "What the hell's an X2B?"

"Ex-husband to be. A down-and-out budding divorcé? That's with one e and an *accent aigu*."

"Don't try to sweet talk me with all that French stuff, but I accept. I wouldn't miss the Old Ebbitt even if I do have to pony up."

They decided to save cab fare and walk the three blocks. Once there, they hurried past the security guard and the parking valets and through the revolving doors. Inside they found the predictable crowd of cherry blossom tourists around the maitre d' desk. When their turn came, Gene asked for a reservation for two in the name of Simmons.

"Charlene will seat you." The maitre d' handed two menus to the smiling blonde who led them up the three stairs to the main dining room.

Once seated, they ordered wine—Chardonnay for Nettie and pinot noir for Gene—and sampled the bread.

"Who's 'Simmons,' if I may be so bold?" Nettie said.

"The person who made the reservation, then had to bow out."

"Male or female?"

"Female," Gene said.

"Tell me about her."

"We've sort of been seeing each other."

"And?"

The wine arrived, and they ordered lunch.

"Seared salmon?" Gene asked.

"Goes with Chardonnay. Didn't want to order another wine."

Gardenias. That was the scent, so faint it was almost subliminal. Gene studied Nettie. Her smile radiated warmth. She was pretty in a buttoned-down sort of way with red hair cut close to her head, a scattering of freckles, green eyes, and brows permanently raised. She always wore heels but didn't even come up to his shoulder. Something about her aroused yearning in him. He pushed away the hurt. He couldn't risk it. When she leaned forward to sniff her wine, he found himself watching her bodice. He immediately raised his eyes, only to encounter the naked breasts of the three nude bathers painted on the wall. Odd he'd never noticed Nettie before.

Not so odd, maybe. Priss was a good screw, nothing more. Nettie . . . A real woman who'd want commitment he couldn't give. He couldn't risk the agony of losing again.

"Why was Clem having lunch with Hacker?" he asked.

"I wasn't privy to their conversation. Doctor Yancy simply told me to put it on his calendar. Had to reschedule a meeting with DIRDIA to do it. I had to block out two hours next Wednesday for lunch with Senator Prowley."

Gene straightened. "What's going on? He didn't tell me—"

"Gene, forget what I said. I talked out of school. Violated executive secretary rules."

"Thought I might find you here," said a voice beside the table. Priss frowned down at him.

"Priss," Gene breathed. "I thought—"

"So she's the one." Priss glared at Nettie. "Didn't know you were attracted to the mousey type, Gene. Makes you feel more in control?"

He tried to slide out from the table, but Priss blocked his way. "Priss, this is Nettie Follander. She—"

"You son of a bitch," Priss hissed at him. "Not dating anyone else but not ready for an exclusive relationship. *You prick.*"

Heads turned toward them, and the hum of conversation died.

Gene managed to get to his feet. "Hey, let's not—"

"And I'm supposed to put up with it, right?" Priss said, her voice rising. "Well. I'm *not* the mousey type." She slapped him hard. The crowd gasped. "And you, you little whore, you'll—"

The maitre d' and waiter had their hands on Priss' arm and shoulder.

"Please, miss," the maitre d' said, "if you'll just—"

"Don't *touch* me," Priss screamed.

The waiter tightened his hold. "This way out, miss." They pulled Priss away from the table.

"Let me go," she cried. "*Take your hands off me!*"

The security guard hurried up. "Come outside with me, ma'am."

As she swung at him, he caught her wrists. The three men hustled her toward the door. They had gotten her to the street before the shrieking became inaudible.

"She drunk?" the woman in the adjoining booth asked her companion.

"Probably drugs," he said in an undertone. "We're in Washington now, honey."

Shaken, Gene slid into his seat. "I'm terribly sorry, Nettie. I can't imagine—"

"Who is she?"

"Priss Simmons. We've been having differences."

The maitre d' came to the table. "I'm terribly sorry, sir. She rushed right past us."

Gene waved his hand. "Not your fault."

"Are you all right?"

"We're fine," Nettie said.

The waiter appeared with two fluted goblets. "Veuve Cliquot. Please accept it as our apology for the disturbance."

"Thank you," Gene said.

The maitre d' and waiter withdrew. The babble of lunch conversation resumed, but the patrons watched them furtively.

"He said her name was Simmons something," the woman in the next booth said. "Is that someone famous? Do you recognize them?"

The man shushed her.

Gene wiped his sweating palms on the napkin.

"Never let it be said that you don't show a girl the exciting side of life in the capital." Nettie laughed. "And champagne, besides."

Gene put his index finger to his lips and tilted his head toward the adjacent booth.

Nettie laughed harder. "And now I'm a celebrity to boot."

When they split the check after the meal, Gene saw to it that they left a thirty percent tip.

Monday, after a lunch of leftover pot roast and canned peaches, Gene walked to I Street and found the offices of Tilden and Blankenship on the sixth floor of one of many buildings of stainless steel and glass. Barry Tilden's secretary brought him coffee and asked him to wait. A moment later the door by her desk opened. A bearded man, looking for all the world like the movie version of a sea captain, walked to Gene and held out his hand.

"Gene Westmoreland? Barry Tilden. Come on in."

Seated by the sleek desk, Gene told Tilden that Nettie had recommended him.

Tilden grinned. "How's my little carrot top? We go way back. We're both in WASP."

"She told me." Gene explained that his estranged wife was preparing to proceed with a divorce.

"Has she filed?" Tilden asked.

"From what she said, I expect her to at any moment. I wanted to be ready."

"You want to file? What grounds?"

"I don't know if I should. She was a lousy wife."

"Did she withhold sex?" Tilden said.

"No."

"Mistreat your son?"

"Neglected him."

"Criminally?"

"No."

Tilden frowned. "Physically hurt him or you? Abuse alcohol or drugs? Spend recklessly? Abandon you? Sleep with someone else?"

"No."

Tilden sighed. "Is there another woman?"

"There wasn't when I left my wife."

"You're still married to her, Mr. Westmoreland."

"The truth is I didn't see anyone for over two years. Now I do."

"We don't have anything to talk about until one of you files. Unless she's willing to cooperate in an amicable divorce."

"She's not."

"Try again. It'll save a lot of money and suffering. Meanwhile, stay in touch. Call me if you hear anything."

"Thanks, Mr. Tilden."

"Make it Barry."

"And I'm Gene. By the way, do you sail?"

Barry gave him a puzzled look. "Me? Not a chance. I get sea sick. Say hi to Nettie for me."

On the morning of the next scheduled hearing, Gene and an anemic Clem went by cab, carrying only the shell budget, not the real one. They were escorted into the unlighted hearing room by the Blue Boy who promptly disappeared. No one else was at the table or in the gallery. The Blue Boy and Vince Dellaspada held the curtain open for Prowley. The two younger men sat in the shadows while Prowley plumped down, put on half-glasses, and flipped on the reading light. It lit him from below. Where were the other subcommittee members? The microphones were off.

"Doctor Yancy?"

"I'm here, Senator," Clem said.

"Who's the gentleman with you?"

"Doctor Eugene Westmoreland, the Senior Budget Reviewer for Nuclear Defense Intelligence."

Prowley adjusted his glasses and peered. "Good to see you, Westmoreland. Pete Hacker spoke to me about you."

"Nothing untoward, I trust?" Gene said.

Clem kicked Gene beneath the table. "That's not the way to address a senator," he whispered.

Prowley frowned. "Untoward indeed." He growled. "Of course not. We're gentlemen here."

"My apologies, Senator," Gene said. "My levity itself was untoward."

"So we're glib, are we?" Prowley's frown deepened. "Enough. Let's get to work." He opened a binder in front of him. "Page 26, line item 13B, subpara 21. Clandestine transportation. Why only 115 million?"

Gene found the spot in the shell budget and opened the fact book to the corresponding page. Clem toyed with his tie, snuffled, and answered.

For the next hour and a half, Prowley, with occasional assistance from Dellaspada, grilled Clem on line items and repeatedly proposed to raise the amount in the president's budget. Clem responded in a halting voice, stopping frequently to drink from his glass. His hands left wet prints on the table.

Finally, Prowley closed the binder. "I trust the message is clear, Yancy. In these uncertain and threatening times, we must not stint on defense of the nation." With that, he got to his feet. Vince and the Blue Boy parted the curtain, and Prowley disappeared behind it. A door opened and closed. The Blue Boy gathered Prowley's papers, then followed his boss.

Dellaspada came around the desk and descended the three steps to the floor. He shook Clem's hand. "How've you been?"

Clem stood. "The old boy plays rough."

"Preparedness is his sandbox. He doesn't take kindly to interference."

"All we did was stay within guidance." Clem patted his forehead with his handkerchief.

"If the senator's changes take you over guidance, you'll have to find other places to cut."

In the cab, Clem and Gene were silent until they were stuck in traffic on Pennsylvania Avenue.

"You going to do it?" Gene said softly enough that the street noise prevented the driver from hearing.

Clem took a vial from his pocket, snatched a pill, and tossed it down. "It's already done."

"Prowley's add-ons come to something like a billion and a half. You'll have to cut someone else's program. National Reconnaissance Office? NSA? Defense Intelligence?"

"They'll howl," Clem said, "but the president has the final say."

"Maybe Prowley has the final say. If the changes appear in the president's proposal, Prowley's protected from a veto."

"Gene, this is chicken feed. The president favors the increases."

"You could go to the National Security Council," Gene said. "Or Office of Management and Budget. Let them fight it out with Prowley."

"I'll send the NSC a memo."

"It's obvious that Hacker's gotten to Prowley. End run out of channels. The president would have our scalp."

Clem gave him an edgy smile. "Gene, let me make this clear. Hacker, Prowley, and the president are on the same team."

"But it's illegal."

"We can't discuss that here."

Chapter 4

We're Gentlemen Here

The proverbial April showers never materialized. Gene watered with the sprinkler every day, prayed there wouldn't be a watering ban. Grass emerged in the newly cultivated earth, first as stubble, then as a low-lying haze.

One Monday morning Gene found the revised FIBO portion of the president's budget in his in-box. All of Prowley's changes were there. His door chime sounded. Mark Forrester.

Mark slammed the door behind him. "DIRNSA's furious."

"Durnza? Does she know me?"

"Director, NSA, smart aleck. Clem reduced his funding in the 2020 budget. The so-called 'special revision' just came out. DIRNSA's budget guys have been all over me since I got in. Clem told me to tell them he had to cut to keep the budget within the president's fiscal guidance." Mark collapsed into the chair next to Gene's desk. "I'm not cleared for the NPO budget, but the revision summary shows the total for each agency. NPO is almost two billion higher than it was in the original. NSA is two billion lower."

"Did Clem cut any funds from PRISM?" Gene asked.

"Increased them. Warrantless wiretapping and data mining are thriving. Training, travel, research, and personnel got cut. What happened?"

"Prowley put Clem on the rack."

"Why didn't Prowley just make changes in the Congressional version?"

"He couldn't get the support of the Democrats and the moderate Republicans if he did."

"Is that legal?" Mark said.

"Probably."

"Clem would nail us if we connived with Congress to change the president's submission."

"Crucifixion," Gene said, "is reserved for peons."

"What am I supposed to tell NSA?"

"Don't tell them about the NPO changes."

Mark paced. "They were the ones who pointed out the changes in the total request."

"Prevaricate. Get DIRNSA to take it up with Clem directly."

"I don't get you, Professor. A couple of weeks ago you were fighting like a cuckolded banshee."

"I did everything but fall on my sword. Clem was unimpressed. It's a DIRNSA-NPO fight now. The rhinos are making love."

"This isn't like you," Mark said.

Gene sagged. "I fought as hard as I know how. I lost."

"You giving up?"

"Just licking my wounds and regrouping. Battered and bruised, yes. Dead, no."

Mark stood. "That's the gladiator I know and love. Gird your loins for the next battle, buddy."

Gene started in on the bitter work of correcting FIBO numbers to reflect the new figures in the President's revised 2020 budget. By mid-morning, he had finished all but the sanitized fiduciary files, but the work delayed his progress on the 2021 line items due to be ready for incorporation into the complete budget by the end of the summer. The intercom buzzed.

"Hey, Gene." Nettie's voice. "You'll be getting a call from Shafter. Seems General Hacker wants to see you at his Pentagon office, probably this afternoon. I wanted to give you time to shine your shoes and put on a new tie."

"Wants to see *me*? I thought Clem always handled—"

"Doctor Yancy's not even invited."

Gene's secure line rang.

"Catch you later, Nettie."

Gene pushed the blinking button on the phone.

"Hey, buddy." Shafter's gravelly voice. "General Hacker would like you in his office at fifteen-thirty. We'll send a car."

"What's the subject, Hugh?"

"He didn't tell me."

By two-thirty, Gene had secured and put on his suit jacket. At two-forty, his door chime sounded. Through the crystal, he saw Cutter standing at attention. Gene opened the door.

"This way, please, sir," Cutter started down the hall.

Cutter was silent throughout the trip across the Potomac, sitting next to Gene in the rear seat of the black Lincoln Continental. The driver dropped them at the Pentagon mall entrance, and Cutter led Gene through security, using his passes, to the elevator, and into the anteroom of Hacker's office. Shafter greeted Gene, then stood aside and allowed Cutter, his face filled with awe, to accompany Gene to the inner office, a space large enough to accommodate the entire FIBO. Twenty feet in front of them was an expanse of tinted glass overlooking the river. Hacker sat at a massive desk of dark wood, his head bent over papers.

He raised his head, saw Cutter, and smiled. "Thanks, son. That will be all."

"Yessir." Cutter did an about face and exited, closing the door behind him without a sound.

"Thank you for taking time from your busy schedule." Hacker came around the desk and gestured toward a plush sofa with teak coffee table. As they sat, an Air Force enlisted man appeared with a tray.

"Coffee?" Hacker asked.

"Thank you."

The aide placed porcelain cups in front of both and poured from a matching carafe. He put sugar, cream, and a miniature pitcher on the table and vanished.

Hacker sat straight, a fist on each knee. "You're so new in your job that we haven't had time to get acquainted. I owe you an apology. We've been preoccupied—thanks to all the budget work—and haven't properly oriented you. Hugh will see to that as your schedule permits. Our mission is complex, multifaceted, and urgently important. Milk, sugar?"

"No, thank you, sir."

"I personally prefer honey." Hacker tilted the pitcher over his cup. "We won't get into anything technical today. Just get to know one another. You're from Pennsylvania, I understand?"

Gene blinked. "Yes."

"You lived for a time in Burrell? Lovely town."

"Only as a child," Gene managed.

"And your son will enter his senior year this fall at George Washington. My own children are older."

Gene tried to think of something to say.

Hacker stirred his coffee. "Many in the rank-and-file are unable to grasp NPO's mission. I find that I often have to mollify the more plebeian, even in Congress, who, in their naïveté, cannot encompass our enterprise. One is grateful for men of integrity and intelligence like you." His eyes twinkled. "All men are not created equal after all. That's hardly news."

"No." Gene wondered where all this was headed.

"You ask the uninformed citizen," Hacker went on, "what form of government we have, and he'll say democracy, but he's mistaken. It's a constitutional republic. The founders knew perfectly well that the rough-and-ready farmers, shopkeepers, and common laborers were ill-equipped to govern a great nation. So the framers set up a system whereby the most able represent the vulgar masses and use the levers of power in the name of the people. Hence a few select men, yourself among them, move the nation forward, assuring that the common folk are spared coping with matters they can't understand."

"Government by the elite—" Gene began.

Hacker waved his hand. "I dislike provocative language. It serves to arouse emotion and obscure issues. That's one reason we must preserve secrecy and avoid press scrutiny."

"Surely," Gene said, "our system of classification is to keep information out of the hands of enemies."

"Of course, but those of us seasoned in the world of covert endeavor learned long ago that so-called transparent government is an invitation to disorder." Hacker paused as if considering. "And the president uses classification to avoid meddling by the uninitiated." He folded his hands in front of his chest. "Do you know the philosophy of Leo Strauss?"

"My training is in mathematics."

Hacker gave Gene a forgiving smile. "You should delve into alien disciplines. It keeps the mind nimble. Strauss understood that leadership is restricted to those of superior ability who have a moral obligation to reshape reality for consumption by the people, in short, to tell them what's good for them. That's why religion is essential for the masses even though the leaders should avoid it."

Gene looked at the carpet.

Hacker's face lost its warmth. "Before you pass judgment, consider that men in the forefront of government and journalism today are disciples of Strauss. I have never discussed Strauss with Senator Herman Prowley or the president, but their actions show them to be on the side of the angels." He laughed. "Forgive my philosophical meanderings. I simply wanted to welcome you to the fellowship. I had misread you, but your recent work in correcting the 2020 budget, in accordance with Senator Prowley's guidance, made it clear to me that you have the wisdom to understand our goals. Now FIBO and NPO can work together to accomplish the mission. And all of us in the preparedness business owe you a vote of thanks."

Hacker finished his coffee and stood. The meeting was at an end.

Back in his cubicle, Gene replayed Hacker's monologue in his mind. He guessed that this was as friendly as the general got. Hacker was a victim of his own ideology. The clarity of his rectitude forced him to assume that the angels he spoke of would see everything as he did. The proof that Gene had drunk from the font of wisdom was his changes in the budget to suit Prowley—and Hacker. Had Clem misled Hacker? More likely, Hacker had reviewed the chain of events in the context of his certainty and concluded, wrongly, that Gene had shucked the clouds from his eyes and achieved enlightenment.

Work on the 2021 budget would quickly dispel the illusion unless Gene could continue Clem's ruse of protecting NPO from unfriendly members of Congress by pointing out the obvious padding. Meantime, could Gene exploit Hacker's misjudgment? He'd start by using his good graces to get his hands on the compartmented annex to the NPO charter. He dialed Hugh's secure number.

"This is Colonel Pierce, sir. Mr. Shafter is on leave. He won't be in the office until the eighteenth."

Should Gene mention he had just seen Shafter in the office? "Who can I talk to about the NPO charter and its annexes?"

"I'll speak to Mr. Shafter as soon as he returns."

Gene hung up. Another delay. He would have to complete his review of the 2021 budget without knowing what the annex authorized NPO to do. He dialed Clem's secure number. Nettie put him through. Gene described his coffee with Hacker.

Clem laughed. "Tit for tat, Gene. When we work with NPO, they work with us."

"The budget changes?"

"That smacks of bribery. Let's just say we have good relations."

"You knew about this?" Gene asked.

"Hacker phoned me this morning after he saw the revised budget. I expected your call."

"Meanwhile, I'm still waiting for the orientation and a glimpse of the compartmented annex. Have you ever seen it?"

Another laugh. "Don't push too hard. Let's keep Hacker happy."

When Gene got home, Carl, in bow tie and evening jacket, was running through material at the Steinway.

"Be here for dinner?" Gene asked through the arch from the foyer.

"Soon as I finish memorizing this, I'm out of here for the Côte d'Azur."

"Hank here?"

"Haven't seen him. Probably out job hunting."

So only George would be home. Gene changed and started cooking—chicken parmigiana and pasta in marinara sauce. George, in his usual evening attire of silk dressing-gown and ascot, volunteered a Chianti Brolio. After the dishes were cleared, George brewed coffee from his private stash and opened the French doors to let in the spring evening air.

He brought the coffee and cups to the table on a tray. "Have you noticed a green Honda parked out front? I usually see it when I've been working late and go out for a breather before bed."

"No," Gene said, "but I'm usually in bed earlier than you."

George poured. "There's always someone sitting in the driver's seat. I've seen it three or four times."

Gene tried the coffee. "Wonderful. Where'd you get it?"

"The co-op. Grind my own. *Très raffiné.*"

"Close to twenty-five dollars a pound as I remember. Too *raffiné* for me."

George sniffed. "The Parisians are right. Foreigners should never attempt French."

"Do I detect a more-Parisian-than-thou attitude?"

"I was born in Paris."

"I didn't know that."

"I'm not quick to share my private life," George said, "least of all with my tenants, but for a man who knows how to train dogs and plants lawns—anything." He tasted his coffee. "As a teenager, my mother went to France and became a *chanteuse* in the Josephine Baker tradition. Used the name Juliette Berthier—taken from Louis-Alexandre Berthier, Prince de Wagram, one of Napoleon's marshals. She was a regular at the Théâtre des Champs-Élysées and the Follies-Bergéres in the mid thirties. She never said who my father was. Maybe she didn't know, but she named me Jean-Marie. One of her ardent admirers was Jean-Marie-Gabriel de Lattre de Tassigny, a general of some repute. When the Nazis occupied Paris, we watched. Anybody not blond, blue-eyed, and Nazi was targeted. My mother used her connections, mostly with those by then in the underground, and we got to Marseilles. From there to Lisbon. And then the United States and Alabama. I began using the name George."

"That explains why you taught French."

"For forty years. Part of our legacy as Americans is that we are too chesty to speak another language well. We are particularly vicious to French. Like one of those doo-wop singers who's never on pitch. And corruptions of French are insufferable. Creole is an abomination, Canuck an insult." He chuckled sourly. "Like the no-trespassing sign on a cemetery wall in Québec—*Défense de Trépasser*. In Parisian French, it means, 'No dying allowed.'"

Gene laughed. "Your good humor is showing."

"*Roturier* gossip. I have no good humor. More coffee?"

Gene refilled his cup. "You're pampering me."

"You've a noble nature."

"You give me too much credit."

"My insights are rarely wrong." George raised one brow. "I've watched you for the better part of three years. Sometimes you're a little too sure of yourself, but decency is your middle name."

"I don't have a middle name. In fact I have no name. No one knows where I came from. My earliest memories are from

Westmoreland County, Pennsylvania where I was in the first of many foster homes and orphanages. Kept running away. Best guess is that the name Westmoreland came from the county. My second name, Burrell, was one of the biggest towns. So maybe I was born there. There are no records."

"Not the usual background for a Ph.D. and government senior executive." George poured himself more coffee.

"I was always good with numbers. Got a reputation for compulsive perfectionism. And, frankly, arrogance. Came from learning to rely on myself and not trusting anyone else. Went to college on a math scholarship and here I am."

"A nameless divorcé and a *métis* misfit," George said. "Destined to be allies."

Gene's shoulders sagged. "Paupers without partners. Limbo men."

"Remember one thing, *mon bel ami.*" George smiled. "The strongest man is he who stands alone."

When George went downstairs to the library to resume his research on Massenet, Gene washed dishes, then headed upstairs to face the empty attic. Weeknights were the worst, and this was only Monday. Without switching on a light, he slumped onto his desk chair and gazed at Michael's bed, just out of the reach of the shafts of moonlight slicing through the windows. The smooth bedspread, the blankets, the sheets remained untouched, as he had left them when he made the bed after Michael left two Sundays ago. He longed for Michael to move in. That wouldn't do much to solve his ultimate matelessness, but it would distract him from the void in his gut.

Humbling to admit that he needed his son. Children are supposed to need their parents. Michael was strong, independent—no needing there. Gene chuckled to himself. He pictured Michael's sappy face atop his agile body, that grin he got when he was being a wise ass. Too articulate for his own good. Cocky. Michael came by his swaggering honestly.

But Gene couldn't expect Michael to be an analgesic for the throbbing nothingness inside. Even after all this time, Gene was still grieving over the death of his marriage. He needed the love of a woman. No, he needed to love a woman. Still not right. He needed both. Until and unless that happened, he needed to stay busy to keep the hollow place anesthetized.

Could he ever love again? And if it went bad again? Could he live through that twice in one lifetime?

He forced himself to his feet and moved to the window. Brightest moon he could remember, cold blue and shimmering. Edgy objects on Jessamine street, three stories below, stood out in black and blue bas relief. He watched a car park in Carl's usual place next to the tallest maple. A figure got out of the car, walked toward the house, and disappeared under the dentiled porch roof. In the distance he heard the peal of the Big Ben doorbell.

George and he were the only ones home, and George would have trouble getting up the basement stairs. Gene hurried to the foyer and called, "I'll get it." In the entrance hall, he flipped on the lights and opened the door.

Priss in a trench coat and a floppy rain hat faced him. "May I come in? I wouldn't blame you if you said no—" She stepped inside.

"You expecting a storm?" Gene said. "That outfit—"

"I just threw on the first thing I found."

He moved aside, and she trudged up the steps to the foyer and into the dining room. Gene switched on the light and motioned to a chair.

She sidled into it. "I'm here to apologize. I made a fool of myself and embarrassed you and . . . that Nettie person."

"Apology accepted. You came all the way up here to tell me that?"

She took off her hat. "I thought maybe I could make it up to you. Elizabeth's going to be at her father's this weekend. We could have my place to ourselves."

"We're finished, Priss. Let's make it a clean break."

She tilted her head. Tiny lines stretched from the corners of her eyes. Blue smudges, like misapplied eyeshadow, darkened the skin beneath them. "I have a standing invitation to participate in a group sex session. They're once a month. Couples only. Would you—"

Gene suppressed a shudder. "Not my thing."

"Okay. I know how men are, so I thought maybe—" She rubbed her forehead. "I'm truly sorry. Forgive me."

"I do, but we need to go our separate ways."

"Please, Gene." She lowered her head, then raised it. "I won't make the same mistake twice. All I ask is that you stop seeing Nettie."

"I'm not seeing Nettie, but the answer is still no."

Priss turned toward the French doors as if to watch the moonlight on the veranda. "The first time I saw you, when you came to me across the dance floor, I knew you were for me."

"That's not what you said."

"I was right for *you* that night, wasn't I?"

"A roll in the hay doesn't make for a relationship."

One side of her face smiled. "You kept coming back."

"Then the accusations started. You know as well as I do it'll never work."

"It *will* work." She took a deep breath. "I was going to suggest you move out of this haunted house and come to my place. Elizabeth likes you. You'd be closer to the office—"

"Not a chance."

She unbuttoned the top of her coat. "I know what you want." Her fingers moved from button to button. "And you know what I want." The coat opened exposing her naked breasts.

"Jesus." He turned away. "Go, home, Priss."

She reached for him, but he stepped aside. She let her hands fall to her sides. "Is Nettie as good as I am?"

"Have you been drinking?"

"Come on, Gene. If you're not getting it from me, you're getting it somewhere."

"Go home," he said. "Now."

"The woman scorned." With measured calculation, she buttoned the coat, put on the cap, adjusted the angle of the brim. "All right." She rose and drifted into the foyer. By the door, she put her arms around his neck. "Have it your way, sweetheart. Go ahead and sow your oats. When you come to your senses, Priss will be waiting. Don't take too long."

She gave him a dry kiss and was gone.

Gene doused the lights. She was out of his life. It was over. Relief was like coming up for air after too long under water. The substitute Priss had embodied hadn't even created the illusion of palliation. The empty part of him hurt more than ever.

Thursday the twenty-sixth, the April Monthly Intelligence Budget Overview convened in the NPO conference room. As usual, Clem and the agency heads sat at the table, and Gene and the other NPO budget monitors were relegated to the gallery with staff people from the agencies. After the opening formalities, NSA's director spoke first, seconded by the directors of the National Reconnaissance Office and Defense

Intelligence, to protest Clem's issue of the revised 2020 budget after it had been submitted to Congress. Clem, obviously uncomfortable, declined to discuss the issue. He said he'd received his marching orders. Members around the table were clearly displeased but said nothing more. Moving on to new business, General Hacker, fists clenched on the table as though ready to hammer, said he had forwarded his latest revision to the 2021 budget but hadn't received any response.

"General," Clem said, "I'm afraid we're going to need more justification for your proposed increases. As you know, some members of the Senate Preparedness Subcommittee are inclined to view proposed expansions with skepticism—"

"The justification," Hacker said, "is compartmented. I'll take it up with the subcommittee members who are cleared for it."

Clem's nod to Gene was barely perceptible.

Gene stood. "Sir, the problem is that the justification given in your draft speaks of threats without specifying what they are. We need to take that language out of the document or be specific. The uncleared members of the subcommittee will want to know what data you have that would support the increase."

Hacker flushed. "Doctor Westmoreland, once again I ask you to leave Congress to me."

"Sir, forgive me, but Doctor Yancy must also appear before the subcommittee. He will be asked why he agreed to include your proposal, and we have no information to answer with."

"Pete," the Director of NSA said across the table, "without getting into detail, what's the gist of the justification?"

"We need more resources to monitor indications that China might target Diego Garcia with nuclear weapons."

Gene closed his eyes. Why hadn't Hacker run the justification by him or Clem before bringing it out during the overview? Maybe the honeymoon was over and Hacker saw through what Gene was doing.

The directors of CIA and DIA laughed aloud, and the NSA director swallowed a chuckle.

"Pardon me, Pete," NSA said, "Diego Garcia? The island in the Indian ocean?"

"As you know," Hacker said, "the United States has extremely valuable assets on Diego Garcia."

"Yes, but—" NSA lowered his head to hide his grin. "*Diego Garcia?* This is the first I've heard of the threat." The other agency heads nodded. "May I ask what agency has provided this information?"

"I'm not at liberty to name the source," Hacker said. "The president has directed that the organization providing this data shall not be identified."

Clem coughed. "Gene, take this up off line with the NPO staff, and—"

The Director of CIA interrupted. "I think I speak for all members of the board when I object. Granted, we don't get a vote in the final disposition of intelligence funding. That's the president's prerogative. Nevertheless we're all significantly affected. The president is cutting out budgets, and then one of us gets a disproportionately large increase, as NPO has over the past several fiscal cycles. That money is also coming out of our programs, and we'd like to know as much as possible about the deliberations."

Clem raised both hands in a hold-it gesture. "I'll fill you in on the outcome in next month's session. Can we move on to the next item?"

When the session ended and the principals moved toward the exit, Gene caught Hugh Shafter by the arm. "How soon can we get together?"

"Have to get back to you after I talk to the general."

This time, Gene and Mark met in Gene's cubicle for the port-mortem.

"Did you see the faces around the table?" Mark asked. "Can Hacker get away with that? And what's this unnamed organization?"

"The rhinos are frustrated, Mark. My view from the trenches ain't all that great, but it's clear that this so-called unidentified source is the tool the administration is using to justify what it wants to do when intel findings don't fit the ideology. You remember the Office of Special Plans set up under President Bush? It maintained that Saddam Hussein had WMDs and close ties with Al-Qua'ida. It told the White House what it wanted to hear, that our forces would be greeted by the Iraqi populace with flowers and hugs. It was the source of reporting that led to the warrantless wiretap. The administration set it up in the Pentagon to stovepipe unevaluated intelligence, including rumors, statements of unreliable defectors more interested in telling us what we wanted to believe anyway than in giving us facts, and data gained through torture—which any intel pro will tell you is the least dependable of all.

"Now we have this unnamed organization. It's the Office of Special Compartmented Intelligence, OSCI, the old Office of Special Plans under a new name—which was itself a new name for Northern Gulf Affairs Office (NGA). It shapes intelligence to suit policy. If it says China going to hit Diego Garcia with nukes, the increase will go into the budget, and Prowley, with his party support in the subcommittee, will approve it. When policy is formulated on the basis of ideology instead of fact, this is what you get."

"And," Mark said, "the tax payers foot the bill."

"Nope. We just add it to the deficit and the national debt. The president will be the first one to tell you that deficits don't matter. Besides, some conservative commentators actually favor fattening the national debt to the point that the government will be crippled. That would force us to reduce programs like Medicare and Social Security and food stamps, thereby curbing 'the culture of poverty' by cutting off enabling handouts." Gene dropped into his desk chair. "I think Hacker's found a way to defeat FIBO's efforts to control his budget. Its name, Office of Special Compartmented Intelligence, is unspoken."

After Mark headed to his own cubicle, Gene lifted the receiver of the secure phone for his weekly call to Mavis, as mandated by Senator Danley, then hung up again. What could he tell her? Not the Diego Garcia story. Not about his daily attempts to hold the NPO budget in check. Not about Hacker's growing animosity. Hacker obviously made a point of keeping Prowley informed, while Danley was blissfully ignorant. Clem's guidance was clear: say as little as possible.

Carl stopped playing and looked up from the Steinway as Gene came into the foyer.

"To what do we owe the grace of your esteemed presence?" Gene asked. "Côte d'Azur getting too rich for your blood?"

"They're having a special day-early Cinco de Mayo evening—you know, mariachi, margaritas, even a piñata—a day early. No need for a tinkler like me."

Gene stopped his chuckle. "You might want to reconsider your phrasing there. 'Tinkle' also means . . . never mind. So you'll be fixing dinner. George and Hank going to join us?"

"Not George. He's out doing fund raising for that clinic. Haven't seen Hank in days."

"He's been here. Saw cigarette butts on the veranda."

Carl tilted his head toward the motorcycle. "Right. He wouldn't leave the bike, the love of his life, behind. Dinner in an hour, okay?"

Gene came down early to set the dining room table and pour Foxhorn Merlot, the cheapest drinkable wine he could find. Carl served hamburger patties and salad.

"So," Gene said, sliding his chair under him, "how's life among the spit-and-polish-erati—or should I say erotic?"

Carl grimaced. "Your humor is like your sex life: into graceful degradation. Heard from Priss?"

"Not since I kicked her out, after a scene you wouldn't have believed."

"Could have avoided all that if you'd listened to me."

"I got away," Gene said, "with my scrotum intact. No hits, no runs, no errors."

"Be patient. My instincts tell me you haven't heard the last of Miss Priss."

"If I let your instincts be my guide, I'd be eight inches shorter with thinning hair and too many teeth."

"Not genes," Carl groaned. "Instincts. *Instincts*. Want me to write that down for you, big fella?"

"Not with the mood you're in. Did Sharon substitute saltpeter for your Viagra?"

"Sharon's gone the way of all good women. I got a new honey. Adelaide. She lets me call her Addie. The mood I'm in? Ever wonder why? My ex sees no reason to remarry when she can keep squeezing me for alimony. She's been shacked up with the same guy, in *my house*, no less, for three years. I keep trying to increase my gigs so I'll have extra income. No luck. Been passed over for promotion three times. That means I'm forced to retire. The icing on the cake is I come home from my gig after midnight and there's someone in my parking place. Three times in the last week and a half. Same green Honda. Last night I decided to check it out. Soon as I got close, the guy behind the wheel burned rubber getting out of there."

Gene frowned. "Funny."

"Like I said, your sense of humor's gone south."

"Funny in the sense of: 'This meat smells funny.' Speaking of which, what's new at the Funny Farm?"

"Sameoldsameold," Carl said, "except for one development. Rumor has it the Grand Inquisitor has identified a new heretic. A certain Doctor Westmoreland."

Gene's fork stopped in mid-air.

"Yeah," Carl went on. "Seems this guy was a member of the faithful and became an infidel. Air Force Matériel guys have started a new pool. Five dollars a shot. The guy closest to the date of actual termination wins."

"Hacker's not even in my chain of command. He can't touch me."

Carl shook his head. "We're in a new era, buddy. Loyalty is the touchstone. Not competence. Not hard work. Least of all expertise. In defense and intel, you ain't a lick-spittle to the president, you're out on your ass. Doesn't matter whose chain of command you're in. The power brokers in this administration can reach across the hierarchy. Never heard of lateral firing?"

"My boss will stand behind me. He put me in the job to counter Hacker's tactics."

"You and your boss," Carl said, "are in the executive branch, right? So are we military. We've learned to keep our mouths shut and follow orders. When we don't, we find ourselves stationed in Iceland. You saw what happened to Sally Yates and David Shulkin and Michael Flynn? Forced out faster than you can say 'Yessir, yessir, three bags full.'"

"I'm not a political appointee and not the military."

Carl took a deep breath. "I'm low enough on the totem pole that nobody notices me. You're not."

Gene pushed his plate away. "All right. Suppose you're right. Hacker's doing things that could lead to—never mind what. Should I stand aside and let him do his worst?"

"How much are you willing to sacrifice for your principles? Your job? Your reputation?"

Gene shook his head. "It would never come to that."

"Don't count your blessings before they're hatched."

"Is that the best one-liner you can manage?" Gene said.

"Been learning at the feet of a master, Master. And don't say 'bator.' That's even worse than hatching blessings. Dishes are yours. I'm off to see my honey."

Gene sat across from Hugh Shafter and the blond, balding Colonel Pierce, Hugh's assistant, doing a markup of the proposed shell budget for 2021. The NPO Conference Room and its table for twenty dwarfed them, and their voices resonated.

"Hugh, we'll never be able to sell it. How can you pretend to need three hundred million for foreign travel? A hundred thousand? Maybe."

"Okay." Hugh ground his teeth. "Where would you put it?"

"I can't find a place. Every line item is bloated. The subcommittee will laugh it off the table."

"Perhaps," Pierce said in a voice so soft Gene had to strain to hear him, "we could create a new category. I was thinking of something like nuclear engineering research, compartmented of course. We might ask to fund a reactor for cutting edge testing, ostensibly to keep pace with the competition."

"Duplication with DOE," Gene said. "Danley and the moderate Republicans would never go for it."

Shafter threw down his pencil. "Shit, Gene, how about working with us instead of fighting us on every fucking line item?"

"I'm not fighting you. Clem and I are both working to get the budget through Congress. Even multiple compartments can't obscure obvious padding. Yes, I know, Prowley and the Republicans have a majority on the subcommittee but only by one vote. If even one Republican gets antsy, we're in trouble."

"The general thought you were one of us. Now he's changed his mind."

"You want me to let these swollen proposals go to the subcommittee? Get their ire up and you won't just lose your increases, they'll cut you. Like the argument that China might target the Aleutians for nuclear attack. That's just plain laughable. Nobody in the intelligence community supported you on that one, and subcommittee ended up reducing your funding for Asia research."

"Right," Hugh said. "You egged them on."

"And General Hacker's justification?" Gene sat rigid with palms flat on the table. "'An unnamed source has picked up communications chatter revealing that the Chinese have targeted the Aleutians.' Come on. Does he even know what 'communications chatter' means? Comms chat is unofficial give and take among radio communicators, usually about things like scheduling and frequency and number of messages waiting to be sent."

"Not anymore. Thanks to NSA, we now have access to terrorist telephone conversations. People say things, unaware they're being overheard."

"Who said what to whom?" Gene asked.

"It's not clear."

"So it might have been Aunt Mai talking to Cousin Wang in the next village? Was it in Chinese? How many calls were intercepted? Over how long a period?"

"Stop playing intelligence analyst," Hugh said. "The general believes you torpedoed us on that one."

"I know that's what the general thought. My problem was I couldn't defend the position NPO took. I took the same line of reasoning in talking privately with you."

"My contacts tell me that our unnamed source," Pierce said, "is researching the Chinese threat."

Hugh straightened. "No shit?"

Pierce nodded.

Hugh gave Gene a triumphant grin. "You'll be seeing that line item again."

"Hugh," Gene said, "if you play the 'unnamed source' card too often, even the Republicans will get queasy."

"The boss blames you for the cut," Hugh said. "Things were rough around here last week. As we say in the Air Force, ain't the general happy, ain't nobody happy."

"Doctor Westmoreland—" Pierce cleared his throat. "I'm a mere drudge compared to you, but I think it not indecorous to suggest that arousing the wrath of a general the president is fond of is unhealthy. Witness what happened to the gentleman originally nominated for your current position."

Gene gave him a sidelong frown. "He withdrew for security reasons."

"That was the conventional wisdom," Pierce said, "but it's booted about among the *conoscienti* that he and the general had a disagreement of some import after his name was submitted."

Gene's pulse quickened. "Are you threatening me?"

Shafter laughed. "Of course not. We're gentlemen here."

That afternoon, as Gene tallied 2021 budget requests, he answered a call on the outside line.

"Doctor Westmoreland, this is Andrew Brinkman with Spicer, Brinkman, and Klauthammer. We're representing Mrs. Westmoreland." Here it came. "She doesn't know the name of your attorney, so we're required to ask."

Gene flipped open his address book and gave Barry Tilden's address and phone number. "Is Mrs. Westmoreland filing for divorce?"

"I need to discuss issues like those with Mr. Tilden."

When Brinkman hung up, Gene dialed Barry Tilden.

"She's probably filed, Barry."

"Who's representing her?"

"Spicer, Brinkman, and Klauthammer."

"From Philadelphia?" Barry asked. "They specialize in the legal problems of the rich."

"Her father's lawyers. That means she must have told him we've split."

Silence on the line, then Barry said, "He didn't know?"

"Long story. When can I see you?"

"Let's wait until I hear from Spicer *et al.* I'll call you."

All the way home on the Metro, Gene watched, unseeing, the passage of stations and buildings and people. Donna was about to make it final. He'd have to battle her to avoid losing everything he owned. He'd so hoped to avert the bloodletting. On the walk between the station and the house, he went over the struggle with Hugh and Pierce. Hacker had seen through him.

The house was empty when he arrived. He changed and began his workout, his mind still churning. Something wasn't clicking. During the one-arm rows, Gene thought through the scene in NPO's Conference Room. What had Pierce said? *My contacts tell me that the unnamed source is researching the Chinese threat.* Hugh had been surprised. Why would Pierce know that if Hugh didn't? What contacts? Who was Pierce anyway?

Gene got to the office earlier than usual the next morning. When the computers were booted, he entered his passwords and searched through NPO personnel files. No Pierce. He typed in the FIREFANG passwords and searched again. Nothing. Who was this guy? On a hunch he did a search of Defense Department personnel archives. In the staff of the Office of Special Compartmented Intelligence (OSCI) he found a brief entry: "Roderick O. Pierce, Colonel, USAF, Temporary Duty."

He dialed the OSCI.

"Colonel Pierce, please."

"Just a moment, sir."

Gene was put on hold. He fought off the temptation to bite his nails. He'd gotten after Michael for that. Ran in the family. How could he chastise Michael if—

"Sir?" a voice said. "Colonel Pierce is no longer assigned here. He's returned to his home office."

"Oh," Gene said in his most business-like tone. "I didn't realize he wasn't permanent party. Where was he assigned from?"

"The President's intelligence staff."

Chapter 5

Obstruction

Gene's intercom rang. Nettie.

"If you and Michael aren't doing anything Sunday the thirteenth, maybe you could stop by my place. Just a few friends. Informal. Hamburgers on the grill."

"Let me talk to him."

Might be fun. All he ever did with his son was yard work. Michael had finished his finals, so he'd have time.

That evening, while Gene was changing into jeans and boots to take Scarpia on a training run, his cell phone rang.

"Dad, big favor. Can you come pick me up and let me use your car tonight? I have a date."

"Sylvia?"

"Naw. Sylvia's severely passé. Leila's really special. I'll stay the night at your place so you won't have to take me home."

Dressed for a hike along Rock Creek, Gene picked Michael up in Takoma Park and let him take the Mustang for the evening. Gene stayed up until ten-thirty on the off chance that Michael might be home early. Before heading to the attic, he flipped on the outside lights and took one last look out the living room window. No Michael. In the place Carl usually parked, next to the tall maple, was a green Honda. The headlights of a car coming down Jessamine lit the Honda from behind. For a few seconds, the silhouette of a man at the wheel flashed through the windshield. Gene hurried to the front door and out to the circular driveway. As he approached the car, its engine started. With the headlights off, it swept away from the curb and lurched down the hill toward the entrance to Rock Creek Park and vaporized into the darkness.

Gene frowned after it. Was the house under surveillance? He went in, climbed the stairs to the second story, and knocked at George's room.

"Come."

George, in his dressing gown, was at his computer. Scarpia lay at his feet.

"I'll only be a moment," George said. "I'm on line."

Scarpia wagged across the room for the ritual ear scratching, then returned to his place next to George. Gene moved a stack of books and orchestral scores from the chair to the bed and sat. The room had once been the master bedroom. It had its own fireplace, private bath, and two large windows, neatly curtained floor to ceiling in a coarse green material. Plaques and black-and-white pictures of George and others lined the walls.

The computer beeped discreetly. George took off his glasses.

"What're you up to?" Gene asked.

"Saint-Sulpice."

"French?"

George straightened. "You don't *know* it? *N'est-ce plus ma main que cette main presse* . . . Arguably the finest thing in *Manon*. I've been analyzing the authenticity of the scene and practicalities, for example, could Manon have reached Saint-Sulpice quickly from Cours La Reine where she learned that Des Grieux was about to enter the priesthood. But of course. *Manon* was written for Paris. It couldn't have the blunders of the Puccini version—like the barren deserts of Louisiana." George allowed himself a generous laugh. "The Puccini is *so* vulgar—"

Gene raised both hands, palms out. "That guy in the Honda is back. I went outside to check, and he drove away. I couldn't make out the license plate."

George's jolliness withered. "Is Hank home?"

"Haven't seen him."

"I never should have allowed him into this house. He's a tragedy waiting for the final act. I'll call the police."

"Michael will be staying here tonight," Gene said. "He'll get in late. Don't mistake him for an intruder."

"When will he be moving in?"

"June."

"And Carl's boys will be staying the weekend. A house with children." George smiled. "It'll be like a real home."

Gene shrugged. "I hope someday. For now it's just a stopping-over place."

"You and Carl and Hank are fortunate. You have children."

"You must have family."

George shook his head. "My southern relatives rejected me when I came out."

Gene froze.

"I'm gay, Gene. No one in this house knows, and I'd appreciate it if you didn't share it, especially with Hank. Don't worry, though. I'm celibate. Too bad. If you were thirty years older, you'd be my type."

"Why did you tell *me?*"

George took a score from the bed and paged through it. "I need an ally. The blacks don't want me because I'm too white. The whites reject me because I'm black. The gays pull away—I'm not into the gay culture. The straights hate me because I'm gay. Carl and Hank think I'm too old and finicky. Like you—I didn't come from anywhere, I don't belong anywhere."

"You belong here. This house is yours."

George laughed. "If I can keep up with the taxes and maintenance. My annuity doesn't cover much."

"You bought this house."

"Inherited it. Did you ever hear of Alex Fournier, the architect? We were lovers for twenty years. He died of AIDS at the beginning of the epidemic, in 1985. He sold me the house for a dollar and set up a trust to help me with expenses. When I retired, the money wouldn't stretch, so I started renting out rooms." George put aside the score. "I could have tried to find a job, but I wanted to help. Don't tell the others, but the clinic where I volunteer is the Whitman-Walker, the gay establishment. When nobody in the medical community would touch Alex, the clinic stepped in."

Gene blew the air from his lungs. "I had no idea—"

"Remember," George said, "not a word to Hank. When I brought him into the house a year ago, my money was running out—I took the first renter who applied. Scarpia took a dislike to him. That should have alerted me."

At the sound of his name, Scarpia raised his head expectantly. George patted him and reached for the telephone. "What's the number of the police?"

"I'll call them," Gene said. "I got a good look at the car."

But when he did, the sleepy police sergeant sounded like he'd heard it all before. "If he comes back, try to get the license plate number."

Right. In the middle of the night with the car's lights off.

When Gene's alarm woke him in the morning, Michael's bed was untouched. His clothes were not in a heap on the floor. No scrubs were missing from Gene's shelf. The shower and the floor in front of it were dry.

Gene recovered his cell phone from the jeans pocket and poked in Michael's cell number. Six rings, then—

"Hello?" The voice was muffled.

"Michael? You okay?"

"Why the hell are you calling me at this hour?"

A woman's voice said, "What's the matter?"

"My dad," Michael said.

"I was worried about you." Gene tried to keep his voice calm.

"I'm fine. I'm at Leila's. It was so late I didn't want to call and wake you."

Gene took a deep breath. "Well, okay. Um, how about returning the car tonight? Stay for dinner and—uh—bring me up to date."

"See you about six."

The woman's voice was talking when the line went dead.

Gene showered, shaved, and dressed. So his son was no virgin. Surprise, surprise. If it had a heartbeat and looked good in a tight sweater, Michael was on it. He'd be twenty-one in June. He'd been dating since he was fourteen. That was when Gene gave him condoms. "I don't want you to use them, but I'd rather you used them than not." Michael had understood. At least three times during high school, Michael had let Gene know that he'd been with a girl. At least he'd stopped drooling in the presence of women.

The sexual revolution had passed Gene by, but Michael was riding the wave. So, apparently, was this Leila. For no reason Gene could put his finger on, Leila worried him.

As he put on his shoes, he reminded himself that the boy he played football with on the front lawn, taught to drive, showed how to use a razor was a man now. They'd talked about sex openly, especially since the split with Donna, and Gene had made no pretense about his affair with Priss. He could hardly demand celibacy of Michael when he himself had been sleeping with a woman he wasn't married to. Worse, now that he'd stopped seeing her, horniness was rearing its delightful head at every opportunity. He pictured Nettie. *Don't get distracted.*

He draped his suit coat over his arm and picked up his briefcase. Would he sleep with a woman again if he had a chance? Of course. Could he require Michael to abstain? Nope.

Michael didn't arrive until six-thirty, and the father-son conversation had to wait. Carl and George were happy to have Michael as an extra at the table, and George was pleased with Michael's compliments on his fish in white sauce. After dishes, Gene and Michael retired to the attic.

Michael stretched on his bed and put his hands behind his head. "You want me to bring you up to date, right?"

"First," Gene said, "we have an invitation for a cookout on Sunday. Want to go?"

"Can I bring Leila?"

"I'll have to clear it with the hostess."

"You're seeing Priss again?" Michael asked.

"This is someone else."

Michael cast him a side-long glance. "And she's single, right? And available."

"Yeah, I guess. She's an attractive woman."

"My own father a masher." Michael shook his head sadly. "Who'd have thunk it?"

"I'm not seeing her. It's Nettie, Clem's secretary."

"Don't tell me the thought of hooking up with her never crossed your mind."

"I have hormones, too, you know. I figure we need to be open with each other, especially since we're going to be roomies."

"I'm cool with that, but, um—" Michael bumbled. "I haven't been up front with you. The woman I'm seeing. Leila. She's older than me, Dad. Two years out of school."

"You're *seeing* her?"

"Last night was the first time I stayed overnight, but we've been, uh, doing it for a couple of weeks." Michael gave full attention to the rafters disappearing into the darkness above him. "She says men reach their sexual peak between seventeen and nineteen. So I'm over the hill. Women come later. She thinks we as a society have the age thing all wrong in our mating rules."

"Younger man, older woman—not ideal for reproducing."

Michael nodded. "She says that's what's wrong—we're geared toward reproducing when the world is overpopulated. It wasn't until the nineteen-hundreds that the Catholic church admitted there was any reason for sex other than making babies. Leila thinks that's bassackwards."

"Does she respect your mind? Or is she only interested in your body?"

"Who cares?"

"Maybe she hasn't had experience with older men," Gene said. "They're more sensuous, subtle—"

"And can last longer, but younger men make up for it by being ready for more sooner. Besides, she's teaching me to take my time."

"Jesus. She'll turn you into a sex machine."

Michael cocked his head. "Fine by me."

"She sounds, I don't know, unusual."

"No way." Michael shook his head emphatically. "Huh-uh. You got it wrong, doofus. Try gnarly—so far off the bell curve it can't even be explained as an outlier, to say nothing of an anomaly."

"No more statistics courses for you. Anyway, you really like her?"

"She's okay. Sort of immature. Favors more rigid enforcement of the death penalty. Thinks people without kids shouldn't have to pay taxes to support schools. Blames the Kurds for the mess in Syria and Iraq. Fierce supporter of the president. She'll grow out of a lot of that in time. Want to grab a beer?"

"Michael, I don't want you hurt. Among other things, I'm not ready to be a grandfather."

"She's on the Pill."

"There's disease, too."

"She hates condoms."

"You need to be careful," Gene said. "She's probably had lots of partners."

"Not so many. The men she's known haven't interested or haven't satisfied her."

Gene took a slow, deep breath and let it out. "Okay. You're an adult, only one month shy of attaining your majority before the law. I wish you weren't in this relationship, but that's your choice. Meanwhile, I hope you'll always tell me what's going on."

"I will." Michael swung his feet to the floor and leaned forward. "You tell me the truth about yourself and you talk sense. So I listen." Michael studied his father. "Where did you learn so much? Not from your parents—"

"From my imaginary parents. I constructed in my mind a perfect father, the one I wanted. Then I decided I'd be that father when I had a child. I did my imperfect best."

Michael watched him without moving. "For an imperfect father, you are fan-fucking-tastic."

"You're embarrassing me."

"Let's agree that we'll always be open with each other."

"Haven't I always been?" Gene asked.

"Promise me you'll tell me as soon as you and Nettie start sacking out together."

Gene laughed. "Deal, since it's never going to happen. Guess you're going to need to borrow the Mustang a lot now, huh?"

"Leila has her own car. It's been in the shop. About that beer—"

"By law you're a minor for another month," Gene said, "but you've never been very open with me about alcohol. Have you ever been drunk?"

"Only once really bad." Michael looked at the floor.

"When?"

"Remember before Christmas my senior year in high school when I got the flu? It wasn't flu. I was hungover."

"Why didn't you tell me?"

"You were pretty uptight at the time, and Mom would have killed me."

"Listen," Gene said. "We can't screw around like that anymore. It's just us now. We have to take care of each other."

"If it happened now, I'd probably ask you to join me. Getting laid has really loosened you up."

Gene's cheeks burned.

"Mashers don't blush," Michael said.

"I'm really a doofus."

"Then how come all these hot and cold running women?"

"They think I'm cuddly."

Michael laughed so hard he choked.

Nettie's place was a Cape Cod nestled among white azaleas atop the highest of the rolling hills in Takoma Park, a mile from the Victorian manse Gene still owned. He had to leave the Mustang on a side street and walk into the cul-de-sac due to the parking overload of Nettie's "few friends." A sign on the front door told him to proceed to the deck at the rear of the house. As he rounded the corner, Nettie, in shorts and a halter top, gave him a radiant smile, trotted down the steps to the lawn, pressed a beer into his hands, and kissed his cheek.

"Wow," Gene said. "I feel like Bill Bailey come home."

She blushed. "No Michael?"

"His date is picking him up at his mother's."

"She let him go out on Mother's Day?"

Gene blanked. "That's today? Went right past me."

"That's the theme of the gathering."

The party had spilled from the deck into lawn chairs in the back yard. Gene ambled across the lawn and sat between Nettie's daughters, Rachel and Sarah. The smell of cooking hamburgers reminded him he hadn't eaten since breakfast.

"So you're Gene," Rachel, the younger, said.

"So you're Rachel. I've seen your picture on your mother's desk."

"We just had Mom's description of you to work from," Sarah said, "but we recognized you."

"I'm flattered," Gene said.

The girls giggled.

Gene glanced at the deck. A woman was staring at him while every man in the place was gawking at her. Her dark eyes, hooded under perfect hemisphere lids, challenged him. Her nose was long and regal, her cheeks hollow, as though she were sucking them in. Her lips were large and full over teeth prominent enough to be ugly in another face. Her hair was dark brown, cut above the shoulders, loose and swinging. She wore a snowy sleeveless top with a high neck that made her full breasts all the more prominent.

Rachel and Sarah followed his gaze.

"Wow," Sarah breathed. "Who's she?"

Standing at the woman's shoulder was a man a head taller than she was. He was smiling at Gene. *Michael.* Was this Leila? Nettie gave each a beer and tipped her head toward Gene.

Michael and the woman came down the steps. Gene stood.

"Dad, this is Leila Spencer."

When she raised her eyes to Gene's, he felt singed.

"A pleasure," Gene said.

"All mine," she said in a voice that was pure honey.

Gene introduced Rachel and Sarah. They responded with chilly graciousness. Michael and Leila pulled up deck chairs, and the five of them tried to make conversation. Sarah brought up a White House official's mockery of John McCain, noting that he "doesn't matter. He's dying anyway." Rachel said it was scandalous, so typical of the administration. Leila opined that the White House had it right—McCain didn't matter any more.

While Leila talked, Gene watched her. She was not beautiful, he decided, but gave off electric vibes. Every laugh, word, gesture bespoke erotic promise. Rather crude—if it was intentional. Maybe it wasn't. Maybe carnality was simply her defining characteristic. Would he condemn her for that?

As he watched her, he saw that she was more than three years Michael's senior. About thirty, he guessed. So she took a younger lover. So? So nothing. But why did it have to be his son?

"Hamburgers ready," Nettie called from the deck.

Gene buzzed Nettie.

"Got Congressional staff people with him, Gene. Problem?"

"He sent me a job announcement. Senior Budget Executive slot at CIA. Scrawled a note across the top— 'Perfect for you.' What gives?"

"My guess is he's looking out for you. We all know you're foaming at the mouth about your next promotion."

"Be nice," Gene said.

"How long have we known each other, Professor? You think he doesn't know you took your current job for the promotion? Then the possibility for an SES1 opens up—"

It didn't ring true. Clem had bitched when Hugh Shafter moved to the NPO to get his SES1.

"How long'll he be?" Gene said.

"A while. Unexpected visitor hot under the collar."

"Uh-oh. Who?"

"The Senate Preparedness Subcommittee Chief of Staff. Stormed in really pissed."

"Dellaspada? What's he want?"

"I just work here," Nettie said.

"Maybe I'd better come up there. Dellaspada—"

"You weren't invited."

"But it's my bailiwick—"

"Cut it, Gene. I'll call you if the man summons you."

Off the phone, Gene flopped in his chair. What was going on?

An hour later, Clem buzzed him. "The announcement? You're part of the FIBO family, Gene. I watch out for my boys. Great opportunity for a career change. Lots of travel. With a little finagling, you could take Michael with you to, say, Madrid or Moscow."

Gene was stumped. "Who would you get for my slot? You know who'd be perfect? Mark Forrester."

Silence. Then, "We'll put out an announcement and see who responds."

"Bet Hacker'd see to it that one of his lackeys applied. If he got one of his guys into my job this time around, he'd have the whole thing sewed up."

Ping. Was that what this was all about?

Clem laughed. "Guys at NPO are rank-ambitious, too, Gene. Anyway, let me worry about that. If you applied for the CIA job, I could pull strings behind the scenes to give you a leg up."

"What did Dellaspada want?" Gene couldn't keep the coldness out of his voice. "Nettie said he was pissed."

"Prowley's in a snit."

"I stayed by the phone. Thought you'd want me to run interference."

"Vince wanted to talk to me alone. Seems Prowley got his hands on your 2021 budget forecast from somewhere. He's ticked that there was no mention of Hacker's latest set of initiatives."

"Prowley and Hacker are colluding behind your back, Clem. Be thankful FIBO is an independent agency."

"Got to go, Gene. Think about the CIA position."

Gene's night to cook. Everybody in the house would be there, and Michael was coming by bus for dinner—before going to Leila's for the night. Carl wandered into the kitchen, still in uniform.

"The apron is lovely, Gene. Where'd you find it? They have it in pink?"

"How about setting the table? You know how to cook minute rice?"

Carl took the rice from him. "Instructions right here on the box. Want me to read them to you?"

"Set an extra place. Michael will be here."

"Let me get into mufti first."

As Carl started up the servants' stairs, the doorbell rang. Gene wiped his hands and went to the door.

"Hey, son." Gene clapped an arm around Michael and hustled him toward the kitchen. "You can give me a hand." He gave Michael the rice. "Make enough to serve five. Instructions on the box."

Hank, more wizened than ever, stuck his head in the door. "What time's dinner?"

"Seven or so," Gene said.

Hank offered Michael a grave appraisal.

"You know Michael," Gene said to Hank. "He'll be moving in soon."

Hank's frown deepened. He headed up the servants' stairs.

"Is it something I said?" Michael asked.

"Hank's pissed with me. Long story."

Just before seven, Carl came down the stairs in shorts and a tee-shirt. "Hey, pup. Sponging off the old man for eats, are we?"

Michael held up both hands, palm out. "I was summonsed. This *is* the woodpile, isn't it?"

"You're not in trouble," Gene said. "I just think we should talk."

"Help me set the table," Carl said.

George, dressing gown in place, descended the steps with dignity. "I have the pleasure of greeting the new college senior, I see. I trust they promoted you?"

"Passed my exams," Michael said.

They were seated when Hank hurried in and took his place.

George passed the rice. "Has anybody seen the green Honda out front lately?"

"Once last week," Carl said. "It was just pulling out when I got in from a gig."

"What green Honda?" Michael said.

"We see it parked outside at night." Gene handed him the chicken platter. "Drives off when you get too close."

"Weird," Michael said. "Who's at the wheel?"

"Best we can tell," George said, "it's a gentleman wearing a baseball cap."

"How can you tell it's a gentleman?" Michael said with a grin.

George examined his fingernails. "I assume everyone is a gentleman until proven otherwise. Present company excepted, of course."

Gene nudged Michael. "You'll have to practice being an otherwise. It's not the same thing as being a wise guy. You'll learn the difference."

"How's the book coming?" Michael asked George.

"Splendidly." George warmed to the task. "I've been working through Massenet's curious harmonic writing of a military theme, first in the overture, then in the last act of *Manon*. I'm trying to understand how he creates such a sense of foreboding. Through a series of augmented chords, he carries the listener enharmonically from F to D-flat to A and back to F, all in seven measures—"

Hank banged down his fork. "God Almighty. Get a life, George."

Movement around the table came to a halt.

Hank picked up his fork and resumed eating. "Nobody's interested in that shit."

"I'm interested," Michael said with a cherubic smile. "Just finished a course called Music of the Nineteenth Century. They talked about Massenet's use of harmony for dramatic effect."

Hank looked to heaven for aid. "Gawd. Two of them. In the same house."

"Two what?" Michael's good humor was wearing thin.

"Intellectual assholes," Hank said through his teeth, "who fart away their time on useless crap."

"Maybe," Michael said, "if you farted away of little of your time on this useless crap, *you* could get a life, too."

Gene grabbed Michael by the bicep. "Don't."

Hank's eyes blazed. "Who do you think you're talking to, shit-head?"

"*Stop this at once.*" George slammed the table with the palm of his hand. Glasses and silverware shuddered. "I will not have this in my house."

Hank glared at Michael. He stood, overturning his chair, and thudded from the room.

"That man," George said quietly, "is toxic. By the end of next month, he'll be three months in arrears. Then I can evict him."

Michael uprighted Hank's chair. "I apologize, George. I should have kept my mouth shut."

George patted his hand. "*Ne derangez-vous pas.* You said what I was thinking."

The rest of the meal was consumed in silence.

Carl and Michael worked together cleaning up while George and Gene shared coffee on the veranda.

"I think I've figured out the green Honda," Gene said. "My wife's probably hired detectives to keep track of me."

"Perhaps," George said, "but did you notice Hank had no comment? I suspect he's involved."

"How could he be?"

"Seek not to comprehend the deviant mind. I am deeply concerned that he will make trouble. I had hoped he'd move on his own. June is the month for the house party and he'll still be here."

"I'd forgotten. What date?"

"A Saturday night. How about 9 June? I'll ask Carl and Hank."

Gene glanced at his watch. "Time for Scarpia's training run."

He walked to the edge of the veranda and called Scarpia's name. The dog trundled up the stairs from the terrace.

"What's happening?" Michael came through the French doors drying his hands on a kitchen towel.

"Time to work with Scarpia. Come with us. I want to talk to you."

The sun had dipped behind the hills on the far side of the creek. They slipped and slid down the brush-covered thirty feet between the property line and the Rock Creek Park bridle path. As they treaded toward the sand flats by the Beach Drive Bridge, Gene worked with Scarpia, starting with the easy stuff—stop, go, heel, come. First he used voice commands, then went through hand signals, rewarding the dog with congratulations, ear rubbing, and Liva Snaps. When the ground leveled out, Gene put Scarpia through the more difficult tasks Gene had taught him after he took over from George. The *tour de force* came when Scarpia sat on command and stayed in place while Gene and Michael moved away through the twilight to a spot under the bridge, clearly beyond Scarpia's field of vision. In a speaking tone, Gene said, "Scarpia, come." The dog bounded to him, then screeched to a halt when he was close enough to see Gene's hand, palm facing out on his extended arm.

"Wow," Michael said. "He's good. Why did he stop?"

"He saw my hand signal."

Gene went on one knee and ran both hands through Scarpia's fur. "Good dog." This time he gave Scarpia two Liva Snaps. He got to his feet and pointed to a fallen tree near the end of the bridle path. "Let's sit."

The three of them walked to the log. Scarpia rested at Gene's feet.

"Getting late." Michael scanned the darkening sky. "Leila'll be here soon."

"She'll wait."

"Why do I get the feeling you don't like her?"

Gene considered. "I like her all right. I don't even disapprove of her."

"I know. You're worried about me. I can take care of myself."

"I think she's older than she told you," Gene said.

"Does it matter?"

"It does if she lied. What do you know about her?"

"What's to know?" Michael said. "She works at the World Bank as a financial analyst, has a sweet place in Foggy Bottom close to campus. I met her in my Nineteenth Century music course. She got permission to audit toward the end of the semester. Doesn't know shit about music. Asked me to help her out. Let's see. She drives an Audi, likes conservative clothes, has lots of jazz CDs, has a great home theater setup in her living room."

"She buying or renting?"

Michael paused. "Damned if I know. No, wait. She talked about condo fees, so she must own the place. Why do you want to know?"

"She bothers me. It's like a piece to a jigsaw puzzle that seems right, but you have to force it. You don't know the fit is wrong until you find the correct piece—"

Scarpia jumped to his feet, tail wagging. They followed his eyes. A dark shape was making its way down the embankment from the end of the bridge on their side of the creek. When Scarpia bolted toward him, the figure spun and stumbled back up the incline through the trees.

"Scarpia, come," Gene called.

Scarpia came to a stop, watching the retreating shadow, then ran to Gene and danced around him, tail wagging. He started toward the bridge again, then doubled back, prancing in place.

"Scarpia's happy about something," Gene said. "Wants us to go with him."

Gene and Michael followed Scarpia, and as they scrambled up the slope, an unseen car started and drove off. When they broke through the brush at Beach Drive, they peered south into the darkness across the bridge, then through the uncertain light of street lamps up the hill to the north. Scarpia, still in a fit of doggy joy, nuzzled Gene's hand and whimpered.

"It's okay, boy." Gene tousled the hair on Scarpia's head.

"We better head home," Michael said. "Leila—"

"Let's go."

All the way up the bridle trail, Gene frowned. The phantom was someone Scarpia was happy to see, but the man fled when he saw the dog. Things were getting dicey. When he got home, Gene checked the street in front of the house. Carl's Rabbit, George's ancient Buick, Hank's Nissan, his own Mustang. No green Honda.

At breakfast, Gene's cell phone rang.

"Dad, Leila's bought a rosewood coffee table. She doesn't think it'll fit in the Audi. I told her maybe we could borrow your car to cart it to her place. What's the model name of your hatchback? We'll check the specs on the web and see if it's big enough."

"Mustang GLZ."

"All right with you," Michael said, "if we pick up your car today and bring it home tonight?"

"Sure. I'll let George know so he doesn't think someone's stealing it."

Mid-morning in the office, Gene's secure phone rang.

"This is Hugh, Gene. I went over the changes you made to the draft budget of 8 May. What the hell do you think you're doing?"

"Trying to piece together an NPO budget we can get through the Preparedness Subcommittee. Despite my warnings, you put back in the increases for office space in Karachi and Singapore. That'll never fly. And buying a courier aircraft? Come on. Nobody'll go for that. And that's just for starters."

Long silence. Then, "Gene—" Shafter's voice was low and tight. "The general wants those increases included. I've told you repeatedly that Prowley has the majority of votes. We'll get it through."

"I doubt it," Gene said. "Sooner or later, Danley or one of his supporters—" How was Gene going to make this stick? Of course Prowley could get those line items through. They were nothing but a cover in the shell budget for further missile expansion in the covert budget. And one of these days, nuclear warheads were going to appear magically.

"For the last time, Gene, General Hacker has ordered that those items appear in the budget that goes to the subcommittee."

"Let's get this straight," Gene snarled. "I don't work under Hacker's command. I'm not bound by his orders. If you want to overrule me, talk to Clem."

Shafter slammed down the phone.

An hour later, Gene's outside line rang.

"Westmoreland?" a grainy male voice drawled. "Herman Prowley here."

Gene's scalp tingled. "Senator—"

"My chief of staff tells me there's a problem, and I thought maybe we could solve it with an off-the-record chat."

"Excuse me, Senator, but this is an insecure line. Perhaps—"

"Our problem is personal, not technical. I talked to Pete Hacker. He tells me he's having trouble pushing through budget proposals I'm prepared to support. Seems there's an obstruction in the system. He hopes we can introduce a laxative before we proceed."

Gene heard his own pulse thumping in his ears. Best to say nothing until Prowley got to the point.

"Pete and my subcommittee chief of staff have both talked to the head of your operation," Prowley said. "Frankly, Westmoreland, Vince sized up your boss as a ball-less wonder. We decided we could save time by a direct approach."

"Senator, anything I can do to—"

"Can't talk specifics here. The message is blunt. Get with the program, Westmoreland. We're losing patience."

Gene swallowed.

"You there, Westmoreland?"

"Yes, sir."

"For the record, this conversation never took place. I wouldn't want to put your career in jeopardy."

The line went dead.

PART TWO

Triangulation

Chapter 6

Manifest Destiny

Michael ostensibly came to Shepherd Park for the weekend, but Leila picked him up Friday night before dinner. When he got to the house Saturday morning, he went for a run while Gene worked out. After a rest, they tackled the front yard, weeding, pruning yews and arborvitae, and restoring the lawn in the semi-circle formed by the driveway.

Gene mopped his forehead. "Next year, we'll get George to buy annuals for the empty beds. It's sunny enough on the eastern side of the house for blooming perennials. Maybe peonies and iris."

"I won't be here next year." Michael leaned on his rake. "If I get into grad school, if I get a scholarship, and if I get a good job next summer, I might be in Berkeley or Boston."

First time Michael had mentioned grad school. Gene grinned to himself at the proud prospect of having two Doctors Westmoreland in the family. "Let's get lunch."

They took their sandwiches, chips, and cokes to the dining room table—the sun was too fierce for them to eat on the veranda.

Gene munched. "You never came for the car Wednesday."

"We looked up Mustang GLZ on line. No such model."

"Not GLZ. GLX. What did you do?"

"Leila had the store deliver," Michael said. "Cost her a bundle, but she didn't care. The table matches these rosewood chests she uses for end tables. Got them in Hong Kong. She's on the personal staff of the President of the World Bank. Makes big bucks, doesn't have to pay income tax."

Gene smacked his lips. "Marry her. Or at least let her keep you."

"She practically does. Pays for everything, just about. Took me to Citronelle the other night. She likes high tea at the Four Seasons. Always with Dom Perignon."

Gene took a swig of coke and watched through the French doors as a hawk circled over the Rock Creek ravine. "Hope you're not planning on this lasting too long."

"Hey, she's having a fling with a younger guy. I'm just along for the ride. She'll give me my walking papers before fall."

"How did she land a senior staff position at her age?"

Michael shrugged. "She said something about her father. Made it sound like he's some kind of big wig."

"Spencer." Gene rummaged through his memory. "Doesn't ring a bell. You're seeing her tonight?"

"Are you kidding? When I got a perfect alibi? Don't have to explain where I was all night."

"No wonder I'm suddenly so popular. I thought it was filial love brought on by budding maturity."

"Naw. Love in bloom. Well, at least lust in full flower."

Michael bathed and dressed in the late afternoon. Leila's Audi appeared in the driveway at six, and they were gone.

Another empty evening to get through. Gene envied Michael. He had to admit he missed Priss. He'd already worked out. Scarpia didn't need to be trained tonight. Maybe after dinner he'd listen to Bach, something he rarely had time for these days. Then there'd be Sunday. He'd go to the office. Plenty of work waiting for him there. He sat on the terrace stroking Scarpia, wishing he had someone to care about.

George cooked late that night. Carl was working, but Gene and Hank both ate. At the table, with the television droning news about the on-again off-again summit between the president and Kim Jong-un, Gene told George what he and Michael had accomplished in the yard. Hank said little. When the dishes were half done, Gene told Hank he'd finish up, and Hank went to the veranda to smoke.

Gene worked on in the kitchen, finding things to do. He scoured the lasagna pan thoroughly, cleaned the oven, dried the dishes, and put them away. After he'd swept the floor, he was trying to decide if he should mop when he heard George's slow tread on the servants' steps.

George came into the kitchen in his dressing gown and ascot carrying a tray, a decanter, and two snifters. "I have Armagnac I save for special times. Would you share with me?"

"What's the occasion?"

"Your sad face."

"That bad, huh? I'd love to but—you think I should mop first?"

"Never postpone joy. Especially for mopping."

They sat close to the open French doors, letting the night breeze roll over them. George poured a tablespoon of brandy in each snifter and offered one to Gene. They cradled their glasses in their hands.

"Is your sadness something you want to talk about?" George said.

"I'm a pariah at work. Got a vicious divorce staring me in the face. My son's hooked up with an older woman."

"Gayness, like deafness, is not a total curse." George sighed. "One is spared some sorrows."

"And some joys."

George nodded. "When one has a friend like you or Carl, one is allowed to share a parent's joy."

"I wouldn't trade with you." Gene swirled his brandy, held it to the light. "Nothing in my life has equaled the pleasure— and pain—of being a father."

"The Armagnac is sufficiently chafed."

George lifted his snifter. Gene touched it lightly with his. Both sampled the brandy.

"Lovely," George said.

"Sharp," Gene said.

"That is why, my friend, one has only a very little to warm one for sleep."

"I'm sure your lifestyle has its sorrows, too."

"The AIDS epidemic. I lost many people I loved."

"You're really celibate?" Gene asked.

"AIDS persuaded me."

"I don't think I could ever abstain completely."

"Amazing what tragedy will do to you. I came to equate sex with death."

"To me sex is life." Gene took brandy on his tongue and held it.

"Don't rush the brandy," George said. "I'm not giving you any more."

Gene chuckled. "One of the things I like about you is your out-of-left-field honesty."

"Gays see life from a different angle."

"How's the book coming?"

"Would you believe it?" George sat tall. "I've finished the second draft in English. I'll do the translation after I do another edit."

"Why not write it in French?"

"I want to take advantage of both markets, see where I can sell it. Rumor has it that both Sony and Deutsche Grammophon will be coming out with new *Manon* recordings and maybe a DVD. If I could publish the book at the same time the recordings came on the market, when the opera world was focused on Massenet—well, you see—"

Gene should have known better than to get George started on Massenet and opera. Now there was no shutting him up. Gene sipped until the Armagnac was gone.

"That was scrumptious, George. Thank you. You're a good friend."

"Worth it to see you smile again. The warmth has spread though my blood and made me sleepy, so I bid you *bon soir*." He held up his hand. "Please don't say *bon soir*. I don't want my system subjected to your pronunciation before I sleep."

"Good night, then," Gene said.

When George started his deliberate march up the stairs, Gene decided against mopping. The floor in the dining room wasn't immaculate, either, but it was good enough for this house. He swabbed the table, glanced over the room, and switched off the dining room light.

As the room retreated into darkness, a speck of red on the veranda caught Gene's eye. The end of Hank's cigarette, close to the door. He was close enough to have heard the conversation between Gene and George.

Friday morning, Clem summoned Gene to his office. "Cancel your afternoon calendar. Hacker wants you at the NPO War Center."

"What War Center? Why? What if I said I was too busy with the budget cycle?"

"Gene, don't push him."

"Right. He's used to having his commands obeyed."

Clem reared. "That was uncalled for."

"Clem, we were set up as an autonomous agency for a reason. You don't report to Hacker. He's bulldozing you."

"Two o'clock. Hacker's guy will come for you."

At two sharp, Gene's door chime rang. Cutter.

He led the way as if Gene were in strange territory, past security, down the elevators, to Seventeenth Street.

"We can walk if the gentleman is willing." Cutter quick-marched up Seventeenth to Jay Street, right to the Harrison Square Metro station, and down the escalator.

"Does the gentleman have a Metro card?" Cutter said.

Gene pulled it from his breast pocket. They passed through the fare machines. Cutter guided Gene away from the train platform toward an unmarked exit and into a dim chamber. Cutter slipped a plastic card into a slot. When a door opened to reveal another door, Cutter entered a code in the keypad, then gestured for Gene to enter ahead of him.

They were in a small reception room of reinforced concrete, the wall ahead of them pierced by a square window and a leaden gray door. Behind the glass were two men, both in gray jumpsuits. One, in a helmet, held an automatic rifle; the other, in latex gloves, sat at a desk with a keyboard and several monitors.

Cutter spoke through a microphone in the wall. "This is Doctor Westmoreland."

The man in gloves pressed a button on a microphone next to his keyboard. "ID, please."

Cutter opened a compartment beside the window. Gene laid his card in it. The compartment door snapped shut, and the turntable rotated. The man withdrew Gene's card from the far side, passed it through a scanner, studied Gene, and returned the card.

"You vouch for him, sir?" he said to Cutter.

"Yes."

The man poked the keyboard. The lead door slid open with a purr. Cutter escorted Gene into a tunnel. As the door closed behind them, Gene caught two pairs of eyes watching them through glass slots. Another door whished open in front of them. They passed through a metal detector. Ahead was another window, two more sentries in jumpsuits.

"Doctor Westmoreland, welcome." The voice came from a speaker in the wall above the window. "Please stand close to the mirror, so that your nose is almost touching, look through the translucent square at the rotating green light, and speak your full name, no initials."

Feeling awkward, Gene stood on two painted footprints before a full-length mirror. He stooped until his eyes were level with the square, then stared into the light, and spoke his name.

"Again, sir. Please wait at least one second between each name."

"Eugene. Burrell. Westmoreland."

"Thank you, sir." The man typed at his computer, and a door glided open. Cutter and Gene stepped through. An elevator. Cutter activated it with a key from his pocket. The elevator dropped. Gene's stomach lagged behind. The doors opened silently.

"This way, sir," Cutter said.

Gene followed him and swallowed a gasp. They were in a room perhaps fifty feet wide and sixty feet long. The high ceiling, the floor, and the walls were blue-tinted mirrors. In an inverted U along the three walls opposite the elevator were two dozen computers on desks. Four men in business suits worked at keyboards. The air was suffused with the scent of damp cement with an undertone of coffee.

"Doctor Westmoreland, sir," Cutter said.

A man in navy blue rose. Hacker. He smiled at Cutter. "That'll be all, son."

Cutter, at attention, quivered. "Yessir." He disappeared into the elevator, and the door closed.

Hacker extended his hand to Gene, his smile gone.

Gene shook hands. "My apologies, General. I didn't recognize you in mufti."

"No one comes here in uniform," Hacker said. "And we don't use the entrance you did. Coffee?"

"No thanks."

"I'd like some. Boyden—"

The man at the closest computer rose smartly and disappeared behind the U, returned at once with a blue mug inscribed with three silver stars.

"We have all the necessities," Hacker said. "Ten men could survive here for a year. Have a seat." He motioned Gene to a rolling chair and sat beside him. "I wanted you to see our nerve center so you'd understand better what we're trying to accomplish. In this room—" He raised both arms and swept the mirrored walls with his eyes. "—you see the remoted triggers for hidden missile sites around the world. I exaggerate only slightly when I say that with the proper warheads we could destroy the war-making capacity of targeted nations within fifteen minutes."

Hacker nodded. Boyden clicked his computer. A panel in the wall opened disclosing a glass projection screen. Boyden clicked again, and a map of the world appeared.

"The threat nations are in red," Hacker said. "Those we can strike from NPO sites are cross-hatched. As you can see, Iran, Iraq, Syria, Turkey, Venezuela, and North Korea are covered. Libya, Congo, Angola, Vietnam, most of the republics of the former Soviet Union, and much of China and Africa are not."

Gene examined the map. "Argentina, Brazil, Egypt, Israel, Pakistan, and South Africa, and let's see—Britain, France, Canada, Mexico, India, Japan—these are threat nations?"

"Potentially."

"They're not hostile to the United States"

"A temporary situation, perhaps. Aside from the United States, the world is volatile."

Gene squinted. "Russia is not included as a threat nation?"

"Russia is one of our few solid allies."

"But—" Gene frowned. "What would have to happen for you to launch a strike?"

Hacker bestowed a forgiving smile. "Unlike the overt ICBM sites, we have dispensed with the cumbersome Permissive Action Links, the Two-Man Rule, and multiple layers of activating codes. A simple command from the president authorizes me to launch remotely." He pointed to a blue telephone. "Secure line to the Oval Office."

"How could you be sure it was the president?"

"Same voice recognition technology that allowed you entry."

"You didn't have a recording of my voice."

"Of course we did. Multiple recordings. Meetings, telephone conversations."

A wave of lightheadedness passed over Gene. "How can you assure that a rogue element won't penetrate here and launch?"

Hacker laughed. "First of all, secrecy. No one knows of the existence of this site except those who are both cleared *and* have need-to-know. Among those, only a few *professionals*, intelligence officers like yourself, have access to the details of our mission. You've seen our physical layout. What may not be obvious is the bullet-proof glass, the air-tight protection against chemical or biological attack, and retina scanning. We'd scanned you covertly in the past, of course, and the system verified your identity. The metal detector checked for the microchip we embed under the skin of assigned personnel. The guards, on my orders, overrode the system to permit you entry. Beyond that, even if non-authorized personnel somehow penetrated our defenses, only I know the keys needed to set a launch in motion. There are no copies. I've memorized everything. Obviously, I never leave Washington. If I am incapacitated, the president can pass the keys to others as he sees fit."

Hacker inclined his head. Boyden clicked off the display, closed the panel.

"Gene," Hacker said, "I invited you here, to the very soul of the most secret operation of our nation's security apparatus, to impress on you the urgency of our need for additional funding."

"You want to add more sites than are currently in your five-year plan?"

Hacker tented his fingers. "If you keep up with daily news reports, to say nothing of intelligence alerts, you know how unstable the world is. Threats are everywhere." He tasted his coffee. "Some nations are simply irrational, perhaps even suicidal. Who could attest to the sanity of Kim Chong Un or Nicolás Maduro? And since the election of the president, the G7 heads of state have shown signs of hostility. We must be prepared to obliterate trouble before it starts."

"With missiles?"

Hacker's eyes sparkled. "Missiles armed with nuclear warheads." He put down his coffee cup, clasped his hands, and leaned forward until his face was inches from Gene's. "It's taken us years. We have the core network of missiles in place. By next year we'll have more. All that's left is to arm them. After that, no entity on earth will be immune to our lethal touch."

"But why? We have ICBM's on land, on subs. We can arm aircraft with missiles—"

"The redundancy principle, blanket coverage, surprise, target saturation, reduced warning time, decreasing the likelihood of misses to a statistically negligible margin. And, most important, complete secrecy." He put his coffee to his lips. "Boyden."

"Yes, sir."

"Coffee's cold."

Boyden whisked away Hacker's cup.

Hacker again fixed Gene in his gaze. "Look at history. One nation has emerged from the last hundred years as the finest the world has ever seen. We have a moral duty, a manifest destiny, to see to it that the rest of humanity follows in our footsteps."

Boyden placed a steaming cup on the desk within inches of Hacker's hand. Hacker lifted it to his lips without looking at it. "Never mind the unassailable logic of the strategy. Think of the American lives we could have saved in Africa, the Balkans, Afghanistan, Iraq, Syria—"

"Would you use your system now in Syria if it were operational with nuclear warheads?"

"Of course."

"The collateral damage—" Gene began.

"We have honed our targeting with microscopic precision."

"Even so, the civilian casualties—"

"The concept of civilians is obsolete. Our immutable enemies are no longer governments with armies and fleets and warplanes. They are populations poisoned with hatred, unfaltering in their determination to oppose us. A ten-year-old German student of today is the suicide bomber of tomorrow."

Gene shuddered. He'd awaken from this nightmare at any moment.

"Fortunately for them," Hacker continued, "our experience with Japan at the end of World War II made it indelibly clear that even the most recalcitrant populations can be terrified into submission. It took only two nuclear strikes."

"Shock and awe?" Gene said.

Hacker's face hardened. "It would be a great deal easier for both of us if you had the breadth of understanding to grasp what I have told you."

Gene waited.

"Don't forget," Hacker said, "who you are and what you're up against. The Senate Preparedness Subcommittee under Senator Prowley supports us. Prowley himself has seen this room. The president is not only supporting us but urging us on."

"Has the president ever been here?" Gene said.

"That is information I cannot share."

"So very few have detailed knowledge of your intent."

"I know from painful experience that briefing elected officials invites leaks. Security professionals are less of a risk. I personally brief those, like yourself, who must know."

Gene took a breath. "Your classified charter only mentions clandestine operations in passing, General, and that in the context of intelligence gathering. There is no authorization for missiles, to say nothing of a nuclear capability."

"You are not permitted access to the compartmented appendix authorized by President Reagan."

"Reagan . . . this operation has been around since the 1980s?"

Hacker nodded. "It was initiated at his behest. It prospered during the Bush administration and waned under the Democrats, but none, not even the Obama misadventure, ever succeeded in uprooting it entirely. Even before he was elected, our current president threw full support behind it."

"What else does the appendix authorize? Has the president seen it?"

"That is a matter too sensitive for me to discuss. Does the term 'deniability' have meaning for you?"

Gene clasped his hands to hide the shaking.

Hacker smiled. "We're getting too intense. Have some coffee. Boyden—"

"No, thank you."

"Gene, you are a gentleman, tough and strong-willed. I'm told you've even mastered a large attack dog which acts as your personal protector."

Gene sat rigid. *How the hell—*

"You're my kind of man," Hacker said. "You have the requisite qualities to join that select group of leaders who rule by virtue of sheer superiority. That's why I brought you here. No one has ever left this site unpersuaded." Hacker's smile dissipated. "If you oppose us—" He paused. "It wouldn't cost much to remove you from the game."

"Is that a threat?"

"Of course not. We're gentlemen here. Just be very sure of your ground. You're taking on those anointed by history." Still watching Gene, Hacker said, "Cutter."

Boyden pressed a button next to his computer keyboard. The elevator door opened. Cutter stepped out. "Ready, sir?"

Gene followed him into the elevator.

Back at his desk, Gene was still off balance. Hacker was a pinnacle of unwavering determination, but his judgment was clouded by arrogance. He'd shown his hand, certain Gene would rush to join the team. He'd seen Gene's repulsion as the failure of a stunted intellect.

Gene took an edgy breath. He was nothing but a bean counter. He couldn't hope to outmaneuver Hacker. He couldn't plead the Eichmann defense, either, not if he wanted to go on being Gene Westmoreland. He had to act, the sooner, the better.

He dialed Nettie. "I have to see him."

"Gene, he's in the small conference room with DIA muck-demucks. Can't be disturbed."

"Break in. I can't wait."

"No way, Gene."

"I'm on my way up there. I'll crash the meeting."

Nettie gulped. "Okay. I'll tell him."

Clem was behind his desk when Gene burst into his office.

"Clem, we have to stop Hacker . . ."

"Calm down, for Christ's sake. What's this about?"

"Hacker showed me his war center. Told me his next step is to get funding for nuclear warheads."

"Gene, chill out."

"It's time to expose Hacker."

Clem shook his head. "You're getting paranoid."

"Listen. Hacker wants to set up a network of clandestine nuclear missile sites world-wide. He thinks we can control the world that way. He's manipulated the bureaucracy and the classification and compartmentation system so that no one sees what he's up to. He tried to co-opt me. The only way I can block him is by lobbying to withhold funding, but *you* could talk to the NSC, maybe even to the president—"

Clem rotated his chair toward the window. "Gene, you're a budgeteer, not a policy wonk."

Gene flinched. "You know about this?"

"I stay out of matters that don't concern budgeting."

"Clem, we have a moral responsibility—"

"Morality is not our business."

"We can't sit by. If the president understood—"

Clem turned back to Gene. "What makes you think he doesn't? The president is going out of his way to assure quick funding for the nuclear warheads."

Gene stopped breathing.

"The president . . ." Clem closed his eyes. "The president has created a subterranean bureaucracy to assure that the U.S. can dominate the world. It includes NPO and the Office of Special Compartmented Intelligence and other organizations." Clem looked down and breathed deeply. "I call it the Secretocracy."

Gene suppressed a shudder.

Clem gave Gene a look of profound sadness. "I'm sorry, Gene." He reached into a desk drawer, took a brown medicine vial, and popped a tiny pill in his mouth. "One more time. Stick with budgeting. Stay clear of policy." He struggled to his feet. "I can't keep flag-ranks waiting." He exited through the side door into the conference room.

Fighting to keep his stride normal, Gene reeled to his cubicle. Arming missiles with nuclear warheads didn't happen overnight, especially not on foreign soil. Since Hacker wanted to do it secretly, without informing host governments, ruses and camouflaged shipments and clandestine portage—God only knew what all—would be required. Before that ever got started, there was the budget process. Gene was still a key player.

His intercom buzzed.

"Gene, you all right?" Nettie said.

"Shook up. Thanks for asking."

"How about a stiff martini and a shoulder to cry on? It's almost quitting time."

"Deal," Gene said. "Meet me at Goldoni's at quarter to six."

"This is sounding better all the time. Maybe I'll spring for dinner. Ever had their tuna? They truck it in fresh every day."

As he opened Goldoni's cut-glass door, he spotted her in a booth, waving.

"I took the liberty of ordering you a double," she said. "Drink up then spill the beans. What's going on?"

The gin was sharp and cold, diluted by nothing more than a nodding acquaintance with Vermouth.

"Let's just say the mother of all storms is brewing," Gene said, "and I'm getting triangulated on."

"The triangulators?"

"Two gentlemen whose three-star rank and senatorial positions shall remain unmentioned. And the boss isn't blocking the tacklers."

"Gene, cut Doctor Yancy some slack. He isn't well."

"Ever since the trip in March. What happened?"

Nettie tasted her wine. "All I know is he's lost so much weight that his clothes look like sails becalmed. And he obviously isn't sleeping well. You're a little under the weather yourself."

"Momentary stress. I'm fine."

"Is your, you know, *job* in jeopardy?"

"Only if Hacker can lean hard enough on Clem. Or—"

Nettie cocked her head. "Or?"

"I don't know. The president could order my dismissal on any trumped-up charge."

"Come on, Gene. This isn't the Nixon Administration."

"I've gotten a couple of not-so-veiled threats." He laughed. "If Hacker or one of his people ever tells you 'we are gentlemen,' head for the bomb shelter."

As they ate, the martini and the wine that followed it kicked in. Nettie had a way of tipping her head to one side when she laughed. She was wearing eyeshadow of the faintest green that set off her eyes. She used her hands for emphasis, as an orchestra conductor does, creating a waterfall with a wave of her fingers. And beneath the scent of tuna and the aftertaste of wine, Gene detected a tinge of gardenia.

He pushed away his plate. "We're having our annual house party on June ninth. Would you come as my date? I wouldn't be able to pick you up. We'll be getting ready right up to the moment the first guest arrives."

"I'd love to. Formal?"

"Shorts and tank top. Lots of people. You'll get to meet my idiosyncratic house mates. That alone is worth the trip."

"I'll ink it in on the calendar." She finished her wine. "Meanwhile, I need to skedaddle. It's pinochle night in the Follander household. Anything to keep them away from TV and the computer."

Scarpia jigged with delight as soon as Gene was in the door. No one else around. Still light enough for a training run. In jeans and a tee-shirt, Gene led Scarpia down the hill to the bridle path. While they were practicing a new command, "freeze," Gene's cell phone rang.

"Hello?" No answer. He could hear breathing. "Hello? Anybody there?" A sound like a catch in the throat. "One last time. Hello?" Nothing. He hung up.

As they reached the house, the phone rang again. Once again, no one answered Gene's greeting. He switched the phone off and went into the kitchen. Nothing to be done here—everything clean and put away. The house phone shattered the silence. More like a fire alarm than a phone. He answered. The sound of breathing.

"Whoever this is, the joke's not funny. Cut it out."

He dropped the receiver into its cradle and swore. He was about to start up the servants' stairs when the phone rang again.

"Now look," Gene began.

"Dad?"

"Michael? Sorry. Someone's been playing telephone games."

"Your cell phone's not answering."

"I shut it off. Never mind. What's up?"

"Can you come get me?"

Gene tensed. "What's wrong?"

Michael sighed. "Mom told me to be ready to leave for Pennsylvania a week from Saturday. I told her I wasn't going. She lit into me like the Witch of Endor with flatulence. Said it was like inviting Grandpa to disinherit me. Told me if I didn't agree to come with her she didn't want to find me here when she gets home from her counseling session at Saint Boniface tonight."

"What?"

"Yeah, she threw me out. Said if I couldn't abide by the rules of the house I could find my own place to live. Then peeled out like Dale Earnhardt on uppers."

"For Christ's sake," Gene said. "How're you doing?"

"I've seen better days. There's no food in the house, I don't have wheels, and I don't have any cash. I'm kinda hungry. Do you suppose—"

"I'll be there in twenty minutes. Start packing. Everything you own that's not nailed down. We'll move you tonight."

By the time Gene got to the house, Michael was sitting on the front lawn with his stereo, computer, television, five cardboard boxes, three oversized laundry bags, and a suit on a hanger.

Gene got out of the car. "God, you're fast."

"I had most of the stuff on the porch before I called. I figured tonight was the night."

On the way to Shepherd Park, they stopped at Target for bed linen and towels. Hauling Michael's things up the circular staircases to the attic took the better part of an hour.

When Michael's bed was made with the new sheets, he set up his computer and used the tail of his tee-shirt to mop his forehead. "Where's your cable hookup?"

"Don't have one. Still use dial up."

Michael stared at him in disbelief. "My God. A Luddite in my own family."

"Where'd you hear that word?"

"You."

"You know what it means?"

"A fugitive from Lower Luddovia with acute allergy to the digerati."

"Close. Anyway, nobody in this house can afford cable. Get over it."

"There go my on-line war games and my chat room conquests. Okay. What's for dinner?"

"Just a sec. I want to give you a heads up. Hank's big trouble. Steer clear of him."

In the kitchen, they found the chopping board and large knife wet with onion fragments and an empty pickle jar and plastic wrap from hamburger on the counter. From outside, they heard shouts and laughter. Gene went to the veranda. Carl and two teenage boys were at the barbecue.

"Hey, Gene," Carl called. "Bring Michael on down so he can meet my boys."

Chapter 7

The Coon Fairy

Summer wasn't supposed to show its face until the third weekend in June, but here it was on the first—heavy air, humidity that leeched color and blunted light, seamless clouds that gave new meaning to "greenhouse effect." Gene and Michael went in together on a window air-conditioner that made the attic bearable but not really comfortable. The ancient pedestal fan, donated by George the first summer Gene had rented the attic, cranked between their beds like a robot watching a tennis match. Despite its clank and wheeze, it allowed Gene to sleep with damp hair. Better than a pool of sweat.

The breathy calls on the cell and occasionally on the house phone came in clusters—two or three a night then nothing for days. The only pattern Gene could detect was that they were nocturnal and most often on his cell. He called Verizon to complain and asked to have them traced. The lady with the Indian accent told him to report the caller to the police. When he did, the police told him to have his phone company trace the calls. To frustrate the caller, he decided not to answer the phone. He told Michael, when he called, to let the phone ring three times, hang up, and dial again. Now Gene only had to contend with intermittent complaints from house mates and recorded messages of wordless exhalation.

The green Honda had vanished, and the shadowy figure on the hill by Beach Drive had not reappeared, unless Gene counted the night he thought he saw someone cross the lawn near the property line. Donna's lawyers were mum, too. Was this the summer of our discontent? The bad guys of all stripes were on leave until fall when business picked up?

Gene and Michael fell at once into a rhythm of shared chores. They alternated doing the laundry that was becoming more plentiful now that the sweating season was in full swing. Gene insisted that Michael keep his side of the attic orderly and use his earphones if he listened to rap. And would he please stop wearing Gene's scrubs? Each morning, Gene left for work as Michael was getting out of bed in time to catch the bus to his construction job. Each evening Michael went for a run, giving Gene time for workouts and dog training. The only snag was the overworked shower stall since both had to bathe before dinner and breakfast. That was Monday through Thursday. Friday night after work, Michael cleaned up and dressed in time for the Audi to appear in the circular driveway at six-thirty. Sometimes Gene didn't see him again until Monday evening.

The week before the ninth of June, everyone in the house, even Hank, devoted all available time to scouring and polishing. George, with the vocal support of Gene and Carl, insisted that Hank move the lame motorcycle to the garage and scrub the marble floor. Gene and Michael lowered the chandelier in the living room, washed the crystal, and dusted the frame. George and Carl cleaned the windows and French doors, while Hank was in charge of the kitchen and the basement party room. Carl bought beer and wine cut-rate from the supplier of Côte d'Azur and split the cost five ways. Hank promised to pay his share as soon as he found work. Scarpia, into everything, was banished to a corner of the living room with repeated "stay" commands.

Saturday night, as nine o'clock approached, Gene retreated to the attic to check his appearance in the mirror. Was the crimson shirt too bright? Should he leave a button open to show the hair on his chest? Did loafers go with dockers? He splashed on after-shave, then, panicky, tried to deodorize it. He studied his image in the mirror. What was going on? Then it came to him. He wanted to cut a dashing figure for Nettie.

When he got to the first floor, Carl was doing a last wipe-down of the Steinway.

"Your date coming on her own?" Gene said.

Carl raised the lid and fitted the brass cup over the end of the hinged arm. "You'll meet her tonight. Tillie." He shot a glance into the foyer. "Hank's acting snarly, the way he does when he's swacked. Michael and me agreed to watch him. You want to help?"

Big Ben sounded. Gene hurried to the door. Nettie, with the same blooming smile he remembered from her party, stood tall, heels together, hands clasped on her white purse. She wore white shorts and a halter top that promised more than it showed.

Gene took her hand. She smelled of gardenias.

"Champagne?" he said.

They headed for the kitchen. He poured them each a paper cup. "Don't tell. It'll be gone."

She giggled. "Oh, goodie. Secret champagne"

"Come with me. I'll introduce you to Carl, the token normal guy of the house."

Carl was on all fours polishing the Steinway's pedals.

"Um, Carl," Gene said.

Carl saw Nettie and jumped to his feet. "Hi."

"This is Nettie, Carl."

Carl was obviously impressed. "What's a nice girl like you doing with an old lecher like our Doctor Westmoreland here?"

"Enough," Gene said. "Back to your pedal polishing."

Carl looked hurt. "You don't have to make it sound shady. Actually, it's very sustaining, even damping." He offered Nettie his toothiest grin.

Gene led Nettie to the kitchen and topped off their cups. "The celebration's downstairs, in the party room. You can get there via the servants' stairs from the kitchen or do a grand entrance by the formal stairs from the foyer."

"I haven't had enough champagne to feel very grand. Let's make like servants."

He gave her his arm and they descended to the unused second kitchen. At the foot of the stairs, Gene balked. He'd forgotten they'd have to pass through the laundry room. With a choked sigh, he led her through the door. The room, lit by a naked bulb, was blocked by piles of jeans, socks, and tee-shirts alternating with plastic baskets of unsorted clean clothes. They ducked to avoid Gene's and Michael's jock straps hung to dry on ceiling pipes.

"Nice homey feel your party room has," Nettie said. "Casual, unpretentious."

Gene conquered his chagrin and escorted her through the door at the end of the room.

The party room, beneath the dining room, was dominated by a curved bar backed by mirrors that ran the length of the room. The outside wall was all French doors that opened to a portico under the veranda. Stairs from the foyer joined the room at the end of the bar. Beatles music came from Carl's boombox.

Gene lowered the volume on the stereo and turned the dimmer switch down. "We don't use this room much these days."

"Tells you what the fuck's the matter with us, don't it?" Hank was on the love seat by the stairway, one arm around a woman on his lap, the other hoisting a beer.

"Nettie, this is my house mate, Hank."

Hank shifted to get a better view of Nettie. "Hi."

Gene and Nettie waited an awkward moment for an introduction to the woman in Hank's lap, then Gene waved toward the French doors. "Want to see the terrace?"

Hank cackled. "Oldest come-on in the book." The woman laughed.

Nettie moved quickly out the door.

On the terrace, they found George, dressed for the occasion in beige slacks and a paisley shirt. Gene introduced Nettie.

"Where's Scarpia?" Gene asked.

"He scares everybody," George said, "so I shut him in the library."

By ten, most of the guests had arrived—a handful of sedate older men, friends of George; Carl's buddies from the Pentagon with their wives, and what seemed like the entire staff from the Côte d'Azur; and a younger, rowdier bunch whom Hank must have invited. Michael and Leila came in breathless, both flushed and starry-eyed, as if they'd just come from bed. By half past eleven, dancers filled the party room floor. Gene, as co-host, moved from group to group greeting and meeting. He and Nettie tried to gossip with Mark Forrester and his wife about Clem—who had declined the invitation—but noise finally got the better of them. After Carl introduced them to

Tillie, Nettie tried to teach Gene the Booty Call. Giving it up as a bad try, they exited to the terrace and went down the steps to the lawn. Carl's florid rendering of "All the Things You Are" from the living room clashed with the Strauss waltzes on George's stereo in the portico.

"Cooler out here." Gene patted his forehead with his handkerchief. "No moon. Must be clouding over."

"No roses," she said, "no violins."

Gene was taken aback. "I came out here to cool off, not to make a pass at you."

"More's the pity."

Gene stared at her.

"Do you ever relax?" she snapped. "You work ten-hour days and spend your evenings and weekends—when you're not at the office putting in extra hours—lifting weights, training a dog, and doing yard work. How much time do you spend with Michael? Don't you ever date?"

He was *not* going to mention Priss. Besides, she wasn't talking about what was pissing her off. She was taking random shots.

"I must have done something to annoy you—"

"*Men.*"

The wind was rising.

"We'd better go in." He took her elbow and led her up the steps to the terrace. "Let's get champagne in the kitchen." Hank, his girlfriend, and two other couples sprawled across the stairs to the veranda, beer bottles in hand, laughing and smoking. When Hank saw Gene, his smile curdled.

"Excuse us," Gene said.

Hank didn't move, "Stay put, guys. The asshole can use the inside stairs."

Gene tightened.

"Him and his little redhead squeeze," Hank jeered.

Gene pushed toward him.

"Gene, please." Nettie tugged him away and pulled him to the party room doors.

Hank cackled. "Pussy."

The others laughed.

Inside, Michael, slow-dancing with Leila, caught the look on Gene's face. "What?"

"Hank."

"Stay away from him, Dad. He's more sheets to the wind than he has sheets."

Jaw still locked, Gene followed Nettie to the bar. She refilled their cups with Chardonnay.

"Thank you," she said in an undertone. "Takes courage to back down. What's that guy's problem?"

"Hank's hate-sick."

A Carlos Santana number on the stereo set their feet to tapping.

Nettie cocked her head. "Shall we?"

As they moved through other dancing couples to the middle of the room, lightning painted the landscape beyond the open French doors. A clap of thunder made them jump.

"Hope it pours," Nettie said. "We haven't had rain for days."

Gene encircled her waist with his arm and led her in a slow foxtrot that utterly ignored Santana's beat. He hadn't danced in years, but when he felt the warmth of her body next to his, an old longing touched his heart. That was why he didn't relax. He had to keep the hurting away. He wished he could explain to her.

The song ended, and a new one started. They danced again. Nettie hummed along. The vibrations of her voice penetrated his chest. The ache blossomed.

Lightening stabbed the sky. Thunder cracked. Rain flogged the terrace cobblestones. Gene closed the doors.

Couples—Michael and Leila and Mark with his wife among them—stood waiting for the next song. The trees beyond the new lawn were suddenly illuminated again. Nettie spoke to Gene, but her words were engulfed in a close explosion of thunder. The music started again. Couples joined and rocked gently. Another splash of lightening simultaneously stopped the music and dimmed the lights. Hank, his girlfriend, and the other two couples burst in from the terrace as if propelled by the rolling thunder. They ruffled their hair and shook water from their hands. Droplets flew in all directions. The guests cried their protest.

Hank laughed. "Bunch o' wussies. Water won't hurt nothin'." He grabbed his girl around the waist and gave her a sloppy kiss on the mouth. "Let's go upstairs and get naked."

She pushed him away with a laugh and stumbled to the bar. "More beer in here?"

Hank and the three men with him, red-faced and bleary-eyed, went behind the bar and opened the refrigerator. Hank tossed two bottles to his girl. She flapped her arms, and the bottles clattered to the floor. Hank reeled from behind the bar, bent to pick up the bottles, and lost his balance. His girl grabbed him by his belt and pulled him upright. He opened their beers and swaggered to Gene.

He leaned close. His breath smelled like a beer hall men's room. "Where's our spade landlord?"

Gene stiffened. Mark's head turned.

Hank gulped beer and wiped his mouth with his hand. "You know who I mean. The coon fairy who lives next to me."

Michael grabbed Hank by the bicep. "Shut up, Hank. You're smashed."

The doors swung open. George came in. "Got soaked," he said to Gene. "Had to bring in the stereo." He headed toward the laundry room.

"There he is," Hank said loudly, "the nigger faggot."

George stopped.

"Hey, honey—" Hank's girl put her hand on his arm.

"You want to suck my cock, boy?" Hank yelled across the room to George. He undid the top button of his jeans. "That's what you homos like, isn't it? A big cock shoved down your throat?"

The room was quiet. George swiveled slowly to face Hank.

Hank leered. "It's perverts like you going to mess up my son. Not while I'm breathing." He strutted toward George, a vein throbbing in his forehead. "Didn't know I knew what you are, did you, boy? Heard you and Gene yacking about your life-style. Maybe you want it up the ass." He grasped the front of George's trousers and wrenched. Buttons flew as the cloth ripped.

George reached for his pants and dropped the stereo. Gene caught Hank by the shoulder. Without taking his eyes from George, Hank elbowed Gene in the gut. Gene stumbled into the crowd. Michael started toward them, but Hank's buddies yanked him back.

Hank took a step closer to George. "Maybe you'd like something else crammed up your ass." He gripped his beer bottle by its top and smashed it against the antique brick behind George's head. Beer and glass shards showered the room. Hank held the jagged neck in George's face. "You want it, boy?"

Mark hurtled across the room and swung Hank to face him. Hank swiped with the broken bottle, but Mark ducked. Hank's buddy grabbed Mark from behind.

Gene sprang. Hank fell backwards and hit the floor with a thud, Gene on top of him. Hank stabbed wildly, gouged

Gene's scalp, ear, and shoulder. A woman screamed. Gene seized Hank's wrist and bashed his arm against the floor. The broken bottle skittered away. Blood spattered across Hank's face and blinded Gene. Hank brought his knee up hard between Gene's legs, flipped Gene over, went for his throat. Gene clawed for Hank's eyes, but Hank jerked his head away. Hank's face, red, sweating, veins bulging, vibrated as he forced both thumbs into Gene's throat.

The world swayed. The lightning was inside Gene's head. His ears filled with cries and thumps and toneless music. His hands grabbled over Hank's body, pulled at his shirt, pushed his shoulders. Hank's face faded and the music got louder.

Gene put his hands beneath Hank's wrists. He locked his fingers over the sweat-drenched skin. With every ounce of strength he had left, he tensed his muscles to drive up Hank's arms. Hank's fingers tightened. Gene's muscles burned. He pushed harder. Hank was laughing. "Big fuckin' muscle man."

Rage shot through Gene. He'd kill the son-of-a-bitch. Hank's quivering wrists moved. His fingers slid a quarter of an inch. He drove in his nails. Gene forced the arms up. The nails ripped his flesh as the hands lost their hold. Breath rushed into Gene's lungs. *Harder, push.* The wrists quavered. *Up, all the way.* Hank's arms were jammed straight out. His face, almost touching Gene's, was contorted in fury.

Gene twisted and kicked. Hank spun away, landed on his stomach. Before he could recover, Gene was on him, belly to back. He snatched one wrist and forced it up behind Hank's spine. Hank screamed. Gene grabbed a handful of hair and bashed Hank's skull against the floor. He knelt on Hank's pelvis and put his mouth to Hank's ear. "You're shit, you hear me? Get your ass out of here and don't come back."

Gene let go. The head wobbled. The arm flopped to Hank's side. The fingernails were bloody. Gene slid off him and stood with his legs bent, ready to pounce.

Nettie reached for Gene. He pushed her away.

Hank put his face to the floor and covered his head with his arms, as though to ward off blows. Gene relaxed his arms and legs, stood straight, and let Nettie come close.

Tears ran down her cheeks. She swabbed his neck with cocktail napkins.

Silent sobs shook Hank's body. One of his buddies knelt beside him. "Hey, man." Hank's arms tensed. The buddy shrugged.

Hank's girl dropped to her knees on the other side. "Come on, sweetie."

Hank cringed away from her and pulled his arms beneath his chest. As he rose to his feet, his friends reached for him. He shoved them away, stumbled to the French doors, flung them open, and staggered out into the pelting rain. A burst of lightening showed him lurching down the stairs to the lawn.

"Will you *please* let me drive you to the emergency room?" Nettie sat on the edge of the sink. Gene's blood streaked her right shoulder. "I've been through every bathroom and the kitchen. No tape, no gauze—"

Gene needed air. He kicked his bloody dockers out of the way and opened the dormer window beside the toilet. Cold air blew across his chest. The rain had disappeared. "How about telling someone to start the fan?"

Nettie folded her arms and crossed her legs. "No disinfectant, no antiseptics—"

He eased down on the toilet seat and adjusted his skivvies. The room was swaying. "I was waiting for a sale."

"Oh, for Christ's sake." She lunged to her feet. "I left scrubs, shoes, and socks next to the shower. Put them on."

She stomped to the bedroom. The fan started. He unwrapped the wash cloths from his neck, dropped them in the sink, and daubed his shoulder with the hand towel. Blood from the gash on his elbow—he didn't know he had it until Nettie found it—was coagulating. His left knee was bruised, but the skin wasn't broken. His ribs hurt. The blood in his hair and on his ear was clotting. Nettie'd been wrong—no other wounds under his clothes. He'd secretly enjoyed letting her strip him. What he could remember of it. He must have lost consciousness.

The cell phone rang. Gene heard Nettie answer it.

Mark trotted through the door. "You better get to a doctor."

"You okay?" Gene said.

"Cut tongue and sore chin. Michael took care of me. Go get yourself sewn together."

"Not as bad as it looks. Scalp wounds bleed like Niagara during a flood. Hand me the scrubs and shoes."

Mark passed the clothes. "I'll take you to the emergency room."

"I got it covered," Nettie called from the bedroom.

"Go take your wife out of this massacre site," Gene said. "And give her my most shame-faced apologies."

"Professor, your parties are freakin' screams. See you when you're well enough to come to the office. I'll tell Clem what happened."

Gene groaned. "Great. Just what I need."

Mark headed down the stairs. Carl craned his neck around the door. "Decent?"

"No. Don't let that stop you."

"Going to drive Tillie home." Carl leaned on a towel rack. "Thought I'd check on you first." He smiled his sunshine smile. "I followed the blood trail."

"Where's George?"

"He went upstairs after the fracas. Bet this isn't the first time he's been through something like this."

Gene peeled the towel from his shoulder, put another in its place. "What'd Hank do?"

"His car's gone. One of his friends took the lady home."

"Everybody went home after the fight?" Gene rubbed his elbow, wished he hadn't.

"Like kids at recess bell. Looks like you're in good hands—" Carl tipped his head toward the bedroom and winked. "I'm outta here." He was gone.

Michael loped in. "You all right?"

"I'm healing nicely, but don't tell Nettie." Gene put on his scrubs. "She wants to nurse me."

"I heard that," Nettie said.

Gene tied his shoes. "Take Leila home."

"I'll stay with you," Michael said.

"Like I said, Nettie's on the job, and I'm not as bad off as what I look like."

"If you weren't slashed up, I'd have used that line on you."

"Get out of here," Gene said. "And don't come back 'til tomorrow."

"But—"

"Out. And be careful. Hank's on the loose."

Michael opened his mouth to protest, then emptied his lungs and disappeared.

Nettie marched in with her purse and a stack of towels. "You ready?"

They trundled down the stairs.

"Who was on the phone?" Gene asked.

"Somebody breathing."

"Christ."

Nettie drove quickly, with cool efficiency. At Washington Circle, she wove her way across the lanes of traffic and whipped down Twenty-Third Street where she parked illegally and herded Gene up the stairs into the emergency room at the George Washington University Medical Center. When the woman at the reception window asked them, without looking up, to take a seat, Nettie gave Gene a wink, then screamed and broke into hysterical sobs.

Gene grabbed her. "Nettie—"

She threw her arms around him and put her mouth close to his ear. "Bleed, dammit. You want me to do this by myself?"

Two nurses and a tech in sea-green scrubs escorted them into the treatment area. As they stretched Gene on a gurney and cut his shirt off, Nettie magically regained her composure.

The senior physician in charge, an intern, and a nurse wheeled Gene to a cubicle. With the precision of a drill team, they cleansed his wounds, applied ointment to his ear, and shaved the hair from around his head wound. After checking for glass fragments, they stitched his shoulder, gave him a tetanus shot, bandaged him, and took Nettie out of earshot to talk to her. She returned, calm and in charge, and helped him into a hospital examining gown over his scrub pants. At the car, she strapped him in and headed down K Street.

"Quite an act," he said.

"You were a big help. Couldn't you have puked or something?"

At Vermont, she veered left.

"Where are you going?" he said.

"My place."

He watched Logan Circle blur by.

"They wanted to keep you overnight," she said. "I told them I'd take care of you." She gave her purse a friendly pat. "I brought insurance forms for you to fill out. They gave me print-outs of home care instructions."

"I should head home. Hank's out there somewhere and Michael—"

"I called the police—while you were fading in and out. They should have been there long since."

"You don't leave much to chance," Gene said.

"You do. How could you guys miss the kind of louse Hank is?"

"George was getting ready to evict him."

"His friends are just as bad. They thought Hank was winning, held back the crowd."

She pulled into her driveway and helped him up the steps. Inside, they passed through the living room to the kitchen. Easing him into a chair at the table, she handed him a tumbler of water and two vials of pills. "Antibiotic and a pain pill. Take one of each. I'm going to check on the girls."

Two sips later she was back.

"Sleeping soundly," she said. "Finish that so I can get you cleaned up and check for bleeding." She tapped her purse. "Doctor's orders. Come on. Take your pills."

"You trying to sedate me?"

"Anesthetize you. Makes me edgy when men scream."

He tossed down the pills. "You heard authentic screams tonight."

She nodded.

"You have a strong stomach," he said.

"All women do."

"You think I'm a beast, right?"

"You smell like one. Did you know that beer mixed with sweat and blood smells like cat urine?" She picked up his glass, put it to his lips, and made him drink. "This way."

At the top of the steps she put her finger to her lips, tiptoed along the carpeted hall to the master bedroom, and hurried him inside.

"Sit on the bed." All business, she untied his hospital gown.

"Pants off, too?"

"Honestly." She pressed gently on his shoulder bandage, then examined the gauze on the side of his head, smoothed the bandage around his neck. "Seems okay. From the condition of your neck, I'd say Hank's manicurist is the Dragon Lady. According to the doctors, the scalp cuts weren't deep. You can get the shoulder stitches out mid-week. I made an appointment for you Wednesday. Meanwhile, the big concern is infection. You're filthy. Go take a shower, but don't get the dressings wet."

She pushed him into the bathroom and closed the door.

He adjusted the showerhead to hit only his chest and below, dried himself, and put the scrub pants on. He left his bloody briefs and sneakers next to the commode.

"Much better," she said as he emerged from the steamy bathroom. She folded down covers to reveal crisp, yellow sheets. He crawled in.

"Give me your pants." She spread the covers over him. "I won't peak."

He struggled out of the scrubs.

She folded them over her arm and sat on the edge of the bed.

He took her hands. "Thank you."

"You're worth every penny. You risked your life to help George."

As she started to move away, he pulled her close. Their lips met, and his arms went around her. The scent of gardenias intoxicated him.

He opened his eyes. No rafters. Seamless white ceiling. Colonial chinoiserie wallpaper in yellow and gray, a maple chest-of-drawers with brass pulls, sunshine pouring between shutter slats. Far off music. Rap? He tried to sit. Sharp pain at the base of his spine spreading across the top of both buttocks. He rolled on his side and raised himself with his arms. His shoulders and upper arms ached. When he slid his legs over the edge of the bed, they dangled painfully. A high bed, complete with a two-stair maple step-stool on the carved Chinese carpet. When he raised his arms, pain stabbed his left shoulder. He fingered his neck, ear, and head. Gauze and tape. The contusion on his knee was livid. His head was throbbing. Splotches of dried blood on the pillow. Brick red streaks on the sheets.

He slid to the floor. Everything hurt. By the time he got to the bathroom door, he was getting his sea legs. He pissed, then rinsed his face in cold water. His sneakers were still next to the toilet, but his briefs and socks were gone. In the bedroom, he searched for his scrubs and hospital gown. His watch lay next to the brass candlestick on the bedside table. Ten-thirty. Christ. He couldn't go hunting for Nettie naked. He eased into bed and remembered Hank's twisted face dripping sweat, Nettie weeping, consciousness fading while she examined his wounds. The drive, the shower, the delicate scent of gardenias. And then . . . He must have passed out. Or fallen asleep. He wanted to kick himself but knew how much it would hurt.

Beer mixed with sweat and blood smells like cat urine. God, what had he put her through?

The door swung open. Nettie tiptoed in with a laundry basket on one hip. She was in jeans and a tee-shirt. "You're awake." She put the basket down and came to the bed. "How do you feel?"

He slid up with a groan and leaned against the headboard, hugging the sheet to his chest. "I hurt."

"Get dressed and have breakfast," she said.

"I don't have any clothes."

"Your scrubs, hospital top, socks, and underwear are in the basket."

"Nettie, about last night, I hope I didn't overstep my bounds."

She gave him a blank look.

"I made a pass at you," he said, shamefaced.

"You did? I thought I made a pass at you. Lot of good it did me. You fell asleep in the middle of a kiss. Good thing that aphorism about a woman scorned is just an old wives' tale." She patted him. "Never mind. You'll have a chance to make amends. I'll personally see to it."

Before breakfast, Gene called Michael's cell. He and Leila were going to Great Falls for a picnic. "Clear skies and sunshine for the first time in a week." Nettie, after extracting a promise he'd call her later, dropped him in Shepherd Park at noon. In the dining room, two large black plastic bags, loaded with party detritus, stood by the French doors. The vacuum waited in a corner. He stuck his head in the kitchen. George was at the sink.

"Hi," Gene said.

George scowled over his shoulder. "From your appearance, I'd say the jabberwock won."

"George, I'm sorry about last night."

George returned to scrubbing the sink. "Not your doing."

"Where's Hank?"

"When I got up this morning, his door was standing open. All his belongings are gone. By the way, it's not my place to judge, but don't you think you ought to get dressed?"

"I'm dressed. This is Washington. People wear scrubs and blood-stained nighties on the street all the time."

"Not people of our class."

"You got me wrong, George."

"No. After last night, I'm sure. You're a member of the nobility."

Carl came down the servants' stairs in a neon green polo shirt and tan slacks. "I know you," he said to Gene. "You were in that movie, *The Thing*?"

"So much for empathy," Gene said.

"Got a date, but I thought I heard your voice. Wanted to be sure you're ambulatory."

"Pretty much, thanks to Nettie."

"Off to see my honey." He got as far as the door. "Remember our friend in the green Honda? He's out there again."

George turned from the sink.

"Yeah," Carl said, "but he's switched cars. After the dust-up, when I went out to take Tillie home, I noticed a black Toyota parked in Hank's place. Same car I saw twice earlier this week. Guy in a baseball cap at the wheel. I had Tillie on my arm, so I let him be. Catch you later."

As Carl's footsteps retreated and the front door closed, George stood still, sponge in hand. "It's starting again."

"We'll get to the bottom of it," Gene said. "Try not to worry."

"In my childhood, the Klan started by watching. Then came the anonymous warnings. Those phone calls—"

"George, this is about me. I suspect my wife is gathering evidence for a slam-bang divorce. I'm sorry."

"In occupied France, homosexuals were exterminated. It always starts with harassment."

"Tell you what," Gene said. "The next time Michael and I are both here and we see the Toyota, we'll confront the guy."

George dropped the sponge on the counter, pulled off the apron, and trudged up the servants' steps.

After a brief call to Nettie, Gene decided to hit the sack early. He removed his bandages except from the head and shoulder. The wounds showed no signs of infection. He was in the shower when he heard clumping on the steps. He dried, put on new dressings, and slipped into clean scrubs. In the bedroom, Michael, fully dressed, lay on his bed, hands behind his head, gazing at the joists.

"I came home to check on you," Michael said.

"Thanks." Gene eased down on his bed. "How's Leila?"

Michael grunted.

"What's the matter?" Gene asked.

"You ready for this? Jesus." He jumped from the bed. "She's missed a period."

Gene slowly filled his lungs, closed his throat, let the air leak from him. "How long have you been—"

"Since the night we met in class, in April. She says she started on the Pill right away. But that night . . . What are we going to do?"

"Wait and see if it's true."

Michael swung around. "She wouldn't lie to me."

"You sure? What about her age?"

"About being pregnant, I mean. She'll go to her gynecologist this week. She says marriage is out of the question. She's opposed to abortion." Michael pulled his golf shirt over his head and took off his shoes. "I never thought . . ." He yanked a pair of Gene's scrubs from the shelf. "I just can't *believe* this."

"Go with her to see the doctor."

"She won't hear of it. Wants to attract as little attention as possible."

Gene managed to get his legs onto the bed, eased onto his side, and lowered his body. Everything hurt. He breathed carefully and listened to his heartbeat slow.

Michael pulled his desk chair to the dormer overlooking the park.

"What are you doing?" Gene asked.

"Watching the raccoons in the trees. It's better than counting sheep."

The pain in Gene's chest wasn't from his wounds. Nothing he could do to help his son. Whether Michael realized it or not, the father—God, it was hard thinking of Michael as a *father*—the father would have nothing to say about the outcome. Leila was in the driver's seat.

Chapter 8

Playing the OSCI Card

Gene got to work before seven and kept to his cubicle. The story of his scrap would be common knowledge by nine. Nettie buzzed him to ask how he was and suggested lunch. He said he'd rather keep out of sight. Mark stopped by to check on him. Clem called at ten to tell him he didn't need to stay at work if he was too banged up. Gene ate his bag lunch at his desk and snuck out close to six after everyone else had left.

Michael was with Leila, and Carl was at the Côte d'Azur, so it was a quiet dinner with a silent and edgy George. Gene cleaned the kitchen thoroughly, waiting for George to reappear and talk. Finally at nine, he went to the attic to face the sweltering heat. He switched the fan and air conditioner to their highest setting, changed his dressings, and got in bed. Too early to sleep, despite his exhaustion. Too much on his mind. His wounds and bruises, wet from his own sweat, kept him from finding a comfortable position. He got out of bed and stumbled down to the kitchen. He took two beers from the fridge and drank them on the veranda listening to the cicadas in the moist air. With a slight buzz but no sleepier, he made his way upstairs and resumed tossing and turning.

When the cell phone rang, he realized he'd been asleep. The clock radio showed ten after two. He let the phone ring and straggled to the front windows. There it was. The black Toyota. He phoned the police.

"License plate number?" a tired voice asked.

"Can't see it."

"Did you have the calls traced?"

Gene clenched his teeth. "I tried. They told me to call the police."

A pause, then, "Okay, we'll check it out. Address?"

After he hung up, Gene watched from the window. Ten minutes later, a police car cruised slowly past the house. When it was out of sight, the Toyota started and drove away. A minute later, the police car came by again, going the opposite direction.

Wednesday morning, Nettie buzzed. "Time to take your stitches out."

"I was going to do it on my lunch hour," Gene said. "You made the appointment for eleven-twenty."

"I'll drive you—brought my car today."

"I can walk."

"In your condition? I made a picnic lunch last night, so we can eat in Farragut Square. Doctor Yancy has to attend another PowerPoint briefing at the OEB, something called 'The Final Lap: Achieving Victory in the Congressional Election.' It's an all-day affair, so I can take the time."

"Another Hatch Act violation. Why doesn't someone call foul on that stuff?"

"I only keep his calendar, Gene."

At eleven, he took the elevator to the street. There was Nettie, in a candy-apple red Chevy of uncertain vintage, waiting at the curb. At the hospital, a nurse practitioner took out stitches and congratulated Nettie for her skill as a caregiver. Nettie dropped him in Farragut Square with the picnic basket and drove off to park. By the time he'd found a bench shaded by a gnarled tree, she was beside him.

She pulled fried chicken, potato salad, and Sprite from the basket. "It's really too warm to eat outside."

"Only in Washington," Gene said. "Overcast and hot with no dry air."

"Never mind. We make a handsome couple, don't you think? The nurse was impressed."

"She was more interested in the walking wounded than the handsome couple."

Nettie nodded. "You make a more interesting maimed hero than you do a budgeteer."

"Flattery will get you everywhere."

"Even to dinner and a movie?"

"If you play your cards right," he said. "Seriously, I'm embarrassed about Saturday night. I'm deeply in your debt."

"In that case, make it dinner at the Capitol Grill and the opera."

"Rich I'm not."

"Yes, you are," she said. "In more ways than you know."

"Miss Nettie, you are an outrageous flirt."

She tilted her head, thoughtful. "Guess you're right. Never was before. I'm about to reach that certain age—you know, strike now or forever hold your peace. I made it my business to dig out your personnel file. Talk about impressive. You taught Stochastic Processes at MIT? What's that?"

"That's against agency rules. And impressive? Come on. An orphan, probably a foundling. Came from nowhere."

"Did everything on your own hook. Much to be proud of."

"Living in a world of hurt." He wrapped his chicken bones in a paper napkin. "Pathological house mate, a maenad for an estranged wife, losing a battle of wits with a general and a senator, being shadowed, about to be a grandfather—"

Nettie stopped in mid-chew.

"Michael's friend," Gene said. "You met her, Leila."

Nettie wiped her fingers on her napkin. "Leila." She squinted. "You know, I've seen that girl somewhere. I can't place her. And you think—"

"We'll know soon."

Nettie stared off toward Connecticut Avenue. "Bummer."

"Nettie," he said, "you might want to think twice about getting tangled up with me. No matter how my scrap with Hacker ends, it ain't going to be pretty."

"I'll stick around if you'll let me."

He was oddly touched. "About the dinner-and-movie, would you settle for a free performance in the Kennedy Center Foyer and a picnic afterwards?"

"Deal."

For what was becoming a weekly frustration, Gene met Hugh Shafter and Colonel Pierce in the NPO conference room after lunch the next day. As soon as they were seated, Hugh put his hands flat on the table, leaned forward, and fixed Gene in his glare. "The Chinese have made a back-channel protest about our site in Taiwan. They hinted that they don't believe our cover story—that it's there to detect missiles fired from Vietnam."

"They think it's a missile site?" Gene said.

"They were unspecific," Pierce said. "We surmise that they either suspect a surveillance facility targeted against them, or they may have somehow discovered the truth. We've launched a major counter-intelligence endeavor to uncover and eliminate the source."

"Next subject." Hugh slapped a slick-covered document on the table in front of Gene. "Here's your justification."

Gene read the title, *Chinese Nuclear Threat to the Pacific.* Above it in smaller print was "Office of Special Compartmented Sources." TOP SECRET CODEWORD was printed in red at the top and bottom.

"Page seventeen." Hugh opened it. "Here."

Gene read.

> Recent indications from several sources point to growing hostile interest by the Chinese nuclear forces in the U.S. installations in the Aleutian Islands, particularly on Adak and at Dutch Harbor. As reported on page 7, the Chinese possess several missiles armed with nuclear warheads with a range sufficient to strike these locations.

Gene flipped the page. A new section titled "Southern Pacific" began. "That's all?"

"Certainly enough," Hugh said.

"Come on, Hugh. How'd you get them to put that in?"

"All we did," Pierce said, "was to ask that they cast a glance in the direction of the Aleutians and see if they perceived the threat we did."

Gene heaved a sigh. "Pierce, we all know that the Office of Special Compartmented Sources is the laughing stock the intelligence community. Have you talked to the CIA estimates guys? Any supporting evidence from signals intelligence?"

"Unnecessary," Hugh said. "The OSCI has the president's ear. We've got justification, so quit fighting us."

The bile of defeat snaked through Gene's intestines. "I'll see what Clem says."

Hugh and Pierce visibly relaxed.

"I need some java," Hugh said. "You can leave your stuff. It'll be secure."

They rose and left the room, locking the door behind them. In the ante-room to Hacker's office, they went to the coffee mess behind a carved sandalwood screen.

"Black," Gene said as Pierce poured. "At some point, Hugh, you'll overplay the OSCI card and—"

"With all due respect, Doctor Westmoreland," Pierce said, "we can't discuss that here. We're not in secured spaces."

"Sorry," Gene said.

In the uncomfortable silence that followed, all Gene could think of to say was *How 'bout them Nationals?* He kept his mouth shut.

"The general," Hugh said, "has suggested that you would be the ideal candidate for a TDY trip to Moscow. Can't go into detail here, but it's similar to the jaunt Clem took for us. Big meeting of scientists. Our folks are too easy to identify. You get the drift?"

"Like the trip Clem took—" Gene began.

"Ever done any sight-seeing in Russia? Red Square, the Kremlin, Saint Petersburg."

Instinct warned Gene to be leery. "Don't see how I could take the time right now."

"Needs to be right away. We'll fix it with Clem—"

"Can't do it, Hugh."

Hugh's face cooled. "The general frowns on refusals." He let the thought linger, then turned to Pierce. "Rod here is about to get his star. Effective the twenty-eighth, he's a brigadier general."

"Congratulations," Gene said. "How long did it take in coming?"

Pierce's grin was predatory. "Minimum time in grade."

Hugh nudged Pierce. "What're you going to do with the extra money?"

"A new car initially," Pierce said. "With the best air conditioning money can buy."

"Might want to think Japanese," Gene said. "The U.S. car industry has improved but still can't match their workmanship."

"I dislike buying foreign products," Pierce said. "You have an Mustang GLZ, correct? Has it served you well?"

"It's been an excellent car," Gene said, "but even their quality has declined in recent—"

Hugh hustled them toward the conference room. "Better get to it, guys. The afternoon's wasting away."

As Gene rode the Metro from the Pentagon to his office, something nipped at his consciousness. He'd missed an important indicator. He went over the conversation. The OSCI justification, so obviously trumped up? When operations start dictating intelligence findings instead of the other way around, disaster was always just around the corner. Like basing decisions on ideology instead of fact. Nothing new here. All of it made him uneasy, but there'd been something else. *Scan the data without bias and you'll find it.* Let the unconscious mind drift over the terrain of interest. How did Pierce know what kind of car Gene drove? Come to think of it, how did Hacker know Gene had lived in Burrell as a child? And then the TDY offer? He remembered the effect Clem's trip had. He didn't know what had happened, but the notion of a trip under the aegis of NPO sent a chill down his spine.

As soon as he was in his cubicle, Gene opened his secure email. Sure enough, Hugh had sent Clem and him a draft program memorandum asking for another half billion. The justification was OSCI's reports on the Chinese threat to the

Aleutians and Chinese interest in Diego Garcia. The best Gene could do was recommend to Clem that FIBO demand justification from a source other than OSCI. Clem knew as well as he did that OSCI was generally ignored by intelligence professionals. Besides, both knew that the Chinese initiatives were a sham to cover expenditures for missiles and, maybe, nuclear warheads.

Gene dialed the front office on his secure phone. He got a recording. Nearly five-thirty. Nettie and Clem were both gone for the day. He'd use intra-office email.

> Boss, I strongly recommend you reject NPO's latest. We both know what it's really about, and the OSCI justification will persuade only those who are eager to believe. Danley and company will tear this to pieces and make us appear foolish or spineless or both.

At four on Sunday, Father's Day, George served steak to Gene and Carl and their respective sons. Jock and Jake, Carl's boys, thirteen and fifteen, didn't finish theirs, but Michael helped them. The meal closed with George's chocolate mousse. The boys, reminded that it was the day to honor their fathers, agreed to do the dishes. Gene volunteered to take Carl's boys home later, so that they could stay a while longer. Carl changed to his white dinner jacket and left for the Côte d'Azur. While the three sons were rinsing and stacking and scrubbing in the kitchen, George and Gene took their coffee to the terrace to escape the racket. There, with Scarpia between their chairs, they settled in to share an early summer evening.

"I have a task for you or Michael, if you're willing," George said.

"Name it."

"I want to plant hybrid tea roses behind the garage, in front of the climbing roses."

Gene hesitated. "How soon? Got a lot on my plate."

"Next couple of weeks."

"You're on."

"A gentleman called me about you," George said. "Your security officer."

"Harry Breighton?" Gene said.

"Didn't give his name. He'll be coming to talk to me about you tomorrow. Are you being investigated?"

"Must be time for my security update. They do it every five years. Guess they're being more thorough than they used to."

"He told me not to mention any of this to you," George said. "I thought you should know that you don't know."

"I'm glad we never talked about it."

"Got another one of those calls from nobody Saturday afternoon while you were watering the lawn."

Gene sat forward. "What time?"

"Around two. I remember because the first act of *Bohème*—WETA broadcasts an opera each Saturday—was about half over. Damned call made me miss half of Mimì's aria."

"Bingo," Gene said. "My cell phone had a message at 2:03 p.m. Nothing but breathing. Did you see if the Toyota was parked out front?"

"You think there's a link?"

"All I can tell you is that there's a pattern. The calls come when the Toyota's there and my car's outside."

George set his cup on the bistro table. "Gene, tell me the truth. Is the security man behind this? If so—"

"I can't imagine he would be. Security folks are open and above board. They don't sneak around."

But Hacker's people do. Could this be a Hacker job? No way. Hacker was the consummate pro. The Honda and then the Toyota were the clumsy work of an amateur. The only clod in NPO ranks was Cutter. Could Hacker, in his fondness for the adoring kid, have trusted him with surveilling Gene?

Michael came down the stairs. Scarpia bounced to him, tail beating the air. "Started the dishwasher. Jake and Jock want to know if they can come with us for Scarpia's training walk."

"Sure," Gene said.

Michael gave a come-hither wave to the veranda. The boys trooped down.

"If you'll excuse us, George," Gene said.

George gestured toward the park. "*Je vous en prie.* I'll await you here."

The two men, two boys, and dog descended to the lawn and crossed the property line into the woods.

"Let's take Jake and Jack to the knoll," Gene said. "We can watch the sunset."

"Too cloudy," Michael said.

"The sun usually comes out as it gets to the horizon."

The boys ran on ahead, then doubled back while Gene worked with Scarpia. Eventually they arrived at the hillock overlooking a widening of the creek. Gene and Michael sat cross-legged atop the mound while the boys and Scarpia frolicked on the rock shelf jutting into the water below.

"Has Leila gotten the test results yet?" Gene asked.

Michael shook his head. "She's sure, though."

The sound of a splash. They leaned forward. Scarpia was swimming furiously while Jake hopped on the bank. The dog snatched a stick from the water and paddled toward shore.

"Hey, cut it out," Gene called. "He has to have a bath every time he goes into the creek."

Scarpia heaved himself onto the rock, dropped the stick at Jake's feet, and shook. Both boys were seriously splattered and complained loudly.

"Forget to tell you," Michael said. "Last week after you left for work, I got a funny call on the house phone."

Gene groaned. "Nobody there? Just breathing?"

"Nope. A guy asked me if I was one of your house mates. I said yes. He said he was security and he'd like to interview me about you. When I said I was your son, he hung up."

"Jesus, this is getting out of hand. I'll talk to Harry tomorrow. That's just plain rude."

George was still on the terrace when they climbed through the forest to the property line.

"Scarpia took a dip," Gene called to him from the lawn.

"Bath time for Scarpia," George said to Jake and Jock. "And Scarpia hates baths."

The first order of business in the morning was to call Harry Breighton.

"Harry, is it time for my five-year security update?"

"Let me check." Sounds of Harry typing at a computer. "Nope. Not until 2020."

"Somebody's investigating me, doing interviews. They claim they're from 'security.'"

"Could be CIA. Are you in for any special compartment clearances?"

"Not unless NPO put me in without asking."

"Bet that's it. They should have notified me. Let's see—" More computer sounds. "No record. Maybe they haven't punched it in yet. Let me call my counterpart over there and see what's going on."

Ten minutes later, Harry called back.

"NPO hasn't put you in for anything. Ran it by CIA. They're not processing you. Called the Federal Investigative Service just to be sure. *Nada*. What's going on?"

"Harry, if someone decided to investigate me pretending to be from the government, is that legal?"

"Legal-schmegal. It's not SOP. Why would they be doing that?"

"Got some hunches. Should I talk to my lawyer?"

"Damned if I know. Never heard of anything like that."

"Okay. Tip me off if you get wind of anything."

"It's printed in final," Mark said on the secure line.

"The 2020 Budget Forecast Summary for the National Security Council? Couldn't be. Nothing in my mail."

"Nettie has all the copies in the front office. I only know because I caught her flipping through one."

Gene shook his head. "We never did the final edit."

"Guess Clem's changed procedures without telling us. Not the first time."

Nettie was on the phone when Gene pushed through the double doors. She waggled her fingers at him while she finished the call.

"The NSC BFS," Gene said before the handset was in its cradle. "Mark said it's been printed."

She handed him a paper-bound volume the size of a small telephone book. "Haven't sent it out yet, but—"

"Why didn't we get a chance for a final review?" Gene said. "We always—"

She shrugged, but her face held both apology and embarrassment.

"Nettie?"

She shook her head.

In his cubicle, Gene opened to the tabbed Nuclear Defense Intelligence section. The one-page introduction was the text he'd given Clem—the short, blunt sentences, the straight forward prose. The third paragraph, however, was new.

> Faced with the proliferation of rogue state threats, the proposed funding for nuclear defense intelligence has been modestly enhanced. The modernization of sites in New Mexico and the addition of two new facilities in Turkey, due for completion in FY 2022, will strengthen detection capability and reduce reaction lag.

Detection? A new tack. Hacker was now pretending missile sites were monitoring stations.

Gene opened to the details section. There they were, Hacker's add-ons. Gene read the whole section, then slammed the book shut. Someone had changed his work without telling him. He dialed the front office.

"He won't be here today," Nettie said. "He's in a session at the NSC until five, then he's picking up Mrs. Yancy for a reception in Georgetown."

"Hacker's?"

"You know I can't tell you that, Gene."

Gene hung up. He'd have to get to Clem before Clem sent the budget forecast summary to the NSC. Once they and everybody else on the distribution list had it, the budget was set in concrete.

At six-thirty, Gene stepped from a cab before Hacker's restored Georgian home. Carriage lanterns on both sides of the double doors were blazing, despite the gray glare in the sky. Through tall windows, Gene made out the milling figures— men in suits, women in cocktail dresses.

A maid admitted him to the air-conditioned chill. With a forced smile, he moved from the entrance hall into a candle-lit room thronged with guests. The air was laced with polite murmurs, tinged with the odor of a wood fire and melting wax. By the corner window, Dellaspada was talking to a blank-faced young man in a khaki summer suit—Cutter. Gene turned his back and accepted a glass of champagne from a passing server.

"I don't think we've met."

A young man with dark hair almost to his shoulders gazed up at Gene. At first Gene couldn't place him. Ah, yes. The Blue Boy from Prowley's staff.

"Gene Westmoreland, FIBO." Gene said.

The man's graciousness ebbed when he heard Gene's name. "Dennis Hodgings. Senate staff."

"Have you seen Clem Yancy anywhere?"

"He's around. I hear via the grapevine you're heading for Russia soon, *sub rosa* of course. General Hacker—"

"Odd," Gene said. "I hadn't heard about it."

"The general has a way of persuading people to do his bidding. Be sure to take in the Novodievich Monastery. It's awesome."

Gene, irritated, scanned the crowd.

"Doctor Westmoreland," Dennis said. His smile had soured. "The general does not take kindly to obstruction."

Gene's eyes snapped back to Dennis' sneering face.

Gene pushed past him. "I need to find Clem."

Dennis tipped his head. Locks fell across his forehead. "In the dining room feeding his face. And don't miss the cathedrals of the Assumption and the Archangel."

Gene moved toward the wooden arch. Hacker was holding forth to a clump of men from an overstuffed chair, his face dancing in the flicker from the fireplace. "We can't be held responsible for the failures in Syria. In the last analysis, it's *their* country. And they have failed." A bald, mild-mannered man standing opposite bobbed his head enthusiastically. Christ. The newly promoted Rod Pierce.

Gene slipped through the crowd and edged under the arch. He waited for his eyes to adjust to the brightness of the banks of candelabra that dominated the dining room table. There was Clem, more desiccated than usual, with Hugh Shafter at one elbow. Gene worked his way around the buffet sampling the *foie gras* and lemon tarts until he was beside Clem.

"Sometimes," Clem was saying to Hugh, "you have to bite the bullet and do the right thing." His lips were trembling. "Not everyone, of course, will be happy with my decision, but sometimes—"

"Evening, Clem." Gene gave close attention to the pagoda of cheese cubes on the table. He heard the double intake of breath.

"I didn't realize," Clem said in an unsettled voice, "that the general had asked you—"

"He didn't." Gene toyed with the pickles on a cut-glass platter. "I saw the BFS. Wanted to catch you before it reaches the NSC."

"I personally delivered their copies this afternoon."

Gene whipped his head toward Clem. Hugh waved at someone across the room and shuffled off.

"Why did you change it?" Gene said hoarsely. "Without consulting me—"

"I'm still the FIBO director," Clem said, his voice rising. "I'm responsible for the decisions we make. To keep peace in the family, it was time to—"

"So you caved."

The talk around them flagged. Several partiers darted glances toward them.

"Who *is* that?" a woman's voice whispered. "The one with the scars."

Gene put his stemmed glass next to the skewered artichoke hearts and eased around the table to the arch, through the room with the fireplace, and out the front door into the summer heat. It was done. Hacker would get his billions. There weren't enough Danleys to stop him. Gene limped down the hill to M Street. The budget fight was getting bloody. He threaded his way along the sidewalk through clots of young men in baggy, low-slung pants, girls with bare midriffs and jeans. He couldn't win by being an obstacle anymore. The passers-by watched him curiously. He was out of place here. Just as he had been at Hacker's party. Just as he was at the office.

By the time he got to Shepherd Park, it was almost eight. Scarpia did his ritual bark in the distance when Gene let himself in. He passed through the dining room. Dinner was over. In the kitchen he found left over noodles with an unidentifiable sauce. Carl must have cooked. Gene carried his plate and iced tea to the veranda.

"Is this the wounded Gaul I see before me?"

In the horizontal rays of the sun below the clouds, Carl sat feet up guzzling a pink martini.

"Martini is a before-dinner drink, Carl."

"Battlefield martinis are an anytime drink. Without your bandages, you're downright grisly. When does your hair grow back?"

"Might get a buzz cut so I'll fit in."

Carl laughed. "Question: is George really gay?"

"Do you care?"

"No. Curious."

"At his age," Gene said, "he's celibate, so what difference does it make?"

"What difference would it ever make? I'll tell you. When your security officer is a fundamentalist Christian graduate of Regent University put in place at the president's request. A kid of thirty-something hired by the DOD undersecretary who started the Office of Special Compartmented Sources. My stripling security officer wants to know if I have *associated* with any known homosexuals. I wanted to tell him it was none of his fracking business. Instead, I said no."

"Tainted by association."

Carl slurped. "It's enough to make you resort to drink. Then I get a call from some guy who says he's doing a security update on *you*. Asks to come and talk to me. Tells me not to tell you."

"Something funny's going on. I'm not due for my update."

"I'll call the guy's bluff."

"Don't," Gene said. "Give him phony data, and we'll see if it shows up anywhere."

"Run that by me again?"

"Ever hear of Spicer, Brinkman, and Klauthammer? My wife's father's lawyers. They're the only people I can think of who'd be investigating me."

"What about Hacker and company?"

Gene shook his head. "Too ham-handed. Too easy to detect. They're experts."

"So you think it's these lawyers passing themselves off as government security? Isn't that illegal?"

"At least unethical. I'll call my lawyer and tip him off."

"Right on. And speaking of illegal, you know the black Toyota? I noticed something. It's only here when you're here. Anything going on I should know about?"

Gene swung toward the front of the house, as if he could see through the walls. "Is it here now?"

"Damned if I know."

Gene headed for the darkened living room and moved from window to window. Hank's old parking place was vacant. Another empty spot on the far side of the street. No Toyota. He returned to the veranda through a French door off the living room.

"No one out there now," he told Carl.

Carl drained his glass. "I'm snockered enough to sleep."

The attic was dark. Gene undressed and sank into bed, listening to the Goldberg Variations through earphones to blank out the buzz and clank of the fan. Nothing like wrapping your mind around a fugue or two to ease achiness and silence a restive mind. In the middle of the third variation, his cell phone rang. He let it ring twelve times before it stopped. To be sure, he checked for messages. Breathing.

He settled himself again, swearing under his breath. Soon his thoughts dissolved into random visions of fugal imitation.

A creak on the stairs woke him. Two fifty-five.

"Dad?" Michael whispered.

Gene sat up.

"It's out there again."

"The black Toyota?"

Michael nodded.

Goddam. "Let's go after him."

Gene grabbed his scrubs and sneaks. They snatched a flashlight and hurried to the foyer. Michael eased the front door open and tipped his head. In the faint light of the street lamp, Gene saw it, a black sedan. A dark figure in a baseball cap was on the driver's side.

"We'll charge him," Gene said, "before he can drive away. I'll take the driver's side. Ready? *Go!*"

They sprinted to the car. The door on Gene's side opened and bashed him. Michael had the door on the other side open and had one knee on the seat. The driver started the car and screeched away from the curb. Michael flew out the door and landed hard on the pavement. The Toyota roared down Jessamine into the mist.

Gene was on all fours beside Michael. "You all right?"

"Think I skinned my knee."

Gene helped him to his feet. Together they hobbled into the house. In the downstairs bathroom, Gene cleaned the blood from the laceration.

"It's a small break in the skin," Gene said, relieved. He cleaned the wound with peroxide, applied Neosporin and a band-aid. "It'll heal in a day or two."

When Michael headed to the attic, Gene called the police. The weary sergeant listened as Gene described the incident. "Notify us if he reappears. And try to get the license number." That was all. Gene hung up doubting that the police would do anything.

He stared through the French doors into the darkness. He never should have gotten Michael involved. The thought that his son might have been hurt brought a shudder.

Upstairs, he found Michael sitting by the dormer, his face in his hands. He put his hand on Michael's shoulder.

Michael raised his head. "I counted seven raccoons tonight, more than I've ever seen."

"Get some sleep."

Michael shook his head. "The test results came. She's pregnant."

Gene started the workweek with a headache. Mid-morning and three Advils later, the intensity of the throb had retreated from thunderclaps to pounding surf. The secure line rang.

"Hey, buddy, Carl." His voice was barely above a whisper.

"How'd you get my secure number?"

"Bitch at me later," Carl said, talking fast. "This is important. Gene, it's not Donna. It's *Hacker*. The security guy, right? The one who was supposed to interview me about you? First of all, the guy came straight into my office. He's got the clearances. Fishy as hell. Security guys don't have clearances—don't need them. Second, he's this pink-faced kid. Looks like he should go back to high school and give himself up. And he keeps calling me 'sir' all the time. I read the fine print on his ID. He's from the National Preparedness Office. First Lieutenant William M. Cutter, USMC."

Gene gave his head a fast shake.

"He implied he had information that you were mentally ill," Carl said. "Wanted to know the name of your therapist."

"What'd you tell him?"

"I said you spent time with your boy, dated, worked out, gardened. I implied that you're a born-again fundamentalist. He liked that. Told him I never heard of any therapy. Thought you should know right way." Sound of a door opening. "Gotta go." Carl hung up.

Cutter. No wonder the ruse was so obvious. Hacker should have known better than to assign a task that delicate to a kid so wet behind the ears he couldn't find his cock in the dark. Hacker had let his fondness blind him to Cutter's ineptitude.

Chapter 9

Manifest Obstructionism

The smart-ass Michael had evanesced. In his stead was a tense young man of few words. The waggish grin gave way to an occasional polite half-smile. The jibing was replaced with grunts. Gene's attempts to draw him out were met with silence. He stayed most nights at Leila's.

During a workout, Gene hit upon a plan—he'd ask them out to dinner to celebrate Michael's twenty-first birthday. He'd get them to talk to him, maybe even decide what they were going to do. He arranged the party the night of Michael's birthday, Wednesday the twenty-seventh. Carl got them the best table for three at the Côte d'Azur. Michael sullenly accepted the invitation.

Gene bought and wrapped a pair of New Balance 991s (the only shoes Michael would run in), and, after close of business, carried his gift to the Côte d'Azur. Its heavy mahogany door opened to a facsimile of pre-World War I riviera bistro—carpet the color of sand, potted palms, festooned drapery. Carl had reserved a corner booth under a tangle of wrought-iron tracery with frosted globes. As Gene was seated, Carl, at a white concert grand on a dais in the center of the room, nodded to him, then launched into "April in Paris." The patrons scattered around the room ignored the music.

Gene ordered a gimlet and calamari and asked that a bottle of Schramsburg be put on ice to be served after his guests had finished their cocktails. Gene nursed his drink. No sign of Michael. Carl shot him a worried glance without missing a beat in "Falling Leaves."

The massive door opened, and Michael stepped in, pale and edgy. He walked toward Gene, not with the easy gait of the runner, but with the stiffness of the overstressed.

Gene shook his hand. "Welcome to the *man*. With the full privileges attached to the title. Happy birthday." He hugged Michael and flagged the waitress. "Gimlet."

Carl struck up "Happy Birthday" as the waitress brought Michael his drink. The diners turned to peer at him, sang along, and applauded.

"Leila can't make it," Michael said.

"Did she have to work late?"

"No." Michael teased his drink. "Something funny's going on. She almost got run over Monday night when she crossed the street to get to her place. She said a pickup truck was double-parked and drove to the wrong side of the street to get to her. She jumped between two parked cars, and the driver roared away. This afternoon, before she picked me up, she got a phone call telling her that next time they wouldn't miss."

Gene's breath froze in his throat.

"They told her," Michael went on, "that her boyfriend's father had become an obstruction. If he didn't change his tune, she'd get hurt. They said you'd know what they meant and warned her not to call the police."

Gene's heart thudded. "Did she?"

"She was afraid to."

"Call her now. Tell her to report it right away."

Obstruction. Prowley's word. Was Prowley behind this? Or Hacker? Or maybe both. A joint task force. The word *Syndicate* felt appropriate. No, *Secretocracy.* Clem's word. More bureaucratic.

The following morning, Nettie promised to buzz Gene the moment Clem came in. While Gene waited, he reviewed the classification of the First Strike Office's compartment codewords. He verified that the codewords themselves and their existence were TOP SECRET and compartmented under the administrative codename COBRAWING, for which he, Danley, and Mavis Evans were cleared. He could talk to the senator about the existence of the compartments without violating security. Danley was known for the size of his ego. If Gene could let it slip that Hacker, Prowley, and the staff were deliberately bumfuzzling Danley, there'd be hell to pay.

The intercom buzzed. "Clem wants to see you."

"I'll be right there."

Clem was standing at the window staring blankly.

"Before you start," Gene said, "I've got an emergency." He told Clem about Leila, the near miss, and the threatening call. "They used the word 'obstruction,' same word Prowley used with me."

"Chill out, Gene, and let the police handle it."

"Clem, you should report this to the FBI. A federal official subjected to extortion—"

"Get a hold of yourself. No one's been hurt. All you have is words."

"Then I'll call the FBI."

Clem spun from the window. "*You'll do nothing of the kind.*" He straightened his tie. "I know you're upset. I'll put Harry on it right away."

"Clem, for God's sake—"

"Chill out. That's an order."

Gene bit his lip.

Clem walked from the window and sat on the edge of his desk, close to Gene. "Hacker wants to send you on a trip to Russia."

Gene lowered his eyes.

"He'll pressure you." Clem's face turned deadly serious. "Don't go."

Gene watched him. "Clem, did something happen on your trip?"

"Of course not. Now on to the most important item. Prowley has summoned you for nine o'clock."

"There's no hearing scheduled. What's going on?"

Clem smoothed his hair along the temples with tremulous fingers.

"This can't be testimony," Gene said. "Are the other subcommittee members in town? No notice, no time to prepare . . . besides, why me?"

Clem turned back to the window. "Tell them we'd like the tape and transcript of the hearing first thing in the morning pouch."

Gene dashed to his cubicle for his briefcase, then hurried through the gray mist to the Metro. A train was just arriving as he reached the platform. He clambered aboard, took a double seat, and put his briefcase beside him.

"Is this seat taken?" A cultured male voice in British English, faintly accented with Slavic sibilants. Gene glanced up. A tall blond gentleman in gray flannels smiled down at him.

Gene placed his briefcase in his lap. "Please."

The man slid into the seat. "Warm, isn't it? Nicolai Vassiliev." He offered Gene his hand and cocked his head. "Gene Westmoreland?"

Gene stared at the face only a shoulder's length from his.

Nicolai shook Gene's hand and held it a moment longer. "A fortuitous coincidence. I was going to ring you up."

Gene hid his surprise. "Business?"

"Purely pleasure. I remember you too well." Nicolai's face was conspiratorial.

Gene moved closer to the window. "You have me mixed up with someone else—"

"Impossible. I was going to inform you that I could arrange for you to spend time with the young man you were so interested in. With complete discretion, I assure you. All I'd ask in return is a bit of counsel to help me in my work."

"You're mistaken." Gene leaned away. "The only young man I'm interested in is my son."

Nicolai raised his eyebrows. "I didn't realize you are married. Surely you remember Greg—you loved the way he danced."

"If you'll excuse me." Gene half stood. "The next stop is mine."

Nicolai stood to allow Gene to pass. "I'll call you."

Gene hastened down the aisle and out the door. What had the man said his name was? Vassiliev. Gene reviewed the conversation. His instincts screamed danger. He'd report the incident to Harry Breighton as soon as he got back to the office.

Still edgy, he got to the Russell Building at eight thirty-five, went through security, and raced to the hearing room suite. Senator Danley in a sports shirt, coffee cup in hand, came up the hall.

"Doctor Westmoreland." Danley, self-consciously jolly, pumped Gene's hand. "What brings you to these musty caverns?"

"I was summoned."

"I'm incognito." Danley winked. "Only time I can get any work done is when I'm not supposed to be here."

So Prowley hadn't informed other members of the Preparedness Subcommittee that Gene was to testify? Danley continued down the hall.

Gene rang the bell, went through security, and sat on the bench alone in the anteroom. No one else was in attendance?

Nine-fifteen. Was Prowley deliberately making Gene wait? Nine-thirty came and went. Gene fidgeted, wished he'd brought something to read.

The Blue Boy appeared. "Doctor Westmoreland? This way."

He abandoned Gene in the darkened hearing room. The only illumination was a single ceiling spotlight trained on the mahogany table. Gene sat in the middle chair and looked around. No one, not even the Blue Boy. He checked his watch. Nine-forty. Maybe his treatment was deliberate, designed to intimidate. The Blue Boy hadn't addressed him as "sir."

The red jewel light on the microphone lit. A door closed. Three men came in through an opening in the middle of the curtain—the Blue Boy, Vince Dellaspada, and Prowley.

Prowley eased into the center chair and flipped on his reading light. "Westmoreland?"

"Yes, sir."

"Westmoreland, I want to know why you are ignoring one of the country's greatest assets, letting an unmatched opportunity slip through your fingers, refusing to face facts." He stared at Gene, waiting for an answer.

"My apologies, Senator," Gene stammered. "Could you restate the question?"

"I'm told that you are the major—" He paused for emphasis. "—*obstruction* to inclusion of sensible funding in the president's budget for NPO's operations."

Gene tightened his throat muscles. "Senator, my job is to provide an independent review—"

"The bureaucracy is overrun with independents these days, people who think their pay-grade entitles them to make policy."

"Not at all, sir. My job is to assure that the president's budget, or at least the piece of it I review, is completely justified in the light of available information and in keeping with the president's policy guidance, before it is presented to Congress."

"Oversight is the job of this subcommittee."

This was no hearing. Gene's cunning kicked in.

"Senator, I would never attempt to usurp the prerogative of Congress. My apologies, sir, but my job description requires, among other things, that I review the NPO's budget requests—"

"Job description? Is that the best—"

"—to be certain that they are in accord with the law and NPO's charter."

Gene heard the silent ping in the heads of the three men facing him.

Prowley stared at his microphone. "Dennis, I told you—" He glared at the Blue Boy who disappeared behind the curtain. The red light on Gene's microphone went dark.

Prowley leaned toward Gene. "Westmoreland, stop sabotaging Hacker's operation."

"With all due respect, Senator, I'm bound by the law. I don't have the authority—"

The senator's face reddened. "Cease your manifest obstructionism and help us move our cause forward. If you do not, you have only yourself to blame for the unfortunate consequences."

Gene took a deep breath. "Senator, I'm mandated by statute, the FIBO charter, and my sworn oath of office to ensure that budget initiatives are in keeping with the law and binding treaties. Targeting for first-strike *nuclear* attack—" Gene glanced up. Prowley twitched. "—violates our international agreements to limit and eventually eliminate thermonuclear weapons. Launching a single nuclear missile would kill hundreds of thousands, perhaps millions, and invite savage retaliation. NPO has on its target list *all* nations that possess or are working toward nuclear weapons and even our closest allies. I know of no legal, policy, or moral justification for NPO's clandestine operation, let alone its expansion and, especially, the arming of its missiles with nuclear warheads."

Gene waited for the onslaught. Prowley and his two aides were staring at the rear of the room. Willis Danley was standing inside the door.

"My apologies," Danley said, voice dripping with irony. "I didn't realize a hearing was in progress. I certainly would have attended."

Prowley gathered his papers. "Not a hearing. Just a chat. We've finished, Willis. What brings you in today?"

"Work with the staff." Danley walked to the end of the desk and took a seat behind his nameplate. "Doctor Westmoreland, please continue."

Gene opened his mouth to speak.

"We've wrapped it up, Willis." Prowley stood.

"Doctor Westmoreland is right here," Danley said. "Wait. The sound system is off. Dennis—"

The Blue Boy's head swiveled to Prowley.

"No need." Prowley put a sheaf of papers into a briefcase Vince held for him. "We've really covered it, Willis. No sense in repeating—"

"Dennis," Danley repeated, this time with steel in his tone.

The Blue Boy went behind the curtain. Gene's mike light came on.

"Willis," Prowley said, "this is why we have a staff—to weed out the chaff and let us deal with the real issues. I was kibitzing."

Danley spread his arms. "Delightful. I'll kibitz with you."

Prowley examined his watch. "Lovely idea, but I'm to see the president at eleven and Doctor Westmoreland is to accompany me."

Gene started.

Danley stood. "Then I won't detain you."

"My superior," Gene said, "asks that a copy of the tape and a transcript of our interview be forwarded to FIBO by the first pouch in the morning."

"In matters this sensitive," Prowley said, "I am not inclined to honor such requests."

"Come on, Herman." Danley smiled at Gene. "I'll send you copies." He frowned at Prowley. "Tell the president I send my regards. I trust you'll give the plenary subcommittee a complete report." He gave Gene a quick wave and left.

"Dennis." Prowley tipped his head.

The Blue Boy slid behind the curtain, the mike light went out, and he reappeared grinning with puckish delight.

Prowley bent toward Gene and placed his palms on the desk. The reading light shining below his chin turned his face ghoulish. "If you value your career, if you care about providing for your family, if you cherish the well-being of those close to you—" He breathed deeply. "For the last time, Westmoreland, play ball or—" Prowley's voice was grinding now— "have the bat rammed up your ass."

Prowley switched off the reading light and moved with deliberate dignity through the curtains. Dellaspada followed.

Prowley's words ran in an endless loop through Gene's brain as he fought to make sense of them. The Blue Boy fetched Prowley's briefcase and paused, watching Gene with amusement.

"Am I free to go?" Gene managed.

"Of course," The Blue Boy said.

"The president—"

The Blue Boy laughed. "Cancelled." He passed through the curtains.

The spotlight over Gene's head was extinguished, leaving him in the dark.

He'd have to get to Clem at once. Prowley's words proved it. This was extortion, Mafia style.

Gene exited the Metro station and sprinted to Seventeenth Street. As he crossed L, traffic was snarled in front of the New Executive Office Building. An ambulance flashed red lights at the entrance. He picked his way through the crowd around the door, but a policeman barred his way. Gene locked his jaw. He could walk around the block to the rear entrance. The news for Clem couldn't wait.

As he swayed from one foot to the other, trying to gauge the delay, four paramedics pushed through the double doors with a gurney. The police held back the crowd, and the rescue squad made its way toward the open doors of the ambulance. Gene stretched to see the patient. The grizzled face at first sparked no recognition. Gene tilted his head to the left to get a better view.

"*Clem!*" Gene pummeled his way past the police and grabbed Clem's hand.

A hand on his shoulder yanked him. "He's not conscious. Out of the way."

The police and medics eased Clem into the ambulance, slammed the doors, and butted the vehicle, siren blaring, into the Seventeenth Street traffic. Gene and the rubberneckers watched until the ambulance turned left on K Street and disappeared.

Gene bolted past the police to the elevator. When the doors hissed open on the seventh floor, he bounded to the front office. Nettie, pale and disheveled, was pacing.

"Gene." She threw herself into his arms. "I found him on the floor next to the door. He must have been trying to get to me. I dialed 911. Harry sanitized everything before they got here."

"Where'd they take him?"

"George Washington."

Gene started out, then stopped. "Want to come?"

"Go ahead. I'll catch up."

Gene sprinted the five blocks to the George Washington University Medical Center emergency room. The same bored woman was at the admissions window.

"Please take a seat. We'll be with you as soon as possible."

"I'm here to see a patient. Just admitted. Clem Yancy."

She consulted a clipboard. "You can't right now. We'll be with you as soon as possible."

Gene sat in a plastic chair between a man staunching blood from a head wound and a woman with her head over a bucket. He breathed through his mouth to avoid the stench of vomit blended with odor of unwashed bodies.

Nettie plunged in and went straight to the admissions widow. After a querulous exchange with the woman, she waved to Gene and headed through the entrance to the care center. He scrambled after her. Nettie stopped at the sixth cubicle and whipped open the curtain. Clem lay on an examining table, half naked, his face gray and contorted.

"Here's his ID." She handed a card to the startled male nurse. "I'm his secretary. This is his next-in-charge. What's the diagnosis? Have you called his family?"

The nurse stammered. "They're not supposed to let anybody in—"

Nettie grasped Clem's hand. "Doctor Yancy. It's Nettie. You're going to be fine."

Clem lay silent, eyes glued shut, breathing shallowly.

"Ma'am, you'll have to wait outside," the nurse said. "The doctor—"

Nettie was eerily calm. "This is Doctor Clement Yancy, Director of the Federal Intelligence Budget Office. If he dies before a doctor sees him, the investigations won't be pretty. Call me as soon as you have a diagnosis. My number's on the ID card."

With measured deliberation, she passed into the corridor between the cubicles and headed for the waiting room. Gene tailed after.

Once on the street, her calm evaporated. She clutched Gene's arm. "Let's stop somewhere."

They headed down Pennsylvania toward the White House. At a bistro he guided her to the nondescript bar.

"Hot tea," she breathed.

"Coffee for me," Gene told the bartender.

"I knew this was coming." Her voice was so low Gene could barely hear her. "You think he's going to die?"

"Jesus, Nettie, get a grip. It could be anything."

"Did you see him? Death has taken over his face."

"I saw a sick man," Gene lied. "Wait until we know something, then—"

"I should have done something." Tears trickled down her cheeks. "I should have—I don't know."

Their beverages arrived.

Gene started. "My God, I've got to call Michael. Is there a payphone?" he asked the bartender.

"In the hall with the restrooms."

Gene followed the restroom signs through a corridor and dialed Michael.

"Listen, the threat to Leila is real. How about if she stays at our place? I can sleep in the living room or something."

"What are you talking about?" Michael said.

"If she doesn't want to come to our place, you could stay at hers for a while."

Long pause, then, "You're scaring me."

"Prowley threatened us," Gene said. "There's no doubt now."

"Who's Prowley?" Michael said.

Gene sighed. "Call me tonight. I'll fill you in."

When Gene got back to the bar, Nettie was standing, purse in hand. "I've got to get to the office. The hospital might call."

"Can you walk?"

"Let's take a cab."

In his cubicle, Gene assured that everything was locked up, then buzzed Nettie. "I'm heading home. Anything yet?"

"Nothing," she said. "I called them and gave them my home phone, too."

"Call me on my cell as soon as you hear."

As he was lifting his briefcase, the secure line rang. Shafter.

"Gene, the general wants an affirmative from you for attending the conference in Moscow. It's July and—"

"Hugh, I don't know how to make it any clearer. The answer is no."

"Hold one for the general," Hugh said.

The line went dead for an instant, then Hacker said, "Gene, this is an urgent matter. I won't hear of a refusal."

"My apologies sir. I—"

"As you probably know, Gene, I have more than a little say in Senior Executive Service promotions. I understand that you feel you should have gotten your SES1 when you took your current job. With the weight of my support, your promotion would be a certainty. All I ask is a little cooperation."

Gene stumbled. "I'm more than a little grateful to you, sir, but—"

"Beware the hasty decision, Gene. My influence over careers cuts both ways."

Gene inhaled deeply. "I've thought it through thoroughly, general. I am beholden for the offer. I regret disappointing you. But I must say no."

Hacker's voice constricted. "The consequences of your obstruction will be unpleasant."

The general hung up.

It was the first time Gene had ever arrived home from work before mid-afternoon. He stopped by George's room to let him know, then went to the attic and stripped. A cold shower quieted the nettles in his belly and washed away the grit from the smog-laden air. He put on workout shorts but lay on the bed. First the gay Russian, then Prowley, then Clem, and finally Hacker. His mind was haywire. If he could sleep, maybe the wrinkles would smooth out in dreams. Instead, he wriggled and jittered and finally got to his feet. He needed hard physical work to lock in his catapulting psyche, but he could no more lift weights than he could do the Booty Call. He changed clothes again, this time to grubbies and boots. He'd prepare the ground for the hybrid teas George wanted planted by the garage, in front of the climbing roses Gene and Michael had put in last March.

He stopped in the garage for the pick and shovel, then dug holes four feet apart, as George had specified. That done, he mowed the lawn, even though it didn't really need it yet. He ate cold leftovers in the dining room, cleaned up, and returned to the attic. He lay on his bed, stared at the joists. His mind spun.

Just before six, Michael tramped up the stairs.

Gene sat up. "What're you doing here?"

"Leila wants to chill out for a while. Says she's feeling suffocated."

"She's not safe there by herself."

"She says she can handle it," Michael said. "The police are investigating."

"That's comforting."

"She got another call while I was out buying groceries. They told her they're watching the house. They knew when I was there and when I wasn't. They'll know when I leave or she goes out. Then they'll get her."

Gene put his face in his hands.

"She promised to call the police to report the second call," Michael went on. "She'll double lock the doors and windows, won't answer the telephone while I'm gone."

"She must be as jittery as a cat on speed," Gene said.

"Calm as that statue of death. The one in the cemetery in northeast you showed me one time? She just sits there, her face motionless. Scares me."

"It's panic time. There's more." Gene told Michael about the session with Prowley and Clem's collapse.

Michael dropped onto his bed. "Jesus. What are we going to do?"

"Are the police monitoring Leila's phone or watching her house?"

"I don't think so, from what she said. I got the feeling they didn't think it was any big deal."

"With Clem out of the picture," Gene said, "I don't know who I can turn to. Not many people are cleared for the compartments in my portfolio. The president's men are in control of the National Security Council and the Office of Management and Budget. Running to them would make things worse. I'll talk to the FIBO security officer tomorrow. Should have done it today. Too rattled. Meantime, I don't like the idea of Leila staying alone. You should insist that either you stay there or she come here."

"Great idea, except—" Michael was on his feet, pacing. "We, um, like, had a fight. Or rather she fought and I listened. She said it was my fault. She had a good life before she met me. Told me to stay away from her."

Gene held his breath.

That night, as Gene tried to sleep, Michael sat by the window watching raccoons.

On his way to his cubicle the next morning, Gene stopped by the front office.

"Still haven't heard from the hospital," Nettie said. "I'll call them at nine."

"Do you know," Gene asked, "if Clem spoke to Harry after our session yesterday morning?"

"Couldn't have. You'd just left when General Pierce showed up insisting on seeing him. They talked behind closed doors for an hour. After he left, Doctor Yancy asked me to get his wife on the phone. He usually just dials the number himself. They talked a long time. I know because I was watching the phone light so I could remind him about his luncheon appointment. Finally, I figured I'd better interrupt him. That's when I went in the office and found him on the floor."

"May I use your phone?" Gene said. He called Harry Breighton and said he'd be right down. Something important.

Harry's office wasn't much bigger than a walk-in closet, but at least it wasn't an enclosed cubicle. Gene sat across from him and told him about the threats to Leila.

"Any idea who the perpetrators are?" Harry asked.

"Prowley, Dellaspada, and Dennis Hodgings, an aide to Prowley, are in on it."

Harry frowned at his desktop. "Bizarre. Anyone else hear all this?"

Gene shook his head.

"Your son didn't see or talk to any of these people?"

"No."

Harry grimaced, played with a pencil. "Wish we had corroboration. Let me call the police and see what they've uncovered."

"I think we should bring in the FBI."

Harry studied Gene. "I'll get back to you."

Gene climbed the stairs to his office with the distinct feeling that Harry didn't believe the story.

Mid-afternoon, Nettie buzzed him. She'd just taken a call from Clem's wife.

"Guess I scared the hospital staff. They chose not to call me, but Mrs. Yancy thought we should know the diagnosis. Heart attack. Serious. Won't be able to work for six to eight weeks, and he'll be on a strict regimen. Seems he was tense about work, not getting enough rest, not eating right. Mrs.

Yancy thinks he pretty much brought it on himself, asked me if I knew what was bothering him."

"How soon can we visit?" Gene said.

"Not for a week or two. I'll check with the hospital every day."

By the time Gene left the office, Washington was quieting down before the Fourth of July, the following Wednesday, amid rampant gossip about who the president would name to replace Justice Kennedy who had announced his retirement. The Metro crowd was light, little traffic on the streets. The highways and bridges leading out of the District of Columbia would be jammed, especially the bay bridge. Everyone was celebrating. Everyone except Gene and Michael.

After dinner, Michael dug out the chess set Gene had given him when he was twelve. Father and son played half a dozen games at the dining room table, before Gene, who was losing consistently, said he had to call it a night. They turned in early, but neither slept. Finally, Michael got out of bed and dragged his chair to the dormer.

Gene stretched out, knowing he wouldn't sleep until he heard Michael go to bed.

"Dad," Michael said, "there's someone out there."

Gene went to the window.

Michael pointed. "Under the big oak."

Gene made out a shape in the moonlight—a troll in a baseball cap and a long coat belted at the waist. "Who'd be out in the woods at this hour?"

The shadow raised its wrist and read its watch.

"My God, there *is* someone." Gene spun to the shelves. He tossed clothes to Michael and pulled on jeans, a tee-shirt, and boots. "Come on. Grab a flashlight. We'll circle around and come up behind him through the woods."

"Dad, we should call the police."

"He'd hear them and take off."

Downstairs, Gene ran to the French doors in the dining room. "Scarpia," he said in a low voice. The dog bounded up the veranda stairs to him. Gene petted him briefly and headed to the foyer. The two men and the dog skittered out the front door into the darkness. There it was, the black Toyota. No one in it. They ran down Jessamine to the park entrance and followed the trail to the bridle path, then downstream until they were in line with the house. The moonlight offered little help in finding the steep footpath through the woods up to the lawn. They finally located it and began the quiet climb.

Twenty feet before the woods ended, Gene signaled Michael to stay put and hold Scarpia back, then slipped off the trail into the dense foliage. He tested each step before he put his boot down to avoid breaking a twig and alerting the man in the belted coat. The tension in his muscles made his legs tremble. After ten minutes of careful going, he was directly in line with the dormer. He peered through the dark toward the lawn. Nothing he could identify as a human. A motion, fifteen feet to his left. The silent watcher shifted weight from one leg to the other. Gene edged toward him, one step at a time. He had to get close enough to tackle before the man could run. Another step. Another.

The ground gave way under his boot. He stumbled but immediately regained his footing. The man whirled with a gasp. Gene crashed forward. The watcher dashed across the lawn toward the west end of the house.

"Scarpia!" Gene pointed. Scarpia bolted past just as Gene broke free of the vines and started across the grass. The man's trench coat flapped open as he charged up the slope toward the garage. Before Gene reached the corner of the house, the man let out a cry and fell. Scarpia was on him instantly. By the time Gene reached them, Scarpia, growling, had his quarry pinned to the ground, face down.

"Scarpia, back."

As the dog stepped aside, Gene grabbed the collar of the raincoat and flipped the driver over. The cap went flying, and long black hair flopped loose.

"Priss!"

"Help me," she cried, "I'm hurt." She sat up and reached for her right ankle. When she touched it, she whimpered. "I ran into holes."

The holes. For the hybrid teas. He massaged her ankle with his fingertips.

She screamed. "Don't." Her hair was wild, hanging over her face. Her legs, bare beneath the coat, were smeared with dirt.

Michael came running up the hill and shined a flashlight on them.

Gene sat on his heels. "What the hell are you doing?"

"Watching," she said. "I saw Nettie drop you off the Sunday after your party. She answered your cell the night before. You stayed overnight at her place, didn't you?"

Gene stared at her.

"There are others, aren't there, Gene? You must go to their places. Or they come in through the park."

"You're out of your mind."

"I love you, Gene. I won't give you up."

"If I ever catch you here again, I'll have you arrested for stalking."

"Come off it, Gene. Nobody'd believe it."

"Get out of my life, Priss. And no more of those silent phone calls."

"I'm in love with you."

"It's over, understand?"

She shook her head. "Not until *I* say it's over."

"That's not love, Priss."

"You know what love is?" she cried. "*You?* How many women do you have, Gene? How many have you used and tossed aside? You can't do that with Priss Simmons. *She's* the one who decides when enough is enough." She covered her face and sobbed.

Gene clenched his teeth. "Can you walk?" He unlaced her tennis shoe and slipped it off. "Raise the big toe."

She did. He felt her ankle. She gasped.

"Not broken," he said. "Nasty sprain, though. I'll take you to the emergency room."

"No," Priss cried. "Take me home. I'll go to the doctor tomorrow."

"Get on the other side," Gene said to Michael. "On your feet, Priss."

They lifted her by the armpits.

She yelped. "My arm. I twisted it."

"Put your weight on your good leg," Gene said.

Priss swayed between them. A cell phone fell from her coat. Michael retrieved it.

The three of them hobbled around the garage through the bamboo to the street. Scarpia followed.

"I'll drive you home," Gene said.

They stumbled across the street to the Mustang, pushed and dragged Priss until she was propped up against the window on the passenger side in the rear seat.

Gene edged out of the car and closed the door. "Go on in," he said to Michael. "Take the dog. I'll be home as soon as I get her settled." He started the car. "How is it?"

"Hurts like hell," Priss said.

He turned south on Sixteenth.

"I didn't think you'd see me," Priss said.

He veered right on Arkansas, pulled into a parking place. "I'll walk you in." He got out and opened her door. "Come on." With ooches and whimpers, she worked her torso forward until her legs were hanging out the door.

"Okay, stand up." He put his hands under her arms and lifted.

"Easy on my arm." She tottered upright holding her right leg bent. "Damn, it hurts."

"Lean on me," he said.

"I can't walk."

He studied the steps to the porch. "I'll carry you."

With one arm around her shoulders, he bent and spread his other arm behind her knees. "Ready?" He swept her into the air, surprised at how little she weighed.

She wrapped her arms around his neck and rested her head on his shoulder. "What a waste, what a goddammed waste."

At the door, he was breathing heavily. "Give me the keys." First one lock, then the other, and he stepped across the sill. She pushed the door shut behind them, and he climbed the stairs to her bedroom door. "Open it." He carried her to the bed, laid her carefully beneath the canopy, and set her keys next to her.

"Close the door," she said. "I don't want to wake up Elizabeth."

She slid her arms from the coat and lifted her body while he pulled it from under her.

"Let me sit up," she said.

He slid her against the headboard.

She unbuttoned her blouse and took it off. "Undo my bra."

"Priss—"

"Don't be squeamish. My arm is hurt. You've seen it all before." She twisted her shoulders toward him. He unclasped the bra. She slipped it off and unbuttoned her shorts.

"I'm going," he said.

"I need your help." She wiggled the shorts over her hips. "Take them off me."

He pulled the shorts by the waistband to her knees. No underwear.

"Easy," she moaned.

He inched them off, one leg at a time. She cringed.

"Pull back the bed covers for me." She eased over onto the sheet.

Before he could lift the covers over her, her arms went around his neck and pulled him down on top of her.

"You don't know how much I want you," she murmured in his ear.

He snatched her hands away and stood. "Stop it. You keep hounding me, and I'll take you to court."

"And charge me with what? Stalking?" Her laugh was laden with scorn.

"Goddam you."

"Keep your voice down," she said.

"Nothing going on now that Elizabeth hasn't heard before."

Elizabeth. Of course.

"I don't have to charge you with anything." He smiled. "I only have to testify. At custody hearings."

She stopped moving.

"Yes, Mrs. Simmons was stalking me, your honor. She left her daughter alone for hours in the middle of the night while she spied on me. Her ankle? She sprained it trying to outrun me when I caught her in the act."

"There are no custody hearings."

"There will be—when I go to your ex with my story."

She laughed. "You don't even know who my ex is."

"Patrick J. Simmons, the real estate developer. His downtown office isn't far from where I work. I could saunter over there—"

She blanched. "Gene, cut it out—"

"You want to lose her, Priss? Maybe they wouldn't even let you have visiting privileges." He thrust his face close to hers. "Maybe he'd move to the west coast so you couldn't see her. What if the court decided you were a bad influence?"

"You have no evidence." Her eyes were as terrified as if he were preparing to strike her.

"I have your cap, your cell phone, your tennis shoe. I have a witness."

He seized her arms and pulled her so close that her face blurred. "You telephone me or show up one more time at my place, and Elizabeth's gone." His saliva splattered across her face. "You hear me?"

"Yes," she whispered.

She fell with a muffled thud and lay quivering, naked, white-faced, smudged with dirt.

He walked out.

Saturday morning Gene called the police.

"You know his name?" the police sergeant asked.

"No, a woman," Gene said.

"I mean the stalker. What's his name?"

Gene started over again. He hung up certain they didn't believe him.

Chapter 10

Secretology

The following morning, Saturday, Gene explained to his house mates what had happened—Priss was the culprit. The anonymous phone calls should now cease, and there'd be no more strange cars parked outside.

Carl shook his head. "I told you, Gene. She's a borderline personality disorder waiting to shatter. I doubt we've heard the last of her."

"I scared her bad," Gene said. "Elizabeth is the most important thing in her life."

"Borderline personality deficients respond to fear in unexpected ways," George said.

"Dad," Jock said, "what's a borderline deficient?"

"Yeah," Jake joined.

"A person who's so bag o' cats she makes Godzilla look sweet," Carl said.

Gene spoke in a low voice. "I apologize for bringing this on."

"Guess you can relax now without Priss nipping at your you-know-whats." Carl clapped Gene on the shoulder.

"Priss is an amateur nut-nipper," Gene said. "I'm up against pros."

Carl shot him a puzzled look.

"Later," Gene said.

He moved toward the servants' stairs. His cell phone rang.

"Gene Westmoreland? Nicolai Vassiliev here. A good day to you."

"Surprised to hear from you," Gene said.

"I mentioned that I would call. Greg would welcome a rendezvous with you. He will be free tonight after his midnight show. You could come early, have a drink with me, investigate the other dancers. As you Americans say, there is more than one fish in the sea." He laughed. "There is also one hairy boy you have not seen, a new hire. He puts on a wonderful performance."

"I don't know where this is coming from," Gene said, "but—"

"Could you stay the night?"

Gene's face burned. "Don't call me again." He slammed the phone shut.

"What was that about?" Michael said.

"Damned if I know."

On the way to the attic, Gene said, "Michael, call Leila, be sure she's okay."

"Called her this morning while you were out planting roses," Michael said brightly. "I'm staying at her place tonight. She apologized. Said she's scared of being alone. Hates being afraid to go out. Can I borrow the GLZ?"

Gene wished he could laugh. "Guess I'm getting muddled in my old age. Sure, you can use the *GLZ*." He humphed. "Guess it tells you something that I take it as good news that she's frightened."

When they got to their bedroom, Michael put on running shorts. Gene changed to dog-training clothes. "GLZ" was running through his mind. "Michael, remember when you asked me what model the Mustang was and I told you it was an GLZ when I meant GLX—when was that?"

"A while ago. I was at Leila's."

"So we were talking on the phone?"

"Right. Why?"

"Someone used that word—" He combed his memory. "Pierce. He asked me how I liked my Mustang GLZ. Why would he—" The chit-chat at NPO, during the break. Hugh had broken off the conversation.

"My God," Gene said aloud. "They're tapping our phones."

Michael gawked.

"Shafter and Pierce," Gene said. "The Secretocracy."

"The who?"

"NPO and Prowley. They justify it under the PRISM program."

"Thought that was only international calls to or from the United States," Michael said.

"Right. And the president is in bed with Robert Mueller."

Michael stopped tying his running shoe. "Goddam." He sat straight. "So they know about Leila and . . . *everything.*"

"You got that right." Gene said. "I'll get a new cell under a different name. You'd better do the same. Meanwhile, assume that every word you say on the phone is going straight into the ears of our enemies."

In the park with Scarpia, Gene ran through everything he remembered saying on the phone. Nothing he wanted kept secret. Nothing that could be used against him. But they *were* closing in on him. No one he could turn to. The president had placed his people in key positions throughout the bureaucracy. Gene didn't stand a chance.

Maybe he should give in. After all, it wasn't his responsibility to guard the American people against illegal and illicit goings-on. *Oh, yes, it was.* Even his job description said so. His oath of office did, too. Should he sacrifice Leila and put Michael in danger? And yet he couldn't capitulate and live the rest of his life in shame.

He and Scarpia ascended the bridle path. He wished he could avoid human company until he had all this figured out. They trudged through the trees to the property line. Carl and his sons were roasting wieners at the barbecue. Gene waved at them, moved across the lawn and up the steps to the veranda. If he told anyone about Hacker's clandestine operations, he'd be violating security and asking to be arraigned.

George met him at the French doors. "Such a dour face. What's the trouble?"

"Nothing I can talk about."

"You got a call on the house phone. Nettie."

"Thanks, George."

Gene trotted down the steps to the lawn. "Carl, can I use your cell phone?"

"What's wrong with yours?"

"Tell you later."

Gene went to the terrace and dialed Nettie's home number.

"Gene, I'm so glad you called. I got through to Clem. He's arranged for calls from me to be put through to him. Only one a day. They want him to rest, regain his strength, but he's going to ask that they let me in to see him. I'm going tonight. He wants to talk to you, said for you to call him tomorrow at three o'clock. He'll get them to allow your call."

Gene thought. "You and I need to talk. May I come to your place tomorrow and phone Clem from there?"

"Of course." He could hear the smile in her voice.

Gene carried the phone down the stairs to Carl. "Thanks, buddy. Would you take a little walk with me?"

Carl turned to the boys. "You guys take over. Remember, no ashes on my hot dog."

They started for the east side of the house.

"Hacker and company are tapping my cell phone and the house line," Gene said. "I've got urgent calls coming up. I'd like to tell people like Nettie and my boss to call me on your phone until I can get a new one."

Carl stopped dead. "Wait a minute—"

"I can't tell the whole story. Compartmented stuff is involved. What it comes down to is that I'm standing in Hacker's way, and he's using thumb screws."

Carl took a long breath, held it, and let it go. "This isn't the Nixon Administration."

"You with me?"

"Jesus." Carl wiped his mouth with his palm and rubbed it on his tee-shirt. "Okay. For now."

The Mustang pissed and moaned about the hill up to Nettie's place, but Gene showed no mercy. When he'd parked and switched off the ignition, the engine ticked as if panting.

She met him at the door, her face grave. "I've got lemonade on the deck." She led him through the house, stopping long enough to snatch her wireless phone. "Doctor Yancy's expecting your call at three."

"Where are the girls?" Gene said.

"At the pool working on their tans. Never mind that there's no sun. Don't expect them before twilight."

They sat at a glass-top table in the shade of a poplar. She poured drinks.

"Okay," she said. "You wanted to talk?"

He told her about Prowley's threat and the phone taps.

She sat motionless until he stopped talking. "What have you done to make these men hate you so?"

"They don't hate me, any more than you hate a mosquito. You just keep swatting until you get it. The long and short of it is that I won't help Hacker fund facilities that are illegal. He and Prowley and their staffs are in this up to their receding hairlines. I haven't doped out all the links yet, but it looks like the lynchpin is the president."

Nettie's breathing quickened. "If I didn't know you better, I'd swear you were paranoid."

Gene laughed. "Maybe I am, but I can't bring myself to give in. Even the threats to Leila—"

"What threats?"

He took a deep breath and recounted the Leila story.

Nettie angled her head. "She wasn't so stressed out when I saw her."

"Where?"

"Vince Dellaspada hosted an early Independence Day weekend cocktail party at the Omni. I called in Doctor Yancy's regrets, and Mr. Dellaspada insisted that I come in his place. She was there, the picture of health. Utterly gracious, though she didn't remember me."

Gene leaned closer. "She was at a *party*?"

"Not surprising since she's Dellaspada's daughter. She introduced herself as Leila Dellaspada."

Gene's breath stopped.

"I remember her now," Nettie went on. "I only saw her at a distance—at a lawn party at the Dellaspada place in Potomac last summer. Everybody in the missile defense business was there, even Senator Prowley. Quite a gathering. The *Post* did an article on it. I had never spoken to her—until Michael brought her here."

Gene frowned and shook his head. "Let me think this through. Dellaspada's daughter shows up as an auditor in April, end of the semester, in one of Michael's classes, befriends him, sleeps with him. Says she's pregnant, carrying my grandchild, and she's being threatened if *I* don't cooperate."

"Did Michael go with her to the doctor?"

"No."

"Did he see the test results that showed she was pregnant?"

"No."

"Was he there when she got the threatening call? You see what I'm driving at."

Gene reached into his memory for every detail. Each element of Leila's story came from Leila. "Okay if I use your phone?"

She handed it to him.

He called Carl's number. "Remember our conversation yesterday about telephones? I need to talk, privately, with Michael. Would you put him on?"

"He's not here. George says he didn't come home from wherever he went last night."

Gene ground his teeth. "Hey, if he shows up, ask him to use your phone to call me at Nettie's."

"It's three o'clock," Nettie said. "Here's the number for Doctor Yancy's room."

Gene dialed. After one ring, a wispy voice answered.

"Clem?"

"Thanks for the call, Gene." It was Clem all right, but the sound was papery without depth. "I need to see you."

"Will they let me in?"

"Come at four in the morning Wednesday. That's the fourth, so nobody will be out and about. If my keepers see you, I'll tell them you work at night and can't be here any other time."

"Why four a.m.?"

Clem coughed. "Hacker's people are in the lobby checking to see who visits me. They wander up here from time to time and peep through the door at me. My wife recognized Cutter. She met him at Hacker's party. They're military in business suits. Easy to spot. She's seen them at eight in the morning and after they lock the front doors at ten at night." Another cough. "Avoid the front lobby. They'll see you. I'm in 627."

"Why—"

"Wednesday morning." Clem hung up.

Gene stared unseeing into the yard.

"What's happening at four a. m.?" Nettie asked.

"That's the time Clem wants me to visit him on Wednesday. Hacker's men are snooping around. I have to sneak in."

Nettie paled. "Good God. So they'll see me when I go to see Doctor Yancy tonight."

Gene nodded.

She grasped his hand. "I want you to tell me what's going on."

"Brace yourself." He told her everything—FIREFANG, the fake security interviews, the threats from Prowley. "They've got me in a vise, and Clem's acting like he doesn't want to get involved."

"Doctor Yancy's ill. I . . ." She put her hand to her mouth. "That's why he's sick, isn't it? Something happened to him on that trip Hacker sent him on, the one to China."

"I don't see the connection."

"I don't either, but . . . Jesus, Gene. Now you've got me scared silly."

"Take it easy. You're not involved."

She massaged her hands. "I'm to see Doctor Yancy at seven. I'll call you when I get home."

He gave her Carl's number.

As soon as Gene got home, he went to Carl's room to borrow his cell, but Carl was out, presumably for a gig. Gene decided to risk calling Michael on his own phone. No answer. He tried again both before and after dinner. Michael must have turned off his cell.

As Gene was finishing the dishes, Big Ben boomed, announcing a visitor. He opened the door to find Nettie on the threshold.

"May I come in?"

"What's wrong?"

"If you want a short answer, ask what's right." Then, with her arms loose at her sides, she said, "Gene, would you hold me for a minute?"

He folded her in his arms.

"Thank you." Her arms went around his waist.

When he stroked her hair, the sobs started, as if against her will. He held her and let her cry. Tears soaked through his shirt to his skin. She snuffled. He pulled out his handkerchief. "Let's talk." He led her to the dining room. "Sit down. Can I get you something drink?"

She sat. "Thought you'd never ask."

"Red wine okay?"

"Bring the bottle."

He set his bottle of Foxhorn and two glasses on the table and poured. As she drank, he watched her. "Now—" He eased into a chair next to her. "—tell me what's the matter."

She squared her shoulders. "When I got to the hospital, these two yahoos in the lobby watched me the way people watch someone eating worms. I'm sure they were Hacker's men, all dressed up in suits and ties, pretending to read magazines. Then, when I got to Doctor Yancy's room, he barely spoke to me. His skin is gray. I don't think he's going to survive. On the way out, the Neanderthals watched my every move. The whole way home, 'what if Doctor Yancy dies?' ran through my mind, over and over. That got me to thinking about my own life. Pretty soon, my girls will be on their own, and I'll be alone. I made overtures to a guy—" She gave him a you-know-who look. "—but he's not interested."

"Who told you that?"

"He didn't reciprocate."

"You misread me, Nettie. My life's been steroids on steroids."

She guzzled her wine and handed him the glass. He filled it.

"It's more than I can cope with," she said. "Doctor Yancy's dying. I can't unload on my girls. I'm on my own from here on out, and I can't deal with it."

He pulled her to him, and she rested her head on his chest. Her hand sought his. He smelled her hair, and old yearnings flickered to life.

"Just hold me," she said. "Sometimes I need a little backup."

"I'll help all I can."

"You feel so good." She rubbed against his chest.

He tightened his hold and kissed the top of her head. "You're going to be fine. You're tough."

"I want to believe you."

He kissed her ear.

She shivered. "Do it again."

He did. She raised her head and kissed his lips. He pulled her face to his. She pushed away.

"I'm sorry," she said. "This isn't what I intended. Forgive me."

He took her hands and kissed her again.

"Gene—"

He looked down at her. "You want me to stop?"

Her eyes stayed on his. "No."

His arms went around her waist, hers around his neck. They kissed.

"Stay with me tonight," he said.

They kissed again.

The alarm clock woke them. It was past dawn. He slipped from the bed and got her a pair of scrubs. "Put these on. I'll start coffee."

She pulled him down on top of her and kissed him, then tousled his hair. "You're beautiful."

He laughed. "And you're *strong*."

They chortled together.

"Let's—" he said.

"No. We'll be late for work. Come to my place tonight?"

"You bet."

They ate breakfast on the veranda. She was quiet.

"You okay?" he asked.

She breathed deeply, watching the table top. "I want to be sure of one thing."

"Which is?"

"Was last night a pity fuck?"

He was taken aback. "Did I act like I felt sorry for you?"

"No." Her glower gave way to an embarrassed smile. "More like you'd been leching after me for years."

"How do you know I haven't?"

"Women know these things, Gene." She giggled. "You've been spending too much time in the company of men."

"That's the worst understatement you've ever been guilty of."

"And you're very good at squelching unwanted feelings."

Gene straightened. "How could you possibly know that about me?"

"I've known you a long time. Last night taught me a whole new side of you I suspected existed but had never seen."

"If I get my way, you'll see a lot more of that side."

"I'll be sure you get your way."

After Nettie headed home to change for work, Gene checked Carl's room. The bed was undisturbed. Carl's Rabbit was not parked in its usual place. He must have hooked up with a woman. Gene swore and called Michael again using his own cell. This time he got an answer.

"I'm on my cell," Gene said. "Okay?"

Short pause, then, "Okay. You know where I am, right? Figured I'd stay here for a couple of days to, you know, kind of keep an eye on things."

"Fine by me, but how about coming home for dinner tonight? We're fixing your favorite, sweetbreads, and I need your recipe."

Michael hated sweetbreads, couldn't cook anything but breakfast, and never owned a recipe in his short life.

"I could tell you on the phone," Michael said. "It's all in the spicing."

Smart-ass kid. "I'd really rather you showed me in person." Gene's voice turned serious. "Don't give me a hard time. This is important."

"Important enough for me to, uh, leave my post?"

"No question. I'll be home around six. See you then."

At the office, after stopping by Nettie's desk for a clandestine kiss, Gene went to his cubicle. The first order of business as to look for Leila Spencer in the Washington, D.C. phonebook. No listing. He did a reverse check on Leila's phone and was told it was an unlisted number. Next he did a GOOGLE search on Vince Dellaspada and found a *Washington Post* article in the Style section from a year ago reporting on the lawn party Nettie had attended. A picture of the Dellaspada family on the steps of their mansion showed a smiling Vince with an arm around a woman who might have been Leila. The caption identified her simply as his daughter. The text didn't mention her.

Next Gene queried for a personnel listing for the World Bank and went through the staff positions. No hits. Then he ran through the personnel listing for office of the bank president. "Leila R. Dellaspada" was shown as a personal assistant. Back to GOOGLE to search on her name. He unearthed a news photo titled "New World Bank president chooses his personal staff." The picture showed the bank president in the middle of a line of smiling young people. Next to him was Leila. Unmistakable. The caption identified her as Leila Dellaspada.

The secure intercom buzzed.

"Harry Breighton, Gene. I've talked to the D.C. police. No record of any reports of threats against a Leila Spencer. No threat reports that week, matter of fact. Thought you said she called the police."

"That's what she told us, Harry. Never mind. Fits with what I've found out since I talked to you."

"Gene, you sure this really happened? Pretty wild story."

"It didn't happen. She was lying."

"Wait a minute. She lied about Prowley and Dellaspada and Hodgings?"

"No, that's for real. She's working with them. It's a set up."

"Uh-huh. Yeah. Well." Harry clicked his teeth and hung up.

That night, Gene was home by quarter of six. He left his briefcase on the steps, doffed his tie, and opened his collar to let his skin dry. Breathing more easily, he wandered from the foyer to the kitchen and back again. Where was Michael?

Just past six, Michael let himself in. Gene was sitting on the stairs to the foyer.

"Let's grab a beer," Gene said.

"Oh-oh."

Michael followed Gene to the kitchen. Gene opened two Budweisers left over from the party and headed for the terrace. Scarpia, all wags and grins, came up from the lawn to sit with them.

Gene handed Michael a beer. "Sit down and get ready for interesting news. Leila's a plant." He told Michael everything, from Nettie's recognition to Gene's research on Leila's name. "The pregnancy is almost certainly a lie to pressure us. The threats to her never happened."

"We've been hornswoggled." Michael watched the afternoon sky. "We should have caught on. So obvious—"

"We can't let the Secretocracy know we're on to them. Go on seeing her. Act like the horny bastard you've been for real."

Michael wrinkled his nose. "I'm not a whore."

Gene jerked. What was he asking Michael to do?

"That skank." Michael bounded to his feet and paced. "I could kill her." He kicked the balustrade. "And she said I was such a great lover. All so she could humiliate me and laugh at me behind my back. How evil do you have to be to make your daughter into a whore to control somebody?"

"Power corrupts."

"And does being the quarry corrupt, too? What's happening to us?"

"No," Gene said. "If we lose our moral sense, they've defeated us."

"Then we can't use their tactics."

"But, Michael, we can't confront them. We have to outfox them. Let them think they've got us by the short hairs. We'll go on using our cell phones as if we didn't suspect. I'll go on interacting with NPO and the Senate Subcommittee as if everything were normal."

"And I'll go on seeing Leila. My decision, not yours. I've got the chops for it." Michael hawked and spat. "But I can't bring myself to touch her again. Call her on your cell and tell her I have the flu."

"Lying isn't using their tactics?"

"Not when they've forfeited their right to the truth." Michael got to his feet unsteadily. "You know what I want for Christmas? The complete works of Christopher Marlowe. Started reading him last semester. He writes about the powerlessness of morality in the face of determined evil. I'm living in his world." He turned toward the steps. "I pay a high price for being the son of Gene Westmoreland."

Tears blurred Gene's vision as he watched Michael head in.

Two-thirty Wednesday morning, Nettie's alarm brought Gene upright in bed. He'd slept feverishly, alternating deranged dreams of Clem on a beach by the sea, in a torture chamber, floating above the horizon, but never in the hospital. Gene kissed Nettie and told her to go back to sleep, then dressed in the sea-green scrubs he'd brought from home and clipped his FIBO badge, turned backwards, to the breast pocket. Carrying his wallet in the single hip pocket of the scrub pants, he drove through the city, sinister in its muggy darkness on the morning of a holiday. He parked across from the George Washington University Medical Center on Twenty-Third Street and mounted the double set of steps to the glassed-in the emergency room. Standing outside the reach of interior light, he peered through the floor-to-ceiling windows. Several street people slumped in chairs waiting to be treated. Next to them, two young men with crew cuts, ties loosened, sat side by side, one snoozing, the other reading a *Playboy*. Hacker's men.

Gene waited. Maybe the Hackerites would have to go to the men's room or something. Ten minutes later, two women and a man, all in scrubs and sporting GWUMC badges, came into the waiting room from the hall to his far left and headed towards the entrance. Gene timed his steps so that he reached the door just as they were coming out.

"Off at four?" he said breezily.

"Just out for a smoke," one of the women said. They stepped out and held the door for him.

"Thanks."

Gene walked in, taking his time. Ahead of him, at the wide door to the corridor, a security guard sat behind a lectern. Keeping his face turned away from the suited men in the waiting area, Gene loitered at the admissions counter.

"How's it going?" he said.

The admissions clerk glanced up. "Quieter than usual. Won't get swamped until mids tonight."

"Typical holiday rush, right? You on again tonight?"

She nodded.

From the corner of his eye, Gene noted that the security guard had seen him talking to the woman at the counter.

"Gotta get back. Take it easy."

He drifted toward the corridor door. As he passed the guard, he smiled and waved. The guard nodded absent-mindedly.

The short hall led to the rounded mezzanine above the main lobby. He stopped at the railing and looked down. Cutter, in a tan summer suit, sat rigid on a bench by the front door.

Next to him was another man, who might have been his twin. Gene backtracked out of their line of sight and turned toward the elevators. One stood open. He took it to the sixth floor.

When the doors hissed open, he headed north, past Intensive Care and a nurses' station to the northeastern corner of the building. There he found room 627. He pushed on the door. It opened silently.

The only illumination came from a curved wall of windows on the right overlooking Washington Circle. To Gene's left was the bed, its chrome rails reflecting the blinking traffic signals. On both sides, beyond sterile curtains on runners in the ceiling, were glowing indicators on machines in racks. Wires connected them to the patient. Plastic bags on T-frames swayed in the intermittent light. A faint aroma of alcohol and ether obscured a deeper, sour smell. The only sound was the soft swish of air conditioning and a faint machine hum.

"Gene."

The same papery voice. Gene moved to the bed. A hand reached for his. It felt like ashes crumbling in his grasp.

"You want the light on?" Gene said.

"*No.* The staff'll come in."

Gene enveloped Clem's withered hand between both of his.

"I expect by now Hacker has you in his sights," Clem said.

"Let's talk about that when you're better. Can I do anything?"

Clem's hand tightened its grasp. "Listen to what I have to tell you. Promise me before God that, no matter what happens to me, you will never repeat it."

"You have my word."

The hand relaxed. "Beware the Secretocracy. It's rooted in the president and has tendrils everywhere. NSA sends the president transcripts of other officials' phone conversations. Don't trust anyone." Clem paused to cough and spit into a cloth. "I know you see Hacker and Prowley as the arch-villains. They're not. They're nothing but extensions of the president's power." He panted, rasping. "If Hacker asks you to travel for him, say no. He uses the president's clandestine connections abroad to ensnare the Secretocracy's enemies."

"I already turned him down."

"He'll find a way to punish you. The Secretocracy works outside the chain of command. I wouldn't be able to protect you."

"How could he touch me?"

"He's good at thinking of ways to remove roadblocks," Clem said. "What I want to tell you, no, what I *have* to tell you—"

The fitful light from the window showed the moisture gathering in Clem's eyes. "I'm a coward, Gene. I was too close to the end of my career, thought I could ride it out, save my retirement. Hacker understood that I was undermining him. He thought if he got me in his power, he'd get what he wanted. He didn't count on *your* resistance. I should have gone to higher authority as soon as I realized . . . and yet . . . the president—"

He reached for a tissue on the bedside table. "A coward." He ran a shaking finger under his nose. "However you judge me after you've heard me out, don't ever believe that I did anything depraved."

His voice faded to a whisper punctuated by wheezes.

"The trip in March. To Shanghai. Hacker's people set me up. At a reception, they put something in my drink. I woke up naked in my hotel room in bed with three Chinese men. Other men, westerners, were taking videos. When I called for help, they cleared out. The Chinese police came, found nothing.

The day I got back, Pierce came to see with eight-and-a-half by eleven glossy color photos of me and the Chinese men engaged in acts—I'm too ashamed to tell you what. Pierce told me that NPO had things sewed up at the Senate Subcommittee. FIBO had become an obstruction. If I didn't cooperate, the videos would find their way onto the web. I'd lose my clearances and my job and my retirement. My wife and child would be publicly shamed."

"Take it easy," Gene said.

Clem raised his chin and opened his mouth to gasp for air. Gradually his breathing slowed. He wiped his forehead with his fingertips.

"After that, I did the best I could for Hacker, overruling you, redacting your work. Vince Dellaspada rewrote your stuff without your knowledge. You became the obstruction. I tried to get you to take the CIA job, but I underestimated your tenacity. Pierce showed up without an appointment and gave me the rest of the day to remove you from your position or he'd post those hideous videos on the web, identifying me in acts . . . That's when my heart gave out."

Clem paused. "The videos will show up any day now. I'm finished, Gene, one way or another. Point is, I'm not going to be there to run interference for you. You're on your own, and the whole Secretocracy, with the power of the president behind it, is ranged against you. I *had* to warn you." His eyes glistened. "The greatest shame is that I betrayed you, the man I had come to think of as the son I'd never had."

Gene's throat burned.

"Listen to me." Clem's eyelids fluttered. "You're next on the hit list. Pierce all but told me. You could resign before they get you fired for cause and you can't get a job anywhere in government." Clem coughed, then lay silent, rasping for breath. "You'd better go." His hand tightened on Gene's. "Remember. You've promised you'll never reveal anything I've told you. That's a vow you must keep."

"You have my promise."

"Don't let anyone see you. If they find out we've talked, they might get panicky."

"Clem, anything I can do—"

"Get out of here, goddammit. *Now*." He pushed Gene's arm away.

"I'll stay in touch."

"No, don't."

Gene held his breath.

Clem's wide eyes were fixed on Gene's face. "Good-bye, Gene."

Gene put his hand over Clem's, then moved silently into the hall.

Clem's words followed Gene home, to bed for sleepless tossing, up again at dawn. He was in more trouble than he thought. These guys had no conscience. Why did that surprise him? Hacker and Prowley were as driven as any jihadist, and in their cosmology, the end justified any means.

After breakfast, Gene took out his cell to call Nettie, then stopped. The tap. He dressed in slacks and drove to the office, knowing he'd be able to park on the street—Fourth of July. At his desk he decided to make a list of every point he could think of that might make him vulnerable to attack. He tapped his pencil regularly staring at the blank page. What might they use against him? He'd never violated security, committed any crime, been involved in any shady dealings. What might they have heard on his phone that could be construed as evidence against him? The affair with Priss. Nothing there. Donna? Michael? Certainly not. Nettie. No. Wait. The call from the guy who approached him on the Metro. What was his name? A Russian. Nicolai Vassiliev. Gene wrote the name. He tried the phone book and found him. On Rosecrest Place Northwest.

On a hunch, Gene went to the web page for the Russian Embassy and found the name again. In the office of the Cultural Attaché. He remembered Shafter or Pierce saying that the Russians were our allies. Might the Russians be trying to recruit Gene? It was just after noon. A holiday. Maybe he could find Nicolai at home and confront him.

Gene drove north on Sixteenth. Just after Florida Avenue, he turned left into a maze of hilly streets crowded with stately Victorian apartment houses overlooking Washington in the flatland to the south. From Crescent Place, he edged the Mustang into Rosecrest Place. The address turned out to be The Rosecrest—a four-story stone edifice with inset gardens on both sides of its art-deco entrance. Inside the double glass doors, Gene skimmed the listing of residents with a button next to each. He found Vassiliev's name and pressed.

"Allo?" said a man's voice from the brass covered speaker beneath the names.

"Mr. Vassiliev?" Gene asked.

"Yes?"

"This is Gene Westmoreland."

Long pause. "Yes?"

"We talked on the Metro and you called me."

"I believe you are mistaken," said the Russian-tainted voice. "I do not ride the Metro—"

"Can you spare me a moment, sir?"

Muffled voices in the distance. "Wait in the lobby, please."

Gene passed through another set of glass doors onto a mosaic floor with "Rosecrest" spelled out among twirls of tile fronds and ribbons. The lobby, decorated with angular nineteen-twenties chairs and sofas, ran the length of the building ending at the reception desk where a funereal gentleman kept careful watch on the elevators. Gene planted himself on a couch and waited.

The elevator swooshed open, and a burly blond man approached him.

"You want see Mr. Vassiliev, yes?" The man's words were barely recognizable as English. "You show ID."

Gene gave him his driver's license.

"You come."

Gene followed him to the elevator.

The man spent the ride frowning at the floor indicator. When the doors opened, he went ahead of Gene down the corridor. He paused at a door marked 404 in curlicue brass and gestured for Gene to go before him. Gene passed through an entrance hall ten feet long and entered a living room with marble floors, a fireplace at one end, and a grand piano at the other. Sitting on a balcony beyond a wall of glass doors was a sixty-something man in a white shirt with a Nehru collar and white slacks. He watched gravely as Gene approached. The muscle man mumbled something in Russian, and the man in white nodded.

"My apologies, sir," Gene said. "Are you Mr. Nicolai Vassiliev?"

"I am he."

"The man I am searching for is not you, sir. Do you know of anyone else with the same name?"

Vassiliev was faintly amused. "No, I do not."

"Do you have any idea why someone might be using your name?"

Vassiliev laughed. "Indeed. We are in Washington, no? Espionage and deception are the profession of half the population. I am no longer surprised by devious games. The reason I admitted you . . . Off the subject. However, in point of fact, I have heard of no such duplicity."

"I'm sorry, Mr. Vassiliev," Gene said. "I have been wrongly informed. If you will excuse me."

Gene bowed his head courteously. As he started to leave, the bouncer returned his driver's license.

Gene barely remembered driving to Nettie's. Who was the fake Vassiliev and why did he cotton on to Gene? To set him up?

Late in the day, Nettie did the best she could to create a private Independence Day celebration for Gene, Rachel, and Sarah. She grilled chicken on the deck, made milk shakes, and steamed corn on the cob bought that morning at the Takoma Park farmers' market. The girls were chatty and hinted broadly that they wanted to understand what was going on between their mother and Gene. While he did dishes, Nettie herded the girls to the basement rec room, ostensibly to assure herself that the movies they'd rented were suitable for teenagers. Gene had started the dishwasher and dried the corn pot by the time she returned. They took coffee to the deck.

"I told them the truth," Nettie said, "that you'll be staying here sometimes. They'd already figured that out."

Gene sucked air. "Are they upset?"

"The opposite," Nettie laughed, "they're thrilled I'm finally coming out of my shell. Besides, they really like you."

He sighed. "One little load off my shoulders."

"You saw Doctor Yancy? Why did he want to talk to you?"

"Um . . ."

"You're not going to tell me?"

"It's confidential," Gene said, "What you need to know is that things are worse than I thought."

"He told you what happened on his trip, what made him sick."

"I can't talk about it."

She crossed her arms. "We're on intimate terms, you and I. You can tell me."

"I promised never to say anything to anyone."

"So we're not on intimate terms."

"It's not that," he said.

"Yes, it is."

She sat quiet. He waited.

"Someday," she said, "you'll have to take down the walls you've built around yourself and trust me." She got to her feet and picked up the coffee cups. "The girls will be up half the night watching movies. Let's go to bed."

Gene was at the office by seven the next morning. In Clem's absence, business of substance was on hold. He and Mark shook their heads over Clem's condition. Nettie told him she'd forward urgent calls to him as second in command, but Clem's illness was common knowledge—she didn't expect many calls. Gene spent the day going over every line of the current NPO budget, including the First Strike version. Still nothing he could identify as funds for nuclear warheads. He called Pierce on secure.

"When will you start funding action for the warheads?"

Pierce laughed. "We're way ahead of you. The funding started more than a year ago."

Gene paused. "I can't find it in the budget."

"It's not in our budget. It's safely ensconced in the National Nuclear Security Administration budget. We have presidential approval to assign members of our staff to work there on temporary duty."

Well past six, Gene dragged himself home. He was surprised to see Carl's Rabbit in its usual place. As he opened the door, an overblown piano arrangement of "Moon River" swamped the foyer. Gene went down the steps into the living room, sat on the workout bench, and took off his suit jacket. As he was loosening his tie, Carl noticed him.

"Haven't seen you around," Gene said.

"Got a new honey, and I've been doing extra gigs. Money's short, and the regular at the Moonpenny was out sick."

"Taking the night off?"

Carl shrugged. "Need to practice. Technique's slipping. Want to get smashed? I have gin. Got any vermouth?"

"How about cabernet?"

"Back to battlefield martinis."

While Carl mixed drinks, Gene changed into scrubs. They met in the dining room. Scarpia wagged in from the veranda and sat at their feet.

Carl leaned his elbows on the table. "Your boss is sick?"

"Now you know why I'm nothing but smiles. You're a bundle of giggles and grins yourself."

"Took the boys to their mother's today." Carl stirred his drink with his index finger. "She and her boyfriend are home from Europe. She went out of her way to tell me they have no wedding plans, so I'm stuck with alimony forever."

"Ah, the joys of the divorcé."

"By the way," Carl said. "I ran into an old friend of yours in the most unlikely place."

"I don't have any old friends. I'm too young."

"Good line. Anyway, I was in the Pentagon Concourse at lunch, and who should I see walking toward me in a suit and tie, clean-shaven and hair neatly combed, but your old buddy, Hank."

"Come on. He doesn't own a tie."

"He does now. He saw me and veered away, but I caught up with him. Doesn't want to be called 'Hank' anymore. He's *Mr.* Henry Shelby, GS-12. That makes him rank-equivalent with me. The fucker wanted to be sure I knew that. He got a job in Air Force Matériel."

"How the hell—"

Carl poured them both more pink martini. "That's what I asked him. 'Best qualified among the applicants,' he said. Bull*shit*. He's got an uncle somewhere in the hierarchy pulling strings. You can tell, too. He's twitchy, like he's got a kink in his ass. Couldn't get away from me fast enough."

Gene lumbered through the rest of the week, spending as much time as he could with Nettie. Friday, she told him that Mrs. Yancy had called to report that Clem was improving. He was off the IVs and machines and twice had been out of bed and walking.

Michael was home that night for dinner. Sullen and restless, he told Gene he'd played sick, hadn't touched Leila, but he didn't know how long he could keep up the charade. One new development: while Leila slept, he'd taken the key to her desk from her purse. Her mail was addressed to Leila Dellaspada.

Gene spent the weekend at Nettie's. She asked no more questions about what Clem had told him, but she was silent and distant. They made love Sunday morning before Gene headed home to get ready for the week at work. Their coupling was sad and quiet.

Monday was another dead day at the office. Mrs. Yancy reported that Clem was walking regularly with the help of a patient care technician. Gene stayed at home that night. He had just come downstairs for breakfast the next morning when the house phone rang. He hurried to answer it before it woke up the rest of the house.

"Gene," Nettie said, "Clem's dead."

Gene's heart banged against his chest.

Nettie choked back a sob. "He killed himself."

Chapter 11

Manifest Insubordination

Clem's death was on the front page of the *Washington Post*.

A source, who asked not to be identified, said that Dr. Yancy was found around midnight with a bed sheet tied to the coat hook on the back of the door to his hospital room and looped around his neck. Initial indications suggest that he forced his neck against the sheet and shut off the flow of blood to the head. When he passed out, the weight of his body kept the throat closed until he suffocated.

Clem had been heard weeping about an hour before. He'd been given a diet coke, and he was checked every twenty minutes. Around midnight hospital personnel had had to force the door. The paper added that Clem had left a note, contents withheld by the police.

As soon as Gene got to work, he went to the front office. Nettie was pacing. He took her in his arms.

"Harry sanitized the third-floor conference room," she said. "The police are interviewing everybody there. I just got out. Mark's in there now. Harry's already been. You'll be called."

He felt her shake her head.

"Why did he do it, Gene? What could possibly be so wrong in anyone's life that they'd want to end it? He must have suffered terribly."

Gene had no sooner hung up his jacket when the cubicle chime sounded. Harry Breighton, paler than Gene had ever seen him, stood outside with bowed head. He waited until Gene sanitized, then dropped into Gene's visitor chair.

"I'm talking to each person before they're interviewed," Harry said. "Remember that the police investigators are not authorized access to any classified information. Tell them as little as possible."

"Understood," Gene said.

Harry shook his head. "I've never been through anything like this. Can't believe he did it. Didn't he stop to think of the anguish he'd be putting everybody through?"

At eight-thirty, Gene was summoned to the conference room.

"Doctor Westmoreland?" The middle-aged man, in suit and tie, stood. "Special Investigator Henley. Please take a seat." He indicated the chair on the far side of the table.

"How well did you know Doctor Yancy?" Henley asked.

"Met him more than twenty years ago, worked directly for him the past eleven years."

"Had you noticed any change in his behavior recently?"

"Something's been wrong with him since the spring. I guessed that he was ill."

Henley inspected his notes. "Did he ever mention anything about videos that upset him?"

Gene hesitated. He had given Clem his word of honor. "No."

"Did you have any reason to suppose anyone was blackmailing him?"

The whole affair was shot through with compartmented data. Henley wasn't cleared. Gene was too vulnerable. "No."

"Did you know of any troubling relationships Doctor Yancy had, in his personal or professional life?"

"No."

"Had his work life been unusually stressful?"

Gene considered carefully before he spoke. "It's been a rough year for us."

"How so?"

"We do budgeting. It's been hectic."

"Give me an example."

"I'm sorry. Everything we do, even who we work with, is classified."

Henley jotted something. "Do you know of anyone who wished harm to Doctor Yancy or might have threatened him?"

"No."

"Thank you, Doctor Westmoreland. We'll be in touch."

Mark was waiting at Gene's cubicle.

"Well?" Mark couldn't hold still.

"Come on in and sit down."

Gene poked in the code, went in, and closed the door after Mark. Gene sat, but Mark rolled on the balls of his feet.

"What did you tell Henley?" Mark asked.

"Nothing."

"Did he ask about videos? What's that about?"

"Damned if I know."

Mark fidgeted. "You think they'll talk to DIRNSA? And Hacker and his crowd?"

"Not unless someone told them who our clients are. Did you mention the NPO to Henley?"

"No," Mark said quickly. "Anyway, they took Clem's calendar and phone log. They'll talk to everyone he's been in touch with."

Gene hadn't thought of that. They'd at least question Pierce. No, maybe not. Nettie'd said he wasn't on the calendar the day he talked to Clem just before Clem's heart attack.

Mark paced, his hands hysterical. "I've never known anyone who . . . Jesus, Gene, this is creepy. Did you see the paper? He must have been wacko."

Wednesday evening, while Sarah and Rachel watched the latest *Pirates of the Caribbean* movie, Gene and Nettie tried to relax on the deck with sodas.

Nettie touched a paper napkin to her mouth. "You think the police will be back?"

"I hope so. I pray they get to the bottom of Clem's death."

"You know more than you're telling me."

Gene sat quiet.

"You're good at hiding things," she said. "Like how you feel."

He wished he could share what he knew about Clem's death.

"You ever wonder where we'll be ten years from now?" She gazed into the sky, past the tops of the trees.

Gene opened the top button on his shirt. "Haven't had time for thoughts like that."

"I think about it. You suppose we'll be together?"

"Haven't the foggiest."

"Will we be together in six months?" she asked.

"I may be in jail by then."

"Gene, stop avoiding the issue."

"What issue?"

"Do we have a future?"

He looked at her. She was serious.

"I'm in love with you, you know," she said.

He looked away. "Be patient with me. My attention hasn't been on us."

"I want you to think about us. Sometimes I think you're here because you feel sorry for me."

"I've watched you overcome emergency room bureaucrats, care for the walking wounded, stand up to overbearing generals. You take on challenges I couldn't cope with."

She folded her arms. "So. You're sorry for me. And I'm a good screw."

"Jesus, where's this coming from?"

"I'm not getting any younger. I want assurance you won't tire of me and pull out."

He kissed her, leaned away. "The truth is that I'm so confused, I don't know what I think. Besides, what have I got to offer you?" He shook his head. "I don't know if I'm even capable of love anymore. It's like asking a man on his way to the guillotine if he likes Mozart. Will you forgive me?"

"I don't know."

"Our love making," Gene said, "is better than I knew it could be, but that's because of the way we feel about each other."

"That's an understatement. You know the end of the first act of *La Bohème* when Rodolfo tells Mimì he loves her?"

He shrugged sheepishly. "No."

"He says, 'In you I see the dream I always want to dream.'"

"You're getting mushy."

"And? Love is mushy. Don't you ever feel sentimental?"

He hesitated. "Sometimes. I don't like it. It hurts."

"Since when is Gene Westmoreland afraid of a little pain?"

His head bowed. "Hey, if you don't mind—"

"You know how much it can hurt. You don't want to risk it again."

"Nettie, please—"

She pushed out her chair and stalked to the edge of the deck. "You're a coward, Gene."

She'd ripped open the scab, and he was bleeding. He grasped the arms of the chair, lifted himself to his feet, and forced his legs to walk to her. Standing behind her, he put his hands on her shoulders. "I'm sorry. I know I'm a casualty. It's the best I have to offer." His grip tightened. "I don't want to lose you."

She turned to him, tears in her eyes. "Then love me."

He shifted away. "Give me time. We've only been together a week."

"I've loved you for years."

"I don't want to lose you. Stay with me."

She eyed him. "Say more."

She was testing him. The pain in his heart made his eyes water.

He took her hands. "I need that look on your face when you're about to say something irreverent. I need your smile. I need the way you say my name."

She put her arms around him. "You can't say it, can you? You ask so much of me, that I go on loving you and ask nothing in return."

"Nettie—"

"It's all right. For now. Just for now."

Friday dawned steely, the latest in the series of colorless days. Gene and Nettie knew without talking about it that they needed to keep their relationship confidential, at least for now. Mark brought his car to work and drove them to the funeral at Faith Lutheran in Potomac. The pseudo-Gothic church was resplendent in black hangings and white roses. Air conditioning did nothing to dispel the cloying scent. Passing an eye over the assembly, Gene estimated that three hundred were in attendance. Pierce, in uniform, sat in the third row, immediately behind the family. Behind him were Dellaspada and Dennis Hodgings in his perennial blue summer suit. The service opened with a chorale prelude by Bach, and standard hymns—the only one Gene recognized was "A Mighty Fortress"—echoed from the vaulted ceilings. The readings dwelt on resurrection and the paradise to come. Clem's daughter, Jane, offered a eulogy, followed by the homily in the life-is-a-veil-of-tears mode. As the family followed the casket down the aisle, the organ played Bach's "Es ist genug."

Gene, Nettie, and Mark joined the caravan to Hopewell Cemetery and listened to the grave-side prayers. The casket was lowered, and Julia Yancy threw a white rose and a handful of dirt into the grave. The service at an end, the congregation milled in uneasy silence and edged toward the parking lot.

Julia, a stately matron in black, stayed by the grave alone. Gene told Nettie and Mark to go on without him and went to the grave.

"Julia?"

She turned her head slowly. "Gene. How good of you to come. I was going to call you."

"I'll help any way I can."

"Perhaps—" She watched the cars straggling from the parking lot. "Would you be kind enough to come to the house? Maybe you could stay for lunch. There's something—"

"Mom, you all right?"

Gene looked over his shoulder. Jane Yancy was coming toward them.

"Of course," Julia said. "You remember Gene. He'll be coming to lunch."

Jane shook Gene's hand. "Good to see you again, Doctor Westmoreland. Why don't you ride with me?"

The Yancy residence, surrounded by mature trees lush with foliage, lay in a vale at the end of a narrow road. The two-story stone homestead had originally been a farm house. Generations of owners had expanded and modernized it without changing its resemblance to a rustic country inn. Jane left Gene at a Dutch door at the side of the house and walked toward the main entrance.

The upper half of the door opened. "There you are," Julia said. "I told Jane to leave us alone. Come into the kitchen. I have tea brewing."

Gene opened the bottom half-door and stepped onto a cobblestone floor. The kitchen walls were rock-in-mortar, the table to which she directed him wrought iron, sturdy, and square.

Walking as if her feet hurt, Julia brought a tray with tea-things to the table. "I wonder how long it will take me to get back to normal." She set a cup in front of him. "Normal." She laughed. "Why would I want to return to that?" The teakettle whistled. She carried it to the table and poured into an earth-enware pot. "Things have been, what shall I say, putrid for months. Clem didn't kill himself. Something inside him did it. I don't know what. He never told me." She lowered herself to a chair.

"I can't tell you how sorry—"

She put her hand over his. "Please. Don't make me cry."

Gene lowered his eyes.

"From what he told me," she said, "I think he respected you more than anyone he worked with. The last time we talked, on the phone the night he died, he told me I could depend on you. He had no friends and no patience with acquaintances. Said little but did a lot. I knew when things were not going well at the office, but he didn't confide in me. Habit. From the years he worked with compartmented material."

Gene looked up.

"Yes, I know the business," she said. "I retired from CIA three years ago. Clem stayed on to get the maximum retirement benefits. I know who Hacker is. We went to a party at his place. Who's Pierce?"

"Another Air Force general. He was at the funeral."

She stared into space. "Both of them have something to do with Clem's death. They called here, several times. Each time, Clem went into his study for an hour or so. Then he'd be irritable. What did they do to him?"

"Julia, I'm not at liberty to talk about that."

"I have the feeling we're in this together. So what they did to him is classified?"

Gene clamped his teeth. He'd promised.

"It's not secret, is it?" Julia said. "Tell me."

Gene shifted. "I gave my word I'd never speak of it."

"To Clem? That was before he took his life. Things have changed."

Gene fidgeted.

Julia rose. "I wanted to show you something." At the sideboard, she used a key on a chain around her neck to open a dark wooden box. She took out a piece of paper and returned to the table. "Here."

Plain white copy paper, folded. He opened it. A handwritten note in blue ink.

My dearest Julia,

By the time you read this, my shame will be public information. I want to assure you that none of it is true. The videos were taken while I was unconscious. I did the best I could to keep this from happening. Now Gene will have to face them. I failed him, too.

I've been a coward, Julia. Had I been of sterner stuff, I'd have stopped them, even though it might have damaged me.

Instead, I procrastinated, hoping I could make it to retirement. Now I have shamed you and Jane. I have lost my job and my retirement. My life is over.

I hope you and Janey will forgive me for what I have done and what I am about to do. You have always been my first concern and my first love. I failed you. I can't go on living.

No signature.

Gene folded the note and handed it to Julia.

"Were Hacker and Pierce behind this?" Julia asked.

Gene stared at the table.

"What were the videos?" Julia said. "They blackmailed him, didn't they? They trapped him somehow, made it seem as though he was doing something disgraceful."

Gene locked his throat.

"You are a good man, Gene. You won't violate the trust of a friend. Despite that, his daughter and I deserve to know."

"Julia—" Moisture gathered behind his eyelids. "I can't."

She patted his hand. "Never mind. I'll find out anyway. We're partners now, Gene. Whether we like it or not."

"I'd better head to the office," Gene said. "Do you forgive me?"

"Nothing to forgive. You are an honorable man. Proud, stubborn, arrogant, but honorable. Just as Clem always described you. Jane will drive you to town."

At close of business, Mark, clearly unaware that Gene and Nettie were lovers, offered to give them a ride home. They drove up Thirteenth Street with the windows shut against the leaden air.

"Who's going to get Clem's job?" Mark asked.

"Been so long since a new chief was named," Nettie said. "The National Security Council nominates, and Office of Management and Budget confirms."

"Don't confuse the ought-to-be with what is," Gene said. "The president will choose from a list of candidates handpicked by the chairman of the Senate Preparedness Subcommittee with the advice and consent of the Director, NPO."

"Surely you don't think the president would select you," Nettie said.

"Not unless the Second Coming happens first. The new chief will be one of Hacker's or Prowley's right-hand men."

Nettie tsked. "Why do you always assume it'll be a man? Plenty of qualified women—"

"Not in Hacker's domain. In his realm, women have their place and stay in it."

When Mark dropped Gene off in Shepherd park, the Mustang was gone. Disturbed, he hurried up the stairs and knocked at George's room.

"Come."

"My car's gone."

George turned from the computer. "Michael came home after work and took it."

"Did he say why?"

George shook his head.

As Gene dressed for a workout, Michael trudged up the stairs carrying a cardboard box. "The prodigal has returned."

"For dinner?"

"For keeps. Leila threw me out. Said she was sick of me. Guess the flu thing was getting old. I was convincing though. Even threw up in the toilet. Put two fingers in the back of my throat. Really works." Michael dropped the box on his bed. "Couldn't carry my stuff on the bus, so I took the car. Met her father. Tall guy, graying, the Hollywood version of a distinguished gentleman. Ignored me. Couldn't wait until I was gone."

"They must have decided," Gene said, "that you've out-lasted your usefulness."

"Maybe they figure you're too set in your ways to give in to pressure. You know, the old-dog-new-tricks syndrome . . ."

"Your acidity is returning. You must be in a good mood."

Michael grinned. "The best. I haven't enjoyed living a lie. Going to take a shower. See if hot, soapy water will wash away mendacity."

"I'm glad it's over. The whole masquerade shamed me."

Michael's smile faded. "Hot, soapy water washes away shame, too."

Gene, sad and quiet, stayed at Nettie's Saturday night. Rachel and Sarah seemed pleased to have him there. He made love to Nettie that night and again in the morning before he left for Shepherd Park. She said little but clung to him as if he might slip from her grasp.

Monday morning, Gene called Hugh to confirm their meeting for Wednesday. Pierce came on the line.

"The calendar's on hold," he said. "We'll reschedule when things resume relative calm."

"Clem's death?"

"I'm moving to a new job," Pierce said.

"Really? Who's taking your position?"

"So far undecided. Perhaps no replacement will be named. I have been here on loan from my parent organization."

"I didn't know that," Gene lied. "What office are you from?"

"That's discretionary information, Doctor Westmoreland."

"Okay. What's your next assignment?"

"I'm not authorized to discuss the matter," Pierce said.

"What will Hugh do without you?"

"Mr. Shafter is being promoted. He's moving, too."

"Where to?"

Pierce paused as if for emphasis. "To the position of Chief, Federal Intelligence Budgeting Office."

Gene's heart jumped. "He's Clem's replacement?"

"Affirmative. Effective as soon as he's able."

Gene took Nettie to a consolatory lunch at Goldoni's. She told him, glumly, that Hugh would be moving in on Wednesday and assuming full control on Thursday. Ironic. Hugh's takeover of FIBO coincided with the biggest administration scandal yet—the Helsinki summit and further attacks on the U.S. intelligence community by the president. Then, this morning, the president talked about cancelling security clearances for those critical of him. That decision could apply to Gene. How much worse could things get?

Hugh held his first staff meeting Thursday afternoon in the small conference room adjoining the front office. He assured the budget monitors and staff that he would run things much as Clem had.

"I manage on PDL principles. That is, Professionalism, Discretion, and Loyalty.

"You're professionals here and I expect you to behave as such. That means I don't care how many hours you have to work to assure a quality budget that will be acceptable to the Congress.

"What happens in these offices is to be handled the same way we protect classified information. What we say and do here is not to be spoken of outside these walls.

"Loyalty is my first principle. You will support my decisions to the hilt. I expect complete commitment to the goals I set for each of you."

Hugh gave the assemblage a broad smile and gathered his notes. "That's all."As the budget reviewers got to their feet, Hugh beckoned to Gene. In the director's office, Hugh went behind the desk. "Starting today, no more calls every Thursday to Danley's office. That violates my principle of discretion."

"Those calls," Gene said, "are at Danley's personal request. Clem felt—"

"No more calls. Clear?"

They locked eyes.

"Clear," Gene said.

But Gene did place one last call to Mavis, the next morning, "just to tell you that I won't be able to report to you weekly."

"Problem?" Mavis asked.

Problem? She had no idea. "I'm following guidance, that's all."

"From your new chief?"

"Yes," Gene said.

"I get the feeling you're being muzzled. This is Hugh Shafter's policy? FIBO isn't the White House, you know. Hugh can't claim executive privilege."

"Sorry, Mavis."

"Right. I'll have to report this to the senator. He won't be happy. Let's face it, Gene. You haven't been very forthcoming in our weekly talks, but at least we had some inkling of what to expect."

"My apologies." Gene hung up feeling that he'd let down a good friend.

Monday morning, Nettie buzzed him. "Mr. Shafter wants to see you."

Nettie frowned as he entered the front office. "He's really pissed. Look out."

Hugh was pacing before the great window overlooking the Eisenhower Executive Office Building. He halted when Gene came in. "When I say no calls, I mean no calls, shithead."

Gene gulped.

"'FIBO isn't the White House,'" Hugh chirped in a falsetto. Then, in a growl, "From now on I expect my orders to be obeyed."

"How did—"

"All calls into and out of this office are monitored. A manifest insubordination incident will be entered into your personnel record." Hugh dropped into his desk chair. "Get the fuck out of here and get to work."

Saturday morning, Gene used Carl's cell phone to call Julia Yancy. "Was wondering if I could stop by the house sometime. We could pick up our conversation where we left off."

"How about Sunday morning after church? At, say, ten?"

Gene parked the Mustang in the round-about by the Yancy house at ten sharp. Jane greeted him at the door.

"Mom's in the garden," she said.

Gene walked behind her through cramped halls opening onto the library, the dining room, and the sitting room. The rear of the house was an expansive sunroom, all windows, looking out on the shaded garden.

"She's waiting for you." Jane opened the door.

Julia Yancy, in a beige suit, was at a small iron table with inlaid top. Her purse, gloves, hat, and prayer book lay beside a teacup.

"Something to drink, Gene?"

He shook his head.

"I thought we'd sit out here," she said. "Private and comfortable—until the heat sets in. Maybe we'll get more rain. Cool things off." She indicated the chair across from her. "Please."

"How are you doing?" he said as he sat.

"Not well, Gene. I keep forgetting he's gone, living through his death all over again."

"Anything I can do?"

"It's my loss, and I have to cope with it. Nobody can do it for me."

"I miss him, too."

She cocked her head. "You're probably the closest thing he had to a friend. Such a loner. Even with me and Janey. Yet we knew that he loved us. Never forgot a birthday or anniversary. Always chose the most thoughtful of gifts. Not once was he inconsiderate, even during those awful months before he—" She sat very still as if fighting off a tremor. "It's the little things that hurt the most. When I get up in the morning, his side of the bed is undisturbed. No smell of shaving cream in the bathroom. No coffee made when I get to the kitchen. He—" Her voice wobbled. "He loved this house. We bought it right after we were married, and he poured himself into it, heart and soul. He planted the pear tree shading us, took out a second mortgage to have the sunroom built, restored the old stonework. Now . . ."

Gene waited.

"I'm afraid," she said, "we're going to lose it. Even with death benefits, I don't have enough money." She tightened her fist. "I'm sorry. I didn't mean to get into that." She whisked a handkerchief past her nose. "I don't even know why you wanted to see me."

"First of all, if you need to call me, use this number." Gene wrote Carl's number on the blank side of a business card.

She took it. "This isn't your number?"

He shook his head. "The cell phone of a friend."

"Your phone is tapped. Is that part of the story that includes the video?"

Gene chuckled. "You're very quick."

"I was in the business, remember?"

"Second, do you know Willis Danley?"

"The senator?" she asked. "I've met him several times at receptions and parties."

"Would you be willing to make an appointment to talk to him? Would you tell him the same things you told me about your suspicions? You could show him Clem's note."

"Are you confirming my guess about what happened to Clem?"

"If I read you correctly," Gene said, watching her closely, "you want closure, even if it means unsavory facts are made public."

"My God. Things Clem did?"

"No. Ugly, untrue accusations leveled against him."

She folded her hands. "Can you assure me that Clem didn't participate in . . . Never mind. I know he didn't." She fixed Gene in her gaze. "Even if he did, I'd want the truth known."

"I can't assure you of anything. All I know is that we must act."

She leaned toward him, frowning. "Why?"

"You know what compartmented means."

"And you don't want to lay yourself open to prosecution for violating security. Tell me two things. First, have you told me or have I stumbled on any information that's classified?"

Gene pondered. "No."

"Second. Are my suspicions correct? Did Clem tell you about it before he died?"

"I've violated his confidence by coming here today. Don't ask me to make it any worse."

"Why don't you go to Danley yourself?"

"He's not cleared for the compartments," Gene said, "but if he sees Clem's note and hears you out, he might smell corruption."

"Especially if I tell him that this Pierce person visited Clem late the night he died." She smiled at his surprise. "Clem telephoned me at eleven that night. He was upset, though he tried to hide it. Told me he just wanted to hear my voice. Told me Pierce had been to see him and that 'that closes the case.' He wouldn't tell me what he meant."

"Did you tell the police?" Gene said.

"Yes."

"So they've probably had a talk with Pierce before now. Not likely they'll follow up, though."

She got to her feet. "I'll call Danley's office tomorrow."

"Ask for Mavis. She's his factotum."

They followed the walkway around the side of the house.

"May I mention you to Danley?" she asked.

"He knows me. Tell him to call me at the number I gave you, not at the office."

"Your office phone is tapped?"

"The management would deny that. Let's just say it's monitored."

She wrinkled her nose as if to ward off a stench. "What have we come to?"

"The president and the Secretocracy. That's Clem's word, by the way."

"Clem used to say that we no longer have a right to know. That's the first step toward totalitarianism."

"He and I saw many things the same way."

That night, before leaving for Nettie's, Gene brought Michael up to date. "Be careful what you say on the phone, any phone. Even my office phone is tapped."

"Jesus. Is nothing sacred?" Michael said.

"Oh, yes. The power of the president over the rest of us."

"Is this what the framers had in mind?"

Gene humphed. "What did they know?"

"Spoken like a true administration supporter. What I can't figure is why Leila dropped me when she did—as though I wasn't serving a purpose anymore."

"Maybe they reckoned that with Shafter as the chief of FIBO, I was emasculated. But if I were Hacker or the president, I'd still worry that I had a loose cannon on deck in rough seas."

On Wednesday, August 1, the *Washington Post* published an update on the number of falsehoods perpetrated by the president, a total of 4,229, average of 7.6 a day. The next day, it printed an article on something called "QAnon," a movement rife with conspiracy theories supporting the president and denouncing the Democrats. Gene remembered Clem's warning and shook his head. Every day it got worse.

Meanwhile, he had heard nothing from Julia Yancy. He'd successfully avoided Hugh Shafter. Then, mid-morning Thursday, while Gene was finishing his in-basket, the cubicle chime sounded. Harry Breighton, carrying his briefcase and looking decidedly unhappy. After Gene had sanitized and let him in, Harry sat stiffly in the chair next to Gene's desk.

"Gene, I won't waste time. We have evidence you've been engaging in practices that require suspension of your continued access to classified material."

Gene's muscles flexed involuntarily.

"Our sources confirm," Harry said, "that, among other things, you're involved in sexual orgies with other men."

Gene's mouth opened.

"And," Harry said, "that your pimp is an official of a foreign government. You passed him data that portrayed the Russian government in a bad light." He shook his head. "My God, Gene. How could you let yourself . . . I've known you for twenty years. First that cock-and-bull story about Leila Spencer, now this. Should have seen it coming."

"None of this is true," Gene said. "Who—"

"You know I can't divulge sources, Gene. I'm withdrawing your clearances. Effective immediately, you'll be working out of office space at the Bryson Building in Anacostia. May I have your ID please?"

"On the basis of an allegation?"

"The evidence is firm. We have telephone conversations, a video, and three confirming sources. Your badge and ID."

"Harry—"

Harry held out his hand.

Gene unclipped his FIBO picture badge from his shirt collar and handed it over. He pulled his ID from his wallet. Harry lifted a hole punch and scissors from his briefcase. He perforated the face on Gene's ID and cut his badge in half.

"Come with me," he said. "Bring your personal belongings."

PART THREE

Isolation

Chapter 12

Shame

What a difference four months makes, Gene sang to himself. The Bryson Building was his Gulag Archipelago. The chair creaked as he leaned forward and rested his face in his hands. Muffled laughter. The workmen were back with several buddies. Jostling each other to get a peek between the curtains. Maybe Gene should paint over the plate glass. And be fined for defacing federal property? He hadn't even been here a day, and he already hated it. But he probably wouldn't be here long. One way or another. Meanwhile, compulsory idleness would undermine his sanity.

His ruin would be easier to bear if he could feel like a victim, but he'd done this to himself. He could have folded, spared his son suffering, saved his own reputation. No one forced him to confront Hacker, challenge Prowley, resist Shafter, defy the president. They'd isolated him. How long would it take to terminate him?

Telephone conversations, a video, three witnesses. That was the source of the evidence against him. Except for the imposter Vassiliev—that would account for one phone call and Harry's reference to a foreign government official—Gene was stumped. He understood how Clem felt. His own life was finished. Shame crawled through his scalp.

At one, he left the building, found a burrito stand two blocks away, and ate, doing his best to ignore the smoky stench. Heading north in the harsh light, he found a drug store and bought magazines. In his glass cage again—he understood why they called it "the tank"—he inched through the afternoon with *Harper's* essays, *Atlantic* articles, and a *New Yorker* short story he didn't understand.

When he returned from the men's room, the curtain was open again. He closed it. Time to call Shafter. He'd put it off as long as he could.

"He's got someone with him," Nettie said.

"Ask him to call me."

"Subject?"

Nettie'd never asked for a subject before.

"My status," Gene said. "How do I apply for leave, by the way?"

"Just tell me." Nettie was business-like.

He found Supply on the second floor and requested forms to requisition a computer. The elderly black gentleman asked him if he was the current occupant of the tank and explained that he had no forms for anything like a computer. He'd see if he could get some. Could Gene try again after the first of the month? Gene got dust cloths, paper, and government-issue ballpoint pens.

That night he took the Metro to the Takoma station and walked the six blocks to Nettie's. The last block, up the incline to her house, tested his quadriceps. At the top, he squinted at the seamless gray glare. The cloud cover held in heat and humidity. No respite in sight.

Nettie met him at the door, still in her suit. Her kiss was cold.

"You heard, I guess?" he said.

She nodded, started for the kitchen.

"What are people saying?" He followed her.

"Mr. Shafter called a meeting to announce your departure. Hinted that you'd gotten involved in something sexual. Acted scandalized. What did happen?"

"The Secretocracy trumped up phony charges of homosexual behavior. I know where some of it came from."

At the table beside her, he recounted the tale of Vassiliev. "I was the stooge for a perfect setup. But Harry talked about three confirming sources. Wouldn't tell me who was accusing me of what."

"Mark was more upset than he was by Clem's death. He's sure they faked evidence to get rid of you. Told me he'd warned you they were out to get you and that withdrawal of security clearances was now the standard administration method for firing those who don't fall in line."

Gene nodded. "We need to watch ourselves. The office phones are bugged."

She shuddered.

Gene took her hands. "Are you all right?"

"As if you didn't know. My whole life is the pits. Doctor Yancy's death is still freaking me out, and the office is hell on speed. Mark is semi-hysterical, Harry's acting like he's PMS-ing, and Mr. Shafter—"

"You don't have to tell *me*."

"You don't know a tenth of it. He . . . I can't tell you. I'm his executive secretary."

Gene tightened. "Right. Protect the poor guy."

"That's not fair," she cried. "It's my job."

"God forbid you should be disloyal to the son-of-a-bitch."

"Oh, Gene." She wrung her hands. "All right. NSA is monitoring our phones under PRISM and sending the transcripts to him."

"I found that out the hard way."

"He's started weekly meetings, in the small conference room, with analysts from the Office of Special Compartmented Intelligence, people from the president's staff, Vince Dellaspada, and General Pierce. They meet behind closed doors. If I go into the room, they stop talking."

Gene's heart raced.

"He's setting up other sessions," Nettie said, "with the same players and people from PRISM and their counterparts from the Congressional staff. He sees to it that none of this shows on the calendar. No calls between him and any of these people get recorded in the phone log. I'm terrified I'm party to something illegal."

She paused as if trying to decide whether to continue.

"I haven't told you the worst. He made a pass at me. Hinted that my future depended on how cooperative I was."

"Jesus Christ, Nettie. Report him."

"To whom? OMB staffed by the president's cronies?"

"Quit and go public."

"Uh-huh. And who's going to hire me? And the girls soon to be in college."

She was right. Gene hadn't known a tenth of it.

"What's unbearable," she went on, "is I've gotten into a one-sided relationship with the man who's at the center of the storm. Unfortunately, I'm in love with him."

Gene studied his fingernails.

"Do you love me, Gene?"

"Don't ask me if I like Mozart while they're carting me to the guillotine."

She stood. "That won't cut it anymore."

"I'm doing the best I can."

"Not good enough. You're asking me to put my job in jeopardy, maybe even risk physical harm. If I were sure you loved me, maybe . . . but *you're* not sure."

So this was how it was going to be. Gene closed his eyes.

"I think you'd better go home," Nettie said.

Gene found his voice. "I'll come back when—"

"No."

"Nettie, I need you."

"And I need you. But not enough to go on with no commitment from you." She turned her back.

He got to his feet. Maybe if he took her in his arms. Maybe a kiss. He studied her, from her carrot top, suit jacket, business-like skirt, to her high heels. Her back still to him, she had folded her arms and lowered her head. Her body silently forbade him to touch her.

Weary, he made his way to the living room, took his work clothes and shaving kit from the table by the stairs, and left.

The strongest man is he who stands alone. Maybe George was right. Gene had always chosen to rely only on himself. Now he had no choice.

Friday morning, the tank's curtain was again open. Gene, heartsick, closed it, took out his magazines, and spread them on his desk. He'd have to find something to do with his time. Inactivity was unbearable.

Noises in the hall. The curtain opened. Five women in overalls and painter's caps stood outside in hysterics, watching him. Why did they find him so hilarious? He waited until they were gone, went into the hall, and drew the curtain.

The phone rang. Gene jumped.

"Hold." Nettie said. "I'll put him on."

"You wanted to talk to me?" Hugh said.

"I need to see you," Gene said. "Find out what's going on."

"You can't come here."

"Where could we meet?"

"I don't think we can."

"But, Hugh—"

"Someone will be in touch with you when necessary."

He hung up.

Gene held the receiver in front of him. The mute hunk of plastic was as close as he was going to get to pleading his case. Not much help if no one would talk to him. Not enough time for moping. He had to bring Barry Tilden up to date. He dialed Barry's number, told Barry's secretary it was urgent, and got a fifteen-minute appointment Saturday afternoon.

That evening, Julia Yancy called Gene on Carl's cell phone.

"I called Senator Danley's office and talked to Mavis, as you suggested. She told me the senator would be very interested in hearing what I have to say, but he can't see me until the first week in September."

Gene's spirits sagged. He told her he'd lost his clearances and expected to be fired any time.

"So," she said, "they've eliminated all pockets of resistance." A long sigh.

"Any chance you could get to the senator before I get booted out?"

"I'll see what I can do," she said, "but my gut tells me they won't fire you. That's leaving tracks. Instead, they'll outwait you, keep you hanging out to dry until you quit from frustration. Then they won't have to present evidence that can be challenged."

"I'd never considered that."

"Don't resign. Find something to do to keep your mind occupied. How are you at crossword puzzles?"

"I get the picture."

"I'll call you if I have anything to report."

Barry welcomed Gene into his office with a handshake.

"I'm about to be unemployed," Gene told him. He related the events of the previous week.

"My God, Gene, this isn't the Nixon Administration."

"I'm not making this up. I'll start the job search this afternoon, but if they fire me, I don't know how I'll pay you."

"Let's face that when and if," Barry said. "Meanwhile, have you heard anything from your wife or Spicer, Brinkman, and Klauthammer? Everything seems to have come to a halt. Can't figure out what's going on."

"Why would they delay getting on with it?"

Barry shook his head. "If you were about to be promoted, I'd say they were procrastinating in hopes of a fatter ox to gore. You stand to inherit money? Any stocks maturing? About to sell real estate?"

"Nothing," Gene said. "What would happen if I counter-sued—to precipitate action?"

"Might work, but it'd be messy and expensive."

Barry wandered to the window and stared down at the perennial traffic jam on Twenty-first Street. "Their silence makes me uneasy. I'm going to recommend something I usually wouldn't. How about talking to your wife?" Barry turned to face him. "She knows why they're biding their time. Maybe she'll tell you. Or maybe—" He winked. "—you can tease it out of her."

Gene's purgatory of idleness had no end in view, and aloneness was apparently to be his permanent lot, but, at least temporarily, he could distract himself by making job search a full-time occupation. Saturday night at home, he fired up the computer and brought up *www.opm.gov* to check on jobs. Under BUDGET ANALYST, he found seven jobs in the D.C. Metro area, not counting GS-11 and below. Only one, at Forest Service, was an SES-level job. The budget analyst skill requirements were virtually identical for each job except for the level of proficiency. Here and there he found odd twists in the requirements, a tip-off that the text had been written with a specific candidate in mind. He'd try anyway. With his Ph.D. and twenty years of experience in government budgeting, he should have a good shot at each job. He'd apply for all of them, even those labeled "hazardous duty," in places like Baghdad, Kabul, and Brazzaville. The problem, one that might rule him out completely, was that he was unknown outside the intelligence community and *persona non grata* inside. The trick would be to get an interview.

If he couldn't find a job in the federal government, there was always academia. He'd taught at MIT after his doctorate, before NSA hired him as a mathematician. He'd enjoyed teaching—granted, not as much as cryptanalysis and intel budgeting—and he'd been good at it. He might have to leave the Washington area and work in Peoria or Albuquerque, but his only tie to D.C. was Michael, who'd likely move elsewhere after he graduated next June. What if the cause of his dismissal followed him? No, it was federal personnel policy never to reveal reasons for the withdrawal of clearance status.

He didn't give a damn about his own future. He'd be happy to move to Los Angeles and eke out a living coaching body builders in a gym, but Michael needed money to finish school. And if Michael decided on graduate school? They'd face that when the time came.

Gene fell into a routine. By day he carried his job applications to agencies and companies, studied the skill and experience requirements in job announcements and ads, called agencies and private sector companies for information, drafted applications, and filled out forms. By night, he typed the paperwork and mailed it. By the end of the week, he was running out of things to do.

To keep his mind nimble, as Hacker had put it, he'd have to learn something new. Over the weekend, he pondered the possibilities. A quote came to him from the past. *Let your plans be dark and as impenetrable as night, and when you move, fall like a thunderbolt.* Sun Tzu. A general in ancient China. A foster-father had required him to memorize it. His enemy? How could he get to know the Secretocracy better? What had Hacker said? Many prominent conservatives were disciples of Leo Strauss. Hacker himself was. On AMAZON.COM Gene ordered Strauss' purported masterpiece, *Natural Right and History* and two books about him by Drury and Smith.

Late one afternoon, the phone on his desk rang. Nettie.

"I was wondering," she said, "if you could drop by the house tonight and pick up the rest of your stuff."

"What stuff?"

"A few odds and ends. Be here at eight." She hung up.

Nettie met him at the door and asked him to sit down. "I want to be sure you understand why I asked you to come by. I don't want you to stay, but I care enough about you that I wanted to bring you up to date. The pick-up-your-stuff line was a ruse."

"I figured."

"Mr. Shafter will know I called you. He knows we were seeing each other. He chewed me out for keeping company with you, 'an infamous pederast.' I was surprised he even knew that word. Guess he makes up for his lack of education by detailed knowledge of sleaseology. He said, 'Your future is my hands, baby.' The images *that* brought to mind. Anyway, tomorrow I'll explain that I still had a few items that belonged to you and I wanted you to come to the house and get them."

"Your story makes me nauseous."

"Meanwhile, your replacement has been named. Brigadier General Roderick Pierce. He's moving in this week. He'll be acting Senior Budget Reviewer instead of being officially assigned to the position. Seems he's on loan and no one can be assigned to your job until 'certain personnel adjustments are completed,' according to Mr. Shafter."

"My God," Gene breathed. "They're blatant. Don't even pretend to follow personnel regs."

"One other tidbit. Since no one in personnel is cleared, I had to review General Pierce's personnel file and remove any classified documentation for separate filing in cleared spaces. Did you know he's from the president's office?"

"Found that out a while ago. They hide his connections with the White House."

"The odd thing was TDY orders to Madrid for the period 5 through 19 July. The file has his TDY orders and hotel, taxi, airline, and meal receipts, but something doesn't jibe. On the tenth, the day Doctor Yancy died, the NPO secretary called me from the Pentagon to get the telephone number of Doctor Yancy's hospital room. I told her I wasn't allowed to give out that number, and General Pierce came on the line and demanded that I give it to him. When I refused, he hung up. I went through the phone log. I had entered that call."

"The fifth through the nineteenth," Gene said. "Clem died the morning of the tenth. Sounds like they want to show he was out of town when Clem died."

"That's why I wanted to tip you off." She stopped talking and looked at the floor.

He started to reach for her but stopped himself. "How are you, Nettie?"

She kept her eyes lowered. "I miss you. I wish I could take you back, but I can't."

He nodded slowly. "I'm sorry. I never meant to hurt you—"

She stood abruptly. "Will you go now please?"

He watched her. Her fists were tight at her sides, and she stared at the floor. He nodded. "Okay."

He left.

The third week of August, the press reported the firing of FBI senior counterintelligence agent Peter Strzok. The *New York* Times opined that his dismissal was a warning to government employees: this is what happens if you cross the president. Then came reports that the president had withdrawn the security clearance of former CIA director, John Brennan. Gene nodded as he read. He wasn't the only casualty.

The Strauss books arrived. In the long hours in the tank, Gene became oblivious to his tormentors outside the glass as he immersed himself in "mendacious populism," "radical illiberalism," and "the natural order of domination and subordination." The reasoning inherent to philosophical thinking was alien to him. No concrete rules here. Everything was abstract logic, plausibility, and—he realized with a start—preference. Turned out that, in the realm of philosophy, one believed in accordance with one's taste. Just like everything else in life, except science and mathematics.

His desk covered with job announcements and draft applications, Gene homed in on the concepts of relativism and absolute truth. For a full week he ruminated over Strauss' assertion that "the inalienable rights of man" was a "ridiculous and pitiful" idea. Only "the principles of the right—fascist, authoritarian, *imperial*" made sense. Gene saw that if one accepted the underlying and unprovable premises of this philosophy, the rest flowed with mathematical precision. In this context, Hacker's logic was unassailable.

His mind was awakening from its stupor. With increasing frequency, he lifted his eyes from his texts to discover that the rubber-neckers outside the glass had gone home for the day and he was alone in the building except for the guard at the front door.

But at a level of consciousness he avoided, he knew he was keeping his mind occupied so he wouldn't dwell on the sorry situation he'd gotten himself into. The worst times were at night, after he'd put aside his book. Unable to rest, he'd lie in bed, listen to the crank, wheeze, and return of the pedestal fan, Michael's untroubled breathing, and the faint hiss of the overworked air conditioning unit. His cockiness had brought him down. Another man would have put the interests of his family ahead of his belief that he had to be true to himself. The same pride that cost him his marriage. And Nettie. And, maybe, the love of his son.

Michael had been subtly different since the day Gene had told him Leila was a plant. *I pay a high price to be the son of Gene Westmoreland*, he'd said. Yeah, the acid remarks, the smart one-liners, the arch rejoinders were back. And yet . . . In ways Gene couldn't put his finger on, Michael had distanced himself.

One evening after a dinner George had cooked, Gene and Michael shared kitchen duties. When the dishwasher was loaded and pots scrubbed, Gene took a beer from the fridge.

"KP duty upsets you so much you need to imbibe?" Michael said.

"Having trouble sleeping these days. Sometimes beer helps."

Michael took the can from Gene's hand and set it on the counter. "Okay. Talk to me. What's going on?"

"You know my situation. Waiting for the axe to fall."

"What about Mrs. Yancy?"

"Hasn't called," Gene said. "That means she won't see Danley until September. Besides, maybe the ploy won't work. It's a long shot."

"What's the worst that can happen?"

"I might not be able to find another job," Gene said. "Nothing's surfaced so far."

"What you did to them was awesomely uncool."

"I crossed a general and a senator."

Michael nodded gravely. "So what happened? Did you get a genator or a seneral?"

Gene did a double take, then threw back his head and laughed long and hard. Michael, in stitches himself, fell forward and threw his arms around Gene's neck.

"Sorry," Michael said.

"My pawky son. I'll never accuse you of taking things too seriously."

Michael wiped his eyes. "You mad?"

"Hell, no. I know where to go to get over my funk."

"Seriously, though," Michael said, "I could probably get a refund from George Washington if I withdrew right away. Classes don't start until next week. Maybe we should think about putting off my senior year—"

"No way," Gene said. "With two more semesters to go—"

"I'm making pretty good money. If I kept at it full time, I could—"

"Michael, shut up. Before anything like that, we'd go to your grandfather."

"You talk like that, I'm going to puke." Michael snatched the beer from the counter and ripped off the tab. "Drink this and quit beating yourself up. A good night's sleep never hurt anybody." He looked down. "You've been so uptight. Sometimes you don't talk. I've been laying low, waiting to see . . ."

Gene took the beer. "I can't tell you how ashamed I am. If anything happens that you can't finish college—"

Michael took him by the shoulders. "*Stop it*. Ashamed for clinging to the right thing even if it cost you your job?" He took his hands from Gene's shoulder. "You listen to me. All my life I've looked up to you. I've always wanted to be like you." His voice dropped. "I've never been more proud to be Gene Westmoreland's son."

Gene looked at his son. Michael's eyes were misted. Gene set down the beer and pulled his son into his arms.

At six Friday morning, when Gene stepped from his bedroom to the attic hall, he found a note taped to the door. Carl's handwriting. "Julia Yancy called." He dashed down the stairs to Carl's room. The door was ajar. No Carl. He tried the bathroom at the end of the hall. Carl stood naked, shaving.

"Need your cell right away," Gene said.

"On top of my briefcase in the chair by the bed."

Gene dashed back to Carl's room, grabbed the phone, and dialed. Julia answered.

"Sorry for calling at this hour," Gene said. "You know my phone problems."

"Don't apologize. I was up," Julia said. "Wanted to bring you up to date. Mitch McConnell reduced the August recess to one week, so they're back in session. I talked to Mavis in person."

"Not the senator?"

"He was called to the floor for a vote. I told her everything I knew. She took me seriously, made a copy of Clem's note, asked if anyone else had information. I said you did."

Gene winced. "Did you give her my alternate number?"

"I asked her not to call on any number but that. She put two and two together and asked why your phone was being tapped. She didn't know you'd lost your clearances, said that fit the pattern the president has started."

"Did Mavis say that the senator will talk to you?"

"She said she'd pass the info on to him. From there, it was his ball game."

Gene considered. "I doubt he'd see me if I called. He likes to be the initiator. You think I should push it?"

"Not from Mavis' body language. Let's wait a week or two. If I don't hear, it's your move."

Gene sighed. "Julia, thank you."

"Nothing to thank me for. I'm doing this for Clem."

To fill his empty hours in the tank, Gene read the *Washington Post* and the *New York Times* from front to back. He studied stories of the Manafort conviction, the Cohen guilty plea, Allen Weisselberg's grant of immunity in exchange for cooperation. The evidence of presidential malfeasance grew by leaps and bounds. That meant that the administration would get even rougher on those who, like Gene, had earned presidential wrath.

By the last week in September, Julia had heard nothing from Mavis, nor had Mavis called Gene. They agreed it was time for Gene to take his chances on displeasing Danley and place a call to him. He prevailed on Carl to lend him his cell during the working day—Carl wasn't permitted to carry a cell inside cleared spaces anyway—and Gene took a day of leave. At nine in the morning, he called Senator Danley's office.

"The senator knows me," Gene told the receptionist. "So does Mavis Evans. I need to talk to the senator about the National Preparedness Office."

Silence on the line, then, "Thank you, Doctor Westmoreland. I'll pass your request to Ms. Evans."

Gene waited. For a week, nothing. Then, the second week in October, before he left for work, he got a call. Mavis' voice sounded like she was talking under water.

"You're breaking up," Gene said.

"I'm on my cell. The senator's in the home state, campaigning. I'm acting as liaison on legislative business. We have an election next month, remember?"

"I've had too much on my mind."

"The senator won't be in Washington until after the election, Gene, but I'm returning Saturday, the thirteenth, to keep the office running. The senator wants to know more about why you want to see him. Could you meet me in his office at, say, ten Sunday, the fourteenth?"

On Sunday, October 14, in the aftermath of the Kavanaugh imbroglio, Gene found the Russell Office Building deserted. He went through the usual security routine at the entrance, then hurried down the gaping corridors to Senator's Danley's office. Inside, Gene greeted the lone secretary, a woman in jeans and an "Ocean City is Where It's At" tee-shirt, and sat on an upholstered Queen Anne love seat. Danley's outer office was a marble room with high ceilings and an echo muted only by the carpet. The door to the inner office, an ornate arch that belonged in a

Byzantine cathedral, was flanked by four mahogany desks, two on each side, with banks of telephones and computers.

The intercom buzzed. The woman picked up the phone, then turned to Gene. "Doctor Westmoreland?" She led him through the door into another ante-room with five desks, through yet another central door, into an expansive office with a marble fireplace.

Mavis, in slacks and blouse, stood. "Good to see you."

She motioned to a carved table near the fireplace, and Gene sat. She moved her chair across from him and slid the three telephones aside to make room for her notebook. "You have something to tell the senator about the National Preparedness Office?"

"Ms. Evans, I've lost my clearances, so I cannot legally talk about everything I know. I *can* tell you General Hacker and Senator Prowley, at the direction of the president, are conspiring to carry out programs I know to be in contravention of our treaties and in violation of the law. The two gentlemen are willing to go to great lengths to achieve their objective. You saw Clem Yancy's note?"

"I have a copy."

"I've been subjected to similar pressures. My phones are bugged, my son was duped into a relationship designed to pressure me, and I've been accused with false evidence of participating in homosexual debauchery. I expect any day to be notified that my employment is terminated."

Mavis raised her brows. "Why would anyone do these things to you?"

"I persistently fought against the illegal programs. The general, the senator, and the president saw me as an obstruction and eliminated me."

"That's quite an allegation. How much can you prove?"

"None of it," Gene said. "It's my word against theirs."

"And what do you want Senator Danley to do?"

"Nothing for me. I recommend he investigate compartmented operations within the National Preparedness Office."

"The senator and I are both cleared for those compartments."

"I suggest that you ask General Hacker if there are other compartments you are not cleared for. Ask if their very existence is itself compartmented. Ask why you were never told about them. Ask to be cleared for them."

Mavis opened her mouth in surprise.

"I have skirted violating security in that suggestion," Gene said. "I hope you'll protect me."

"You want a great deal."

"I don't want to be prosecuted for security breaches."

Mavis frowned at her notebook. "The truth is, Gene, Doctor Yancy's suicide note shocked us. I've had several confidential sessions with the D.C. police, an Inspector Henley, on behalf of the senator. Mrs. Yancy told me that General Pierce visited Doctor Yancy hours before the suicide. A nursing care technician also reported the visit. Attempts to question Pierce have been blocked by claims of risk to national security. If that continues, the Senator may have to intervene. Both Pierce and Hacker called Doctor Yancy at home several times, according to Mrs. Yancy."

Gene grinned. "You've already begun—"

"Don't celebrate yet. Senator Danley is in the minority on the Senate Preparedness Subcommittee. The staff is under the control of Vince Dellaspada who answers only to Senator Prowley. Senator Danley's every move has been thwarted. His attempts to bring General Hacker and General Pierce before the subcommittee for questioning have been stymied. His letters to the National Preparedness Office have been tabled."

She took a deep breath, held it, released it.

"The senator and his colleagues have worked hard to make the American people aware of what the administration is up to. The election will show us how successful they've been. Meanwhile, legislative business is at a standstill. They're all on the campaign trail."

Chapter 13

Manifest Debauchery

Gene caught Carl heading out the door.

"Got a minute?"

Carl scowled at his watch. "Thirty seconds."

"Hank Shelby. Maybe his uncle is a major general."

"You lost me."

"Hacker. His flunky, Cutter, talked to you and George. Who knows who else he talked to? I humiliated Hank. I was in Hacker's way. Maybe they found common cause."

"Getting exiled's made you paranoid."

"When Cutter came to see you," Gene said, "did he leave a number where you could reach him if you thought of something you hadn't told him?"

"Worse. He asked me to watch for anything suspicious and call him."

Gene nodded. "I figure he did the same thing with Hank. I've got to find Hank. If he's smart, he has an unlisted phone. You have any buddies in Air Force Matériel?"

"Sure. We're Jay-Fours—logistics types. A little wheeling and dealing behind the scenes is what saves the military from sinking under the weight of its own bureaucracy."

"Could you get me Hank's address and phone number?"

"I'll give it a whirl."

Gene slugged Carl on the bicep. "You're the great white hope."

"Great white hype." Carl studied his watch. "I've got thirty-five minutes to get to the Pentagon." He gave Gene his killer smile. "They can't fire the military."

Gene returned to his cold breakfast on the veranda. The earth glowed pearl gray in the prelude to the coming day. Hank. He should have guessed. Harry had mentioned other sources. Who?

That night, Carl, still in uniform, interrupted Gene's workout.

"I bribed my buddy at Air Force Matériel. Got a pencil?"

Gene snatched his workout chart and wrote down Henry Shelby's address and phone number.

"I found it on MapQuest," Carl said. "It's an apartment building at the juncture of Route 450 and the Beltway in New Carrollton."

"What shift does Hank work?" Gene asked.

"Early. Leaves the Pentagon at three."

"I owe you one, dude."

The next day, Gene called Nettie and had her charge him leave for the last two hours of the day. He left the Bryson building at three, took the Metro to New Carrollton, and walked down Route 450 to the Beltway overpass. The ragged apartment complex, four stories high, with large numbers over each entrance, was wrapped around an oil-stained parking lot. Gene entered the building, climbed the dim flight of steps, and located the apartment on the third floor. In the tarnished brass frame above the knocker was a hand-lettered name, "Shelby." Gene knocked. He tried the door. Locked. His watch told him it was only three-forty. Hank wouldn't be home yet. Gene went up the flight of steps toward the fourth floor as far as the landing where he had a clear view of Hank's door. He set down his briefcase, took off his jacket, loosened his tie, and rolled up his sleeves.

Just past four, Hank in a tie and blue dress shirt wet under the armpits came into view. He set a plastic grocery bag on the concrete floor and unlocked the door. As he stooped to pick up the bag, Gene bolted down the stairs and collided with him. They careened through the door. A carton of milk splatted on the parquet floor. Hank stumbled across the room. Gene spun him and put all his strength into an upper cut that sprawled Hank on the futon. Before he could recover, Gene was on top of him.

"You son-of-a-bitch." Gene grabbed Hank's tie and gave a sharp yank.

Hank's teeth rattled.

"What did you tell them?" Gene yelled.

"Fuck you." Hank bucked and tried to knee Gene in the crotch.

Gene took Hank by his thinning hair and slammed his head against the wall. "Talk or I'll smash your goddam skull."

"Lay off."

Gene backhanded him hard. "Tell me."

Hank crossed his wrists in front of his face. Gene straightened but seized a handful of Hank's hair. "Don't make me wait. I'm not in a patient mood."

Blood drizzled from Hank's nostril. "They called me last March. Don't know how they found me. A guy named Cutter.

Came and saw me. Asked all kinds of stuff about you. I told them the truth, about training the dog, working out, shacking up with Mrs. Simmons, stuff like that."

"Liar." Gene tightened his grasp on Hank's hair.

"Wait," Hank yelped. "Cutter left me his number. I kept him up to date on what was going on with you. After the party, I told him George was a homo. A creep named Pierce coached me. He said to say that you and George were having sex and using coke and heroin. That you hit on me for a three-some when Michael was there."

"You bastard."

"Gene, give me a break." He ran a finger under his nose. "Pierce wanted me to tell another guy, somebody named Breighton. I said no. He offered to get me a job at the Pentagon. Told me he'd get me a place to live if I'd name someone else who could vouch for my story. I gave him two names."

Two? Gene's heart thudded.

"Priscilla Simmons," Hank said. "Cutter called her, then your wife. Mrs. Westmoreland was willing to say she'd left you because of drugs and your having orgies with gay guys. Cutter told us how to find Breighton, but we weren't supposed to let on that Cutter sent us. We contacted Breighton separately, a week apart, so it wouldn't look like we were in it together. Breighton was really freaked out. Said that corroborated evidence from somebody named Durnsa."

Gene curled his fingers inside the neck of Hank's shirt and jerked him forward, then shoved him backwards. Hank's head banged the wall. He groaned.

Gene got to his feet. Hank and Priss and Donna. And NSA forwarding the recording of the intercepted call from Vassiliev. Shit. Hacker was blessed with maniacal cunning. Gene was so discredited even the press wouldn't believe his story.

Hank struggled to sit forward, ran his hand through his hair, and rested his elbows on his knees. "I called Mrs. Simmons a week ago. Told her what we did probably cost you your job. She said you deserved a lot worse. She's really out to get you. It's like she wants you disgraced or something."

Sure. So Gene's reports of her stalking wouldn't be believed and lead to the loss of custody of her daughter.

"Your wife's the same." Hank attempted a weak smile. "Gene, you really have a way with women."

Gene frowned. Donna hated him, but his loss of income would hurt her. He faced the glass door to the balcony and kicked the leaking milk carton, then walked through the puddle to the murky window. Three floors below him Route 450, asphalt and tar and endless tangles of telephone wires, was clogged with traffic. The sun was feverish. At eye level, the Beltway bridge over the road was smoke gray.

Hank had buried his face in his hands. His body was already old, his clothes rumpled and spotted with blood.

"Call Breighton," Gene said. "Tell him you lied. Call Priss and tell her what happened today. Shake her up."

Hank's lips curled. "I wouldn't give you the sweat off my balls."

Gene was on him in an instant and slapped him so hard his head snapped. "Do it or I'll kill you. Harry's still at the office. Call him now." Gene raised his hand.

Hank cowered. Gene dragged him to the telephone on the kitchenette wall. Hank fumbled with his personal phone book. Gene watched him open to the B's, find Breighton, and dial.

"Mr. Breighton? This is Henry Shelby. Yeah. You said to call if I had anything further to report. The son-of-a-bitch is—"

Gene closed his fingers around Hank's throat.

"Gene Westmoreland," Hank choked out. "No, got a cold. Anyway, I lied. Everything I told you. Huh? I don't know. I guess—"

"I feel bad that he lost his job," Gene whispered.

"I just feel bad about his losing, you know, his job. I never meant—"

Gene released his grip.

"Because we had a fight and he beat me up," Hank said in a shaky voice. "I wanted to get even."

Gene whispered again. "Tell him the guys who live with me will vouch for me."

Hank watched Gene. "You can check with his house mates. Yeah. Mr. Berthier and Major Carl Swenson. Mrs. Simmons and Mrs. Westmoreland lied, too. I don't know. Guess they got their reasons. Mrs. Simmons was Gene's girlfriend, then he dumped her, and Mrs. Westmoreland is his estranged wife. You know how that is. Yeah. Okay. Sure. Any time." He hung up. "You satisfied?"

"Call Priss," Gene said.

Gene didn't need to intervene this time.

"He told me to tell you what he did to me," Hank said into the phone. "Yeah, he's standing next to me. You? Probably. You ever been beat up by a guy Gene's size?" He handed the phone to Gene. "Wants to talk to you."

"Priss, you listen to me. Call Breighton now. Tell him you lied. I'll know whether you've talked to him or not. If you don't, your daughter is gone." Gene gave the phone to Hank.

Hank listened. "She hung up." He let his frame sag onto a stool at the counter. "You won, asshole. You got what you wanted. Don't hurt me any more."

Gene tightened his tie, unrolled his sleeves, and buttoned his cuffs. "You're safe as long as you carry through. See Breighton and tell him the truth."

"I don't mean that kind of hurt." Hank snatched a paper napkin from the counter and held it to his nose. "Beat me up all you want. I can take it." His eyes watered. "They're letting me see my son again. Only every other weekend for a couple of hours under supervision, but it's a start. Now that I have a good job and I'm off the sauce and living decent and all." His shoulders drooped. "I knew I shouldnta done what they said, but it was the only way, you see what I'm saying? Look, I did you dirt and you beat me up. We're fair and square, okay?"

"Depends on what you do next."

"Don't tell nobody at the Pentagon about this. Best job I ever had. I'm good at it, too. They'll tell you. Thanks to that and the apartment and dressing right and everything, they think I've changed. I *have* changed. Don't hurt me that way."

Hank was begging. Gene's stomach bucked.

Without another glance at Hank, he left.

Back in the tank the next morning, Gene tried to rivet his attention on the argument in the Drury book that Strauss' philosophy was the underpinning of neconservatism, but he couldn't focus. He'd ruined a good dress shirt and suit. Got Hank's blood all over them. Should have had the sense to dress in grubbies. Fact was he hadn't intended to attack Hank. He'd acted on instinct. He shook his head and closed the book. *Being trapped unleashes the beast.*

Now he had two acts he was ashamed of—letting Michael go on seeing Leila under false pretenses and using force on Hank. Sure, he could rationalize both, but it troubled him that he was stooping to the tactics of his enemies. *Beat them at their own game.* Right. And degrade yourself in the process.

Not anymore. When this was over, he didn't want to have to justify his tactics to anybody, least of all to himself. He laughed. He'd told himself if he gave in to Hacker, he wouldn't be Gene Westmoreland anymore. Was he still Gene when he resorted to violence against the weak and suggested that his son prostitute himself? For once in his life, he wished he'd stayed Catholic, after one of his many foster parents had him baptized. Then he could go to confession and have a clean conscience.

Okay, you live and learn. From this day forward, he wouldn't allow the Secretocracy to corrode his soul, even if it meant he lost the war.

When his phone rang, he started. After the second ring, he answered.

"Doctor Westmoreland, this is Dennis Hodgings."

Gene tried to place the name. Ah, yes, the Blue Boy.

"Senator Prowley's staff. I dug up info I'd like to share with you. You free for lunch? Meet me at the National Building Museum. Fourth and G Northwest. Noon sound good? I'll look for you at the fountain."

Gene took the Metro to Judiciary Square and entered the museum just before twelve. He passed immediately into the Great Hall dominated by eight four-story tall Corinthian columns over a terra-cotta tiled floor. In the diffused light from phalanxes of windows five stories above, he located the fountain. No sign of Dennis. He moved toward the splashing water. Half a dozen tourists were scattered among the porticos at the hall's perimeter. He stood in the center and revolved slowly, scanning.

A tenor voice echoed through the columns and colonnades. "Up here." Dennis waved from two floors up, in the balcony atop the brick-red galleries. The sky-blue of his suit stood out against the Renaissance orange.

Gene found the elevator. Dennis, briefcase in hand, met him when the door slid open.

"Let's stroll," Dennis said, amiable to a fault. "Great building. I often bring my lunch over here—when I get a lunch break. So serene and only four blocks from the office."

Gene walked beside him the length of the gallery while Dennis chattered.

"One of the unheralded wonders of Washington. They hold inaugural balls here. Can you believe this place was built in the 1880's?"

"What did you want to tell me?" Gene said.

"I'm coming to that. You've been talking to Mavis Evans, Senator Danley's legislative assistant and—" He paused as a pair of tourists came toward them. "Top of the day to you." He flipped his hair out of his face and ambled on until they were out of earshot. "And you've been meeting with Julia Yancy. You shouldn't be doing that."

"What makes you think I've seen either of them?"

"Have you ever heard of the PRISM?" Dennis said.

"Restricted to surveillance of suspected terrorists."

"Precisely. The president interprets the law to allow us to eavesdrop on those who might disrupt national security. Besides, we track your cell phone with radio direction finding, so we always know where you are. And then there's the work of the National Applications Office."

"Airborne and satellite imagery?" Gene said. "But those sources are strictly for foreign intelligence."

Dennis shook his head. "The president changed all that. We have had to reinvent the law."

Gene's stomach tightened. "Congress won't stand for it."

"Only those members who are steadfastly in our camp will be allowed to know. Besides, Congress is in our hands."

"Elections are coming up," Gene said.

"Our strategists have emplaced programs to assure that ours will always be the majority party. The president's Make America Great Again spiel, the privatization of Social Security—really a plan to greatly expand the stock market—medical savings plans. We've made no secret of our need to see to it that everyone is an investor rather than a beneficiary. Why do you think we've avoided regulating the subprime mortgage market? Investors and property owners always vote for the right. And now we're 'starving the beast'—cutting taxes to the point that government will have to get smaller. We've increased that national debt so much that the bleeding-heart programs like Head Start and WIC will eventually be phased out. Medicare and Social Security will be cut. All they do is encourage dependence anyway."

"You're not making sense," Gene said. "Many of the administration's programs have little to no support in Congress."

"Be patient. Our thinking is long-term. Meanwhile, your Mustang GLX, not GLZ, by the way—" Dennis allowed himself a hearty giggle. "—shows up clearly in imagery. We have multiple means of keeping tabs on you. Adding your name to the list of known terrorists helped. And then there's data mining of millions of telephone conversations—"

Gene caught the gasp before it escaped. "You can't stop me talking to anyone I want to."

"We can make things uncomfortable for you." Dennis stopped and surveyed the columns. "Did you know that these are among the largest indoor columns in the world?"

"You've used up your ammunition. Leila Dellaspada—"

Dennis' brows went up. "You know about that?"

"And Vassiliev. I've lost my clearances and soon will be fired. What else can you threaten me with?"

Dennis lifted a manila envelope from his briefcase. "I don't suppose you've ever seen these." He took out a set of photos. "Lovely, isn't she?"

Glossy black-and-white photos showing the glaring distortion of a flash bulb. A grinning naked woman in sexual acts with two men. In the last of them, still grinning, she was being penetrated anally and vaginally.

"Makes me puke," Gene said.

"Be stalwart. You know who she is?"

"I don't want to know."

"I'm going to tell you anyway. She's your mother."

Gene flinched.

"We haven't been able to determine who your father was," Dennis said. "Might be one of the men here. These were taken nine months before you were born."

Gene closed his eyes and turned away.

"Her name was Mary O'Neill," Dennis went on with a news announcer's lilt, "daughter of Irish immigrants. As a prostitute in Burrell, Pennsylvania, she barely got by—as you can see, she wasn't pretty—and did porn on the side to make ends meet. Right after her baby was born, she got into a disagreement with her pimp. Killed him with an ice pick, then hacked off his penis. She abandoned her baby and went on the lam. Took the police six weeks to find her—still in Burrell, by the way. She denied the baby was hers, so it was put in an orphanage. She died in prison sixteen years later."

"You've concocted this story," Gene said.

"We can prove everything. County and city records. All sealed at the time. They wanted to give the child a chance for a normal life."

"Nothing is beyond you, is it?"

Dennis' face sobered. "Extremism in pursuit of the good of the nation is no vice."

"Okay. You've shown me these pictures. So what?"

"We thought your son might enjoy them. Leila says he's quite an earnest and naïve young man."

"That's unspeakable," Gene spat.

"Not at all. I just spoke it and will speak it again. Unless you cease your dealings with Mavis and Julia."

"I'll do as my conscience dictates."

"As you see fit," Dennis said. "Then we might be forced to take yet another step. Your homosexual orgies might accidentally find their way onto the internet—with your name prominently displayed, of course. Would you like to set up another meeting so I can show you the videos?"

"There can't be videos. It never happened."

"Amazing what a little computer tinkering can do. Replace one face with another. I could show the Pope *in flagrante delicto* through the miracle of undetectable modern technology. The videos are masterpieces. Manifest debauchery. You must see them. Let's set a date—"

"You're enjoying this," Gene said. "God have mercy on you."

"I'm not religious anymore. Religion is an encumbrance for the ruling class."

"You want to take everything from me—my family, my good name, my job. How do you expect me to make a living?"

"You can make a bundle in the porn industry. How big's your cock?"

Rage constricted Gene's voice. "Do your damnedest. You'll be unmasked. Hacker, Prowley, Pierce, the president, the lot of you."

"Who?" Dennis tilted his head as if in surprise. "I never implied any of those notables were involved in this. I can even prove *I'm* not implicated. We are gentlemen."

"Plausible deniability."

Dennis laughed good-naturedly. "*Sine qua non.* You enjoying the Leo Strauss?"

Gene moved slowly toward the elevator. Dennis' laughter echoed through the Great Hall.

The walk from the Anacostia Metro station through the graying October afternoon gave Gene respite. His muscles were working, the air, dirty as it was, moved into his lungs, the jitters in his hands all but disappeared. The guard in the entrance shack barely acknowledged him as he passed. He was no longer a figure of ridicule. He'd become part of the landscape.

He flipped on the light in the tank and dropped into his chair. How in the world did they find out he was talking to Mavis and Mrs. Yancy? Jesus, every phone he used must be monitored. Or, more likely, they were tapping Danley's phones. And Yancy's. Maybe they used data mining to know which phones to focus on. They even knew he was studying Leo Strauss. Had he mentioned that on the phone? Yes, when he talked to Mavis. So they'd bugged her cell. The *Post* had reported that telephone companies were cooperating with NSA as part of the PRISM program. The Secretocracy was tracking his car and cell phone. He assumed they were reading his emails. Maybe they were opening his surface mail, too. From now on his business would have to be conducted face-to-face, and he'd have to travel by Metro.

Meanwhile, how much of Dennis' tale about his parentage was accurate? The narrative had the ring of truth, but these men were experts at mixing a molehill of fact with a mountain of falsehood. Did he care that he was the son of a strumpet and one of her johns? Would Michael be troubled? Not enough for Gene to give in. He could attempt to verify Dennis' story—go to Burrell and rummage through the city and county records. No. He'd learned in the string of foster homes that he couldn't claim lineage to anything.

The other threat did worry him. If Gene were publicly disgraced, he'd have a hell of time getting a job anywhere, certainly not in government or education, probably not in the private sector. He felt the familiar cold in his belly. The president's Secretocracy was rasorial. It would exploit any means, moral, legal, or otherwise, to bring Gene to his knees.

More troubling by far was the larger picture. The American people had elected the president who brought the Secretocracy into existence. What would it take to jolt the American public awake?

That night before they cooked together, Gene fetched two beers from the fridge and took Michael to the lawn.

"Beer, huh?" Michael said. "More bad news coming, right?"

"Screw thy courage to the sticking place," Gene said.

"Holey Moley. Shakespeare. We must be sinking fast."

Gene told him in detail about the meeting with Dennis. "Assume every phone you're on is bugged."

Michael eased his body to the grass and sat leaning against the stone barbeque. "So I'm the progeny of a cold-blooded business shark on my mother's side and a whore on my father's."

"It doesn't matter," Gene said. "You are who you are. You're not your ancestors. Besides, it may not be true. Dennis' story about my debauchery is pure fiction."

"I want to know. I'll cut class tomorrow and drive to Pennsylvania."

Gene sat next to Michael and opened his beer. "I can't tell you how sorry I am. I wanted to tell you before Dennis got to you."

"Thank you." Michael shook his head. "God, this must be hard on you."

"My soul's gotten lots of callouses these last few months. I can take it."

"I can, too, Dad, but I want to know."

"Then go find out."

When Gene shuffled in from work the following night, Michael was striding up and down the foyer.

"It's true," he said. "I had to prove I was your son to get into the archives. I went through a dozen different files to piece the story together. Mary O'Neill was arrested repeatedly for prostitution and obscenity. They found an abandoned baby in her rented room. She denied she'd ever had a child, even though the hospital records proved she had. The authorities considered the child a foundling, named him Eugene Burrell Westmoreland, and put him in the county orphanage. She was convicted of the murder and mutilation of William Tuttle—described during the trial as her procurer—and imprisoned."

Gene mopped his face. "How're you holding up?"

"I'm fine. Now I can move on with my life."

"Too bad we don't get to choose our parents. You could have done a whole lot better."

"Huh-uh," Michael said. "I looked at your records, too. Ran away, what, seven times? 'Bright as a new nickel,' your social worker wrote about you, 'but stubborn and self-reliant.' She got that right. For a foundling, you've done pretty well."

They headed up to the attic together.

"I've got a favor to ask," Gene said. "You're in touch with your mother, right?"

"No more often than I have to be. I try to call her once a month or so. Talked to her last week."

They reached the top floor. Gene stripped off his tie. Michael took scrubs from the shelf.

"Find out when she's going to be home," Gene said. "I need to see her but don't want to telephone her for obvious reasons. I'll drop by the house."

"You're out of luck. She's in Saint Michaels. She'll be there until Wednesday."

"You know which hotel?"

"A bed-and-breakfast called the Manse. Used to be a preacher's house. She gave me the phone number in case something came up."

"The Manse is where she and I stayed." Gene set his mouth. "Think I'll drive to Saint Michaels."

The next day, he called Nettie from the Bryson Building and said he'd take leave Monday to catch up on chores at the house.

Set, Gene reminded himself Saturday morning. *A psychological malady in which the patient continues the same pattern of activity and expects the outcomes to change.* He'd known he was risking pain when he let himself care about Nettie. His experience with Donna had taught him nothing. Losing Nettie hurt so much he wanted to go into the fetal position and abandon all activity.

Instead, he was out raking leaves before the sun had cleared the horizon. Hard physical work always got him through. Then came weeding and spading the bed at the eastern side of the house, even though he had nothing to plant there. By ten he had blisters. He'd forgotten to wear work gloves.

Stressing the body relaxed the soul, but physical pain did nothing to ease his hurting heart. The void would stay a void until he filled it with— What? Love. The anguish kicked up a notch.

Monday morning he collared Michael before he left for classes.

"If anybody calls, say I've gone grocery shopping or something. I don't want the Secretocracy to know I'm out of town."

"You're driving to Saint Michaels to see Mom?" Michael said. "She'll be home day after tomorrow."

"Golden opportunity. I'll catch her off guard, confront her in strange territory, not in her citadel. I want to scare the truth out of her."

"About her lying to your security guy?"

Gene shook his head. "About why she's not proceeding with the divorce. My lawyer and I both smell a plot."

"What time will you be home?" Michael said. "Can I use the Mustang tonight? I have a date."

"Drive me to Enterprise Car Rental and you can have it now."

"Why are you renting a car?"

"Because the Secretocracy is tracking my car," Gene said. "Take my cell. They're tracking it, too."

Michael moaned.

Gene grinned. "We'll confuse the hell out of them."

Gene drove his rented Ford out Route 50 across the Bay Bridge, then south to Route 322. The air was sharp and clear, the autumn sun brilliant, the sky a piercing blue. The smell of the earth had changed. Fall was moving toward winter. At Route 33, he turned right and followed it until it became Talbot Street, the main drag through Saint Michaels.

Halfway through town, the double turrets above the Manse's façade caught his eye. He parked and climbed the steps to the porch. The double doors of etched glass stood open. A grey-haired lady put aside her dust cloth and came toward him, ostentatiously gracious.

"May I help you?"

"Mrs. Westmoreland," Gene said. "I understand she's staying here."

The lady frowned and adjusted her apron. "Don't recall the name."

"Donna Westmoreland?"

"Oh, Donna. They went out right after breakfast. You might find them at the House of Lancaster, three blocks south. Red rose over the door. They asked me for a recommendation for lunch."

Gene headed to the street. *They?* Michael hadn't mentioned anybody coming over here with Donna.

It was nearly twelve. He left the car on a side street and headed south on the brick sidewalk. He found the House of Lancaster, a Della Robbia red rose hung prominently on its portico, on the eastern side of Talbot. Gene mounted the steps to the porch and entered the vestibule. There another graying lady, with an armful of menus, greeted him.

"I'm afraid there'll be a wait," she said.

"The folks I'm meeting are seated," he told her. "May I look around for them?"

"Certainly. The dining room's to your right."

The room he entered might once have been a formal parlor, but the aroma of Châteaubriand and Hollandaise left no doubt about its current use. The half-dozen linen-covered tables were occupied, and a jovial hum of conversation and the well-bred tinkle of plates and silverware filled the room from its bright windows to the bar along the inner wall. There a couple lolled, paying attention only to each other—a man Gene didn't recognize and Donna, in sandals, slacks, and a loose-fitting blouse. Gene strolled among the waiters and slid onto the stool next to Donna.

"What can I get for you?" the bartender asked with exaggerated cheerfulness.

Gene put a fifty on the bar. "Pinot noir."

Donna laughed at something the man said and leaned toward him.

"She was quite discreet," the man said. "Told me we could take our time. She'd clean up after we were dressed."

"We should have gotten out earlier," Donna said.

The bartender brought Gene's drink. "Anything else, sir?"

"What do you have for healing moral decay?"

For the first time, Donna turned, saw him, and recoiled.

The bartender laughed. "At the mixology academy, they always recommend a Rusty Nail."

"Bring the lady one," Gene said breezily. He offered Donna a shy smile. "Hi."

She jerked backwards, her face bloodless.

"And see what the gentleman will have," Gene said to the bartender. "Something to bolster a sagging—um—spirit. He'll need it."

The man was on his feet. "Listen, asshole—"

"Wait." Donna quavered. "He's my husband."

The man glared at her. "You told me—"

"The divorce isn't, you know, final yet," Donna said.

"Isn't begun yet, either," Gene added helpfully.

The man's face tightened. "I'll wait for you at the B&B."

He marched toward the door.

"Sir?" the bartender called after him. "Your bill—"

"I'll cover it," Gene said with a never-mind wave.

Donna's voice grated. "What are you doing here?"

"We should talk," Gene said. "Let's revisit the notion of an amicable divorce. Especially now—" He tipped his head toward the door. "—that you've decided chastity is a dispensable virtue."

"You of all people—first that slut, Priss, and now some-body named Nettie." She fixed him with a glare of pure hatred. "You use women and cast them aside. Priss has your number—" She caught herself and closed her mouth.

"So you and Priss have been comparing notes. Did she tell you of any techniques—you know, foreplay, angle of entry—I didn't use with you?"

She slapped him. Diners turned.

She put her elbows on the bar and bent her head to her folded hands. "No scene. Please."

"Why not? Spices things up. Particularly now that I've caught you in virtual *flagrante dilecto*—just like the Pope, only real."

"What?"

"Never mind. Donna, I don't care if you sleep with a whole battalion, serially or all at once—if you like that sort of thing. What I want is to get on with the divorce."

The bartender presented Donna with a Rusty Nail. "Learned to make these from a master of the trade. The secret is the proportions. Another for you, sir?"

"Just the check," Gene said.

Donna massaged her cheekbones.

"How about it?" Gene said. "We could find a separation counselor—"

"I'm not ready to move yet."

"What are you waiting for?"

"Completion of, what do you call it, data collection," she said.

"I think they call it discovery in divorce court."

"Whatever. I'm going to pin you to the wall."

"With a rusty nail?"

Triumph showed in her face. "With evidence. Your sick-ening lifestyle." She was gleeful. "I'll have witnesses and affi-davits. Even a video."

Gene worked to conceal his surprise. She was going to use the security allegations against him in court. He needed a tad more confirmation. He cleared his throat. "You make it sound like I've been participating in—" He took a breath. "—*sexual orgies* or *debauchery* or *drug abuse* or something."

She blanched. He'd found her out.

"You know it's not true," he said.

"I know nothing of the kind."

"You're starting to believe your own propaganda," he said, "like a certain administration which shall remain unnamed." He got to his feet. Long trip to Washington. Plenty of time to think things through en route home. He called to the bartender. "Keep the change."

When he left the restaurant, there was no traffic. At the signal in the middle of town two black SUVs were parked in the cross-walk preventing access to Talbot Street. Three men in suits wearing wires in their ears were pacing behind the roadblock. Gene approached the policeman standing in the middle of the intersection.

"What's the problem?"

"The former head of the EPA." The officer was scowling.

"He's a problem?" Gene laughed.

The officer chuckled. "You might say that. Every time he comes to Saint Michaels, they land his helicopter at the Easton Airport and block the roads while they drive him to his place outside of town. Same when the vice president shows up."

"Must piss off the locals."

"You got that right." The officer grinned. "We fixed his wagon once, though. Every year in March we have shopping cart races—we decorate the carts and people dress up and a guy pushes while a woman rides and everybody gets a little soused. Well, wouldn't you know it, the EPA chief's entourage shows up in the middle of the race and demands we clear the street. Nope, we say. The Secret Service gets downright uppity, but we stick to our guns, and goddam if the EPA chief doesn't have to wait until a bunch of drunks finish their race. We were happy campers that night."

"I'm surprised he didn't send you to Guantánamo," Gene laughed.

"Folks around here are pretty fed up with the guy in the White House. I voted for him. Then—" The officer watched the horizon above Gene's head. "Then came the fracas at the border and separating children from their mothers and no way to reunite families. That was after the big tax break for the rich. And getting buddy-buddy with Kim Jong-un and Putin, and—" He took a deep breath and straightened. "Anyway we got real tickled about the race. Things are changing, buddy. The little guys are talking back."

One of the earplug men waved to the policemen. All three got into the SUV's and drove off.

"All clear," the officer said.

Gene hurried to the Ford.

Things were changing. The people were waking up. For the first time he could remember, Gene felt a spark of hope. Michael would enjoy the officer's story. So would Nettie. *Nettie.* The stab of hurt surprised him.

Barry Tilden's calendar was full. He agreed to meet Gene for lunch at Côte d'Azur the middle of the following week. After pleasantries, Gene told him about the trip to Saint Michaels. "She's going to use the filth in the divorce court, the lies they invented to deprive me of my clearances."

Barry toyed with his lobster bisque. "The federal government would give her that kind of data?"

"No. She's got the stories from what I'm calling the Secretoc-racy—those guys aligned against me. Now all she needs is either willing witnesses or sworn statements to introduce as evidence."

"I doubt that Mrs. Simmons and Mr. Shelby would be willing to perjure themselves. What's the possibility she could get copies of the statements they made to your security people?"

Gene paused. "I started to say 'none.' That's illegal. On the other hand, so much else that's happened with the Secre-tocracy has been, at minimum, extra-legal."

"And the purported pictures of you in orgies?"

"If they post that trash on the internet, she can copy them for free. They're faked, Barry. How easy is it to detect doctored videos?"

"Depends," Barry said. "In the predigital days, it was pretty easy. With computer imaging, it's a lot harder, especially if they're expertly done."

"So even without witnesses or statements, she could give us a run for our money."

"Yep."

"Why?" Gene shook his head. "What's she going to gain? She knows I'll lose my job any day. I won't have money for alimony."

Barry chuckled. "Poor old Gene. You don't get it, do you? She doesn't give a damn about the money. She's got her father, right? He's financing the whole divorce operation. I'll lay you odds he paid for her trip to Saint Michaels."

"If not the money, then what?"

"Your son. The hope, I suspect, is that if your presumed indecency were made public, Michael would turn against you."

"She's never cared about Michael," Gene said.

"It's not Michael, it's you. He's one of the few weapons she has to hit you where it hurts."

"He already knows all about the phony videos."

"*She* doesn't know that."

Gene heard nothing more from Dennis. He waited, sick with anticipation. A week later when he got home from "the office," George told him Michael was waiting for him in the attic. He found his son on his bed, eyes closed, arms behind head, earphones pumping. The music was audible ten feet away. Gene touched his arm. He sat up.

"I didn't hear you." Michael flipped off the earphones.

"I could hear you. You'll puncture your eardrums."

"They came."

Gene knew what he meant.

"Left them on your bed," Michael said. "Fasten your seatbelt. They're pretty raw."

Gene sat on the bed and opened the ten-by-thirteen clasp envelope. The nine photos fell out. Inside, he found a single sheet of paper. "This is your grandmother the year before your father was born," the Courier typescript read. "See if you can guess which one your grandfather is." Gene breathed deeply. "Your father will deny his heritage," the note went on, "but we thought you should know your rootstock."

Gene examined the pictures one by one. Sexually explicit, yes, but how could even the most debased find images this ugly arousing? Maybe people addicted to pornography enjoyed it *because* it was repulsive.

"Let's hold a ritual burning in the barbeque pit," Michael said.

"We have to keep them," Gene said, "for legal proceedings sometime in the future. You okay?"

"I got past the rough part when I went to Pennsylvania. I knew what to expect."

PART FOUR

Redux

Chapter 14

Unraveling Reinterpretation

Six-thirty, Wednesday morning, the seventh of November 2018. As Gene came down the servants' steps, the dining room television's nasal-voiced speaker repeated the news over and over. "In what observers read as a major rejection of the administration's policy and Republican support for the president, the lower house of Congress will pass into the control of the Democrats in January."

"The commentator lacks understanding of syntax," George's voice said.

The television went on to name notable winners in the Senate including Danley and Prowley.

Gene glanced into the dining room. George, in his dressing gown and blurred with sleep, sat at the end of the table drinking coffee. Carl, freshly shaved and bathed, was next to him in uniform. Opposite was Michael, in sleeveless tee-shirt and jeans, eating cereal. All three watched the screen intently.

Gene soft-boiled eggs and microwaved bacon. Breakfast and coffee in hand, he took a chair next to Carl and pulled the *Washington Post* from the middle of the table. Its headlines blared the news—"Democrats seize House." A little reading told him that the Republicans increased their seats in the Senate.

"Wow."

"Shh." George bristled, then riveted his gaze on the screen.

When the news ended, George clicked off the television with the remote, stood, and raised his arms high. "Hallelujah. God's in his heaven, all's right with world."

Michael turned to Carl. "You think things will really change now?"

"The president is still in the White House," Carl said. "The Commander-in-Chief alone controls the armed forces. More important, he has the entire intelligence and security apparatus in his iron grip. And the Republicans increased their hold on the Senate."

"Congress," George said with dignity, "controls the purse strings *and* has impeachment power."

"You think they'll impeach the president?" Michael said.

"Not right away," George said. "But now all those investigations in the House will be reinitiated. And new ones will get underway. The administration will resist, refuse to hand over documents, or allow insiders to testify. It will finish up before the Supreme Court—"

"Which the administration has packed with allies," Michael said.

"Even so," George said, "more scandals, like violations of the Hatch Act and political cleansing at the Justice Department and FBI and violations of the emolument clause will be laid open. Justice is on life support. Interior has changed the definitions of things like 'strip mining' to allow industry leeway. The Environmental Protection Agency encourages polluters, and it's muzzled its employees so they can't talk to the press or Congress. And on the secret side of government, Defense and Intelligence, both under the firm control of the president, warrantless wiretapping, intimidation, and horrors we know not of will come to light."

Gene shook his head. Horrors. George didn't know the half of it.

"Popular sentiment for impeachment is growing," George said. "Polls show that something like half of the population would support it." His face soured. "The abuses of this administration will be recorded as one of the most shameful chapters in the history of the country. Within the year, exposés in books and the press will become a deluge."

"They already have," Carl said. "But I don't know. With so much damage to undo on other fronts, the House ain't gonna rush headlong into that snake pit. Besides, an impeachment motion would tear the country apart. And don't forget—the Republicans control the Senate."

George was righteous. "They simply must impeach, whatever the cost. The nation cannot tolerate flagrant violations of the Constitution."

Gene laughed. "You underestimate the administration. It can be diabolical in crushing threats."

"You are too cynical, *mon bel ami.*"

"So," Michael said, "the best we can do is hope."

"And pray," George said.

The rains came. The wet summer did nothing to forestall a wet autumn. For a week, heaven bathed earth with downpours followed by drizzle. Temperatures dropped to just above freezing. Gene stored his summer suits and short-sleeved dress shirts next to Michael's shorts and tank tops in the closet at the top of the steps. Out came the woolens, the sweaters, the cords. As Daylight Savings Time ended and the days shortened, Gene discovered that heat in the tank was scarce. A complaint to the management brought no response. Gene sat at his desk in sweaters reviewing job announcements and drafting applications. After running out of jobs to shoot for, he worked his way through Strauss' assertion that only the elite, the natural leaders, are capable of accepting the fact that moral truth doesn't exist. The masses must be misled for their own good. Hacker himself couldn't have said it better.

By late November, the tank was too cold to work in. A thorough examination of the room revealed a plethora of electrical outlets—this place must have been a workshop—and two heat vents in the ceiling, both cold to the touch. The building management informed him that his home office needed to reduce expenses and had trimmed the monthly cantonment payment to the Bryson Building. The office had told Bryson to cut amenities, including air conditioning and heat, to offset the decrease. Gene argued that the tank was becoming uninhabitable. It hadn't been cleaned in months, and the chill threatened to freeze his morning coffee. His quartering there, Bryson said, was intended to be temporary. There were three options: take leave, take leave without pay, or resign.

The next Saturday, Gene bought a space heater at Sears. He drove to the Bryson Building and carried the heater, a broom, dustpan, mop, liquid cleaner, and rags into the tank. By evening, the room was clean. Plugged in with an extension cord and placed next to his chair, the heater freed him from the need for gloves.

Then, during the second week of December, the curtain disappeared. Next, the fluorescent bulbs in the ceiling fixtures were missing. A floor lamp borrowed from George gave him enough light to work. For good measure, he bought the cheapest coffee pot he could find at Target. He considered moving in a cot and chest of drawers to make his intent plain.

Repeatedly, during the long, cold hours in the tank, his mind's eye wandered from Strauss' imperious prose and sought out an image that, like a contusion on the mend, both hurt and comforted him—a carrot top with green eyes and irreverent freckles. His fingers pressed the ripeness of her breasts as their bodies folded together. His ears remembered her pert laughter. A hint of gardenias brought tears to his eyes.

Surprised at the depth of his feeling, he berated himself for sliding into vulnerability. The sooner he hardened himself, the better. As he forced his attention back to Strauss' text, his brain recalled eyebrows always arched as if in permanent surprise.

At home, he searched the internet for anything resembling an exposé of his putative homosexual forays. He opened YouTube and spins offs, ran his name through GOOGLE, and hunted using the YAHOO search engine. Plenty of hits on the town of Burrell and Westmoreland County and on the Vietnam general with the same name. Nothing on him except his doctoral dissertation and academic articles he'd published while at MIT. Why were they delaying? Maybe their monitoring showed no calls to Danley's office or the Yancy home. Maybe the Secretocracy had concluded he was prostrate.

On the other hand, none of his job applications resulted in an interview. The Secretocracy might have poisoned the personnel system against him. Easy enough to do. Word gets around with nothing ever appearing in writing. No bites from industry or universities. The panic in his belly was gathering strength.

Still he hadn't been fired. The Secretocracy was using every weapon it could garner to force him to resign. These guys were smart. By not terminating him, they avoided the possibility of litigation. Not that he could win, of course, but during the hearings he might level unsavory accusations. The president didn't need that. Especially if he could freeze Gene out.

Christmas was only two weeks off. George had let the day pass unobserved the last couple of years, and Carl did his celebrating with his boys. Gene told Michael that neither of them should spend money on gifts this year—every penny had to be saved against the possibility that Gene's income would cease with no warning. But the thought of giving Michael nothing at all sickened Gene. On AMAZON.COM he found the complete works of Christopher Marlowe, a handsome five volume set at eight-hundred dollars. Out of the question. He searched Barnes and Noble and Powell Books for something he could afford.

At six that night, without thinking, he got off the Metro a stop early, at Takoma, and found himself climbing Nettie's hill. As he approached her house in the autumn dark, he asked himself what in the world he thought he was doing. Her windows glowed warm, and the porch light welcomed him. He rang.

When she opened the door, her mouth dropped open. She was wearing sea-green scrubs many sizes too large.

"Scrubs?" he said.

"They're yours. You forgot them."

They stood staring at each other.

"May I come in?" he said.

She stepped aside, and he entered.

She gestured toward the back of the house. "Come in the kitchen."

He followed her.

At the stove, she turned off the burners and covered the cooking food. "Sit down. Coffee?"

"Thanks."

He stirred and sipped, wondering what to say. "How are you?"

"I've seen better days. You've lost weight."

"Things are rough all over."

They sat silent. Why the hell was he here?

"Shafter still after you?" he asked.

"The weekend after I saw you last, I told him I couldn't spend the night with him because my period was due."

"He bought it?"

She sighed. "He said it wouldn't bother him if it didn't bother me. I told him I'm Jewish and a menstruating woman is considered unclean. He said that was fine. His thoughts about me weren't very clean anyway."

"Shafter makes me feel slimy for being the same gender."

"When he touched me, I felt his lust. When you touched me, I felt your awe."

Ouch. Gene looked away.

"Right after that," she said, "unbeknownst to FIBO, I applied for administrative assistant slots at beltway bandits, and a job with Wellbourne Security Systems came through. They've arranged for my clearances to remain in effect when I transfer. The day after I received their acceptance letter, Shafter told me he was tired of waiting for me. He was going to bring in his secretary from NPO to replace me. I resigned on the spot to avoid having a dismissal on my record. I'll start at Wellbourne after the beginning of the year. Higher pay and shorter commute with better benefits."

"I'm happy for you," Gene said.

"Thank you."

"You're welcome."

Sarah, in high-heel boots and jeans, swept in. "Mom, what time—" She saw Gene. A hopeful smile flashed briefly across her face.

"Sarah . . ." Nettie began.

Sarah waved her hands, palms out. "Say no more." She turned toward the door. "Good to see you, Gene," she tossed over her shoulder and disappeared.

Nettie folded her hands. That told him she was thinking. He drank coffee.

"Are you, you know, *dating*?" she asked.

"No. Are you?"

She shook her head. "When I met you, I knew I'd found the man I want to spend my life with."

That stung. He looked at the door. He could leave any time.

"I sent you away." She bowed her head. "I was wrong. I know I hurt you. Will you forgive me?"

"If you'll forgive me. You called me coward once. You were right on the money."

"Most men are afraid of commitment because they don't want to lose their freedom. Commitment wouldn't take *your* freedom away. With you, freedom is in-born. What you fear is the anguish of loss." She drummed the table with her fingers. "You don't know how many times I almost called you."

"I wish you had."

She took a pained breath and stared at him. "This hurts. Let's get on with it. Why are you here?"

"I miss you," he said.

Her brows wrinkled, and her mouth opened, then shut. "So you're the one to make a move." Her laugh was ironic. "I thought you were too proud."

"Pride's my downfall."

"No, fear is your fatal flaw. I don't like that. Maybe you'll always be that way. But sometimes I have to take what I can get."

He watched her.

"I have no pride," she said. "I don't want to be without you another day."

Gene slowly filled his lungs. A trace of gardenia wakened bittersweet memory. Set himself up again? Risk loss all over again? Accept vulnerability? "Yes."

Her lips trembled. She shut her eyes and hunched forward. "I didn't call you. I was so sure you'd say no."

"I do hold you in awe."

She moved close. "Hold me now."

Gene wrote to Julia Yancy, warning her that the telephone taps were widespread. Best to contact him by regular mail. No answer. He wanted to wait for Mavis to call him, but the edginess was getting the better of him. He never knew when his income might end. Besides, she might telephone him, and the Secretocracy would know what he was doing.

Monday, a week before Christmas Eve, Carl was home— Côte d'Azur had hired carolers for the week—and was therefore stuck with cooking dinner. Michael was folding his laundry in front of the dining room television while Gene worked out. As Gene did concentration curls, Michael's voice echoed from the arch.

"You know that senator you told me about? He's on TV."

With a groan, Gene finished the set, snatched a moist towel, and went to the dining room. Michael's full attention was on the screen. Gene clumped down next to him, dried himself, and set his teeth, prepared to see Prowley's porcupine hair and eyebrows. Instead, he saw the jovial figure of Willis Danley, backed by the marble fireplace and an American flag.

"We are caught in the odd dilemma," Danley was saying to the camera, "that to keep our enemies from knowing something, we also have to keep it from the American people.

Frankly, there are times when the need of the public to know outweighs the importance of secrecy for national security."

The screen split. On one side, labeled "New York," was a smartly coifed woman in a business suit looking at the camera. On the other, called "Washington," was Danley.

"Senator," the woman said, "are you persuaded that your proposal to put more classified information within the reach of the Freedom of Information Act won't result in tipping off the Bashar al-Assads, the Vladimir Putins, and the Kim Chong-uns to strategic data?"

"It could provide them insignificant bits of intelligence," Danley said, his merriness unscathed, "but I think it critical to the health of the Republic that the citizens know as much as possible so that they can make political decisions based on fact."

"That's my man," Gene said.

"Senator," the woman said, "your colleague, Senator Herman Prowley, has voiced the opposite opinion. How do you respond?"

Danley gave the camera a puckish smile. "Senator Prowley and I do not often hear the same drumbeat."

"And that," the woman said, "will have to be the last word. Our guest tonight has been Senator Willis Danley—"

Michael clicked off the set. "You know this guy, right?"

"He's on the Senate Preparedness Subcommittee." Gene hesitated. "The Democrats took the House." He gasped. "My God. There's a chance."

That night Gene typed a letter to Mavis asking to see Danley as soon as possible and saying he had reason to believe that Danley's office phones and her cell were tapped. He mailed it the next morning and waited. Thursday night, Carl brought his cell phone to the attic. "For you."

"Mavis Evans, Gene. I'm calling on a friend's cell. Can you come to the office at the beginning of the week? Congress begins its holiday recess Friday. Everyone will have left town. How about Monday, the twenty-fourth, at four?"

"I'll be there."

Gene put down the phone and thrust his fists into the air with a whoop. *"All right!"*

Carl winked at Michael. "Hey, maybe he's going to score with that lady."

Michael shook his head sadly. "One of his spells. It pains me when he does that in front of others."

"I have an appointment," Gene said. "Christmas Eve at four p.m."

"Dad," Michael said patiently, "you try to work it so your date will *end* at four in the afternoon, not begin." He turned gravely to Carl. "He requires a lot of retraining."

"Danley," Gene yelled. "He's going to see me."

"Who's Dan Lee?" Carl said.

Michael leaped from his seat and threw his arms around Gene. "God almighty damn!"

By Christmas Eve, the federal government was partially shut down, due to the president's insistence of money for a wall on the Mexico border, a demand Congress refused to agree to. Gene took the Metro to Capitol South to prevent the Secretocracy from following his movement to the Russell Building. He whisked past the empty Capitol grounds just as the Taft Carillon struck three-forty-five. To his right, the mammoth capitol Christmas tree stood desolate in the last of the day's pale winter sunshine. Up one block on Constitution to the Russell Building, then through the empty halls to the third-floor office. Only one security stop the entire way. Dominated by a white Christmas tree with red paper bells, Danley's outer office was conspicuously devoid of human presence.

"Gene?" Mavis in a warm up suit was at the inner office door. "Come in."

He followed her through the second office into Danley's inner sanctum. A fire crackled in the fireplace. A Christmas tree stood beside the flag. Danley, a not-quite-believable Santa Claus in blue jeans and a flannel shirt, sat at his desk studying an open binder with acetate pages. When he saw Gene, he bustled to meet him. "Doctor Westmoreland." No one had called Gene by that title in months. The three sat together at the carved table near the fireplace.

"I trust you won't mind if Mavis sits in," Danley said.

"Delighted," Gene said. "I expect Mavis has brought you up to date on my situation."

Danley nodded, his merriness gone. "I talked to the Senate telephone technicians. They tell me there's no way to detect a tap since it wouldn't be done here. The perpetrators would set up a monitoring operation in the commercial telephone switching facilities. I can't even investigate without evidence."

"You believe," Mavis said, "that the president is responsible?"

"Just inference," Gene said. "The larger issue at the moment is what General Hacker and the NPO are up to. I'm in an odd position. I'm no longer cleared, and even if I were, I couldn't reveal information you're not cleared for."

Danley scowled. "Both Mavis and I are cleared for the compartments in Hacker's operation."

"Forgive me for contradicting you, sir," Gene said, "but you are cleared for a fraction of them. In the legislative branch, only Senator Prowley and Vince Dellaspada have access to all the NPO compartments."

"So." Danley's frown darkened. "Start at the beginning. Tell me every detail."

"Without violating the law, I can tell you only the unclassified part." Gene took a deep breath and launched into the narrative he'd practiced. He described his clashes with Hacker, Vassiliev's appearance, the blackmail against Clem and himself, Prowley's threats, the unspeakable photos, and, finally, Hank's confession. "On the operational side, I can't go into the NPO projects both Clem Yancy and I tried so hard to stop, Senator. I was led to believe that there was a compartmented appendix to the NPO charter that justified ventures you are not privy to. I've concluded it doesn't exist. Maybe President Reagan, who set up a similar program, had a verbal agreement with one of Hacker's predecessors. Or maybe Hacker made up the whole thing. In any case, I was cleared for the compartments dealing with these initiatives through a clerical error. By law, I can reveal to no one what I know, but I can tell you where to hunt and hint at what you should find."

Gene relaxed his tense muscles. Danley and Mavis both looked as though he had told them there was anthrax in the air conditioning. It was now or never. *When you move, fall like a thunderbolt.*

Gene bent forward and folded his hands on the table. "Hire me, Senator."

Danley blinked and Mavis' mouth opened.

"Put me on your personal staff." Gene riveted his eyes on Danley's. "Use your power and my knowledge to bring Hacker down."

The hint of a smile, half amused, half admiring, flitted across Mavis' face.

The senator sat unmoving. "Prowley—"

"—would be defeated and disgraced," Gene said.

"Why not a position on the Preparedness Subcommittee staff?" Mavis asked.

"Not as long as Dellaspada's the chief. He's one of Hacker's men. Before Senator Prowley got him hired for his current position, he was an Air Force colonel and a division chief at NPO."

"You've lost your clearances, Gene," Mavis said. "The executive branch would have to restore them."

"Henry Shelby is ready to recant," Gene said. "Hugh Shafter knows the whole fracas was phony. I have plenty of other witnesses if it came to that, but it wouldn't. If the Senator expressed his desire, my exoneration would be complete in hours."

"And the threat to put compromising videos of you on the internet?"

"I'll risk it if you will. Once I'm in a position of strength, I can tell my unclassified story publicly and recover my reputation."

"And heads would roll," Danley said through his teeth.

"Forgive me, sir," Gene said, "but I doubt it. In this administration, good old boys who screw up don't get canned. They retire with a handsome stipend, are granted pardons, and retreat to think tanks and private industry."

"Gene," the senator said, "how do I know you're not fabricating this story?"

"Have your personal staff review the NPO budget. Go through footnotes to the addenda to the appendices to the classified annexes and the supporting documentation and feasibility studies. You'll find telltale inconsistencies. Price out the line items in the shell budget. The padding will stand out. Check out the sources for the justification. The legitimate intelligence agencies don't support it—it's the Office of Special Compartmented Intelligence—OSCI—against the rest."

"Shell budget?" Mavis and Danley exchanged glances.

Gene considered how much he could say without violating security. "All I can tell you is that the budget you've been reviewing is not the real NPO budget. Until now, the subcommittee staff, under Dellaspada, concealed the duplicity. You may have to go to Federal Intelligence Budget Office or maybe even subpoena documents from the National Preparedness Office itself to get the relevant data. I predict Hacker and Shafter will drag their feet, plead security risks. Prowley may move to stop you. The president may invoke executive privilege. It's going to be a grim struggle. Meanwhile, pinion the guys at Department of Energy and National Nuclear Security Administration. Subpoena all information about negotiations with NPO."

Mavis tensed. "What do DOE and Nuclear Security have to do with NPO?"

"Under the law, I can't tell you what I know," Gene said.

"You're implying nuclear weapons?" Danley said.

"I simply recommend you see where it leads."

Danley and Mavis stared at him.

"That is but one small example of how I can point to fruitful areas of investigation." Gene tried to soften the triumph in his voice.

"You're talking weeks, maybe months, of research," Mavis said. "We have no independent staff cleared for NPO compartments."

"There's another way to prove my case," Gene said. "Mavis, as I remember, the D.C. police told you that General Pierce visited Clem hours before his death."

"Inspector Henley said the patient care technician told him that. Mrs. Yancy told me the same thing. Doctor Yancy telephoned her after Pierce left."

"Call Hacker on his unlisted number, the one the president is supposed to use. No one but him answers it. Tell him it's urgent—that you're concerned about Clem's death because there are security implications. Say you want to talk to General Pierce to see if he can shed any light on what happened."

"Why?" Danley said.

Gene pounced. "Hacker is concealing Pierce's visit to Clem's room that night. He'll tell you Pierce wasn't there."

"But," Mavis said, "we *know* he was there."

"The only evidence of Pierce's presence there that Hacker is aware of is the statement of the patient care technician. He doesn't know about Clem's call to his wife. They can claim that the technician misidentified Pierce. They've faked documents to show that Pierce was in Spain at the time."

"Mavis, call him," Danley said. "Flip on the speaker phone."

"The call may be intercepted," Gene warned.

"Fine," Danley said. "I want them to know."

Mavis punched buttons on the phone. The sound of the connection came from hidden speakers. After a single ring, a man's voice said, "Hacker."

"This is Mavis Evans in Senator Danley's office. So sorry to bother you at home, General, but an urgent matter has come up. Senator Danley was greatly distressed over Doctor Yancy's death. He's just learned from the police that General Pierce visited Doctor Yancy immediately before his death. The senator would like a private, off-the-record interview with General Pierce to see if he can tell us anything about why Doctor Yancy took his own life."

"I see," Hacker said. "General Pierce, as much as he would like to help, can't shed any light on Doctor Yancy's death. We've told the police that in the interest of security we can't allow General Pierce to be questioned. In any case, the man who claims he saw General Pierce at the hospital that night is mistaken. General Pierce was on TDY in Madrid at the time."

Danley and Mavis caught their breath. Gene beamed.

"Hacker," Danley shouted. His pate was reddening rapidly. "Let's get a couple of things straight."

"Excuse me," Hacker said with dignity. "To whom am I speaking?"

"Willis Danley."

Hacker was silent.

"First, don't you ever lie to me again. Got that?"

"Senator," Hacker said in a choked voice, "I had no intention—"

"Second, I want you and Hugh Shafter to meet me on 2 January to review projects in which we have a common interest."

"Senator," Hacker stammered. "I don't see how . . . what with the holidays—"

"January second. You'll both be at the Russell Building. Call Shafter and tell him."

Hacker burbled inarticulately.

"Two members of my staff will join us, Ms. Mavis Evans and Doctor Eugene Westmoreland. I gather there's been a little misunderstanding over his clearance status. I expect you to get that straightened out before the meeting."

As Danley hung up, he turned to Gene. "As a result of the election, the Democrats lost seats in the Senate. Never mind that those who voted for the Democrats outnumbered those who voted for the Republicans by multiple millions. Every state is allotted two senators. So fewer than 600,000 people in Wyoming are given the same representation in the Senate as almost 40 million in California."

Gene frowned.

"So," Danley said, "I'm still in the minority on the Senate Preparedness Subcommittee. I won't be able to demand hearings on what Hacker and Shafter have done at the behest of the president."

Gene winced.

"But," Danley continued, "the Democrats won a strong majority in the House. It so happens that the new chair of the House Preparedness Subcommittee is my close friend and ally, Congressman Bruce Wallace. I'll suggest that you meet with him and hint that perhaps a House subcommittee investigation is in order."

Gene grinned. "Yes, *sir.*"

As Gene left the Capitol complex, he was reminded of the moment when Hank's hands had lost their grip on his throat and air rushed into his lungs. He stood on Independence Avenue in the twilight, spread his arms, closed his eyes, and relished the pleasure of breathing. From a passing car, he picked up a snatch of "God Rest ye Merry, Gentlemen." *Christmas!* He'd forgotten about it. He had so much to do and so little time.

He hurried down South Capitol and turned left into Southeast toward a vacant lot where he'd seen Christmas trees for sale. He looked in vain for a Frasier fir, had to settle for a balsam. Seven feet tall. Biggest they had. For an extra five dollars, the seller threw in his Santa Claus hat and bundled the tree with net. After a hearty exchange of "Merry Christmas," Gene made for the Navy Yard Metro station. On the train, he telephoned Michael to meet him at the Silver Spring station with the Mustang.

When Gene, hat flopping over his shoulder, lugged the tree into the Kiss 'n Ride, Michael was leaning against the Mustang, arms folded. "God Almighty at midnight."

"Open the hatchback," Gene said. "We'll put it in trunk end first."

They got it in, but not without curses and sweat. As Gene drove to Shepherd Park, with the butt end of the tree between them almost touching the windshield, Michael couldn't control his laughter. "You carried that thing on the Metro? Wearing that cap?"

"And?" Gene said without a smile. "This *is* Washington, D.C. I fit right in. The Lesbian couple with bikes and the man carrying a nativity set barely noticed me. Granted, the lady preacher was offended that I didn't have a free hand to take her literature. And a drunk wanted to hug me or the tree— couldn't tell which."

"I thought we weren't going to have a tree."

"I made an executive decision. We've postponed joy too long."

"I assumed you'd stay at Nettie's tonight," Michael said.

"I wanted to be with you. Besides, she doesn't celebrate Christmas."

Michael peered around the bottom branches of the tree. "For a man who drinks beer to get to sleep, you're smiling a lot."

"Danley hired me. The House Preparedness Subcommittee will be tipped off and will undoubtedly hold hearings."

Michael's mouth gaped.

"Yeah," Gene said, "I'm on Danley's personal staff. I'm getting my clearances back." Gene gave him a play-by-play description of the meeting with Danley. Michael whooped.

As they struggled through the door with the tree, Carl was coming down the spiral staircase, mug in hand. "What the hell is that?"

"A baby whale," Michael said. "What does it look like?"

"So we're going to have a tree after all?" Carl said.

Michael gave him a scowl. "Sometimes, Major, you're a little slow on the uptake. Give us a hand."

They got the tree down the steps to the living room and laid it in front of the fireplace.

"What about ornaments?" Michael wiped his hands on his jeans.

"How are you at threading popcorn?" Gene said.

"George has fresh cranberries left over from the Thanksgiving dinner we never had," Carl said.

"What a sorry bunch we are," Gene said. "We should celebrate every chance we get. Instead we let life's little reverses take center stage. Let's agree here and now we'll change that."

"Pine needles," George said from the arch. "From the front door, up the steps into the foyer, down into the living room, leading to a heap in the middle of the floor."

"Merry Christmas, George," Gene called to him. "Time to stop moping and start rejoicing. We have a lot of missed revelry to make up for."

"You are, as usual, arriving at the correct conclusion in arrears," George said.

"I made a batch of Tom 'n Jerry." Carl held out his cup.

"And I baked cookies," Michael said.

"You don't even know how to turn on an oven," Gene said.

"George does."

George scowled. "He wouldn't hear of brioche or biscotti. Had to be cookies."

"I didn't have your recipe," Michael said, "so we used the one from the chocolate chip package."

"Why?" Gene asked.

Michael shrugged. "Looked like it was going to be a bleak Christmas. No tree. Nothing fancy to eat. I remembered how you always made me cookies on Christmas Eve."

"We decided," George said, "to carouse whether you wanted to or not. I baked a Yule cake and prepared egg nog. There's a leg of lamb ready for the oven. Not traditional, but I like it better than goose."

Gene grinned. "Beat me to the punch, the three of you. God bless you."

"Tell the truth, Dad," Michael said. "For you, things are coming up roses."

Gene nodded wryly. "Senator Danley hired me. We're going to bring Hacker to his knees."

"Alleluia," George cried.

"I'll drink to that," Carl said. "Everybody to the kitchen for a round of Tom 'n Jerry."

All talking at once, they trooped through the dining room. Carl spooned rum and batter into cups and added boiling water. He hoisted his mug. "To a happy Christmas among friends."

They clinked cups. "Merry Christmas."

"*Joyeux Nöel,*" George added.

"Carl says you have cranberries," Gene said to George. "We can thread them with popcorn to put on the tree. If we can figure out how to stand it up."

George raised his hand, palm out. "Go to the attic. In the storeroom next to your bedroom, you'll find three plastic boxes the size of steamer trunks. Bring them to the living room."

Gene gave him a puzzled look, then tipped his head to Michael and Carl. They went up the servants' stairs and toted down the boxes. George met them in the living room. He knelt by the first box and unfastened its lid. Inside in cardboard containers were Christmas ornaments, lights, and garlands.

"You'll find a tree stand and a skirt to put around the base of the tree in the second box. In the third is a crèche from Paris."

Gene lifted a silver ball from the box. "I had no idea—"

"Alex and I collected these over our years together. I haven't had the heart to look at them since he died."

Stuffed to the eyebrows with lamb, yule cake, and cookies and mellowed by rum, Gene and Michael wished George and Carl a last merry Christmas at eleven and headed to the attic.

"I want to do a full workout tomorrow," Gene said. "Come next week, I'll be working long hours. May not have the time or energy for weight lifting."

"I'll plan on a run," Michael said.

"I think you should visit your mother. This is the first Christmas she's been without you."

"She threw me out, remember?"

"Michael, she's the only mother you'll ever have. You've got to come to terms with her, at least in your own mind. Besides, a little kindness will cost you nothing and will mean a lot to her."

"Where's all this coming from? Look at the damage she's done you."

Gene began to undress. "I loved her once."

Michael studied him sadly. "Okay. For your sake, not hers." He took a small box in Christmas wrap from under his pillow. "For you."

"We agreed not to exchange gifts this year."

"You paid for it. I didn't."

Gene tore off the paper. A grade report from The George Washington University for Michael Cantwell Westmoreland, Fall, 2018. Straight A's.

"Michael," Gene gasped. "This is wonderful. I can't tell you—"

"You said not to spend any money. I put all my pay into the account to pay tuition for next semester." Michael blushed. "So this was the best I could do. Sorry it's not more."

"Son, this *is* the best you could do. I'm proud and grateful."

"It means I'll graduate with honors. I'll have a shot at scholarships for grad school. I've been looking at Columbia and University of California."

Gene shook his head slowly. "The best gift of all. Through it all, my heartache was what would happen to you if I became an outcast. Now—" His voice failed. He went to his desk and opened the drawer. He handed Michael a wrapped gift.

"Dad, you *said*—"

"I lie a lot. Open it."

Michael did. The Complete Works of Christopher Marlowe in one volume, paperback, with small print. Michael stared at it, mouth open.

"To remind us both how vulnerable we are to amoral will."

Father and son embraced.

Gene found delicious irony in the scene. Shafter and Hacker were at the witness table in the secure House hearing room, the jewel lights on their microphones glowing. On the platform behind the long desk, Bruce Wallace was poised, dead center in the chairman's seat, with other members to his right and left. Dellaspada, Dennis, and Gene sat in the darkened room behind the witness table, next to Mavis and Danley. Two other senators, back from the Christmas recess early, attended. Prowley was conspicuously absent.

Gene was surprised how large the people in the spotlight at the table in front of him appeared from spectator seats. Shafter bowed his head, as if hiding his face from the light. Hacker sat at attention, as though he were trying to appear larger.

Wallace opened the hearing. "Gentlemen, you are addressing the new chairman of the House Preparedness Subcommittee. I expect brief and straightforward answers to my questions. I'll start with you, General. Why are there compartments in the NPO program whose existence have been concealed from me?"

"Congressman," Hacker began, his demeanor belligerent, "prudence dictates that we keep the number cleared to a minimum. Until now, your subcommittee has not requested—"

"You will clear me, all members of the House Preparedness Subcommittee and all members of the Senate Preparedness Subcommittee for *all* compartments this afternoon. I have a list of them here. Tell me if I have missed any." He turned to a staff member. "Bob—"

The man carried the paper from Wallace to Hacker.

As the general read, his face hardened. "Congressman," he said, "we may have a security violation here. The names of these compartments are in themselves compartmented. Someone has breached security in supplying these names to you."

"Not at all," Wallace said. "You will note that the document you hold in your hand is Top Secret Cobrawing. All the compartment names listed are covered under the Cobrawing compartment, for which, as your records will show, I and the subcommittee staff are cleared. I grant you I do not know what the compartments cover, but I shall by this afternoon."

"That may be impossible, Congressman," Hacker said. "I don't have the paperwork with me. There are administrative procedures—"

"General." Wallace gave him a fatherly smile. "We wish to continue funding NPO programs, do we not? Well, then, surely, we can find a way to overcome administrative hurdles. We have secure telephone, fax, and internet connections with your office. They are at your disposal. The clearances will be forthcoming this afternoon."

Hacker said nothing more.

"Mr. Shafter," Wallace said. "I am disturbed that the weekly contact between the Senior Budget Reviewer for Nuclear Defense Intelligence in your organization and the Senate Preparedness Subcommittee assistant, Ms. Evans, was abruptly discontinued some months ago. The liaison at the time was Doctor Westmoreland, now on the senate subcommittee staff. His replacement is, I understand, General Roderick Pierce. General Pierce will, beginning next Thursday, meet weekly with me and Senator Danley, or in our absence, Ms. Evans and/or Doctor Westmoreland. Not by phone. In person."

Wallace looked from Hacker to Shafter. "One more point before we break to allow General Hacker to phone his office. It is your job, Mr. Shafter, to ensure that agencies operate within their charters. NPO's charter makes no mention of the activities we will be investigating this afternoon. I conclude that these programs are unlawful. Unless, of course, there is an appendix to the charter adding other fields of endeavor. Does such a document exist?"

"Not to my knowledge," Shafter said.

"It does not, Congressman," Hacker said. "There were *verbal* understandings about certain activities not spelled out in detail in the charter. A highly placed official authorized activities which I cannot discuss under the current security ceiling."

"And who, may I ask, was that official?"

"Forgive me, Congressman. I am not at liberty to say."

"Pity. Your funding depends on it."

Hacker considered briefly. "Very well. President Ronald Reagan."

"Out of office for some time, if memory serves," Wallace said. "Were those understandings ever put in writing?"

"No, Congressman."

"They are no longer relevant, then."

Hacker squirmed. "They were voiced again more recently."

"By whom?"

"Forgive me, sir, I am not free—"

"By whom?" Wallace said louder.

Hacker clasped his hands on the table and lowered his chin. His face vanished into darkness. "The president."

Gene stifled a gasp.

Wallace leaned toward Hacker. "Whence comes the president's power to alter the mission of an agency of government without legislative action?"

"I am not a legal scholar, Congressman," Hacker said. "I followed orders."

"So the president commanded you to violate your charter?"

"No, sir. He reinterpreted the charter to include certain activities—"

"And those activities were?"

Hacker's clasped hands tightened. "Congressman, I cannot discuss them with uncleared personnel."

"Including me?"

"Yes, Congressman."

"And will the clearances we shall receive later today cover those activities?"

Hacker paused, then bowed his head, hiding his face in shadow. "Yes."

"Would it be a fair interpretation to say that the compartments whose existence were withheld from me are those which cover activities authorized by the president?"

Hacker sat unmoving.

"Let the record show that the general did not respond," Wallace said. "What is to prevent me from concluding that the president ordered and you carried out extralegal activities and attempted to avoid scrutiny by flagrant misuse of classification?"

Silence.

"We'll break now," Wallace said, "to allow General Hacker to use the secure phone. Fifteen minutes."

He left his seat.

The rest of January 2019 was taken up with the reshuffle of House members, the shift of House committee chairmanships to Democrats, the emergence of a new power structure, and the beginning of House investigations into the administration's possibly illegal activities. Wallace, at Danley's urging, wanted to begin hearings immediately. They were to fall into two broad categories: classified sessions on illegal operations by the NPO, aided and abetted by the current FIBO leadership and the chairman of the Senate Preparedness Subcommittee; and open hearings on the blackmail and extortion carried on by NPO employees and the subcommittee staff with the knowledge and encouragement of its chairman, Senator Prowley. As a key player, Gene was back to twelve-hour days and weekend work.

The government shutdown ended on January 25. Slowly, the behemoth federal apparatus came back to life. Government employees were paid for the first time in a month. The general consensus, as reported by the press, was that the president deserved the blame for the disruption. Meanwhile, the president renewed his verbal public attacks on the intelligence community, and one of the president's close allies, Roger Stone, was arrested and charged on seven counts by special counsel Robert Mueller, including witness tampering and lying to Congress.

By mid-February, the press had caught wind of both of Wallace's investigations and was hounding all concerned. Gene wore stocking caps and dark glasses and to and from work to avoid reporters. With his help, Wallace peeled away layer upon layer of compartmentalization and laid bare the entire FIREFANG-First Strike Operation. The D.C. police cooperated in the extortion investigation and even found the Vassiliev imposter, a Russian émigré who worked in an upscale hair salon on Connecticut Avenue. He testified that he had been approached by Pierce who paid him, told him which Metro to take to find Gene, and gave him the script to use. By March, Dellaspada, Dennis—both fired in February—Shafter, Leila, Cutter, Hank Shelby, Michael, George, Carl, Nettie, and Julia Yancy had been called to testify. The president's office refused to allow Pierce to appear, citing executive privilege. Danley subpoenaed him anyway. Litigation on the matter might eventually reach the Supreme Court. The Justice Department, under orders from the president, balked at indicting any members of the Secretocracy, despite the evidence Wallace was accruing. He summoned the acting Attorney General to testify about the delay.

Michael, meanwhile, was in love. Louise was, like Michael, a senior and creative writing major at George Washington. She was blond and sinuous with a passion for jogging. Her taste ran to dark beer, Moroccan decor, and contemporary fiction. She and Nettie didn't hit it off—Gene attributed their frigid relationship to the natural rivalry between two beautiful women. But she went out of her way to charm George, and Scarpia thought her only rival in ear scratching was Gene himself. Because she lived in the dorms and Gene refused to allow

Michael and Louise to use the attic, the relationship remained more platonic than either of them would have preferred.

Late one evening, when Gene, wrapped in a trench coat and stocking cap, trundled wearily through the door, George swooped from the living room, Scarpia at his heels.

"You're exhausted and probably famished," George said merrily.

As Gene doffed his outer clothing, Scarpia gazed up hopefully and was rewarded with plentiful petting.

George fluttered his hands. "You've been so preoccupied. I've resurrected the fireplace in the living room. Have a lovely blaze going. Michael helped me move your weights to one side. Hope you don't mind."

George scooted through the arch and down the stairs. Gene's bench, barbells, and dumb bells had been shoved out of sight, and a Persian carpet was spread across the marble floor. In front of the fireplace was a sofa and coffee table.

"New furniture?" Gene asked.

"Used. The clinic sponsored a rummage sale. Charming pieces. Got them for a song. Gays have divine taste." George poured wine. "I found a new Chambertin that is simply heavenly, and the Camembert you'll find irresistible."

"This feels like a celebration." Gene loosened his tie and eased down on the sofa.

"There's cause. Try the cheese."

"You going to raise my rent to pay for all this?"

"I've come into a small sum," George said. "Decided to use it on the house. I wish I could afford to restore it to the way Alex maintained it. This is a start."

"Certainly different. I've barely been in here since the election."

"In your new job, you've been neglecting maintenance of your body. I notice things like that."

Gene grinned. "Thought I was too young to be your type."

"I don't have to be *amoureux* to appreciate a well-maintained male body. Forgive me, my friend, but you're getting a paunch."

Gene was mildly shocked.

"And," George went on, "Scarpia's training has gone to the dogs, so to speak."

"I'm sorry, George."

"*Ne derangez-vous pas.* You've had other priorities. Bringing down the administration is no small task."

"I'm doing nothing of the kind."

"The *Post*," George said, "has an article almost every day. Not on the front page anymore."

"The notoriety is a pain."

"The strongest man is he who stands alone. You did this. No one but you."

"I wasn't alone," Gene said. "I had the support of Carl, Michael, Nettie, you."

"You did it. We didn't."

George nibbled cheese, washed it down with wine, and kissed his fingertips. "*Que c'est formidable.*"

Gene kicked off his shoes. "Something's making you awfully jolly. Let's have it."

"I finished the book on Massenet before Christmas. Norton is going to publish it as part of their Great Composers series. They gave me quite a nice advance."

"George! I'm so happy for you."

"I've been thinking about doing something on Bizet or Gounod."

"The strongest man is he who stands alone," Gene said softly. "You did this. No one but you."

"I had good friends who saw me through the trying times."

"You did it. We didn't."

Chapter 15

Faithful Toadies and Good Worms

Nettie, of course, had been right. Spring had turned cool, too cool for a cookout. Gene bothered the chicken breasts and flipped the hamburgers. He pulled up the hood on his sweat shirt. It was drizzling. Not cold enough for snow, though—he hoped.

Michael came down the stairs from the terrace with an umbrella and a plate of cheese slices. "Seven mediums with cheese. Don't put any on the three rares for Louise and me."

"You always have cheese on your burgers."

"We're both trying to lose weight."

Gene surveyed him from head to foot. In his extra-extra-large sweats, Michael's body was indistinguishable. "You're overweight?"

"We want to be lean and mean for the Boston Marathon. It's April fifteenth."

"How much weight are you going to lose in a week and half?"

"We're into maintenance now. High protein, low carbs, run every day, long runs on weekends."

Gene chuckled. "When are you leaving for Boston? You driving?"

"The thirteenth. We thought we might stay over a couple of days after the race. Come home, maybe, the twenty-first? Could you make do without the Mustang that long?"

Gene moved the burgers and chicken to a plate. "What about classes?"

"We talked to our professors, got it arranged. Make-up work, an extra short story from me."

"What a guy won't do for a little time with a woman."

Michael grimaced. "I didn't think you'd figured that out."

"I'm a man, too, you know. I know how the hormones work."

"Louise loves it when I first get in from a run all sweaty. She says she gets all moist when my skin is shining and my body flushed."

"Hold it," Gene said. "Some things a father doesn't want to know."

"Just because I'm getting serious, we're not going to talk frankly anymore?"

"Yes. Michael, the woman you care about deserves discretion."

Michael scratched his head. "Guess that's why you broke your promise to tell me when you and Nettie starting sacking together."

"I promised nothing of the kind."

Michael shrugged. "Love sure does cripple the memory."

Gene handed him the meat. "Take these in. Tell everybody to fix their plates."

Gene doused the fire and loped up the steps. Getting easier now that he was working out again regularly. Nettie met him at the French doors.

"Phone for you," she said.

"If it's Danley . . ."

"Can't be. Mavis says he's at a reception."

Gene kissed her forehead and hurried to the foyer phone.

"Mr. Westmoreland, my name is Pat Simmons. Priss Simmons is my ex-wife. I was hoping you could tell me where to reach her."

"I haven't seen her in months, Mr. Simmons."

"The place on Arkansas Avenue is for sale. I understand that you know something about complaints against her for stalking and this Senate hearing thing she was mixed up in."

"I'd rather not go into that on the phone."

A long pause. "Mr. Westmoreland, I'm not interested in the relationship between you and my ex-wife. I want my daughter. Priss failed to show up for the custody hearing. No one knows where she and my daughter have gone. If you can help—"

"I wish I could. The last time I talked face-to-face with Priss was in June last year."

"The night she sprained her ankle?"

"Yes."

Another pause. "Please call me if you hear anything." Simmons gave Gene his home, office, and cell phone numbers and his email address, and hung up.

Poor Priss. Maybe she deserved everything she got. Maybe she couldn't help herself. But maybe he could have done something, at least for Elizabeth who'd end up suffering more than any of them. Like so many of the crises in his life, he could honestly say that he did the best he could at the time, but it wasn't good enough.

"Bad news?" Nettie stood next to him, two plates in hand.

"Not for us," he said.

"Come sit by the fire."

George was in the middle of the sofa with Rachel Follander on one side, Julia Yancy on the other. Mark and his wife, Barry Tilden, Carl, Sarah, Harry Breighton, Michael, Louise, and Mavis Evans were arranged on cushions in the firelight. Nettie patted the floor next to her and Scarpia. Gene sat at the outer edge of the circle and took off his jacket.

"Gounod," George was saying with authority, "often constructed his melodies so that the second phrase is a repeat of the first but a tone or two higher. He keeps his harmonies simple so that when a sudden shift into a new key comes, it has more than the expected impact."

Rachel and Sarah stared at each other blank-faced. Julia listened politely. Mark watched George with a fixed expression. Gene and Nettie traded quick grins and munched.

"Who needs a beer?" Carl got to his feet abruptly.

"Me," Barry said. "I'll come with you."

"They're in the cooler on the veranda," George said.

"We'll find them." Mark stood.

"Let me show you." George rose with creaky grace and put his plate on the mantle.

"Stay put," Carl said.

"I know where they are," Michael said. He pulled Louise up from the floor.

George trundled toward the arch.

Sarah popped up. "I need to find the powder room. Want to come, Rachel?"

"Yes." She followed Sarah into the foyer.

Gene chuckled. "George sure knows how to empty a room."

"Gene," Nettie said, "be nice."

Harry Breighton finished his potato salad, wiped his lips, and set his mouth. "Gene, I have something to say."

Gene gave him a puzzled look.

"I want you to know how sorry I am for the role I played in your troubles. After Mr. Shelby, Mrs. Simmons, and Mrs. Westmoreland contacted me, I thought I should alert the chief before I did verification—didn't want him embarrassed in case it blew up. When I reported the initial findings to Mr. Shafter, I got the impression he already knew the details. He ordered me to go to your cubicle and strip you of your clearances immediately." Harry studied his shoes. "I had misgivings, confirmed the day Henry Shelby called me. Once I began to check, the story fell apart, but Mr. Shafter wouldn't allow me to reinstate you."

"Any word on his replacement?" Julia asked.

Mavis nodded toward Gene. "A certain Doctor Westmoreland—as soon as he finishes his temporary duty on Senator Danley's staff." She laughed. "Gene is technically still on the FIBO payroll, so when Shafter was removed for cause, Gene moved up one step on the organization chart to the chief's position and assigned Mark Forrester to his old job. Meanwhile, Mark's sitting in as acting chief."

Julia's face lit up. "Gene. I didn't know. Congratulations. And Rod Pierce?"

"We'll see," Gene said. "He didn't respond to Wallace's subpoena. Justice Department is in shambles. It'll probably stay that way as long as the current administration is in power. Anyway, the new Attorney General is resisting Wallace's demands that Pierce be prosecuted for Contempt of Congress."

George came down the steps from the foyer, wine glass in hand. "The others decided to brave the elements on the veranda. Rain's let up."

"Think I'll join them." Gene stood.

"I'll come with you," Nettie said.

"No, stay here with Scarpia." Gene snatched his jacket from the floor. "George was just getting to the good part, about how Gounod uses liturgical music so effectively, at the beginning of *Faust* and especially in the church scene where Méphistophélés terrifies Marguerite."

"Arguably the finest thing in the score." George rubbed his palms together.

Nettie quailed, reached for Gene's hand.

"No, no, that's all right," Gene said. "I've heard it before." He headed for the foyer.

Michael, Louise, Mark, Carl, and Barry, in windbreakers and overcoats, huddled at the balustrade.

"Ah, Florida." Carl chafed his hands. "By now the temperature has moved from the seventies to the eighties, I bet."

"Why the sudden interest in Florida?" Gene asked.

"I retire in October. Been looking into possibilities for gigs in Miami, Fort Lauderdale, and Tampa. Lots of older folks down there. They enjoy my music more than kids." He sneered at Michael and Louise. "All they like is gangsta rap. That's not even music. Doggerel in common time. Anyway, Alicia might come with me."

"The one I've seen here weekends?" Gene asked. "So you're going to settle down?"

"Don't rush me." Carl frowned. "You're as bad as she is. Oh. A couple more things to bring you up to date on." He took Gene by the arm and moved him away from the others. "Scuttlebutt around J4 is that Hank's on his way out. Air Force Matériel doesn't take kindly to bad publicity. His case is under review."

Gene shook his head. "Poor Hank. Another one who can't seem to help himself. Anyway, Hacker will protect him."

"That's the other piece of news." Carl gave Gene his luminous smile. "Hacker's retiring early. Seems the Air Force got copies of his testimony before the Preparedness Subcommittee. He'll be lucky to get out without a reduction in rank."

"The bastard." Gene gritted his teeth. "He should be indicted."

"Not in this administration. Justice won't move against him. Gossip has it Hacker's going to work as a senior executive in Academi. That's the new name for Blackwater USA. You know, the mercenary army in Iraq? I hear he's taking Shafter and Cutter with him."

"Damn. No sin goes unrewarded."

"Faithful toadies get good worms," Carl said.

"Gene." Barry touched his arm. "I'm going to have to be on my way. Can you spare me a minute? You're not returning my calls."

"Sorry, Barry. I've had no time to call my own."

"I gathered that from the papers and TV. Anyway, Spicer, Brinkman, and Klauthammer called. Mr. Spicer himself came to my office, all the way from Philadelphia."

"So they're getting ready to strike?"

"Not quite," Barry said. "Spicer allowed as how Mrs. Westmoreland has had a change of heart."

"I don't suppose her testimony before the subcommittee had anything to do with it?"

"Gene, be fair. After what Shelby and Simmons told them, what was she supposed to do? Perjure herself? Anyway, she's become more amenable to negotiation. What it boils down to is she'll settle out of court to avoid having her testimony before the subcommittee admitted as evidence in the divorce."

"Terms favorable to us?" Gene asked.

"You bet. All you have to do is mention 'false statements about drugs and homosexual orgies,' and Spicer gets edgy. I might even suggest she pay you alimony. How soon can you get to my office so we can get everything arranged?"

Gene squinched. "That's a tough one. My work day runneth over. How about one night after work? I'll buy you dinner."

"Call me and set a date?"

"Promise. Meanwhile, let me tell Nettie."

Barry fought back a chuckle. "Feeling a little pressured, are we?"

"What's wrong with a long period of adjustment? Five years, maybe? Anyway, once she knows the divorce is imminent, she'll start beating her drum."

"Us divorcés have to hang together or we'll hang separately."

They headed in. Julia in hat, coat, and gloves waited in the dining room.

"Gene." She hugged him. "I'm in your debt. Not just for today. For what you did to restore Clem's reputation."

"You were the catalyst. Danley would never have listened to me if you hadn't gone to his office."

"I'll be grateful all my life. So will Jane."

"Give her my best. When can you and I get together?"

"I don't know. I'm moving. Yeah, we had to give up the house."

"The house Clem worked so hard on. Julia, I'm sorry."

"Don't be. It's my loss. I'll manage it."

"You always do."

He walked her to the door. As she left, Mavis came into the foyer carrying her coat. "I have to go. Can we sit by the fire for a minute?"

He took her arm, and they descended the steps to the now-deserted living room.

She sat on the sofa and nodded to the seat next to her. "It worked, didn't it?"

"Danley's a scrapper. I hear Prowley's retiring."

"Yes, and we'll fumigate his office before his replacement arrives. It'll be another Republican. The governor will name him."

Gene cocked his head. "Prowley decided he couldn't be re-elected?"

"To put it mildly. The Senate leadership let it be known that if he didn't want to be censured, he'd best go quietly. Censure leads to investigation. Investigation could lead to impeachment. Liberty University—you know, the Jerry Fallwell Christian Fundamentalist outfit? Lots of the current staff positions in the administration are filled by graduates. Dennis Hodgings is a recent alumnus. They've offered to make Prowley the Dean of Humanities."

"Guess there are many ways to kick someone upstairs." Gene said. "No one ever faces indictment in this administration."

"Dennis is being indicted."

"Hadn't heard."

"Prowley and Dellaspada denounced him as the author of the whole blackmail scheme, carried out, they said, without their knowledge or approval. He confessed. Told the authorities there weren't any porno films. He made that up."

"God," Gene said. "And now they're making him the scapegoat."

"Maybe not. We're hearing rumbles that the president is planning a pardon for him. Prowley might offer him a job at Liberty. I suspect that was the deal from the start."

"At least Dellaspada got canned."

Mavis' smile was wry. "He's been offered a position at Halliburton at triple his salary."

"Jesus. These guys know how to take care of each other."

"Gene, tell me the truth. On your deathbed, would you rather relish your wealth or remember the good you did?" She got to her feet. "Tomorrow's going to be a killer."

Gene accompanied her to the door. "I need a couple of hours of leave in the morning."

"Oh, Gene. With all the hearing material, we have to prepare, I don't see—"

"Something I have to do, Mavis. You know I don't stint."

She set her mouth. "Whatever it takes. The work won't go away."

As dusk darkened the horizon, the house mates finished the cleanup. Carl left for the Côte d'Azur, Michael drove Louise to the dorms, and George retired to analyze the orchestration in Gounod's *Romeo et Juliette*. Scarpia went with him.

"Where are the girls?" Gene asked.

"Took my car home," Nettie said. "Want to have brandy by the fire before we head to Takoma Park?"

They carried snifters to the living room. Gene added kindling and a log, and the fire revived. She nestled against him.

"You know some wonderful people," Nettie said.

"And some *summa cum laude*, medal-of-honor, world-class sons of bitches."

"We outnumber them."

"They've got the money and the power," Gene said.

"Bet none of them have what we have."

"Why do people settle for so little?"

She disengaged and sipped the brandy. "Gene, when things loosen up, are you really going to push ahead with the divorce? I worry about the example we're setting for Sarah and Rachel."

"They seem content."

"They think you're a conquering hero." She leaned against him. "That's not what I mean. Did you know that in Europe most couples living together aren't married, the birth rate is in decline, and religion is unimportant to the majority of the population? The United States isn't there yet, but we're headed in the same direction."

"What does that have to do with the girls?"

"I want them to marry and have children. I don't want them to abandon their religion, and they can be influenced, not by what we say but by what we do."

"What are you getting at?" Gene said.

"I can't be hypocritical. My religion tells me that sex outside of marriage is wrong. I don't want to end up cynical like so many people living without religion."

"You want to be one of those mean, pious old spinsters?"

"What I want *us* to be," she said, "is a decent couple giving a good example to our children, offering them a model we want them to follow."

He toyed with her hair. "You're playing bait and switch with me."

"And?" She sat up and drank brandy. "I'm not going to leave you over it, but it's what I want."

"For me to commit to you."

"Gene, you've won. The Secretocracy is destroyed. Can we please get on with our lives now?"

"What's the hurry?"

"We need to grab life by the horns and bend it to our will. Procrastination will wither us. I love you more than any man I've ever known. I love you more than I knew I could love."

He tried to ease the lump in his throat.

"How about a little reciprocation here?" she said. "Does that courageous mouth know how to shape the words, 'I love you'?"

He studied the fire.

"Did you love Donna?" she asked.

"Yes."

"Do you still?"

"No."

"And Priss?"

"I never loved her," he said.

"And me?"

"Yes."

She waited. He said nothing.

"Maybe I understand, a little," she said, "how you grew up without love, how you crave it, how it terrifies you because if you love, it might go sour and you'll be hurt more than you can stand."

He drew away. "Stop it."

"It frightens you more than all the Hackers and Prowleys in the world."

He winced.

"I hate hurting you," she said, "but you've got to come to grips." She straightened, looked into the fire. "I love you enough to stay with you even if nothing changes. I'm not threatening you. I'm offering you something. Real love. The love you've never had."

He lowered his chin to his chest. This hurt. Biting his lip, he made himself look at her. "I love you, Nettie. As God is my witness." Tears came into his eyes. "Will you marry me?"

Her face crumpled. Tears flowed. Her arms encircled him and held him close.

The drizzle of Sunday melted into brisk Monday sunshine. Gene hurried home from Nettie's, bathed, and dressed for the office. With his bag lunch in his briefcase, he drove the

Mustang west to Hopewell Cemetery. He parked at the perimeter and passed over the rolling mounds of grass, by headstones and monuments and markers, to the rise where Clem's body rested. He read the gravestone and walked around the plot, viewing it from every side. Finally he stood at the foot of the grave and folded his hands in front of him. He had to talk to Clem.

"We won, boss."

He raised his eyes as if he expected a response.

"The rhinos made love. We were right in the middle of it, but we survived. Hacker's gone. Shafter's gone. So is Prowley. NPO is working within its charter." He chuckled. "The Democrats even won the House in the election."

No answer. Why did he keep listening for one?

"Your good name is intact. Julia saw to that. I came through it fine. So did Nettie. Oh, we're together now. Thought you'd like to know that."

He imagined Clem smiling and nodding.

"But mainly, I wanted you to know—"

He sank to his knees and folded his hands.

"I'm speaking now as the son you never had. You're the father I always yearned for. And I wanted you to know . . ."

His vision went blurry.

"You didn't die in shame, Clem. You didn't fail. You won."

Lexicon of Government Organizations

The following is a list of organizations that appear in this book. The fictional ones are shown in *italics*; the real ones in standard print.

CIA—the Central Intelligence Agency, the premier agency responsible for collecting and analyzing intelligence for the federal government. CIA is also responsible for clandestine activities of a non-intelligence nature.

DIA—Defense Intelligence Agency, an organization within the Department of Defense responsible for collecting and analyzing intelligence of interest to the military.

DNI—the Director of National Intelligence, overall chief of all intelligence activities of the U.S. government.

FIBO—the Federal Intelligence Budget Office, responsible for preparing the annual intelligence budget for presentation to Congress, assuring that submissions are in keeping with presidential guidance, the charters of the submitting agencies, the laws of the nation, and treaty obligations.

Intelligence Community—the sixteen agencies of the federal government which collect and analyze intelligence, all under the Director of National Intelligence (DNI).

NGA—the Northern Gulf Affairs Office, the new name for OSP when the latter became the subject of controversy.

NPO—*the National Preparedness Office, an intelligence agency responsible for the collection and analysis of intelligence on the nuclear threat to the United States, its allies, and possessions; and for analysis of the United States ability to withstand a thermonuclear attack.*

NRO—the National Reconnaissance Office, responsible for the collection of raw intelligence from satellites. The NRO shares analysis responsibility with other agencies.

NSA—the National Security Agency, an organization within the Department of Defense responsible for Signals Intelligence (SIGINT), the collection and analysis of electronic signals (radio, telephone, email, radar, telemetry). In the Bush Administration, it was assigned the task of the Terrorist Surveillance Program ("warrantless wiretapping") which includes monitoring of telephone conversations between communicants in the United States and other countries and other unspecified activities. It apparently also includes data mining—a technique for searching massive quantities of intercepted signals to locate information of interest and for linking bits of suspicious data—and the intercept of emails. The program was replaced by PRISM which at this writing is evidently still in use.

NSC—the National Security Council, essentially an advisory body to the president on matters of national security.

OMB—the Office of Management and Budget, the accountant agency of the federal government, responsible for preparing and executing the annual federal budget.

***OSCI**—Office of Special Compartmented Intelligence*, the OSP (see below) reincarnate.

OSP—the Office of Special Plans, an operation under the Secretary of Defense responsible for analysis of raw intelligence data, set up by Donald Rumsfeld and Douglas Feith as an alternative to analytic conclusions produced by existent intelligence agencies, i.e., CIA, NSA, DIA, etc. Often accused of shaping intelligence findings to suit the ideology or policy of the Bush Administration. Formerly the Northern Gulf Affairs Office (NGA).

***Senate Preparedness Subcommittee**—a body of seven U.S. senators which oversees nuclear defense intelligence operations and budgeting.*

SES—the Senior Executive Service, a system for selecting and rewarding federal government employees acting as executives. The highest pay level in the government for career employees (as opposed to political appointees) is SES1.

About the Author

Dr. Tom Glenn has worked as an intelligence operative, a musician, a linguist (seven languages), a cryptologist, a government executive, a care-giver for the dying, a leadership coach, and, always, a writer. Much of his writing comes from the years he shuttled between the U.S. and Vietnam as an undercover NSA operative supporting army and Marine units in combat before escaping under fire when Saigon fell.

Between 1962 and 1975, Glenn was in Vietnam at least four months every year. He had two complete tour there and so many shorter trips that he lost count. He was a civilian employee of the National Security Agency, but when in Vietnam, he was under cover as an army or Marine enlisted man; to maintain his cover, NSA redacted his name from its public documents. He was sent to Vietnam repeatedly because he knew North Vietnamese radio communications intimately—he'd been exploiting them since 1960. He spoke Vietnamese, Chinese, and French, the three languages of Vietnam, and he was willing to go into combat with the army and Marine units he was supporting all over South Vietnam. After the withdrawal of U.S. military forces from Vietnam in 1973, he headed the covert NSA operation there. As the fall of Saigon loomed in April 1975, he evacuated his 43 subordinates and their families even though the U.S. ambassador, Graham Martin, had forbidden him to send his people out. On the night of April 29, after all his people were safely out of the country and the North Vietnamese were already in the streets of the city, he fled by helicopter under fire.

What Glenn did after the end of the Vietnam war in 1975 is still classified. But it is public information that he toured the country lecturing on leadership and management, trained federal executives, and was the Dean of the Management Department at the National Cryptologic School. Maryland Public Television interviewed him and fifteen others in its 2016 salute to Vietnam vets, and his memoir article on the fall of Saigon has been published by *Studies in Intelligence* and reprinted in the *Atticus Review* and the *Cryptologic Quarterly*. In late 2017, the *New York Times* featured his story on his role in the 1967 battle of Dak To in Vietnam's central highlands. These days he is a reviewer for the *Washington Independent Review of Books* and the *Internet Review of Books* where he specializes in books on war and Vietnam. His Vietnam novel-in-stories, *Friendly Casualties*, is now available on Amazon.com. Apprentice House of Baltimore brought out his novels *No-Accounts* in 2014 and *The Trion Syndrome* in 2015. In 2017, the Naval Institute Press published his novel, *Last of the Annamese*, set during the fall of Saigon. Adelaide Books brought out his latest novel, *Secretocracy*, in early 2020. You can access his blog at https://tomglenn.blog/